calling on Lily

This is Louise Harwood's first novel.
She lives in London with her
husband and two sons.

LOUISE HARWOOD

calling on Lily

PAN BOOKS

First published 2002 by Pan Books
an imprint of Pan Macmillan Ltd
Pan Macmillan, 20 New Wharf Road, London N1 9RR
Basingstoke and Oxford
Associated companies throughout the world
www.panmacmillan.com

ISBN 0 330 48613 6

1 3 5 7 9 8 6 4 2

A CIP catalogue record for this book is available from
the British Library.

Typeset by SetSystems Ltd, Saffron Walden, Essex
Printed and bound in Great Britain by
Mackays of Chatham plc, Chatham, Kent

For Ant

and in memory of my father,

Graham Hartley Davies

My true friends have always given me that supreme proof of devotion: a spontaneous aversion for the man I loved.

Colette

1

You don't often see a good-looking man in Welshpool. To see four at once, on a rainy Friday in February, with no girls in tow, was too good to be true. Kirsty stopped abruptly and caught Lily's arm.

'Look at them, on the other side of the street.'

Lily screwed up her eyes, wondering what she was referring to, and saw four men, slowly making their way towards them. They were walking three abreast and one behind, dominating the pavement, forcing everyone else to divide, muttering, around them.

Before Lily could get a proper look, Kirsty grabbed her arm and hustled her off the High Street and into a tiny cobbled passageway. Hidden, they stopped beside a deserted clothes shop.

'They're crossing the road,' Kirsty said, edging out to get a better look. 'Keep still and look at the clothes. Any minute now, they're going to walk right past.'

Smiling at the speed with which Kirsty had moved into action, Lily watched her whip out a lipstick from under her coat and slide it quickly across her mouth, then consider herself in the glass reflection. She slapped both her cheeks and wiped her cold nose with her hand.

'You're such a tart,' Lily told her.

'No I'm not!' Kirsty grinned. 'But you have to admit

it's sod's law. If you go out with no make-up on and looking like a dog, gorgeous men *will* walk up the street towards you.'

Kirsty had wild black curls, sparkling blue eyes and pale, flawless skin. Under a thin summer coat, she poured out of a low-cut top that was tucked into jeans so tight she'd been practically vacuum-packed into them. The last thing anyone was going to notice was the lipstick.

Out on the main street the men were getting closer.

'Josh,' one said loudly, the voice now so clear that he had to be almost beside them. 'Do you *seriously* want to look around the castle? It's raining and it's miles away. Or did you say that to get rid of Hal?'

Lily took a sneaky look. The guy who was talking was tall and well built, with cropped brown hair and soft dark eyes.

'No, Hal's safely at home,' Josh replied, looking at his watch. 'Come on, lard-arse, you could do with the exercise. It's only four o'clock. We'll be back by five.'

Kirsty considered them carefully, trying to decide whom she'd say yes to first. Either of the first two, she decided. And the third's not bad either. Lily could have the fourth one. Like his friends, he was probably in his late twenties or early thirties, but while they were growing older gorgeously, he had traffic-light orange hair that was fast receding at the forehead, plump pale cheeks and beady eyes. He was wearing a rugby shirt tucked into his jeans, with the collar up against the wind, and was hanging back from the others, hunched over a kebab and dripping a trail of grease and juice and bits of meat on to the pavement. And if that's from the Taste of the Orient kebab van, she told him silently, you're not long for this earth anyway.

At the front, Josh was wearing a dark coat buttoned high up to his chin and a navy stretchy hat pulled down to his eyes. Kirsty had never seen someone wear a woolly hat and look so good in it, certainly no one older than ten. But beneath the hat were lovely eyes and lofty cheekbones, and the short coat revealed a pair of long, long legs.

'Hey, we could chuck Hal in one of the castle dungeons,' said the one with the kebab. He wiped his chin with his hand, and started to laugh. 'Save us the hassle of looking after him.'

'Oh, ha,' said Josh in a bored voice. 'No. Llanygoed will suit us just fine. The cottage is perfect.'

Lily wondered who Hal was and what was going to happen in Llanygoed. For a second, she thought, quite calmly, that they might be planning a murder. She concentrated hard on the voices, trying to hear everything that they said.

'Don't tell me you lot are bottling out?' Josh challenged them all, stopping suddenly, his words causing Lily's heart to beat even faster in sudden panic. 'It's much too late for that.'

He stared at them, waiting for an answer, but nobody spoke.

'Does anyone have any better ideas?'

The other three stood awkwardly on the pavement.

'Come on, guys,' Josh said impatiently, turning against a sudden gust of wind and rain. 'We've been through this a million times.'

Still the others didn't speak.

'We can't wait here for ever,' Lily whispered from the passageway, her teeth chattering. 'I'm freezing.'

Kirsty shrugged. 'As long as we need to. I'm not moving.'

'And I can't stand these terrible clothes any longer!' Lily hissed back. 'People might think I like them!'

'Don't be such a snob! And don't you dare move. They'll notice you and then they'll shut up. Something is definitely going on.'

Lily rolled her eyes and looked back at the window, noticing that the mustard-coloured dress, which she had come to think of as a permanent feature of Welshpool, had been joined by a pair of matching mustard earrings.

'No, Josh, I'm not happy about this,' someone said. 'I never have been. It can't be the only answer.'

On the street Josh paused and pulled out a packet of cigarettes. His head bent low as he struck a match, long fingers cupping it against the wind and rain, before flicking it out into the road.

'You're not the sharpest knife in the drawer,' he said, looking up at the guy with a grin, 'but can't even you see we have no choice? We've been waiting for Hal to change his mind for months! And we can't wait any longer because the wedding's in the morning.' He stopped for a second, challenging them all. 'We've got him down here, against all the odds and now, what else do we do? You lot haven't produced one single good idea. And in the long run he'll be grateful,' Josh insisted. 'We're saving him from a fate worse than death. Amber's such a bitch she'd win best of breed.'

'But it's his *wedding*!' the other guy replied. 'Think of all the people, the cake, the presents – the matching bathrobes that I chose with such loving care – the vicar, the honeymoon . . .'

'Think of his vows.' Josh was adamant. 'And how he'd never give up on them. He'd be reciting his own prison sentence. As his best man and ushers it's our duty to look after him.' He paused. 'So we'll stop the wedding, stop him marrying Amber.'

Absolutely, thought Kirsty, who hated people getting married.

'But they can't!' Lily cried, and for a moment Kirsty thought she might be about to confront them.

'Shut *up*! Keep *still*,' she begged, grabbing Lily's arm.

'They can't do that!'

Somehow the four men didn't notice them and slowly moved off again. Lily and Kirsty immediately walked out into the street and tucked in behind them.

'We'll have dinner at the Little Goose at about eight.' It was the one called Josh speaking again. 'Then we'll drive back to Llany-welshy-whatever, get him trashed and put him to bed.'

Kirsty bristled at his words.

'He'll probably sleep beyond midday,' Josh went on. 'And by then it'll be too late.'

'How are we going to keep him here? Won't he go

back to Oxford as soon as he wakes up?' It was the dark-haired one talking again.

'Oh no, Charlie,' Josh said, sounding surprised that he hadn't understood. 'If he tries to leave, you're going to stop him. Rich, Alex,' he said, nodding at the other two, making sure they were listening to him. 'It's up to the three of you to make sure nothing goes wrong. When he wakes up tomorrow you mustn't let him leave. I'll have gone to Oxford, to see the bride, break the news that he won't be showing up.' He shrugged. 'She'll get over it,' he said confidently. 'Give her a week or two and she'll have got her claws into some other poor sod.'

'It's all we can do,' said the kebab eater. 'As Josh says, she's a hound.' He moved swiftly up the street, beginning to leave the others behind. 'Forget the castle, we're not here for the sightseeing,' he shouted back to them. 'And we said we'd get some beers. Hal will start to miss us if we're not back soon.'

Kirsty and Lily watched them until all four disappeared into the off-licence.

'Can you believe that?' Kirsty looked at Lily with glee. 'And they're all alone!'

'Can't see things changing for the guy with the kebab. Even with you around.'

Kirsty blew her a kiss.

'And you heard what they said,' Lily went on. 'They're in the middle of a kidnapping, they're not going to have time to get to know you!'

'They don't need time to get to know *us*,' said Kirsty. 'It's just important that they know *we're* here – we're an important local attraction. Pleeease! How often is it we get an opportunity like this?'

'You know,' Lily said, looking puzzled. 'I've always given people such a hard time for calling you Thirsty Kirsty. Why is that?'

'Don't ask what they call you!' Kirsty put her arm around Lily's shoulders. 'Come on,' she cajoled, 'all you have to do is come with me to the Little Goose. We know when they'll be there.'

Lily nodded slowly. She wanted to talk to Kirsty about what they'd heard, wanted to ask her if it could possibly be for real, but Kirsty was too bound up in plotting and scheming and working out how she might engineer a meeting and was almost oblivious to what they'd actually said.

'Home,' Kirsty said. 'We need time to get ready. Let's go back to your sister's.'

*

It was a steep, wet climb. On either side of the wide street were solid, sodden black and white buildings, their ancient gutters pouring arcs of rainwater out on to the pavement. Shouldering space between them, giving the street a lovely higgledy-piggledy look, were tiny cottages and an occasional Georgian townhouse. And all along, branching off at regular intervals, were narrow alleyways with names like Bear Passage, where the lichen and moss grew rampant between the slippery wet cobblestones.

Sometimes these alleys would open on to an utterly unexpected courtyard and it was in one of these that Lily and Kirsty had spent most of Lily's first summer in Welshpool, sitting outside in the shady dappled sunlight, idly eating lunch. They'd met a week after Lily's arrival, sharing the last outdoor table, one hot July day.

It hadn't been entirely spontaneous. Kirsty, preparing for a solitary lunchtime with *OK!*, had looked up to see Lily walking hesitantly down the cobbled pathway towards her. Kirsty had been captivated, not just because she knew everyone in Welshpool and Lily was obviously a stranger, but because Lily looked amazing. A wisp of black lace held back her short blonde hair, and she wore a loosely crocheted black cardigan over a violet bra top, cut-off black jeans and flat leather sandals. She had golden brown legs and dark purple nail-varnish. The kind of girl who Kirsty wished would stay on, would move in down the street, and liven up her beloved, boring town.

Of course she was probably only in Welshpool for a few hours, how many people stayed longer? But even so, as the girl moved indoors to choose her lunch Kirsty made a swift decision and dived in behind her. By the time they'd finished queuing for the soup, they'd begun to talk.

Later, sitting languidly in the sun, their empty bowls pushed to one side, Lily explained that her decision to come had been made on the spur of the moment. That she'd got a sister in Welshpool, called Grace Somerville who'd bought a house about six months ago, and that she was going to spend some time with her. Kirsty had flinched. Of course she knew exactly who Lily meant. Everyone knew Grace, or knew of her. She was their local Miss Haversham, living out a life of miserable isolation in a lovely house in a quiet back street a little way out of the town.

Kirsty had nodded non-committally, waiting to see if Lily was going to say more. But Lily had fallen silent, transported back to the flat in Manchester where she was staying at the time, listening again to her sister weeping brokenly down the telephone, protesting in the same gasping breaths that she was absolutely fine. She had known with sisterly intuition that she should get to Grace as soon as she possibly could.

Lily had shaken the image from her mind, and looking up she'd smiled at Kirsty and had started to describe what it was like being met at Shrewsbury station and driven through the early evening sunlight, into what felt like the middle of absolutely nowhere, where not even Macdonald's had penetrated. Kirsty laughed, but Lily had meant what she said. As the hills had become higher and more beautifully desolate and the villages had fallen away, she had grown silent, looking out of the car window wide-eyed. She had noticed signposts to Welsh Harp Hollow and the Long Mountain and had felt an unexpected glow of anticipation.

'Where are you from?' Kirsty had asked.

'I've been at art college in London,' said Lily, squinting at Kirsty in the sunlight. 'I've just finished a post-grad in three-dimensional design.'

Kirsty was momentarily silenced.

'Call it pottery!' Lily reassured her, laughing and showing even pearly white teeth. 'But I grew up near Chester. We used to come here camping. I don't remember it but I think that's why Grace has come back.' Lily fished a pair of sunglasses out of her back pocket and settled them on her small nose.

'And how long might you stay?'

'Dunno, it depends on Grace. But I'd imagine about a month. She wants me to help her paint her house.'

Kirsty nodded slowly.

'And what about you?' Lily asked. 'Have you always lived around here?'

'Sure,' said Kirsty. ' "*Does neb byth yn ymadael!*" ' She grinned at Lily. 'Nobody ever leaves. The furthest I got was when I was sent to boarding-school about thirty miles away. But I love it. I always have. I couldn't be anywhere else.'

Lily laughed. 'Well, while I'm here, I've got to see you again. Please! You can imagine, I know *nobody*. And Grace can't face a trip to the video shop let alone a night in the pub.'

Six months later Kirsty was feeling confident that Lily would stay put, if not with her sister, then somewhere else near Welshpool, and if not for ever, at least for a few months more. Although the freezing winter winds had put paid to the alfresco lunchtimes and the rain had fallen almost incessantly since Christmas, Lily had stopped talking about when she would move on.

Now it was so dark that the alleyways had become a little menacing, the bright lights of the nearby shops emphasizing how spooky and silent they were. Lily and Kirsty hurried past them, then moved off the High Street and began to head out of the town.

Lily was deeply relieved that her sister had chosen that weekend to go to see their parents and wouldn't therefore walk in to find Kirsty in her house. Grace couldn't even stand to be in the same room as Kirsty, and hated Lily spending so much time in her company – time spent away from her – missing the point that Kirsty provided vital light relief. What others saw in Kirsty – why others felt better for being with her – completely passed Grace by. She could make Lily laugh at nothing, but her loud voice and relentless good humour made Grace itch to slap her. Even more, it was Kirsty's avaricious accumulation of all the most personal, most embarrassing gossip that really drove Grace crazy, knowing that Kirsty would have an absolute feast on all the disastrous details surrounding her own love life.

'She's like a dirty great bluebottle who finds the shit and then just loves spreading it everywhere,' Grace had said bitterly. 'And don't you ever tell her what happened to me.'

*

When Lily had offered to come to stay with Grace she'd had little idea of what she was letting herself in for. She and Grace had had a bust up a year earlier, but it had never occurred to Lily that she might not be able to regain the easy friendship that had always previously been there between them. But she had arrived to find the new Grace was someone she hardly recognized. Alternately weeping or bitingly aggressive, she was negative about everything and everyone, particularly Lily, and still refused to forgive her for her part in what had happened the year before. If Lily had presumed that her arrival would smooth things along, pick up the pace of Grace's recovery, she was wrong. The weeks passed but Grace's black moods did not. Still Lily had hung on, patient and gentle, tirelessly listening, encouraging Grace to talk, night after night, hoping that, in time, she'd come to terms with what had happened to her.

Six months later, Lily was close to admitting she'd failed and, if anything, that Grace was in even worse shape than when she'd arrived. When she announced to Lily that she was going away for the weekend, a miracle in itself, Lily felt a leap of delight at the thought of a whole weekend without her. Now with the stag party in town she was even more relieved that Grace was safely off the scene.

She played the boys' conversation over again in her mind. It was unbelievable that after all that she and Grace had been through, she of all people would overhear such a conversation. To Lily it was amazing that these men could have so much confidence that they were doing the right thing, and were prepared to hurt so many people. She hadn't been able to do it for Grace.

A year ago Grace had had a fiancé. He was someone Lily had disliked at first sight and only loathed more the longer she knew him. At first Lily had been hardly able to do more than voice a doubt, but when they became engaged she'd resolved to try to tell her sister how she felt. It had sent an immediate icy wind whipping between them. Grace had been livid that her little sister had questioned her judgement about anything, let alone her choice of husband. In tears, she'd spat out, an inch from Lily's face, that it was only because Lily was jealous, because she couldn't get close to anyone herself, that she hated Jeremy. Lily had swayed in shock, totally taken aback by Grace's anger. She remembered staring at Grace in disbelief, telling her that she was wrong and that it was only because she loved her that she had decided she must say what she felt.

'And what *was* that exactly? Tell me again!' Grace had demanded.

'That I don't think he loves you. Enough,' Lily had replied quietly, not adding that in her opinion, he was about as good a catch as a bucket of crabs. And he'd probably given her them already.

*

Stop thinking about it! Lily told herself now. She grabbed Kirsty's arm and marched her up the steep hill, putting her sister firmly out of her mind.

'In! In! I'll go all frizzy,' Kirsty cried when Lily eventually unlocked the front door of Grace's house, pushing past her and making her way towards the kitchen. Lily followed, letting her keys and coat drop to the floor. She stood still for a moment, ignoring Kirsty's chatter, and lightly touched the walls. The hall smelled of Green Smoke paint even though it had been dry for a few days. It still surprised her every time she walked in and for a moment she felt almost nostalgic for the anaglypta wall paper and the old pizza-effect carpet Grace and she had ripped up with such relish. But the new colour emphasized the uncluttered simplicity of the house and highlighted the beautiful vaulted ceiling and curving central staircase. It had taken a long time to persuade Grace that style didn't always mean that your clothes were black and your house white, but the effort had definitely been worth it.

'All that work. Bet you wish this place was yours,' Kirsty said.

Lily followed her, thinking that it was true, her footsteps loud on the floorboards, newly stripped and sanded by her. She walked over to the windows, which opened out on to a large garden, and drew shut the heavy curtains. Behind her, Kirsty headed straight for the freezer and took out ice and a frosted bottle of vodka, orange juice already at her side.

With a glass in each hand, Kirsty pushed open the sitting-room door with her foot. She handed one glass to Lily and lowered herself on to the sofa.

'So, who would you pull, then?' Kirsty asked, forcing off her trainers and curling her feet underneath her. 'I liked that one called Josh. Bloody gorgeous. I bet they're all loaded.'

Lily put down her glass. 'I just can't believe we heard them say all those things,' she said. 'And sorry, Kirsty, sorry, but I didn't *like* them. Whoever Hal is, he's picked a bunch of bastards for his friends.'

'You're so predictable.'

Lily laughed. 'I don't care what you think, you old slapper.'

Kirsty shrugged, enjoying herself. 'So what? I keep the

locals happy.' She looked at Lily with a light in her eye. 'You, on the other hand, have no fun at all.'

'Oh, leave it out,' Lily said. 'If I don't choose to shag for Britain that's up to me.'

Kirsty let it rest. She wasn't going to risk irritating Lily tonight. Not when she might refuse to go to the pub. She lay back on the soft, dark brown moleskin sofa, stroking the arm with her hand and wondering if moleskin had once meant real moles.

Kirsty couldn't have admitted it, even to herself, but from the moment they'd first met she had found Lily completely captivating. She stared endlessly at Lily's thick straight eyebrows and olive-green eyes, listened intently to her soft laugh and continually analysed her clothes. How or why Lily did even the most trivial things was of vital importance to her. She followed Lily's example and fitted hair-clips of butterflies and flowers into her own dark curls, sorted expertly through the same piles of gorgeous tops and jackets in the vintage clothes shop, and drove miles in search of the same pair of sunglasses that Lily had worn on that first day they'd met.

To Kirsty, Lily was cool, part of an urban, sleeker world. She wanted to know everything about her: if she coloured her hair, if she took drugs, if she liked sushi and where she lost her virginity, whether she thought ankle boots had had their day, how often she saw her parents, whether she could cook. But they talked about more serious things too, about the collapse of the farming industry and the devastation wreaked by foot and mouth, and urban sprawl, and Kirsty was relieved to discover that the terrible rural crises that one after another were destroying so much of her own family's livelihood hadn't entirely passed Lily by.

Lily was welcome relief. They had been born into similar enough backgrounds, and although Lily had been through art college while Kirsty had gone straight to work from school, Kirsty knew straight away that she had found a kindred spirit. She was happy to sit for hours at the weekends, watching Lily at work on her pottery in the old brick workshop in Grace's garden, warmed by the portable kiln, and enthusiastically reading all Lily's old art college textbooks.

'So what are you going to wear?' she asked now. 'Grey trousers?'

Lily swallowed back irritation at Kirsty's perfect knowledge of her wardrobe and nodded.

'I think I'll make a bit more of an effort,' Kirsty wondered aloud. 'Do you mind if I borrow something?' She looked at her watch. 'It's nearly six now and they're getting there at half seven. Let's get to the bar at about ten past and have a few drinks before they arrive.'

*

After Kirsty had gone Lily went upstairs and flopped on to her bed. Kirsty had been almost humming with excitement. But then, Lily acknowledged, how often did such a potent combination of sex, scandal and gorgeous men land on your doorstep?

The way Kirsty went after men reminded Lily of a fish gliding powerfully across the ocean bed, picking up everything in her path, but spitting most of it out again almost straight away. Lily couldn't remember a time Kirsty had gone out with a bloke for longer than a week.

She didn't doubt that Kirsty would get in with the stag party. It was inconceivable that she would leave the Little Goose without having checked them all over. What they were planning to do wouldn't bother her in the slightest. But it did bother Lily, terribly. Could these guys really be contemplating such a thing? In the low, expectant tone of the conversation on the High Street, Lily had sensed their excitement. They had talked with a mistaken romanticism, as if they were plucking their man from the scene of danger, swooping heroically at the final hour, to hold him in a secret hideout until the crisis had past. They'd been serious, she thought. They were going to do it.

She got up and walked across to the window, drawing shut the blue velvet curtains. Whoever Hal was, however unstable, however lacking in self-preservation, self-awareness, however grateful they might think he'd be; how could they take the chance that they were wrong? If they liked him, even just a little, how could they allow themselves to get so carried away? How could they take it so far?

Lily stood between her curtains and looked out at the deserted, lamplit street, pressing her fingertips against the cold panes of glass and watching the rain streak the window like tears. And what about his bride? It was bad enough that they were doing this to Hal. But what about her? How would she feel, Lily wondered? What might she do?

Grace had been sent four times around the village in her wedding car before it was finally established that her fiancé was not going to turn up at the church. She had still not got over it. Lily could not let it happen to someone else.

2

Alex's grandmother, Peggy Topham, had been delighted for her cottage to be used by her only grandson and his young friends while she went to visit her sister in Cheltenham. In her keep fit class she'd talked about it so much that the group had come to a chattering untidy halt in the middle of a routine and the instructor had petulantly switched off her music and had folded her arms, taking several of them back to their schooldays.

Her cottage was on the edge of a wood, tiny and pretty, with a black cat and three small bedrooms, the sort of place Little Red Riding Hood's grandmother might have lived in. Alex and the others took great care of it, careful not to break the delicate chairs, tread in the plate of cat food or block the antiquated loo. They didn't notice how a couple of pictures had bounced off the walls with the force of the slamming doors, or how the stacked-up beer-cans were threatening to overwhelm the kitchen.

Upstairs old copies of *The Field* were piled high on each of the small, carved bedside tables. In her own bedroom, Alex's grandmother had trustingly left her high, bouncy bed covered in a white lace bedspread, the pillows plump and laundered.

Josh walked along a narrow upstairs corridor his hair wet, a towel wrapped around his waist, his bare feet leaving large wet footprints on the old oak floorboards, and hammered on Hal's bedroom door.

'Go on in. I'm just dropping the kids off at the pool,' came a voice from the bathroom next door.

'Hal! You're an animal.'

Hal laughed over the sound of the flush and appeared in the doorway. 'What do you want?' he asked, bending his head and following Josh into his bedroom.

Hal was tall, easily the tallest of the five of them. He had huge hands and size thirteen feet and a thick thatch of caramel hair that looked as though it had been cut with a Flymo. He loped rather than walked and the tiny cottage bedroom seemed much too small for him. When Josh didn't answer he came round in front of him.

'What's wrong?' He asked, then a shaft of hurt crossed his open, smiling face. 'Don't *do* this to me. I keep telling you. My wedding is not a point for discussion.'

Josh closed the door with a click. 'What do you mean?'

'I mean it's happening. All organized. Dress fitted, guests arrived, speeches written, cake decorated, flowers arranged. There's no going back.'

'But you wish there was?'

'I didn't say that,' Hal said calmly.

There was a long silence. 'Even if I told you I'd slept with her?' Josh said, desperately. He sat down slowly, unable to meet Hal's eye, and picked at the bedspread.

'Yes, you bastard. Even if you told me that,' Hal said eventually. 'I already know.'

'Amber has *told* you?' Momentarily Josh was thrown

off track. 'She cheated on you, Hal!' he said indignantly, quickly back on course. 'You shouldn't be marrying her. What's to stop her doing it again?'

'Nothing. Apart from the fact that we love each other.' Hal stood resolutely in front of him. 'And we didn't when you two got it together. I reckon I can live with it.'

He moved over to the tiny leaded window, undoing the locks and letting in the clean night air, and Josh saw that once again he was getting nowhere.

'How could you still ask me to be your best man?'

'It's hard to explain. Perhaps because I'd probably have slept with her if I'd been in your place. I was like you then. I hated you when she first told me but I forgive you for it now.'

Hal went silent for a moment, looking out into the dark, watching the swing of headlights travel along a distant lane. 'I always knew you'd freak when you realized Amber and I were serious, and I suppose you thought it was a fun way of making sure she forgot about me? You're so bloody heartless, Josh.'

He turned back from the window, bent under the bed and unearthed a pair of black socks. He sniffed at them and then sat down next to Josh to pull them on. 'You should never get married. Remind me to drag you from the altar if you ever get near.'

*

The silence between them was broken by the noise of taps being turned on next door. 'You finished in the bathroom?' Charlie yelled, thumping on Hal's door.

'Yeah. Go ahead.' Hal called back.

'I'm sorry,' said Josh. 'And it didn't happen like that.'

'I know it didn't,' Hal said. 'Amber told me you were so crap in bed that she'd never do it with you again in a million years.' He laughed. 'Hard to believe. And I really do forgive you, Josh. I can forgive anybody anything tonight. You're still my best mate as well as my best man. And, anyway, if we fall out now, I haven't got time to find another one.'

Josh didn't smile. Hal's dignity filled him with self-disgust. 'I'll leave you to it,' he said getting up. 'The others are coming down, we'll open a bottle in about ten minutes. I'll see you then.'

'I'll be there. And . . .' Hal hesitated. 'Forget it, Josh. I have. Please. I don't care about the past.'

Josh couldn't get back to his room fast enough. How impressive Hal had been. How unruffled, unfazed, how certain he'd been about what he was doing. For a brief, terrible moment Josh had to seriously doubt what he was planning. But then he shoved the thought resolutely away. *I am right*, he told himself, *I know I'm right*. He slammed shut the flimsy bedroom door in frustration and the pink rosebud walls shook with the force. He wished he'd been able to talk to Hal properly at some stage, at any stage, before they'd come this far. But the fact that he'd slept with Amber himself had always stopped him dead in his tracks. Hal would never have believed that Josh didn't have some ulterior motive and would only have despised him for bringing her up. And what could he have said? Don't you see that she doesn't love you? Don't you hate it when she rips you to shreds in front of all your friends? Don't you realize that the only two things she finds truly attractive about you are the drop of blue blood and the pile of cash? He couldn't bring himself to say the words even though they were true.

Hal was so impulsively romantic, so happy to see the best in everyone, so quick to fall in love. If he'd only left it a few months longer before proposing, Josh was sure that Amber would have slipped up so badly that even Hal would have seen her for what she was. But he hadn't waited, and so now Josh was going to have to take drastic action. He unwrapped his towel and walked naked into the tiny *en suite* bathroom, feeling overwhelmed by all the doubts and regrets and wishing there was a powerful, painful shower in there to blast them all away.

*

By seven o'clock the main bar of the Little Goose was filling up fast. It was positioned half-way up Vincent Street in a beautiful sixteenth-century timber-framed building with a flagstone floor, head-crackingly low doorways and bulging whitewashed walls. The sort of place, far off the beaten track, that was still unused to tourists.

When Simon Campion, the landlord, had bought the Little Goose and moved in six months earlier, he had been uncomfortably aware of the uncanny similarities between his new acquisition and the Slaughtered Lamb in *An American Werewolf in London*. Sitting in an unobtrusive corner on a weekday evening, trying to decide whether or not to make an offer, he had half expected the locals to surround him and carry him out. A man at the bar wouldn't meet his eye and growled if he came too close, and the landlady's wildly sprouting body hair suggested that she had unwisely left the safety of the pub on the night of a full moon.

In his first six months, Simon had tried hard to change things. He had added five bedrooms, and had bought the next door building, knocked a way through and begun his restaurant. In theory, the Little Goose could now appeal to everyone. The pub went on much as it always had done, with weekly darts matches and a quiz night, and was used by the same old regulars as always as their nightly watering hole. But through a low unobtrusive archway, the restaurant served such enticing, imaginative food that people were being attracted from far and wide. Once they'd established that Simon was all right, the locals were delighted. It was wonderful to have such a place on their doorstep, and they were proud that Welshpool was now being talked of in the same breath as neighbouring gastro-ville, Ludlow.

Tonight there was an old black collie lying like a shag-pile rug on the floor of the pub and a couple of weather-beaten old men standing at the bar in baggy tweed trousers and braces. A game of darts was being watched by most of the room. Good-natured insults loaded with innuendo were being lobbed back and forth between some spotty teenage boys and a table of seven or eight girls.

When Kirsty and Lily walked in they were beamed at by the old men, whistled at half-heartedly by the boys, and given a brief, hostile once-over by the girls. The old dog stretched, stood up and walked over to Kirsty, nosing enthusiastically at her crotch.

'Get your face out of it, Laddie, you can get lost up there,' called out a sharp-faced girl with thin hair held viciously in place by several combs.

The whole room roared with laughter. Kirsty walked over to the girl and put both hands around her neck, pretending to strangle her.

'Join us?' the girl offered.

There'd always been a little friction between them, Kirsty's posh boarding-school preventing her from ever being wholly accepted by this girl and her friends. As a teenager, it had bothered her terribly. Now it had long ceased to matter. But she was grateful for the little peace-offering and at any other time would have pulled up a chair, but just then the door banged open and a gust of freezing air blew into the room.

'I know this place looks like shit but the food's surprisingly good.' The hooray twang sounded even louder in the suddenly silent bar.

Kirsty shifted nervously, knowing just who they were without looking over.

'Shut *up*, Alex, you tactless git.'

So you're Alex, Lily thought, watching ginger kebab man survey the room, his eyes darting quickly from side to side as he looked around for his friends. Standing next to him, a good foot taller, was Josh.

'Hello, gorgeous,' Kirsty murmured in Lily's ear, seeing where Lily was looking, and staring at Josh too. 'You can bend me over a bar-stool any day.'

Almost as if he'd heard, Josh looked across the room and took them both in with a casual glance. Then he let his eyes slide carefully back to Lily. She looked back at him with calm disinterest.

Seeing that the others hadn't yet come in behind him, Josh steered Alex across to the bar. The barman had his back firmly turned away from them and was drying a pint glass with a towel. Josh stood awkwardly, shifting from foot to foot. Next to him the two old men stood quietly drinking their beer, savouring the awkwardness, their eyes alight with enjoyment. Josh was reluctant to call out as it would get everybody else's attention as well as the barman's, but Alex had no such qualms.

'Excuse me, old chap,' he began loudly, 'could we have a couple of beers over here?'

The barman turned.

'We'll have two pints of your local brew. The Shropshire Lad,' Josh said, trying to be conciliatory.

'Two pints, what! I *say*. Oh jolly, jolly good. What a simply smashing idea!' said someone at Alex's shoulder, exaggerating their voices perfectly. Alex turned to him in surprise. The man was about their age and had a face pitted with acne and pale, aggressive eyes.

'You've got straw in your hair,' Alex told him in an amused drawl, not in the least intimidated. Instinctively the man went to touch his head and then stopped himself, furiously. Alex smiled at him with satisfaction, picked up his beer and moved away, threading through the tables, Josh following close behind.

'Still want to score?' Lily asked Kirsty, watching the

exchange but unable to hear what was being said. 'Don't tell me you fancy *Alex*? Look at those jodhpur boots. He probably wears spurs in bed.'

'And keeps a riding whip under his pillow,' Kirsty agreed.

They took the boys' places at the bar, slid on to a pair of stools and ordered a couple of glasses of wine. Lily was quiet, imagining catching the groom alone as he came out of the gents'. 'You don't know me but there's something I must tell you,' she'd begin. Then in another blast of icy night air the other two ushers arrived with the groom himself. Lily and Kirsty looked at him, fascinated to see who all the fuss was about.

The three searched the room until they caught sight of Alex and Josh sitting at the back, then went over to join them. Lily and Kirsty watched Josh leap up to greet them.

'I'll get you a drink,' they heard him say.

'That's unusually generous of you,' Hal grinned, sitting down and rubbing his cold hands together.

'He's got his eye on a chick,' Alex whispered. 'Who happens to be sitting at the bar.'

'Don't you ever rest?' Hal said, looking at Josh.

There was an uncomfortable pause.

Josh said quietly, 'It's your stag night. I think I'm allowed to buy you a beer.'

He got up and left them.

'Alex has booked a table in the restaurant,' Charlie said brightly, pointing at a doorway.

'And? What then?' Hal asked, having visions of lap-dancing Welsh girls in G-strings and stilettos.

'Then we're going back to Pen-y-bont.'

'Penny-a-bonk,' Alex drawled, deliberately mishearing Charlie's awkward pronunciation, 'sounds like my kind of place.'

The Little Goose quickly filled up until all the tables around the bar were crowded with people. Then, just as the boys were starting to talk about moving on, the barman rang a brass bell and announced that that week's quiz was about to begin. Every table was to make up a team. Little blue biros and sheets of paper were hastily handed around and immediately there was a buoyant hush to the room. There were to be twenty questions, the barman explained. A read-through of the answers and then twenty more.

'You're the local, did you know about this?' Josh asked Alex.

Alex shook his head. 'We'll cream them,' he said gleefully, grabbing the paper and pen. 'The peasants will revolt.'

Charlie, already in despair about the plans for Hal, stared at Alex and imagined stuffing the paper and pen into his small round mouth. He adored Hal, and Josh, but several times he had come close to punching Alex. He never wanted to see him or Richard, the third usher, ever again.

But forever in the back of Charlie's mind was the fact that the four of them were Hal's closest friends, and he would never hurt Hal by saying anything too offensive. Charlie knew that, in a simple enough way, the four of them represented all the extremes of Hal's own personality. Alex and Richard had known him through school and then had gone with him into the City. Like Hal they owned thousands of acres and loved dogs and the countryside, and with them, Charlie presumed, Hal could have boring conversations about set-aside and forestry grants. But, Charlie decided, it was with him and Josh that Hal had proper fun. In just a few years of knowing each other, they'd gone running with the bulls in Pamplona, clubbing at the Fridge, drinking in the Red bar and bungee-jumping in Battersea, flying for the weekend to Amsterdam, or Barcelona, and rock-climbing in Thailand. It was because of Charlie that Hal had finally dropped his Husky into a dustbin and because of Josh that he rode a V-Max motorbike to the job he was about to leave. It was with Alex and Richard that Hal had grown old before his time, but with Charlie and Josh that he'd grown young again.

Chill, Charlie told himself now. He took a mouthful of beer and tried to relax, but now he wished he were anywhere else, doing anything else. He loathed Welshpool, loathed the rain, and felt an icy ball of panic rolling around inside him every time he remembered what they were planning to do to Hal.

'Catch!' said Josh, throwing him a cigarette, well aware that Charlie was on the edge, not sure what to do about it.

'Are you ready?' shouted the barman, questions in hand.

'Yes!' everybody roared back, shifting in their seats with anticipation.

'Hang on!' It was the scrofulous youth from the bar,

speaking out from the back of the room. 'I've got a question. Why do posh gits make good ventriloquists?'

The room went quiet.

'Because they always talk out of their arses!'

Then he exploded into laughter.

'And why have toffs got long, thin willies?' a girl shrieked out when the noise had died down a little. She waited for a brief second, looking at the five of them, and then answered with surprising force, 'Because they're tight-fisted *wankers*!'

'And why do all the sheep around here need chastity belts?' shouted Alex angrily, standing up before anyone could stop him.

'Oh shut up!' Josh said in exasperation, pulling him down again, and watched his face glow as bright as his hair.

When Josh plucked up sufficient courage to look around the room again, he saw several people staring in anger and one table of youths that looked as if they'd relish a fight. He gingerly turned sideways and noticed a voluptuous, pretty girl splayed on a bar-stool smiling at him. He grinned back at her, relieved that here was one person, at least, who didn't want him to drop down dead.

'Come on, guys. Let's not hang around here. I'm starving,' he said, laughing in relief and knocking back his drink, eager to get away.

*

'What are they doing?' Kirsty hissed to Lily at the bar. 'They're not staying for the quiz. And once they're eating we've lost them.'

'Undo some buttons and pretend to be a kiss-o-gram,' Lily suggested. 'It's perfect casting.'

'Thanks. But what do we *really* do?' Kirsty said, exasperated that Lily wasn't taking the problem seriously enough. 'We'll have to have dinner too.'

'No way,' said Lily. 'I'm a potter, not a merchant banker.'

'It's all right, I know Simon *very* well,' Kirsty raised her eyebrows suggestively. 'He owes me a lot more than a couple of dinners.'

'Get thee to a nunnery!'

'I'm going to go and ask him.' Kirsty knocked back her wine, jumped off her stool and disappeared out of the room.

Lily waited, listening to the quiz questions with half an ear, and watched the boys with interest as they got up and threaded their way through the tables towards her, noticing even in those few moments how much they all deferred to Josh. He had his back to her, but then he turned, still talking and joking over his shoulder to the others. And looking at him properly for the first time, Lily found herself entranced too, caught up in his wonderful eyes and quick smile and by the golden energy that emanated effortlessly from him. As he walked towards her, he pulled off a thick chocolate coloured jersey, taking half a T-shirt away with it, and gave Lily a quick glimpse of a brown stomach that would have done anybody proud. He caught her watching him and grinned back at her, and unable to stop herself, she smiled back.

All five then slowly filed past her as they made their way to the restaurant. He'll be a complete bastard, she told herself. There was no mistaking that sleepy, sexy, arrogant look in his eye. It didn't surprise her at all that someone who looked like him would concoct such an outrageous plan and think he could get away with it. As she thought about it, Lily was flooded with absolute determination not to let him succeed. If he hadn't exuded such nonchalance, such confidence in his own supremacy, had not been quite so good-looking, quite so able to fool around with the others despite everything he had in mind for later, she might not have felt it quite so strongly.

Would it be enough if she simply caught Hal alone and told him what she and Kirsty had overheard? She doubted it. And even if Hal believed her and confronted the others, there was no guarantee that they wouldn't try to spirit him away immediately. The best thing would be for her and Kirsty to let the evening go ahead as planned but to find out somehow where they were staying in Llanygoed. They could wait until the morning and then pick Hal up and take him back to Grace's. Whatever they had to do later on, what was most important now was that she and Kirsty shadow the group for the rest of the evening. Not something she'd have any problem convincing Kirsty about, Lily reckoned.

Out of the corner of her eye Lily could see her already hurrying back, pushing hard against the wall of people now at the bar.

'We're on,' she said in excitement. 'He's put us right next to their table. Let's go.'

Lily was wearing bootleg dark grey velvet trousers and a silvery blue top edged with downy feathers that she'd found in a vintage clothes shop in Chester. It was nineteen-forties and very skimpy. Her blonde hair was held back by a slide, accentuating her large, clear eyes. As she walked into the restaurant with Kirsty everybody watched her.

'My God, it's Gwynnie,' whispered Charlie.

'She's stunning,' Hal agreed.

Josh considered her. Would she seem quite so lovely if he had caught her eye on the escalator in Harvey Nichols or brushed against her in some club, he wondered? Would she stand out against all the models and actresses who moved through the revolving doors of his offices every morning? Or was it the unexpectedness of finding her here that had knocked him for six? As fast as he asked himself the questions he knew the answers. Lily would stand out anywhere. She was too small to be a model and she didn't have the sleek, expensive look of the girls he knew in London, but she looked even better for that. He wished he was seeing her in different circumstances, some time when he could have engineered an opportunity to get to know her. Tonight he had to concentrate on Hal, and he knew he shouldn't do anything that might jeopardize his plans. She would have to remain forever in his mind as the one who got away.

3

Kirsty and Lily sat down at a neighbouring table. Lily chose a bottle of Pinot Grigio and lit a cigarette off the candle. The wine coursed through Kirsty, who had barely eaten all day, and she looked at Lily, her eyes glittering. She leaned forward, putting the candle to one side.

'Sod the blokes. I'm really pleased to be here with you. This will be one great dinner!'

'I haven't been to a restaurant since I left London,' Lily said.

'So you've never eaten here with Grace?'

'God, no. I can never get her out of the house.'

'Bring her here some time. It would do her good.'

Lily nodded, knowing that she'd never persuade Grace. She arched her back, putting her sister out of her mind.

'So what's it with you and the chef?' she asked. 'And why don't I know about it?'

'I'll tell you in a minute. When I know he's not about to jump out of the kitchen and hear me.'

Lily nodded. 'Okay. Wait until we've ordered.'

'It's not that I've *not* told you anything. There's just nothing much to tell.'

'But enough to get a table and a free meal out of him.'

Kirsty smiled up at the waiter arriving at their table to take their order. 'I'll tell you later,' she told Lily.

When they had both chosen from the menu and the waiter had left them alone again, Kirsty turned back to Lily.

'Let's talk about you for a change. Have you decided how long you're going to stay?'

She poured more wine into Lily's glass and held her breath, hoping that Lily was going to say she would stay on indefinitely. She knew that Welshpool had gradually begun to rise in Lily's estimation, that the isolation, initially so overwhelming, now seemed protective and benevolent, that the clean cold air and the bustling friend-liness of the town had become something Lily loved too. But she also knew that Lily had had jobs lined up in London and that she had to be thinking about what she was going to do in the long term. Working and earning and getting on with her life.

'I don't know,' Lily said, knocking back the wine. 'I could imagine staying for ever, but I can't – I'm in Grace's house, and if I stay much longer she'll drive me crazy.'

Kirsty pulled a face. 'Go! Leave her now! If it was me I wouldn't have lasted a week.'

'I've promised myself that if it gets too bad I'll look for a cottage. If I worked a bit harder I could sell enough stuff to pay the rent.'

When their starters were laid down in front of them, Lily's scallops were dwarfed by Kirsty's plate of roast pumpkin risotto, a Little Goose speciality. Kirsty gazed at her plate in wonder, acknowledging that this was why she was size fourteen and Lily was only a ten, but not caring at all.

As Lily ate she looked around the dining-room with interest, careful not to catch the eye of any of the men at the table. The room was colourwashed a deep pinky red which looked wonderful against the exposed beams in the ceilings and walls, warm and comforting against the cold of the night. Tables and chairs were tucked into alcoves and corners, and twelve more people ate at a Jacobean oak table in the middle of the room. And all around them was the loud drone of satisfied eating and drinking.

They sat in mellow silence for a few minutes more, working through their food and happy to let the atmosphere wash over them, then Lily dramatically put down her knife and fork.

'Kirsty, I'm not going to let them get away with it. I want to stop them,' she said.

Kirsty looked at her doubtfully.

'Don't get involved,' she said. 'You don't know the circumstances.'

'Something like this happened to Grace.'

Kirsty tensed. No one in the town knew what precisely had happened to Grace. There were some facts and of course everybody had speculated, but only in a concerned kind of way. Seeing her out on the High Street, head down, avoiding eye-contact, most people who encountered her were filled with pity.

Kirsty was no longer one of those people. Perfectly sympathetic before she had met Lily, she now found Grace irritating beyond belief and was forever teetering on the brink of telling her so, holding back only out of respect for Lily. She disliked the way Grace wafted around the house in her dressing-gown, pale and tearstained, while Lily bent double dragging dustbin sacks out to the back gate, and how, as far as Kirsty could see, she had taken advantage of Lily's arrival to absolve herself from the responsibility of every single aspect of running her house.

Lily had some idea of what Kirsty thought but she didn't care, confident that if only Kirsty knew all that Grace had been through she would understand how fragile she was, and how Lily had to give her all the help in the world. Until tonight, Lily had never felt like telling Kirsty what had happened but now, suddenly, as they sat together, the words poured out of her.

'Jeremy was never good marriage material,' she concluded with a sigh. 'The last we heard of him, he was swimming with dolphins off the coast of Ireland.'

Kirsty put her hand over her mouth but she couldn't stop herself laughing. Lily grinned tolerantly.

'So, don't you admire these guys for sticking their necks out?' Kirsty demanded, serious again. 'Isn't that just what you should have done for Grace? Surely you're contradicting yourself! You should have done the same for Grace and saved her all that agony. She'd have thanked you for locking her up for six months if it would have saved her from the wedding day!'

'Oh, I don't know, I don't know!' Lily groaned. 'And I couldn't have done anything about it. There wouldn't have been any point.' She shrugged. 'Perhaps in the very, very early days I might have said something without sending her off her rocker, but I didn't. And then she was in love. I tried to say something then and nearly lost my life. So, after that I kept quiet. Anyway, she knew I wasn't bowled over by Jeremy.'

'What about your parents? Did they try to say something to her too?'

'It's not that they don't care,' Lily said slowly. 'I know that they care.' She looked hard at her plate. 'But they don't want to hear about it, or think about it. They like things to be happy ...' she paused. 'Anything difficult, no thank you.' She looked up at Lily. 'They haven't been to see Grace once. They gave her some money towards her house, but they'd never come down and stay with her.'

'I'm sorry,' Kirsty said.

'So it was always up to me. And so I decided to tell her what I thought of Jeremy. And how miserable I thought she'd be if she married him.' Lily winced. 'I was being mild, but it was like I'd lit a rocket.'

She drank some more wine. 'The point I'm getting to is that in the end Grace weighed up everyone's reactions, whatever they were, and made her own decision. And that's what was important. In the end she was free to do that. It was up to her, not me. Who am I to say what makes her happy?'

Kirsty didn't look convinced.

'And the same goes for this lot. Who are they to say how this guy *Hal* lives his life? It's not up to them.'

'But sometimes your friends know you best of all,' Kirsty replied. 'Better than you know yourself. And they can see the disaster you're walking into when you can't. Sometimes a friend will put you straight.'

'No,' Lily said. 'It may be the best thing for Hal. He might be walking into a disaster. But it makes no difference.'

'Surely you're not being much of a friend if all you say is what people want to hear.'

Lily nodded. 'But there's a time and a place, and there's some things you talk about and some things you leave alone. And then there's the point beyond which you've gone too far.'

To Kirsty's dismay Lily's eyes promptly filled up with tears.

'I bet Amber's absolutely lovely. All this will be because those stupid men don't want to lose one of their mates.'

'Okay,' Kirsty said, touching her hand. 'I'm in there with you. You're right. We can't let it happen.' She thought for a moment. 'You know we'll have to drive him to Oxford tomorrow? It's the only way we can be sure that he'll make it on time. Can you get away?'

'But your car's in the garage,' Lily despaired.

Kirsty thought for a second. 'Grace has left hers here, though.'

'There is no way I can involve Grace in this.'

'You don't have to,' Kirsty said, chasing the last grains of rice around her plate. Just borrow it, you're always doing it. We'll be back by teatime.'

Lily knew that Kirsty was right. Grace probably wouldn't ever know the car had gone.

There was a man coming to their table, Lily saw in surprise when she looked up again. He was moving purposefully, wearing a long, expertly tied white apron, and he had Kirsty in his eye. And for once, Kirsty had done well, Lily thought, promptly swallowing the last of her food.

He stopped beside Kirsty and crouched down beside her.

'So why didn't you call?' he asked quietly, ignoring Lily for the moment.

'Don't be boring,' Kirsty said, not looking at him.

There was a nasty silence. It wasn't the first time Lily had witnessed someone being given the brush-off by Kirsty. Lily wondered how much charm she had wielded just a few minutes earlier in order to get them a table, and felt embarrassed at Kirsty's abruptness now. When on the pull, Kirsty was a lethal combination of out-and-out flirtatiousness and down-to-earth good humour and men fell for it over and over again, but when she was no longer interested she showed a brutal detachment that took people completely by surprise.

'The scallops were great!' Lily muttered into the heavy silence, tapping her plate with her fork, but Simon was being bombarded with get-lost vibes from Kirsty and didn't hear her.

'We need time for a proper conversation, Kirsty,' he said, standing up again, 'and we're going to have one.'

Kirsty finally looked up at him.

'Not now!' He caught Lily's eye and smiled. 'I don't want to ruin everybody's dinner. But soon. Okay?'

'I'll call you.'

'Make sure you do,' said Simon, 'and enjoy your meal.' He nodded to Lily and left.

'What was all that about?' asked Lily the second he was out of earshot.

'Nothing much. Honestly, he's not worth the effort.'

'Oh yes he is. Tell me what's going on.'

'You haven't seen him without any clothes on,' Kirsty smiled grimly. 'Best to keep away.'

'You're not serious? Have you seen him with no clothes on?'

Kirsty sighed and didn't reply.

'Hey, I've known you for six months, I see you practically every day and yet I know nothing about this at all. When did it start?'

'About five days before it finished. Not long ago. But it was nothing. A couple of dinners. I didn't tell you because there was nothing to tell.'

Lily looked steadily back at her. 'Are you sure? And if it's all finished, why do I think he doesn't know that yet?'

Kirsty shrugged.

'Okay.' Lily said. 'So we're not going to talk about it.'

She gave Kirsty a long look. In the months since Lily had known her this had happened once or twice before, but as none of the previous guys were anything to write home about it had been a blessing that they'd been binned so swiftly. But this man, Simon, was completely, wonderfully different. Even in the few seconds that Lily had had to take him in, she'd known that Kirsty would be mad to let him go.

'So!' Lily said, changing the subject and nodding in the direction of the boys. 'What are we going to do about them? We'll need to know where they're keeping Hal for a start. Llanygoed's such a tiny place. It shouldn't be hard.' Lily paused, watching them. 'And you know, the more we see of them, the less I like what I see.'

'I agree. I'm sure the ginger one is a gerbil. And the little dark-haired one gives me the creeps. But,' Kirsty looked them over again, 'I'd say the other three have definite potential.'

'So you're including the groom?'

'*Hal*,' said Kirsty, rolling his name on her tongue. 'Maybe. Depends on what happens to him tomorrow. But either of the other two.'

'They're all yours.'

Kirsty grinned. 'So, how are we going to infiltrate? Lose a contact lens?'

'But we don't wear them.'

'So we'll never find it.'

'Okay then,' Lily said, convinced. 'Do it!'

Straight away Kirsty said, 'Fuck!' loudly and clutched her right eye.

'Oh, Kirsty! Have you lost your contact lens?' said Lily. The boys immediately stopped their conversation, scraped back their chairs and all stood up.

'Keep still,' said Charlie, immediately coming over. 'I can see it on the floor.' He moved over to their table, bent down on hands and knees, and studied the floor close to Lily's ankles.

'While you're down there . . .' said Alex.

'No, bugger, it's just some dust.' Charlie gazed longingly up at Lily. 'Hi,' he said. 'I'm Charlie.'

Josh moved swiftly over to intercept.

'You'd better stay away,' he told Charlie firmly, knowing that Charlie had seen nothing remotely resembling a contact lens, and pushed him gently back towards a chair. 'He's as blind as a bat,' he told Lily, shoving Charlie down. 'So he'll only squash it.' Then he held out his hand. 'I'm Josh,' he said.

Next to them Hal started patting the tablecloth in gentle patterns.

'I don't think we're ever going to find it,' he told Kirsty.

'Is it hard or soft?' said Alex, coming to join him.

'Disposable,' said Kirsty.

Alex belched in response and then sat down again and poured himself a glass of wine.

'Better take the other one out,' suggested Charlie. 'Isn't it much worse with only one in?'

Behind them the waiter was hovering with his main course.

'Come and have a glass of champagne with us after dinner to celebrate my stag night?' Hal offered and the others immediately all backed him up.

'Stag night? Congratulations! We'd love to,' said Kirsty. 'Wouldn't we?' she nodded at Lily.

So far, so good, thought Lily. 'Thanks. That would be great,' she said.

'The groom's sweet,' said Kirsty as they waited for their main course. 'I was wondering what he'd be like.'

'Anyone in this room that you don't fancy?' asked Lily.

'You know something?' Kirsty mused, ignoring the question and pouring more wine into her glass. 'One thing

I will never, ever have is a hen night. I can't think of anything worse. No men, all your girlfriends snapping at each other.' She sighed dramatically. 'I *know* none of mine would get on.'

Lily laughed. 'One glass and she's off. And I'm not so difficult to get on with. Don't your friends get on with me?'

'What do you think?' Kirsty said, then she laughed. 'No, they do. Of course they do. But I can think of nothing worse than pissed women with blown-up condoms on their heads throwing up in the loos of some cheap Italian restaurant.'

'No, Kirsty! Think Harvester Inn at the very least.'

Kirsty laughed. 'And you must have some grim friends.'

Lily glanced over to Hal. 'Just like he does.'

They both went quiet, watching them all around him, eating and laughing, passing things for him to try, having a good time.

When their own main course arrived Lily stared at it suspiciously. Having witnessed the fall-out between Kirsty and Simon, and because their meal was for free, she wondered whether it might have arrived raw or doused in pepper, but she had underestimated Simon. When her plate was put in front of her, Lily vowed that it was the most beautiful meal she'd ever seen. Seven wedges of pink Welsh lamb, roasted with anchovies, garlic and rosemary, had been built up into an intricate, layered castle and was sitting above a round of perfect mashed potato. Lily took a mouthful of lamb, so tender it could have been eaten with a spoon.

'Heaven,' she exclaimed with pleasure. 'I wasn't sure about the anchovies but they're not fishy at all.'

'It's the best thing I've ever had here apart from Simon,' Kirsty agreed.

'You can't say that!' Lily told her. 'Not when you're not going to tell me what's going on.'

*

Later, the boys called Lily and Kirsty over to join them and they all squashed up on the two oak settles running down either side of their table and drank a couple of bottles of champagne.

Squashed between Josh and Charlie, Lily saw straight away that Josh was determinedly keeping Hal's glass full. And yet still Hal seemed unaffected, talking coherently about how he'd been left a celebratory bottle of whisky on the doorstep of the cottage by a neighbour. Lily looked at his huge gentle hands and the soft hair falling into his big blue eyes. You're so lovely, she thought. I hope you marry her, and that she deserves you.

She was also aware of Josh's hard thigh pressing against hers. I'm part of the game, she thought. Part of tonight's entertainment. He knows he's gorgeous and he knows he can pull just about anyone, and so tonight he'll try it on with me. For once, Lily found it amusing, her decision to ride to Hal's rescue making her invincible, one step ahead of anything he could do or say.

Opposite her, she could hear Kirsty getting on surprisingly well with Alex.

'Did you have to speak so loud in the bar? You're such a big mouth,' she heard Kirsty tell him.

'Cheers,' Alex replied. 'You have a big mouth yourself. A big, red, beautiful mouth and I want to kiss it.' He refilled Kirsty's glass and opened an engraved cigarette case.

Kirsty looked back at him, for once completely silenced.

'When can we arrange it?' Alex said. He selected a cigarette and clapped shut the box. 'Give me your telephone number.'

'No chance.'

Josh turned to Lily, smiling. 'He won't give up easily, not now.'

'I think she can handle it,' Lily replied, noticing threads of gold in his green eyes.

'It's time he met someone who could keep him in order. She was perfect from the moment she first opened her big mouth.' Josh paused. 'Has she got a boyfriend?'

Lily nodded. 'So, how long have you known Hal?' she asked awkwardly, wanting him to stop staring at her.

'Not long. A couple of years,' he answered, abandoning his decision to leave her alone.

'And what's the bride like?'

'Perfect, they were made for each other.'

He lies so effortlessly, she thought.

'What about you?' he said, softly. 'Anyone made for you yet?'

For a moment Lily paused. I'm drunk and he's good-looking, she warned herself. But in the morning I'll be sober.

'No, not yet.'

He's about to betray his best friend. I don't like him at all. But his smile was as infectious as a yawn and she couldn't stop herself smiling back.

Then, breaking the moment, Charlie tentatively stretched across her and caught Josh's sleeve.

'I need to talk to you,' Charlie told Josh, nodding towards the gents'.

Damn, thought Josh, wondering what was up. 'Don't go away,' he said to Lily.

He tried to stand, then realizing that he had no room, climbed up high on to the bench beside her. Lily immediately felt the hairs rising on the back of her neck even though he didn't touch her. Josh stood for a second to get his balance and then hopped gently to the floor and followed Charlie out of the room.

*

'Sorry,' said Charlie once the door of the gents' was closed. 'Was that bad timing?'

'Don't worry about it. What's up?' Josh asked, sensing trouble.

'I'm sorry,' said Charlie. 'But what I have to say won't come as any surprise. I'm not doing it. I wanted you to know now.'

Josh tested his weight against a basin and then gingerly leaned back. 'It's okay,' he said, well prepared for the conversation. 'I knew you'd feel like this.'

'It's a mad idea. And in any case,' Charlie went on as if Josh hadn't spoken, 'Hal will just go and get married next weekend instead.'

'No, he won't.'

'What?'

'That's the whole point!' said Josh.

'Why? What do you mean?'

'I know that Hal's going through with this only because he's too much of a gentleman not to. He told me so tonight.'

Charlie looked stunned. 'What did he say?'

'That it was too late to do anything else – you know, the guests, the cake, his parents, her parents.'

'My God,' said Charlie.

'But what if we take the decision for him?' Josh looked intently at Charlie. 'Make it easy for him. Don't give him the option of getting there tomorrow. He's not going to go and marry Amber next weekend! He'll be so bloody relieved.'

Charlie still looked unconvinced. 'Are you guessing or did he definitely say he didn't want to go ahead?'

In his own mind Josh was doing the right thing. He took a deep breath and chose his words with care.

'He said that he couldn't back out because it was all organized and because he couldn't hurt Amber that much. But that he wished he could.'

'He *said* that? He said that he wished he could *back out*? Those actual words?'

'Yes.'

'Shit.'

Charlie shook his head, but he was believing it. Because it all fell into place. The weeks Charlie had spent waiting for Hal to change his mind, his own certainty that this engagement was wrong, all convincing him that what Josh was saying now was the truth.

'So we do it for him,' Charlie repeated. 'Do the others know about this?'

'They don't need to. They're on for it anyway. It's only you who's bottling out.'

Charlie walked over to the basin and stared at himself in the mirror.

'Okay, I'll do it,' he told himself. 'You've convinced me. Bloody hell, we'd better be right. What a mess. What a terrible mess. Can you imagine how horrendous it's going to be tomorrow?'

'Awful,' agreed Josh. 'And I'm the one to tell everybody.' He paused for a few seconds. 'What should I do? Tell Amber, or wait till the service is about to begin and tell the whole congregation?'

'You can't do that to her.'

'But if I tell her too early she might still manage to find Hal and persuade him to come back.'

'Not with us there to stop him.'

'That's why you three have got to stay on in the cottage. If we pour enough down Hal he won't wake up till midday. Plenty of time for me to get to Oxford, to Amber's house, and persuade her that Hal's changed his mind. If I manage to convince her she'll start cancelling everything straight away.'

'But if he changes his mind, decides he wants to go through with it all, I really don't think I can stop him,' Charlie warned.

'Charlie! You'll have to. He's very fond of her, he'll feel

absolutely terrible about it. Of course he'll *say* that he wants to go. You'd do the same thing. But you mustn't take any notice. He mustn't marry her! You have to agree not to let him out of the house!'

Charlie looked at him uneasily, but he repeated Josh's words to keep him quiet. 'I won't let him out of the house.'

Josh relaxed a little. 'We're doing the right thing,' he said, putting an arm around his shoulders.

They made their way back to the table and sat down again, but Lily was talking to Hal now and Josh had no opportunity to work himself back into the conversation.

'Hal,' he said eventually, plunging in. 'We should be off. We'll be stripping you,' he joked, 'but don't let it concern you.'

'Is that all of us?' said Alex, immediately unlacing his brogues.

He's so public school, thought Kirsty.

So this is it, thought Lily. We've got this far. Now we must wait until the morning. She got up quickly and moved towards Kirsty, who was still talking to Alex.

'I'm coming, hang on a minute,' Kirsty said, wanting Lily to leave her alone. 'I'll see you outside.'

'Sure, I'll get our coats.'

She stood on the pavement outside and looked up at the sky, then jumped as she felt someone take her arm.

'Good bye, golden girl,' said a velvety voice in her ear. It was Josh. His kiss was as light as a feather, soft on her cheek. 'Finding you was a revelation,' he whispered. 'I didn't know people like you lived here. I wish I'd more time.'

More time for what exactly? Lily thought, looking up into his pussycat eyes. She rested her hands gently on his shoulders.

''Bye,' she said, and leaned forward and kissed him slowly and softly on the mouth. He started, and she watched his eyes as surprise turned instantly into lust, but before he could regain the initiative and grab her again, she moved out of reach.

Seemingly unaware of what Lily had just done, Hal carefully took her hands.

'Next time I'm in Welshpool . . .' he said seriously and then laughed at the look of doubt on her face. 'Honestly! I mean it. I'm coming back – sober. It's a wonderful place and I've seen hardly anything at all.'

'She lives on Green Lane. Over the hill and round the bend,' said Kirsty, joining them.

The rain clouds had disappeared, leaving the night clear and cold, with a deep, black sky and silver stars. The tarmac glittered wet in the dim street-lamps. There was no one else in sight and a wonderful sense of end-of-the-evening quiet.

'We're off,' said Hal, walking unsteadily down the middle of the road with his shoes in his hand.

'Look after him,' said Lily earnestly to Charlie.

She left Charlie and ran after Hal down the road, catching his arm. 'Good luck for tomorrow,' she said, looking up at him.

'I'll need it,' he replied. It was dark, and his eyes were so far above her that she couldn't make out the expression on his face. Then before she could say any more, Charlie joined them and clumsily tried to turn Hal back towards the group.

'How are you getting there?' Kirsty asked Alex.

'I'm driving. And no, I'm not too pissed.' Alex pointed his alarm key at a dark green Golf GTi parked a few cars away. 'Come on, guys, or we'll be here all night!'

He stood holding back the front seat while Charlie, Richard and Hal squashed into the back.

Lily and Kirsty waited until they had driven out of sight.

'So what do you think you were doing?' Kirsty said grinning.

'What the hell. It was good for him – to know he hadn't got me all neatly worked out.'

'Good for you too. I'll bet you're still weak at the knees. And it *is* that cottage on the side of the lane. Off the Builth Road. It's called Pen-y-bont.'

'How do you know all that?' Lily asked, still thinking that up close Josh had been completely irresistible.

'Alex told me. It's no secret, after all.'

'You don't fancy him, do you?'

Kirsty smiled and shook her head. '*Me?* Fancy Alex? Of course not! It was just a bit of fun.'

'Our rescue can wait until the morning, can't it?' Lily said as they walked home. 'I'm so tired.'

Kirsty nodded. 'As long as we get there early enough.

The wedding's at three thirty. Hal should be in Oxford by two at the latest.'

'What if the others wake up and stop us leaving with him?'

'We'll cross that bridge when we come to it. I hardly think they'll fight us for him.'

'Poor Hal,' Lily shook her head.

When the time came for them to go their separate ways, Lily stopped, feeling closer to Kirsty than ever before. 'Stay the night? Grace is away. You can have her room.'

Kirsty nodded and slid her arm through Lily's and they set off down the road, matching strides.

*

The Golf bounced at high speed down a tiny rutted track and came to a rocking halt outside the grey stone cottage.

'Welcome home,' said Alex. He felt in his coat for the key, then shoved against the door and turned the lock.

Hal felt particularly sick. The fresh air outside the Little Goose had momentarily cleared his head but Alex's rally-style driving had done him no favours. He sank to the floor, head in his hands.

'Oh, God. What have you done to me?' he moaned.

Won't be long now, thought Charlie, looking down at him as Alex heaved him up and helped him into an armchair.

'Music, camera, action!' Hal commanded unsteadily from his chair. 'Where are the girls?'

'On their way,' said Josh, appearing in the doorway with a case of beer.

But the beer was barely touched. After all they'd drunk at dinner, and with the plan for the next day cutting a heavy swathe through the party, it was only twenty minutes before Josh and Charlie put their arms around Hal and half carried him into Alex's grandmother's bedroom.

'Like getting into a boat, she keeps moving,' Hal slurred, face down on the bedspread, trying to lift his legs up on to the bed one at a time and ending up half kneeling on the floor.

'I'll get you some water,' offered Josh, going into the next-door bathroom. He found a tooth mug and rinsed out a manky brown sludge from the bottom, deciding as he did so that this would be the only glass he'd allow Hal to drink. He needed all possible advantages, and the worse the hangover, the better.

When Hal and the others had gone to bed, Josh went back downstairs. He sat in the dark, silent sitting-room deep in thought, alternately knocking back sweet sherry from a tumbler and blowing immaculate smoke rings towards the dying embers of the fire. He didn't go to bed and, as the dawn light finally broke across the hills, he quietly opened the back door of the cottage and slipped outside.

4

At five to seven Lily left her bedroom. She'd set her alarm for half past six and had been fully awake the moment it began to ring. Feeling surprisingly clear-headed and energetic, she'd dressed in navy jeans and trainers.

'No, no, much too early,' protested Kirsty drowsily as Lily flung open the door to her bedroom.

'Get up,' ordered Lily. 'The more time we have the better.'

'Make me a cup of coffee,' Kirsty moaned, face down in her pillow, feeling terrible.

Over breakfast, Lily suggested they go by bicycle.

Kirsty's headache gathered force with the thought. 'A *bicycle*!' she repeated in disbelief. 'You are *so* Famous Five!'

Lily stood up, taking their plates over to the sink. 'Don't be pathetic. And anyway, I liked the Famous Five. Dick and Julian were lovely boys.'

'You're sad.'

Kirsty looked a bit more perky after her coffee and Lily judged it the right moment to try again. 'A car could wake them up. It's so quiet there,' she pleaded. 'It's only a couple of miles. It'll do your head good.'

'No! No! No!' shouted Kirsty, her hands over her ears. 'The hills are the size of Everest and it's frigging February!'

'You're such a slob. It's a lovely sunny day. Come on,' Lily begged.

'Listen,' Kirsty paused. 'I am *not* a going-on-a-bike kind of girl! *And* I've just woken up.'

Lily looked at her, knowing when she was beaten. 'Okay, I'll go on my own.'

'See what's going on, how many of them are still there. Try to talk to Hal, then come back and get me and the car.'

'And you make sure you don't do a thing,' Lily told her. 'Not a thing. Actually I know what you're going to do. You'll go straight back to bed.'

Lily left the house by a back door and walked through the long wet grass to the shed that housed her bike and her pottery.

She wheeled the bike away from the house and set off.

As she cycled slowly up the first, hideously steep hill she had to squint against the pale early morning sun. A little while later she stopped for a moment to get her breath and leant against her bike, looking through a gateway at the awesome landscape spread out before her. As always, the vast, panoramic beauty of the scenery took her by surprise. Head down, cycling up a sunken lane, it was easy to forget where she was. Now Lily looked out for a minute across the endless undulating hills and valleys mapped out in the early sunshine for hundreds of miles around her. It was utterly still, utterly silent: no people, no cars, not even the sound of the wind in the trees or the chirp of a bird broke the spell.

She knew that a couple of bends later she would come

to the tiny rutted track that belonged to Pen-y-Bont. Taking a deep juddering breath she set off once more, suddenly feeling overwhelmed with nerves. Her hands, slippery with sweat, slid around the handlebars and, as she cycled towards the track, one foot suddenly kicked itself off its pedal and she nearly came off with it. She freewheeled for a moment and grabbed hold of her back brake, which immediately began a noisy, resentful groan of complaint.

She took some deep calming breaths, trying to steady her nerves and her stomach, and with one eye on the potholes she made her way towards the cottage.

It was as if the house itself was fast asleep. Upstairs, curtains were drawn across the two tiny latticed windows, like eyelids, and the front door was still ajar, like a mouth fallen half open. The Golf was parked outside.

Lily looked at her watch. It was just past eight. She left her bicycle on the grass and slipped silently in.

Much of the kitchen was in deep shadow. She could make out several empty cans of beer and a jar of tomato chutney surrounded by ash and crumbs on an old pine table. The room was filled with the pungent, morning-after combination of wine and cigarette smoke. She walked through an open doorway and found herself in a sitting-room with a large brick fireplace, the ashes still glowing a bright, pale pink. She opened another door and there, lying on a sagging velvet sofa under a brown wool blanket, was Charlie, fast asleep.

Lily quietly shut the door again, tiptoed away and turned towards the stairs. She climbed slowly, trying desperately to outguess the creaky floorboards but choosing the wrong place to put her foot on almost every stair. At the top were two small doors, one to the left, one to the right. She tried the left one, having to half bend her head to get through, and there was Hal.

He was tucked tightly into heavy, white cotton sheets so that only his sleeping face was showing. He was so pale and still that for a moment Lily went cold, but then he made a tiny sound in his throat and she sighed with relief. If I wake you up now, while the others are asleep, I can get you out of the house without them even knowing I was here, she thought. She crept towards him.

'Wake up, wake up,' she said softly. 'Hal!' Hal did not stir.

Have they given him pills? she wondered. If so, they *could* have killed him. She reached into the bed and touched his bare shoulder and again whispered his name, but there was still no response. Lily hesitated for a second, worrying that if she shook him awake he would shout and bring the others in. She crouched down and stroked him gently on the soft skin of his cheekbone, looking down at his sleeping face. Finally Hal stirred and a strong arm wrapped around Lily and drew her close, pulling her on to the bed beside him. For a few seconds she lay stiffly, her eyes wide open, her nose pressed uncomfortably deep into his armpit.

'Hello, sweet pea,' he murmured gently, into her hair.

Lily shot upright. He thinks I'm Amber!

'It's Lily,' she whispered. 'Be quiet!'

'I thought I was dreaming.'

'I had to wake you! You've got to get up. They're going to make you miss your wedding.'

'What?' Hal smiled, opening his large sleepy eyes but making no attempt to sit up.

'I'm really sorry,' she said. 'They don't want you to marry Amber. They've been planning this for ages. They want to keep you here. You've got to come with me now, before they wake up. Before they can stop us.'

Lily was just about to throw back his sheets when a voice from the doorway said calmly, 'I wouldn't do that.'

Lily screamed. It was Charlie, dishevelled and heavy with sleep. He rubbed his eyes. 'I wouldn't do that,' he repeated, 'because he's stark, bollock naked.'

Hal sat up in the bed.

'Did you hear what I said?' Lily asked Hal urgently, and then she turned to Charlie. 'Tell him!' she commanded. 'Tell Hal your plans for today.'

Charlie stayed silent.

'Is it true, Charlie?' asked Hal suddenly completely awake. 'Can you really hate Amber that much?'

'Lily, if you don't mind,' said Charlie, turning to her.

'No. Let her stay. I can obviously trust her more than I can you.'

'You say that,' Charlie said quietly, walking further into the room. 'But I'm trying to stop you making the biggest mistake of your life.'

'How can you say something so corny,' Hal yelled at him, 'about something so important to me?'

'I want to help,' Charlie remained calm. 'I'm not going to stop you going to your wedding. If it's what you really want. But I'm giving you a final chance to get out.'

'But why?' shouted Hal. 'Why would I want to do that?'

'Because deep down you *know* this is wrong.' He stopped, waiting for Hal's response, but Hal didn't speak. 'I'm not going to start cataloguing Amber's faults. That wouldn't do any good, but you have to believe we wouldn't go this far if it wasn't something we were sure about . . . God knows, we've tried everything else.' Charlie fell silent.

'You're wrong,' said Hal. 'You've been wrong from the very beginning. Although why I should need to convince you I still don't know. And I'll never, ever forgive you for this.'

It was as if all the fight, all the uncertainty, suddenly went out of Charlie. He looked back at Hal, nodded meekly and moved towards the door, then turned back again at the last moment. 'I'm sorry,' he said, from the doorway.

Lily followed him downstairs, where Charlie sat down at the kitchen table and put his head in his hands.

'Coffee?' she suggested and he slowly got up again, rummaging in a cupboard above the sink.

'What were you doing up there?' he asked. 'What do *you* know about all this?'

'Not a lot. Enough to decide I wanted to stop you.'

'Interfering woman.' He smiled weakly. 'God, it's a mess.'

'It's not too late. It can all go ahead.'

'What a mess! What a mess! What a fucking mess!' Charlie banged his hand heavily against the wall. 'Of course Josh was wrong. I *knew* he was.'

He looked back at Lily, full of despair. 'How have I let this happen?'

'But it's not too late.'

Charlie ignored her. 'It doesn't surprise me that Hal won't change his mind now, he's a good bloke and he's not going to leave Amber in the lurch. That's why we all thought we should make the decision for him. And Josh is so unimaginably persuasive. You end up believing anything. Anything he wants you to believe.'

He banged two china cups, as thin as eggshells, into their saucers and brought them over to the kitchen table. 'Sorry about these,' he added, pouring in the coffee. 'We can't find any mugs.'

'Tell me what's wrong with her, why you thought it was worth all this? You wouldn't have got involved in all this with no reason.'

Charlie sat down.

'Oh, there's reason,' he said. 'But that's not why we did it.'

Lily looked taken aback. 'But I thought . . .'

'What we wanted to do was give Hal his first real opportunity to think about it. When he's with Amber, it's impossible for him to see straight.'

'And now you're surprised that, thinking straight, Hal has no intention of changing his mind?'

Charlie didn't answer.

'Tell me what she's like,' Lily said instead.

'She's mesmerizing.' He looked at Lily. 'Amazing. I met her with Josh. Hal was still in Japan. Josh and I went to this drinks party in Clerkenwell.'

In his mind Charlie saw Amber walking into the party out of the night. He and Josh had been propping up the banisters, keeping an eye on the new arrivals, when Amber had walked in. Cold and beautiful, with long brown hair as smooth as chocolate.

'When I first met her I thought she was fan-bloody-tastic. When she and Hal got together I would have swapped places with him any time. We all would have done, in theory.' He paused. 'Then Josh put the theory into practice. He had no idea that Hal was that serious about her. None of us realized. And then, just two months ago, they announced they were getting married.' He looked at Lily and shook his head. 'He's completely mad. And God knows why she wants to marry Hal. At least Josh was tough enough to handle her.'

'So when did she and Josh get together?'

Charlie sighed theatrically. 'After the party she got brought in on a production Josh was working on. He's an agent, film and television, and she's into the make-up or something. Then Hal left his job in Japan and came home, Josh had a big party to welcome him back and invited Amber. And she and Hal got together. Josh had lined her up and he wasn't going to let Hal get in his way.'

'And neither was she,' said Lily. 'So why would she want to get married?'

'Well, she probably liked the idea of the dress and the

lifestyle too. She'll have her reasons. Amber always has her own best interests at heart. I'm sure she's worked out that marriage will be good for her.'

Lily felt her enthusiasm for rushing Hal to the church draining away.

'On her part it is not exactly a question of lifelong commitment,' Charlie went on. 'But it would have been for Hal. And he's a good catch. He's classy and eligible.' Charlie nodded to her. 'And he's going to inherit a fortune.'

Lily sat glumly staring at her coffee, feeling depressed. Still believing that Hal had the right to make his own mistakes, but wishing that this didn't have to be such a bad one.

'He'd better hurry up if he wants to arrive on time,' she said, looking suddenly at her watch. 'Who's driving?'

Charlie stirred in some sugar and fished a packet of aspirin out of his jeans. He popped out a row and threw them back with a mouthful of coffee. 'He thinks Alex is going to drive him,' he said, wincing at the taste, 'but he's not. He's never going to agree to drive Hal. Ever. He loathes Amber. He'll hold to the plan whatever Hal tells him.'

'Does anyone else have a car?'

'No.'

'What about Josh?'

'Josh took the other one back to Oxford at five this morning.'

'He did what? And what was he doing, leaving for Oxford so early?'

'Er . . . Well, I think Josh left to talk to Amber.' Charlie shifted in his chair and suddenly wouldn't meet Lily's eyes.

'So by now Josh's been in Oxford for about an hour. And what do you think he might have been saying to Amber, Charlie? While you've been sitting here with me?' She looked at him, thinking he'd been doing it knowingly, deliberately. 'You bastard!' she exclaimed, standing up. 'I thought you were on Hal's side now!'

'Fuck it! I don't know!' Charlie shouted, angry in his confusion. 'What's being on Hal's side? I don't know *what's* right.' He stood up again and walked outside.

'Yes, Josh left first thing this morning to see Amber. Yes, I should have told you sooner. Or even better, told Hal. What will Josh have said to Amber? I don't know!'

'You sat here drinking coffee because you're scared of Josh,' Lily called after him. 'You bloody coward!'

She left him, took the stairs two at a time and charged back into Hal's room. He was sitting on the end of the bed in a white shirt, staring out of the window.

'Which tie do you think?' he asked her, picking a handful off the bed and letting them drop back through his fingers.

'You should call Amber. Now,' Lily said, trying to sound calm. 'Right now. Let her know it's all okay and that you're on your way, with me. Josh left early this morning and he might have tried to convince her that you've done a runner or something.'

'I'll kill him!' Hal dived into his overnight bag and pulled out a phone. Lily left him to it and ran back down the stairs and straight into Charlie, who was waiting for her at the bottom.

'Lily!'

'I'm taking Hal to Oxford,' she told him, pushing him away from her. 'I'm going home to get the car and I'll be back in about twenty minutes.' She stared into Charlie's face, thinking that without Josh to steer him Charlie couldn't come up with anything else.

Then she left them, freewheeling down the lanes, forcing herself to keep pedalling hard up the hills. As she stopped outside her sister's house and got off her bicycle, Kirsty came out of the front door in a stretchy tight pink suit and a large straw hat.

'I know it's February but this is my favourite,' she said. 'And Hal will want us there. We're saving the day.'

'Fine, Kirsty,' said Lily, 'just get in the car.'

'But what about you? You can't go in trousers. You've got no make-up on and you're covered in sweat.'

Kirsty looked Lily up and down. It would be the understated look, but Lily was so striking that no one would guess her outfit wasn't deliberate, and she could do her make-up in the car. Kirsty walked around to the boot, opened it and laid down her pink jacket, then went to climb into the back, leaving the front seat for Hal.

A few minutes later they arrived back at Pen-y-bont. Hal was standing outside the cottage waiting for them, dressed in his morning suit. He looked immaculate and very handsome, his spiky hair flattened wetly down. Kirsty let out a dreamy sigh. 'He looks so young,' she said. 'Like he's waiting to be taken to boarding-school.'

Lily agreed. She could see Hal's blue eyes were dark with worry and his mouth was set in a grim line. Standing next to him, Charlie and Alex were rolling a spliff.

Kirsty was secretly loving the drama of it all and beamed when she saw Alex. She immediately jumped out of the car.

'Get in, because we're off,' ordered Hal.

Lily joined them. 'You okay now?' she asked Hal, gently, ignoring the other two.

'I need to get to Amber,' Hal told her desperately. 'I got through once on her parents' phone and some arse told me it was unlucky to speak to the bride before I saw her in the church. Now there's no answer there at all. And I've tried her mobile and it's switched off. I can call other people from your car. Just get me moving.' He jumped into the car without looking at Charlie or Alex.

'You could come too,' said Kirsty brightly to Alex as she climbed back into the car.

'No fucking way,' snapped Hal.

Lily put her foot down, driving faster through the country lanes than she had ever done in her life before. As they rocketed through the centre of Welshpool, she caught glimpses of startled familiar faces staring after her. All my efforts to mingle with the locals and I'm confirming their worst suspicions, she thought. That I couldn't fit in, that I'm getting out at top speed, and I don't care if I kill half of them on the way. At the Shrewsbury service station she filled up with petrol, drumming her fingers on the roof of the car, for once willing the petrol to suck up the money even faster. As she queued to pay she watched through the window as Hal tried again and again to get through to Amber. Then she raced back out, dumping a hastily gathered bag of Polos and drinks on to Kirsty's lap. Hal took a deep breath and stretched in his seat.

'Thanks, Lily, but you don't have to drive like a maniac the whole way.'

'Be cool. I'll get you there in one piece,' said Lily.

'Mineral water for you?' Kirsty asked her from the back seat as they sped towards the M54, hoping that Lily might have changed the habit of a lifetime and bought herself a sweet, fattening can of Tango. Lily hadn't: she stuck out an arm behind her and took it from her.

In the front seat Hal selected a tape. 'What can that bastard have done?' he muttered, more to himself than to anyone else.

I hate people who prefer the taste of water, Kirsty decided, stabbing a straw into her Ribena, then holding it away from her pink skirt.

She caught Hal's eye in the mirror and smiled and touched him gently on the shoulder.

'Want some?' she offered.

Hal shook his head. He looked out of the window, imagining how it would feel to be running for it, the wind with him, swooping over the fields and hedges in fantastic leaps. He forced himself to sit still.

'You two must be wondering what the hell is going on,' he said. 'Christ, I am!'

He was silent for a few moments then started again, forcefully. 'Whatever *anyone* has said to you,' he looked hard at Lily, 'Amber is a wonderful person. And I don't want to end up with some horsey Sloane who wishes Barbour did a range of underwear.'

Lily and Kirsty laughed.

'Sounds as if you have someone in mind,' said Kirsty.

Hal smiled at her, grimly, in the mirror. 'I do. She's called Lucy and she's my ex-girlfriend. My mother loves her.'

'Well, she's surely not the only alternative,' Lily said.

They hit heavy traffic and crawled towards the M6. Hal wondered who else he might call.

'Your parents?' Lily suggested. Hal grimaced.

'What would they say? They'd be relieved, like everyone else, it seems, if I missed this wedding. Not great for Amber, of course, they'd admit that. Wouldn't wish it on anyone. But they'd be bloody ecstatic when it came to me.'

'Why!'

'I don't know. It's not as if they don't want me to get married off to *someone*. Josh must have poisoned them against her.' Even Hal was aware he didn't sound very convincing.

'They'd help me out now. They're decent, lovely people,' he went on. 'But what could they do that I can't do? At this moment they'll be no nearer to her than I am. I'd prefer they didn't know.'

'Don't worry, it's not far now,' Lily reassured him, putting her foot down again.

Sitting in the back, Kirsty kept missing what was being said. She felt like a child again, swallowed up in the noise of the old car, watching her parents' heads nod and shake. She leaned forwards, squashing herself between the two front seats, butting in to the murmured conversation, determined not to be left out.

'So, Hal,' she shouted. 'What's everyone got against her?'

Hal took a deep breath. 'Different things,' he shouted after a pause. 'Richard and Alex are odd about women, full stop. And they don't like her taking me away from them.'

'I don't understand,' said Lily. 'Loads of other guys must have this happen to them. Gradually no one left to meet at the pub, or do things with at the weekend. One by one everyone getting married. But other guys don't resort to sabotaging their friends' weddings to stop it happening.'

'Look,' said Hal. 'Richard and Alex are much, much worse than the other guys! It's just taken me twenty years to realize it. Josh and Charlie always thought I was mad to have anything to do with them.' Hal shook his head. 'Josh and Charlie too,' he said sadly. 'They've set me up. They'll have had this planned for months.'

'They did it because they care about you,' said Kirsty from the back seat.

'I doubt it,' said Hal. 'This is all down to Josh.' His voice shook. 'Getting me down to that cottage. Missing my *wedding* day!'

'It'll be all right,' said Lily.

'So you'll never ever forgive them?' asked Kirsty.

'Fuck no,' said Hal. 'Bastards.' He looked down at his phone. 'God, I wish I could get through to her.'

'Could Josh have put her off, do you think? Done

something to stop her answering your calls?' Kirsty asked, tentatively.

'There is nothing that Josh could say that would persuade Amber not to be in that church, waiting for me. She loves me.'

When, eventually, they made it to the motorway it was almost empty of cars. It was just past eleven thirty. The sun broke through the clouds and Lily gingerly pushed the car towards a hundred.

They had gone less than a mile when, for the first time in her life, she saw a police car in her mirror and knew it was after her. She braked hard and watched the needle slip back down to ninety, eighty-five, eighty, but it was no good. The police car flashed its lights, gave a burst of its siren and indicated that she should pull over.

Lily watched the pair of policemen saunter over to her in her mirror. She gritted her teeth, knowing there was little point in protesting.

'Run out of runway?' one asked with a patronizing smile.

'I'm sorry,' Hal groaned to Lily. 'I'll make it up to you somehow.'

It took half an hour to be charged and so it was nearly twelve when they came off the motorway. They drove through Evesham and towards Broadway, Hal no longer needing the map, guiding them urgently on through one honey-stoned Cotswold village after another.

Any other time and we could stop for lunch, thought Kirsty, looking at all the tiny shops and the olde-worlde signs advertising cream teas. But it was not really a place she wanted to stop in: architecturally perfect and yet clipped and maintained to such a level that it felt as if the tourists blocking up all the roads, swarming on the perfect green, and flowing in and out of the gift shops, were the only people there.

How serious was that extra half hour delay? Hal wondered, telling himself that if she were waiting for him half an hour ago, she'd be waiting still. In his heart he felt that it couldn't matter. That with this much effort they *must* have succeeded.

They pulled off the main road on to a narrow unmarked lane and, at last, picked up speed again. Every time they turned a corner Lily wondered if this was it, if this time Hal would say *stop*, and they would see his church and know that they had made it. But instead he told her to turn again, and again, leaning up close to the windscreen, one hand on the dashboard in readiness to propel himself out of the car door the second he could. They turned again, into an even smaller lane. Ahead of them and to either side long grassy meadows stretched steeply away from them, the hedges yellow-green in the sunlight, new buds and leaves waiting to unfurl. And then Hal said, 'That's it.' He pointed through a veil of yew trees to a little church set back from the side of the lane.

'Amber's parents live about two minutes further down the lane.'

'There's something pinned to the gate,' said Kirsty ominously as they passed by.

Lily pulled over and parked, tucking the car as much into the side of the lane as she could. Hal got out with

Kirsty and they waited for Lily to climb through the passenger's side before they set off across the road, three abreast, supporting Hal on either side.

'It's Amber's writing,' said Hal, stunned.

They stopped at the gate and looked at the discreet white card, somehow knowing what the words would say. And yet, when Lily did read the words, slowly, one by one, her insides froze with icy shock. It was with regret that Mr and Mrs Aisling announced that the marriage of their daughter Amber to Mr Henry Summer was postponed. Tea was available at Mill House and they were requested not to leave presents.

Hal studied the note long and hard. He finally turned to Kirsty and Lily and raised his fingers to his lips.

'I'd better find out what's happened,' he said. 'Thanks, you've been great.' He took a deep breath and turned away from them.

They let him go, watching in silence as he made his way down a little path away from the church, out of an ornate wrought-iron gate, and then into the lane ahead. They stood, side by side, as his tall, solitary figure loped away from them in the sunlight, until finally he disappeared from view.

5

'We can't go to the reception! It would be like gate-crashing a funeral.'

'Well, if Hal doesn't like it he can tell us. How else are we ever going to know what happens?' Kirsty looked beseechingly at Lily. '*Please*. We can't just turn around and go home. Not now. Don't you want to find Josh? Tell him what you think of him? Don't you want to know what he said to Amber? Don't you want to know if Hal has managed to sort things out?' She paused for a second, racking her brains for something more persuasive. 'Get a quick look at her? See what all the fuss is about?'

'*She's* not likely to be there. She's hardly going to feel like hosting a reception.'

Kirsty reconsidered. 'Well, depends if Hal's found her. They may have sorted it out.'

Lily hesitated. 'I don't think so,' she said doubtfully.

Kirsty lifted her feet off the dashboard and slipped them back into her shoes. 'I am not going home,' she said determinedly. 'So go back without me.' She tried the handle of the car door. 'Unlock it!'

'Hang on a minute.'

'Look,' said Kirsty, 'I'm going to that reception. I don't want to let them all just disappear out of my life. Not yet. It's the best fun I've had for years.'

Lily put her head in her hands.

'I'm only being honest,' Kirsty went on. 'Admit it. We don't *really* care about Amber, or Hal! We don't even know them. It's just a bit of fun. So, stop being so antsy and come and have a cup of tea and a piece of cake. Or go home, alone.'

Lily looked at her. 'Oh sod it. Let's go!' she said eventually and Kirsty heaved a sigh of relief.

It was over half an hour since Hal had left them. For a long while they'd simply sat in the car and watched fascinated as a steady procession of guests had walked past them, clutching hats and bags and presents, on their way to the church. They'd watched as, one after another, people had read the note pinned to the church gate. Unable to hear what they were saying, all the same Lily and Kirsty could make out exactly what they were thinking. Some people seemed horrified, holding hands to their mouths in shock, making big eyes at each other, others couldn't seem to have cared less, and one gaggle of pretty girls had stuffed their fists in their mouths, failing to suppress a great, unanimous gale of laughter.

Kirsty and Lily cruised slowly down the lane, rounded a bend and saw a sign ahead of them with an arrow and 'Wedding Cars' pointing towards a field. There was matting laid down in the entrance and about twenty cars parked just inside. There, ahead of them, was a huge, cream marquee, fluttering and pulling at its ropes, and nestled discreetly behind it, a lovely Cotswold farmhouse. At the sight, Lily felt a familiar thrill of anticipation that turned swiftly into a lurch of sickness. Seeing it all wonderfully spread out, waiting for a reception that was never going to take place, brought a huge lump to her throat. She glanced across to see if Kirsty had felt it too, but Kirsty had almost climbed inside her make-up bag and was oblivious to Lily or anything else.

As they tentatively got out of the car, the sun disappeared behind a cloud and an unsettled breeze whipped at their clothes and hair. Kirsty felt the goosebumps rise on her arms. She grabbed her hat with one hand and Lily with the other.

'You're right. I don't look smart enough,' Lily panicked as they tripped across the field.

'No, you don't. But don't worry about it, masses of people don't dress up for weddings. No one will notice. The important thing is not to tell anyone who we are. We'll find out what's happened, have a quick nose around, and then we're out of here.'

'What if – '

'*No one* will notice us,' Kirsty interrupted. 'It'll be packed full of people – there's nothing this lot like more than a good scandal. They'll all be gossiping away, enjoying themselves. No one will take a blind bit of notice of us.'

'You're right.'

'So don't worry.'

'And what if Josh's there?' Lily said, half dreading it, half relishing the opportunity of telling him what she thought.

'He won't be,' said Kirsty. 'This is the bride's patch. He won't want to hang around.'

They walked in beneath a double arch of entwining pink roses and cream ribbons, and through a short tunnel. Lily just had time to register that it was surprisingly quiet when she found herself in a big, brightly lit, silk-lined marquee, half filled with ornate tables and chairs. Suspended high up on the central poles was an avenue of huge, flamboyant flower arrangements.

Lily took them in at a glance, her attention elsewhere. At the other end of the marquee, sitting in a lone, defiant cluster, were thirty or forty people. Around them hovered a huge army of super-attentive waitresses serving tea and, in the corner of the room, a string quartet was gamely serenading everyone with a complicated piece of Bach. Apart from them, the marquee was completely empty.

As Lily and Kirsty walked in, conversation died immediately away. There was a brief second where it might have been possible to turn on a heel without catching anybody's eye, but the moment passed and neither Lily nor Kirsty did anything.

Lily had never felt such an outsider. She forced herself forwards and walked towards the curious tea party, the music accompanying her footsteps, feeling like she was floating, her feet silent on the hessian floor. At the last minute she lost her nerve, changed direction and veered off towards the tea tables, but a girl rose from her place to bar the way.

The girl was stunning, with porcelain skin and hair that tumbled down her back in long red ringlets.

'Bride or groom?' she asked with an open, friendly smile.

'Bride,' said Lily quickly.

'Groom,' said Kirsty at the same time.

The girl stared at Kirsty long and hard. 'What the fuck are you doing here?'

Lily was aware of the other guests, faces expectant, tea-cups frozen in mid-air.

'Nice to meet you too,' Kirsty snapped back. 'For God's sake! He hasn't murdered anyone.'

Lily jumped in. 'We're friends of Hal's,' she said quietly. 'And we wanted to see if he was okay. We don't want to upset you.'

'Come on Mel, darling. Come and sit down. Stop giving everyone the third degree,' came a rather careworn voice from among the smattering of guests. A heavy, gentle-looking man of about sixty heaved himself off a gilt chair and came across to put a protective arm around the girl's shoulders.

'I'm Jonathan Aisling and this is my *other* daughter, Mel.' He offered his hand and smiled wearily at Lily and Kirsty. 'Need we say more?'

A group of guests, hanging on to every word, all gently shook their heads in sympathy.

'You can imagine that we think unspeakable things about Hal. But that's no reason to lynch you two. Come and have a cup of tea.'

'We're so sorry about all of this,' Lily said to Mel's father.

'He's a bastard. A total, utter bastard,' said Mel passionately. 'You can tell him so when you see him. From me.'

Looking at her, Lily realized that Mel was probably only about sixteen. Her chin, wobbling now with tears, was full and very young and the eyelashes that swept half-way down her cheek were those of a child.

She gently lifted her father's arm off her shoulders. I wonder if Amber looks anything like you, Lily thought, watching the lovely face break into a smile as she wiped her eyes and pushed her father back to his guests, reassuring him that she was okay.

'Can I come and talk to you two for a second?' She asked them more quietly. She glanced around at the other guests. 'You're the only friends of Hal's to come,' she paused. '*Not* surprising.'

'Of course,' said Lily and Kirsty in unison.

'Here, have some,' Mel said, moving them over to where tea was being poured.

Behind her the quartet had moved on to the beautiful, sad adagio from the Bach double.

'Aren't they awful,' whispered Mel. 'I told Dad to shut them up, tell them to go home, but apparently it's Mum's idea. She thinks it'll make people forget what's going on.'

Lily nodded. 'Like on the *Titanic*.'

They took their cups and a plate of tiny sandwiches and sat down at an empty table.

'Sorry about what I said. I'm all over the place.' Mel shrugged bitterly. 'It's all so terrible. You know, I'm more upset about this than Amber! She didn't even cry.'

'Is she here?' Kirsty asked, looking around the marquee.

Mel shook her head. 'Erm, no actually,' she said sarcastically. 'After she spoke to Josh this morning all she wanted to do was get away. She took about an hour to rearrange her flights and then she was gone.' Mel looked at her watch. 'She'll be leaving Heathrow about now.'

'Oh my God!' said Kirsty admiringly.

'She's gone on her honeymoon. My sister's pretty cool.'

'She didn't give Hal much chance to explain. How *could* she leave? Didn't she want to speak to him?' said Lily indignantly.

'Was there something he wanted to say?' Mel shot back. 'I thought he had Josh to do all that for him.'

Lily rocked back in her chair. She was certain that she and Kirsty should not get more embroiled than they already were, that what had happened and was still happening was so precariously balanced that she and Kirsty must not interfere any more. The wrong explanation now, to Amber's kid sister, could screw up everything, ruin what slim chance Hal had of ever sorting things out. If, indeed, he still wanted to. She hoped that Kirsty felt the same way and wondered whether she could count on her to keep her mouth shut.

'Hal was set up by Josh,' Kirsty told Mel, dramatically, right on cue, and Lily's heart sank. 'He didn't mean *any* of this to happen.'

'Don't give me that!' exclaimed Mel furiously.

'Leave it out, Kirsty!' Lily insisted, exasperated. 'It's nothing to do with you, or me, or even Mel. It's to do with him and Amber.'

'But Amber's gone, and Hal's not here. Someone has to tell them all what really happened.'

'No! Everybody has had too much to say already. Let Hal sort it out now.'

'There's nothing to sort out. Amber's gone, and Hal is never going to get her back,' said Mel. 'He was here about half an hour ago. When he realized that she'd gone he went crazy, shouting at my dad that it was him who'd been left at the altar, not Amber. Luckily none of this lot were around,' Mel waved her hand towards the other guests. 'There's nothing he can do now, it's too late. Amber's never going to forgive him for putting her through this.'

'Even if he didn't mean to?' asked Kirsty.

'Wait,' Lily told her, cutting in. 'We only met Hal last night. We don't really know him at all. Yes, he seemed determined to get married but the truth is we just don't know. I think the best we can do is accept that Hal is the one to sort it out, that if they're meant to be together then ultimately, this won't put them off.'

'But what could Josh have said?' Kirsty insisted. 'What could be so convincing that she buggered off without even giving Hal a chance to explain? If Josh's spun some clever lie, by the time Amber gets back from her holiday she'll have had two more weeks to think about it. She'll probably be even more certain she doesn't want to marry him. And Hal can't do a thing. Not unless he flies out to join her.'

'Well, I hope he doesn't do that, because I think Josh's gone with her,' said Mel, quietly dropping an unexpected bombshell.

Lily went cold.

'Just after I'd said goodbye to Amber, I realized he'd vanished too,' she went on. 'All this morning, I kept asking her how she was going to get to the airport, but she always changed the subject and wouldn't answer. And then after she left, I got it.' Mel paused, suddenly forlorn. 'Josh must have driven Amber himself.'

She looked at them despondently. 'There was a bag of his over there in the corner, and then it was gone. He went to the airport with her and I bet he's gone on the honeymoon too. God I hate her!'

'Surely that should be *him*?' said Kirsty.

'I wish I could but I can't hate Josh,' Mel replied sadly.

He wouldn't do it, Lily told herself, acknowledging at the same time that everything she knew about Josh so far suggested that he would. The Josh she'd met the night before would positively relish the idea of eloping with someone else's fiancée. Perhaps, she mused, this was all one big set-up. Carefully worked out so that Josh could get Amber back for himself?

'So you two didn't even know them before yesterday?' Mel said. 'Nothing *you* can tell me then, is there?' Understanding suddenly dawned on her face. 'I bet you weren't even invited to the wedding!'

'Nope,' Lily replied, smiling back at her. 'We met Hal in Welshpool last night. Do you mind?'

A small black and white terrier trotted importantly past with a large pink ribbon tied around his neck. Mel scooped him up into her arms and buried her face in his neck.

'Of course not.' She laughed, balancing the little dog

on her lap. 'My sister hadn't known him much longer and she was planning on marrying him.' She paused. 'And where's *Welsh Pool*?' she said. 'Sounds awful, like the kind of place you get taken to on a biology field trip.'

'It's in mid-Wales, on the border with Shropshire.' Kirsty smiled icily. It was okay for her to knock Welshpool but not anyone else.

Mel set the terrier back on his feet and fed him a sandwich. 'I should get back to my friends.' She scraped back her chair and was just rising to her feet when she noticed that her father was doing the same thing. He chinked a saucer against his tea-cup and looked pointedly across at her and she sat down again.

Jonathan Aisling looked steadily around the marquee.

'When I heard the news, I would go so far as to say that I became concerned for my daughter's sanity,' he announced, staring down at his shoes. All around, people stilled, stricken faces looking up at him. 'Yes,' he added solemnly, 'it really was *that* bad.' He paused for effect and then allowed a smile to twitch the corners of his mouth. 'I'm talking about the day she told me she was marrying Hal!'

The audience laughed appreciatively in a burst of relief.

'I'm not going to say it's better she found out now – I doubt that Amber will ever have a worse day in her life. And I wish I could make it different for her,' his voice wobbled. 'But I can't.' He stopped again and cleared his throat. 'I'd like to thank you all for coming, for support-ing us here today, and I'd like to propose a toast.' He paused again, and looked around the room. 'She's not here because she decided not to waste the honeymoon. So, in her absence, to our dearest, darling elder daughter, Amber.'

The guests started cheering and clapping and hammering the table in appreciation and Jonathan Aisling's face broke into a grin. At his smile, the cheering got even louder and for a while he forgot his speech and gave himself up to them. But eventually the wisecracks and whistling died down again and he raised his glass.

'Amber,' he repeated. 'May you survive this. And when you are ready, have a wildly irresponsible, fantastically indulgent, utterly enjoyable time, *without him*!'

'Hear, hear! To Amber!' shouted people in unison and everybody stood up as one and raised their glasses.

Lily could feel the huge wave of support for the Aisling family, and she thought that if Hal happened to walk in at that moment, the wedding guests would fall upon him like a pack of hounds.

'Finally . . .' Jonathan Aisling hardly had to raise his voice for the guests to fall silent once more. 'There's some tea – if you haven't eaten it all – and then you can push off home and leave us alone!'

Everybody laughed at his abruptness. Mel shook her head, smiling proudly.

'He's always like this,' she said.

Jonathan Aisling's speech opened the floodgates. He had released them from embarrassment and had given them the go-ahead to let rip. Suddenly there were shrieks of laughter, and a mad, animated chatter where before there'd been a decorous, deferential hush. The quartet rapidly switched to a noisy jig and a few people even began to dance, one couple immediately executing a series of complicated rock and roll moves.

'There's *always* someone who does that!' Kirsty commented to Lily. 'Why?'

They watched as the man ostentatiously twisted the girl into what looked like a painful half-nelson.

Lily laughed. 'They're sad people who have no friends,' she said, grimacing as a little girl wandered into the couple's path and was nearly sent flying.

Next to them a rugged, attractive man with greying hair and a too-red face started talking in a very loud voice to a couple of pretty middle-aged women.

'I once gave Hal two pieces of advice,' he said, watching Lily and Kirsty with half an eye, 'and he didn't listen to either of them.' The man paused, picking out his words carefully. 'I said to Hal, one, never dance in public.' The two women smiled, unsure whether this was a reference to the rock-and-rollers. 'And two,' he went on, 'just because you enjoy a good gallop, don't necessarily buy the horse.' He looked at the women with glee. They laughed politely. 'Bloody idiot didn't take my advice and now look at the mess he's in.'

'Really!' one of the women exclaimed, delicately nibbling at a profiterole and seeming to misunderstand him completely. 'How many horses have you bought then?'

'None! But, Kitty, that was a *metaphor*!' He said despairingly.

'The truth is, Kitty,' the other woman explained to her

slowly, shooting a piercing look at the man as she did so, 'Jimmy here can't talk, he's been married four times! And as for horses, he falls for anything that comes between his knees.'

Jimmy raised his eyebrows.

'It's why I adore *you* so,' he said to her. Then added, silkily, 'Although, don't you only come for a title?' He caught her hand.

'Bastard,' she hissed.

'But I adore you,' he repeated, kissing her palm.

'I'm sorry, you've lost me completely,' the dim woman complained.

The man let the woman's hand go.

'Now *she's* rather fetching!' he told them both, loudly, gesturing to Lily. All three looked her over appraisingly.

'If you want to get away, get away now,' Mel advised. 'Jimmy's okay, can even be quite funny, but he's a complete lech. You'll need a Stain Devil to get rid of him.'

Lily had had enough. Jimmy was hurriedly working out the cork of a bottle of Bollinger, so she turned her back on him and grabbed Kirsty's arm.

'I'll let you go. Thanks for listening. Sorry if I was rude,' said Mel quickly. 'Keep in touch,' she called over her shoulder, moving back to her friends.

Walking close together, Kirsty and Lily strode the length of the marquee without looking back. As soon as they were through the entrance they ran, laughing and relieved, back to the car. They flung themselves in and slammed shut the doors.

'Wow!' said Kirsty.

'Let's get out of here,' said Lily starting the engine, suddenly overcome with a violent tremble.

'I'm starving,' said Kirsty. 'Wish I'd got some more of those sandwiches.'

'We'll stop on the M40. Eggs, chips, sausage.'

'And baked beans, bacon, mushrooms and a large Diet Coke.'

6

A week later, Kirsty and Lily knew no more than when they'd left Amber's wedding reception. While Lily was ready to put it all behind her, Kirsty was eaten up with an inquisitiveness that got worse day by day. One answer would have been to ask the Little Goose for a booking number or address and to write to Hal, but that might have meant a conversation with Simon, whom she wanted to avoid at all costs. And so, eventually, she too resigned herself to not finding out any more, guessing there was no likelihood of the boys ever getting in touch with her.

That eventful Friday had been Kirsty's afternoon off. She worked a four-and-a-half-day week and, as usual, had chosen to spend her Friday afternoon with Lily, wandering along the High Street in the rain. They'd meet at the entrance to the covered market before making their way across town to the Courtyard for lunch. Kirsty never wanted to go further afield, not even to Shrewsbury or Oswestry. She made the effort to moan regularly about Welshpool, but actually wanted to be nowhere else.

Her parents tried persistently to nudge her out of the house, comparing her with her younger brother, Dan, who had travelled since he was eighteen, catching up with his family for only a few weeks each year. But Kirsty had no interest in doing the same. Relaxed and confident on her own turf, Kirsty thrived. Away from home for more than a couple of weeks and she always grew desperate to return.

Kirsty worked in a creeper-clad warehouse nestled against the hills on the outskirts of Montgomery, a few miles from Welshpool. She was the general manager of an agricultural suppliers partly owned by her father. Nearly everybody she knew had thought she was mad to take the job. Her schoolfriends had been aghast, arguing that if she had to work in a shop, why couldn't it be somewhere like the florist's, or even the underwear shop on the High Street, where she could have got them discounted Wonderbras? Instead of which, she'd be selling things like chicken coops and cattle prods. Kirsty had retorted that she'd rather help a gorgeous young farmer into a new pair of wellingtons than a fat old bag into a size eighteen corset.

From her first day, Kirsty adored it, as she had known she would. Five years on, she still took pleasure in every sale. She had improved her knowledge of farming to the extent that she could advise with authority, and thrived on all the close relationships she had built up with her customers. They loved her back. Old men who'd never confided in their families or friends in their whole lives would find themselves chatting to Kirsty, taking her into their confidence. She was so good at listening, so disarmingly straightforward, that many people pulled up in the forecourt simply to see her. In the course of her five years, there'd been more and more they'd needed to say.

Even before foot and mouth, the farmers who provided

her with almost every penny of her income had been pushed ever closer towards extinction. Kirsty had become used to hearing tales of desperation, a farmer who had given up his sheep to the RSPCA, another who had shot his calves because there was no point taking them to market. It had been an extreme and yet ever-worsening situation, and Kirsty had veered from despair and anger to disbelief that so little was being done to help, knowing that by the time public attention had caught up with the situation too many farmers would have fallen permanently by the wayside.

And then came foot and mouth. First one young heifer, tender on her feet, and suddenly whole herds of animals condemned to slaughter all around her. Farms closed down, villages empty. The smell of disinfectant heavy on the air. The crack of the gun, the strain and despair etched into faces everywhere.

For a few months public attention had held, but all too soon it was easier to think that because the barricades had come down and the footpaths reopened life in the countryside had returned to normal. In a way it was true – but what had been desperate and relentless before was, too often, impossible now, and for some it had been one crisis too many, tipping some men over the edge, to give up tragically and permanently.

On a practical level Kirsty tried everything she could think of to prevent the warehouse from going under. Gradually she had widened the range of goods on sale, introducing, alongside the sheep dip and baler twine, some pony nuts, tiny plastic bags of hamster food, lawn seed and puncture repair kits for wheelbarrows and bicycles. And as a result she widened her customer base, bringing in the hill-walkers and holiday makers when they started to return, the weekenders and people from the town.

And then one day she'd been stock-taking in the back when the bell had rung and Simon Campion had walked in. Just as she'd always predicted, he was tall, dark and handsome, and was looking for a pair of wellingtons.

'We might not have any your size,' she'd said, doubtfully, staring at a huge pair of Caterpillar boots, surprised to be almost lost for words.

'Hey, my feet aren't *so* big!' he'd laughed, picking a random pair off the shelf. 'These'll do.'

'Try them on?' Kirsty had suggested.

He bent down and unlaced a boot, resting his arm on the wall to keep his balance. He was wearing jeans and a heavy navy ribbed jumper that had tiny wisps of hay clinging to the front. He was rugged and dishevelled, full of energy and vitality. She'd loved the way he'd looked up at her, smiling easily, brown eyes warm. Straightforward, uncomplicated, liking what he saw and not bothering to pretend otherwise.

'I'll have them,' he'd said, pulling out a grubby chequebook from a trouser pocket and stomping back into his shoes, not stopping to retie the laces.

She had taken his cheque, waved away the card and rung it through the till while he looked over her shoulder, studying the flea powders and cat collars displayed behind her.

'What a great place,' he'd said, looking around. 'You've got everything under the sun.' He'd paused, thinking. 'What was it I wanted?' He'd scratched his black hair, searching for inspiration. 'A rabbit hutch! A really big one,' he remembered. 'With a wheel.'

'Rabbits don't have *wheels*,' Kirsty had said dismissively, leading the way to the back of the shop, praying that he wasn't buying it for himself.

'I know I shouldn't ask you out straight away,' he'd said from behind her, making her knees go suddenly weak. She'd managed to carry on walking. 'But I don't want a rabbit hutch.' She'd stopped then and turned around. 'If you say yes, you'll be saving me from coming back hundreds of times to buy all sorts of things I don't need.' He'd looked at the shelves stacked high around him. 'Like wild bird seed and curry combs.'

'But I like the customers who do that,' she'd said.

'Oh damn, of course you do!' he'd laughed. 'Go on, say yes.'

'Go out when?'

'Tomorrow night? I'll cook you supper.'

When Simon had moved to Welshpool the town had been awash with the news, curious as to who this handsome man was, single-handedly taking on crumbling, beautiful Pond House, where he planned to live, and the Little Goose, where he planned to work. Quickly, they'd realized that his cooking was far better than the usual goujons of plaice and melon drenched in port, and that the Little Goose would be flying upmarket. At roughly the same time *World of Interiors* photographers were spotted taking pictures not only of Pond House but of the whole town. Simon was putting Welshpool on the map in more ways than one.

His very public love life provided more rich pickings for the local gossip vultures. Since he'd moved in, there'd been a stream of what the bridge club liked to categorize as 'Twit' girls, all obviously completely unsuitable, showing off their Fendi baguette handbags in the local Co-op, or trying to pay for half-a-dozen free-range eggs with a black American Express card. Confidently, the bridge club ladies had told each other that it was only a matter of time before he met either Lily or Kirsty. It had taken four months.

'Okay. I'll see you tomorrow,' Kirsty had smiled. 'Shall I come to the pub?'

'No, come to Pond House. You know where it is?'

Kirsty had nodded.

'Good!' he'd said calmly. 'And thanks for the wellingtons.' It was only after he'd climbed into an old black Porsche and disappeared in a puff of smoke and dust that she'd realized he'd left them behind.

*

Oh, Simon, Simon, Simon. Kirsty paced in time to the words, her head down, her feet keeping to the squares of the pavement because that would mean she would see him again. I did love your cooking . . . and you, she half thought, before she forced the idea out of her head. She was on her way to meet Lily for a quick shop and was very late. She looked at her watch, swore and broke into a half jog.

At first she'd been confident that she could slip out of the relationship with Simon as simply as she'd got into it but he hadn't given up easily. When the stag party had appeared the week before, it had seemed as if they were heaven-sent, providing her with enough fun to drive Simon out of her head. But it hadn't worked at all.

She didn't want to talk to Lily about it because Lily would never understand and yet, at the same time, she desperately wanted to tell her everything. It had never happened to Kirsty before, this churning panic every time she thought about a man. When she'd arrived at Pond House for dinner, that first time, she'd felt confident, completely on top of the situation, proud of how she looked, at ease with the thought of the evening alone with him. But seconds after he'd opened the front door she'd been engulfed by nerves. It was to do with the way he'd stared at her, and how she'd looked beyond him into a huge dark hall lit only by a log fire. It was a warm, flickering, hypnotizing, flame-lit world and she had suddenly felt as if she were entering the lion's den.

The look on Lily's face, when Simon had come up to them in the Little Goose, had told her better than words ever could that Lily was not going to understand and that her decision to hide her fling with Simon from Lily had been a wise one. Far from being on Kirsty's side, she'd been very impressed with Simon. It was as if she hadn't expected Kirsty to pull it off with someone so cool and so much older. Now, Kirsty knew Lily would be impatient, pushing her to make a go of it with him, not remotely understanding why Kirsty wanted to detach herself before things had really begun.

Rounding the corner, Kirsty saw her propping up one of the pillars at the front of the market-place. As Kirsty approached, Lily smiled and raised a hand in greeting.

It was February the 13th. All around them people were marching in and out of the newsagents and Woolworths, armed with cellophaned red roses, satin padded cards and pink envelopes.

'I'm not even going to think about Valentine's Day,' Kirsty announced later, standing alongside Lily in the card shop, reading poems over Lily's shoulder. 'Roses are red, violets are blue, sugar is sweet, but I'll suck you,' she recited. 'Jesus! Give me Purple Ronnie any day.'

'Sshhhh!' Lily cried, pink with embarrassment, wishing Kirsty didn't have to speak in quite such a loud voice. She shoved the card back into its rack.

'What are we doing here anyway? I'm not sending any.'

'Nor me,' said Kirsty decisively, biting her lip.

Lily took her arm. 'Really? Nothing for Simon? When *are* you going to tell me about him?'

'I don't know. There's nothing more to say. Tell me something about your love life for a change.'

'You know there's nothing to tell.'

'Ah, but surely there was *once*. Wasn't there?'

'Wrong time, wrong place,' Lily said ambiguously, smiling brightly, closing the subject.

'I'll get it out of you some time,' Kirsty said seriously. 'You owe it to me. And then I might tell you about Simon. I'd stay out for a drink,' she added, 'but Dan's come home and I said I'd be back to see him. I'm sorry.'

'That's fine, I'll go home. Cook the dragon some soup.'

'Send her a big kiss.'

'Oh, right,' said Lily.

'I'll call you, we could get together some time over the weekend.' Kirsty turned and walked away, then looked back. 'And if you get any cards, I don't want to know.'

Lily slowly made her way home. She saw that lights were on in the kitchen and guessed that her sister was already there. The hall was in darkness and Lily turned on the overhead light, calling out as she did so. There was no reply.

She went through the house, switching on all the lights, quietly calling her sister's name, until eventually she found Grace in the television room, curled up on the sofa in the dark with a packet of Wotsits, children's television flickering cartoon colours around the room.

'Why didn't you answer? You must have heard me.'

Grace stared at her. 'Drop it,' she said, aggressively. 'You've only just walked in.'

She stood up and brushed crumbs off her jumper, scattering them on to the floor, then scrunched up the crisp packet and threw it into a bin before pushing past Lily and making her way upstairs.

For God's sake, Lily thought to herself, breathing out a shaky sigh, taking in the collection of cups half filled with tea and the crusts of a sandwich lying on the floor. She turned off the television and switched off the light, anger rising like bile inside her.

Needing to get out of the house, she left everything as it was and went back outside, to the small, numbingly cold outhouse built at the back. Her teeth chattered as she opened the padlock on the door and she told herself she was being ridiculous, imagining herself freezing at her wheel, becoming a lifesize piece of ice-art. Once inside, she switched on an overhead light and an electric radiator, retrieved some wet clay and slapped it on to the table in front of her. Still in her coat, she sat down and looked at it, then picked it up again, forcing her stiff hands to begin work.

Boxes and crates of half-finished vases and cups took up almost every foot of space. Huge bowls and fruit plates balanced precariously on top of each other, alongside outsize dishes and milk jugs. In the back were a small portable kiln and several makeshift shelves filled with finished work – bold, colourful designs, flowers, fish and fowl in jewel bright colours. This was the beginning of Lily's studio.

Fingers sticky with clay, she pushed back stray strands of blonde hair, tucking them behind her ears. Every time she bent her head another section came loose and fell forward, and soon there was enough clay on her cheeks to give herself a face pack. She knew she wasn't going to make anything good but still she carried on, stabbing at the piece of clay with a cold finger. She felt like moulding a face of Grace and sticking nails into it but worried that her anger was so strong she might actually make the magic work.

Finally, Lily admitted to herself that it was time to move out. That she couldn't stand staying with Grace any longer. If in all the time she'd stayed she felt she'd helped Grace at all, she wouldn't have been so sure it was time to go. Now all she wondered was what had taken her so long.

How she'd afford to move to anywhere else she couldn't imagine. Once upon a time, as she'd put the finishing touches to her plans for London, there had been a commission from the Registry, a big department store in Chelsea, which was looking for a young designer. She'd complacently turned it down, figuring that moving to Welshpool and looking after Grace was going to take up most of her time, not realizing how unlikely it was that she'd ever be offered anything as good again. Now she kicked herself, only too well aware that she'd sold far too little in the last six months and that her savings were gone.

The Registry offer had come in months ago. When she declined they'd said that she was to get in touch if anything changed. And now everything had changed. It would be a long shot but she'd follow up the invitation in the morning, she decided. And if they said no after all, she'd get off her backside and try somewhere else.

Gradually she brightened up, wondering if perhaps this was the time to move away from Welshpool, to Manchester or even back to London. And yet she didn't feel at all sure about going, not just because she'd miss Kirsty but because she was enjoying herself and she wanted at least one whole summer before she moved on. Somehow she'd get the money together and rent a cottage with a studio, she decided, and Kirsty could move in too.

After an hour she cleaned up, locked the studio door and made her way around the side of the house, letting herself in through the back door into the warm silent kitchen.

She went up to Grace's room, knocked, and then, when Grace didn't respond, opened the door. Grace was lying on the bed reading a magazine.

'Hi,' Grace said, without looking up. 'What's going on?'

'I was thinking how it was time I moved out.' Lily spoke the words before her brain was in gear but Grace didn't flinch.

'About time,' she said coldly, turning a page.

Lily came and sat on the bed next to her and saw that Grace's eyes were filling with tears.

'Don't cry.'

'Please don't go,' Grace whispered. She put down the magazine and looked up at Lily.

Lily moved further up on to the bed, hoping that this was the breakthrough between the two of them. 'If I went it would only be up the street. I'd still see you every day. But admit it, Grace,' she smiled gently, 'I've been driving you insane. I certainly don't make things any better.'

'You ought to have seen me before you arrived.'

'I heard you, on the telephone every night, remember? But this is your house, and you've always said you're better living alone. I get under your feet. Up your nose.'

'Will you please stop telling me what I want. What's best for me. I'm telling you, I don't want you to go. I need you here.'

'No, you don't. I make things worse,' said Lily, ignoring the edge that had crept into Grace's voice. 'I've been here six months and look at us. We're at each other's throats all the time. I can't remember us ever being like this before.'

Lily reached out to touch Grace's skinny thigh, hoping that she might nudge Grace to acknowledge how they once were, but immediately Grace flinched out of reach. 'Grace,' Lily said gently, 'I'm not talking about next week or even next month. But I think I might start looking for somewhere. Somewhere close by.'

'You're serious, then?'

'Yes.'

Grace's mouth hardened and Lily braced herself. The new Grace would move seamlessly on to the attack.

'You go, Lily,' she agreed. 'You're right, I *am* better alone.' She paused and looked at her with cold eyes. 'Mother-so-Superior, with your do-goody crap.'

'What?'

'You heard me.'

Lily bit her lip, holding on. 'What's going on?' she said, still trying to sound gentle. 'How have we got to this?'

'Don't you know?' Grace sat up abruptly. 'You arrive here – uninvited, if I remember rightly – ' She spoke fast, her voice rising steadily, 'Telling everyone who'd listen that I couldn't cope on my own, that you were *so worried* about me.' She paused. 'You stay for six months. Which messes me up completely. And now, you tell me you're moving on again.' Angry tears started to trickle down her face. 'How can you say that!' she suddenly sobbed.

'Grace, please!'

'You never cared about me. You weren't worried when Jeremy ditched me. You were delighted! It was what you'd expected – what you'd told everybody else to expect too.'

Lily had had enough. Of the past six months of letting Grace get away with saying what ever she wanted, of fetching and carrying, listening and supporting, and never retaliating.

'It's not true,' she yelled back, making Grace start in surprise. 'Everything you think is all twisted up.' Lily stared at her. 'And it's been miserable living here with you.'

Grace was still and silent.

'And I'm bored of being miserable,' Lily told her. 'I'm bored of you. It's never even occurred to you, has it? That I might decide to go. In all this time you've never once thought about anyone apart from yourself.'

Lily stared at Grace without seeing her, not noticing how slack and grey her face had become. 'I'm sorry you had a hard time, but I left my friends, gave up my flat, lost a job, all to be with you because I was sorry. And no, since you mention it, I wasn't delighted to do that. It was a lot to give up.'

'Are you leaving now?' Grace asked quietly, in a flat dead voice.

In answer Lily stood up and went over to the door, turned away from Grace without saying any more, and then lifted her hand in goodbye. She walked away, down the stairs, her heart thumping. For a moment she stood silently in the dark hall, then went to the telephone.

'Come over,' Kirsty told her as soon as she heard Lily's voice.

After the phone call, Lily went back upstairs and packed a bag and then she left the house.

It was a black night with no stars visible and the cold night air was like a slap against her cheek. Wheeling her bike out into the lane, she was overcome by everything she'd said, horrified that she could have gone so far. But, she reminded herself, for how many months had Grace been saying far worse? She thought of all the times she'd ignored the insults, turned the other cheek, and her blood boiled again. It had all gone on long enough, and whatever the consequences, Grace had had to hear it.

Street lights hadn't yet come to Green Lane and, as Lily cycled blindly into her third pothole, her bag swinging precariously around her back, she wished she had a light. She began to notice every shadow, and then every clatter in the wind became something menacing. Cycling faster, she felt a cold tightening of fear and imagined her hackles rising like a dog's. She pushed on, holding the bag still with one arm, and kept going until she was out of the side streets, when she could freewheel through the centre of town and then out again, finally tackling the last steep climb towards Little Venus Farm. As she dropped her bike and made her way around the house to the back door, Kirsty opened it and reached out to pull her in before kissing her on her icy cheek.

Later, they sat by the fire.

'Give it time,' Kirsty advised. 'I'm sorry, Lily, it must have been horrible.' She made a face. 'I don't know how you lasted so long.' She paused, savouring the pleasure of finally speaking her mind. 'She was a total nightmare!'

Lily shook her head, not liking to hear it. 'Not always. She used to be great.'

'So,' said Kirsty, changing tack. 'If she used to be great, then deep down, she'll feel awful about you. Some time, when she's cooled off, she'll know what you said is true.'

Lily nodded.

'She'll realize. You'll get her back. She must have some Lily genes in her somewhere! Jeremy can't have taken away her entire personality.'

'He turned her into a nervous wreck. Before him, she was . . .' Lily sighed and looked up at the ceiling. 'Oh, I know you find it hard to believe but she was great . . . *I* was the one who moaned about everything and she'd cheer *me* up.'

'Then give her time.'

Lily nodded, knowing that Kirsty was right. 'Before she met Jeremy, she never had any problems,' she went on. 'She was really *sorted*. Apart from men. She always had useless taste in men. But it never used to bother her.'

'Well, finally there's something Grace and I have in common!'

Lily shook her head. 'You don't have useless taste. You just don't give anyone a chance.'

'I know,' Kirsty smiled. 'I dump everyone too fast. You sound like my mother. But I'm holding out for the right guy. What's the point in wasting time with the ones you know are wrong. I need the tingle factor.'

Lily shook her head. 'Don't give me that! Simon Campion made you tingle! Even in the restaurant, when you were supposedly giving him the push.'

'No, he didn't. It never felt right. And when it doesn't feel right, get out of there.'

'It doesn't always feel right straight away.'

'Rubbish. Think of Josh!'

Lily laughed. 'How has this conversation turned back to me? Okay. *Yes!* Straight away, I thought Josh was . . .' She paused. 'Nice.'

'Lily, this is fantastic! What an admission! And now you're not to change the subject. We are going to talk about him some more.'

'Get away from me! You're striking when I'm at my most vulnerable. I don't need this interrogation right now. How can you do this to me?' Lily laughed.

'Beats talking about your sister. And, for God's sake! What's wrong with you? You're telling me you fancied Josh, that's all. It's not as if we're talking about your serious drug addiction. Or your sexually transmitted diseases.'

'Oh, them,' Lily grinned. 'Anyway, I didn't like him.'

'Of course you didn't. That's how it's bound to start,' Kirsty said dreamily, 'but then somehow, some day, some place, you'll realize that you got him wrong. And fighting, fighting against it all the time, you'll fall in love, get married, and live happily ever after.'

'You should write blurbs for Mills and Boon,' said Lily. 'And isn't our hero currently on holiday with his best friend's ex-fiancée?'

'I forgot about that.' Kirsty screwed up her nose then immediately returned to the pursuit. 'Tell me again. How, *exactly*, did you feel? Was it straight away? You said you didn't fancy him at all when we saw them in the street?'

'It was when we were in the pub,' Lily said. 'I had to wind my legs around the bar stool!'

'To stop yourself doing what?' Kirsty asked, laughing.

'Jumping on him.'

'And then?'

'I don't know. I suppose I imagined him taking over.'

'In the bar or somewhere more private?'

'Enough!' Lily stopped short the conversation just as Kirsty was getting into her stride. 'We'll never see them again. And now, knowing what he did to Hal, I'd never ever dream of seeing him again.'

'Of course you wouldn't,' said Kirsty.

7

At dawn Grace stood motionless in the middle of her bedroom. She'd been making herself wait for seven o'clock but at some point her body had swung itself out of bed and she'd found herself standing there before she knew it had happened.

She sat down in the middle of the floor, then shuffled over to the wall and lay back against the radiator, feeling its heat uncomfortably through her T-shirt but lacking the will to move away. She stared sadly at her feet, picked at a toenail, then lightly ran her hand the wrong way up her calf, taking perverse pleasure in the fact that her stubbled legs looked as unattractive as she felt. Then, for a long time, she simply sat there, arms around her legs, resting her chin on her knees, unable to summon up the energy to think coherently.

When she couldn't bear the burning in her back any longer she stiffly stood up again, feeling as if even the radiator was conspiring against her. She wandered aimlessly around the room. She touched her hairbrush and lifted a pair of jeans off a chair, folded them carefully and packed them slowly away, all the time putting off the moment when she'd confront the fact that she was alone again.

She sat at her dressing-table and applied a layer of

mascara. As she caught her eye in the mirror her mind's eye saw Lily back on her doorstep, finger on the bell. She imagined opening the front door with a great, happy smile, the wonderful flood of relief as she led her back into the house. She imagined all the things they would do together, how she would beg Lily's forgiveness, and talk to her as she had used to and as she had wanted to for so long. They would be inseparable from that moment on, Kirsty cast aside.

It was what she'd wanted from the moment Lily had moved in – a chance to talk about the terrible falling apart over Jeremy, to try to explain why she had been so angry and so unforgiving. She imagined that what had happened between her and Lily must have been played out in one way or another between sisters over and over, across time.

It had been thoughts of Lily, even more than Jeremy, that had eaten away at her in the weeks following her doomed wedding day. Much as she hated herself for falling for such a shallow, worthless, unreliable bastard as Jeremy, she could satisfyingly heap all the blame upon his head, whereas with Lily, kind-hearted, generous-spirited Lily, that hadn't been possible. At the time, she'd been deeply insulted that Lily, her little sister, had had the nerve to challenge her, and completely defeated when she'd been proven right. In the longer term Lily had forced Grace to see things about herself that she wished weren't true, things that made her feel ashamed. It had led to a defensive, corrosive anger that had eventually forced Grace to move away.

Once in Welshpool, Grace had slid further and further

away from the person she used to be. Alone every day, the insecurities born from being dumped at the altar grew and mutated until they dominated her entirely. The only thing that provided her with any energy was her anger. Somewhere, deep down, Grace still knew this was all wrong, that Lily had done the only thing she could, and Grace knew too that she'd never be happy until she freed herself from this bitterness. But until Lily announced that she was moving in, Grace had had nothing to aim for. With Lily there with her, she'd desperately hoped she could break the spell and begin again.

But it hadn't worked out. It was as if her mouth and her mind had belonged to two separate people. She'd sometimes taken *herself* aback with the things she'd found to say to Lily but still, as she'd watched Lily's eyes flicker at a particularly well-placed barb, she had felt a poisonous surge of elation. Why she should want to do this, when deep down she was unbearably grateful that Lily had come to her rescue, she really didn't know. But being bitter and twisted had become addictive, and Lily didn't help matters by being so relentlessly nice. Night after night, Grace would replay in her mind what she'd said and be eaten up with self-loathing and shame, but she never changed, and the further she left her old self behind, the more complicated and difficult the return journey became.

Grace left her bedroom, walked down the hall and paused for a moment outside Lily's door. Much as she wanted to open it, she knew that it would make her feel even worse. So she moved on, into the bathroom, where she could turn on taps and end the awful silence that was beginning to consume her.

As she bent over to drop in the plug, she was acutely, painfully aware of what she'd lost. It was like an electric shock sending a great jolt through her body. She sat down on the edge of the bath. *Lily*, she whispered aloud, startling herself with the sound.

I'm so sorry. She was aware of her loudly thumping heart and she clutched the sides of the bath. Moments from the past, a jumble from across the years, now fell over themselves in their haste to get her attention. I've turned into someone else, someone none of you know, she realized.

Grace remembered driving Lily towards Welshpool on her first evening. At one point she had leaned in towards Lily, smiling conspiratorially, about to tell her some story. As she had done so, she had caught a look of unconcealed relief on Lily's face, as if, unexpectedly, Lily had been told it was all going to be all right after all, and in a fraction of a second Grace's mood had changed. She remembered the swift surge of fury at Lily's complacency and how she had wanted to wipe away her confident smile and cut her down, how much she wanted to retain the upper hand. She remembered what she had said, and Lily's stunned look and the brief surge of power, and hated herself for being such a bitch.

Of course I appreciated what you were doing for me! Sitting there in the car beside me, leaving behind God knows what to be with me. But knowing that only made me feel even worse, even more guilty. And it's been driving me insane.

Grace stood up again in agitation, no longer able to sit still. She moved to the basin and started vigorously brushing her teeth.

And I'm sorry for everything that I said last night, Grace told Lily. She spat into the basin, then allowed herself a brief, grim smile because, actually, Lily owed *her* an apology for the last night. It had been a case of the mouse that roared and Grace had still not quite got over the shock.

You try having a little sister who's such a flaming all-round perfect person, she told Lily, suddenly wanting to defend herself. Who's so organized, and unruffled and so bloody smug. She finished brushing and moved back to the bath, testing the water with her hand. A little sister who makes you feel insignificant and useless. I don't think you would have coped with it any better than me.

And then, she thought sadly, *you* fall in love with someone, and get engaged, and see how it feels when it dawns on you that no one envies you after all. That actually they all pity you for being with such an arsehole. But stand your ground even so, hold firm, have the courage of your convictions, just so that you can find out, as the church bells are ringing, that even he doesn't want you. You'd have gone crazy too.

I'm sorry that I tried to marry someone so useless. I'm sorry that I couldn't see what I was doing. Grace thought back to the image of her father, grey-faced, walking back to the wedding car with the news. And I'm sorry Jeremy didn't want me and that I put you all through so much . . .

After months of trying to talk, this torrent of unspoken words was so loud and clear that she felt Lily had to be hearing them, had to be understanding and forgiving her. But even if she wasn't listening, Grace realized that just thinking the words through had been detoxifying, that she felt a little calmer, a little less desperate.

She wondered if she was glimpsing a new start, one that she still wasn't quite ready to embrace but that was there, just ahead, waiting for whenever she could make a move towards it. It would take one brave casting off of the black robes of her mourning, of the anger and bitterness and isolation that she had wrapped herself in for so long. And with that casting off, perhaps she'd find the confidence to believe in herself again. She picked up an ancient bottle of Badedas and squirted a long green stream into the bathwater.

And then the doorbell rang. She listened carefully, wondering how long it would be before whoever it was gave up. Then it rang again in three short bursts and one long one and suddenly, in a swoop of joy, she knew it was Lily, Lily giving her another chance, Lily arriving like a reward, just as she had turned the corner on her own. She wiped under her eyes and raced out of the bathroom, overwhelmed with gratitude.

'Lily! Lily! I'm coming,' she shouted as the bell rang again. She flew to the front door, her heart thumping. 'Am I pleased to hear you!'

She drew back the bolts, grinning with delight as she swung it open, to be confronted by a swaying, rustling, colossal bouquet of lilies pushed unceremoniously into her face. Around the side of the flowers peeped a bright-eyed gnome of a delivery man.

'Expecting them, were you?' he beamed. 'Aren't they gorgeous? Just sign here and they're all yours. I'm sorry I'm so early, but we've got a lot to deliver today.'

She took his pen.

'So then,' he said, smiling kindly, angling his head to read the little white card attached to the cellophane. 'Would you be the Lily herself? Or are you Kirsty?'

Grace looked up and smiled a grey, ghoulish smile.

'Oops!' said the little man, shocked by the awful emptiness in her eyes.

'I'll see that they get them. Thank you,' she said quietly, taking the flowers off him and stepping back into the house.

She closed the door, feeling as if she could shatter into tiny pieces at any moment. She walked straight to the kitchen, where she laid the flowers carefully on a table and wrenched the lid off the swing-bin. She pulled out the half-filled rubbish sack and opened it as wide as it could go, ensuring that she could stuff the entire bouquet into the sack without the sight of a single flower poking its head through the top. Then she tied the yellow strings tightly together and dumped the sack outside her back door.

Blood roared in her ears. She recognized the same deep

stab of hurt that had assailed her once before, when she had sat alone in her bedroom, looking down at her delicate cream silk shoes.

She leaned her cheek against the cool painted door-frame of the kitchen and wondered if she was about to throw up. So this is what happened when she let down her guard. When she allowed herself to think that just maybe she was turning the corner and that maybe she could hope for a break, a little help along the way. It hadn't been Lily at the door, and disappointing as that was, she could cope with that. But then, for a brief moment, she'd thought the flowers had been for her. A double whammy of rejection. This was an omen, a warning of how strong she had to be. Proof of how foolish she was to hope that fate might have been kind to her now.

She pushed herself upright and left the room. As she reached the stairs she was confronted by water, stealthily sliding down each newly stripped and sanded and polished step towards her. And everywhere there were bubbles made by the Badedas. Some were breaking free from the rest and were hanging gently in the air, catching the light like Christmas baubles, while others, glistening and twinkling, had piled high on top of each other like a huge frothy cake and were being majestically carried towards her down the stairs.

Gritting her teeth, refusing to give up and collapse on the stairs in a heap, she walked through the water. She splashed to the bathroom and found the water slopping and pouring over the sides of her bath. She plunged in her arm and pulled out the plug, then turned off the taps so hard it was unlikely she would ever get them to turn on again. Then she left the room, thinking she should get dressed before she tackled the mopping up.

She opened her wardrobe doors, searching for something to wear, and stared blankly at the tangled knots of dirty black jumpers and thick black tights that seemed to fill every shelf. Suddenly a gut-wrenching wave of hopelessness caught hold of her and threw her back on to her bed.

Tears ran down her face and into her mouth, sliding into her hair and collecting in pools in her earholes. She got back into bed, pulling the duvet high around her face, and eventually, she fell asleep.

*

'He is so safe you could have a picnic under his tummy.' Kirsty waited for a reaction but Lily wasn't listening, all her attention on the big brown mouth that was nudging persistently around Kirsty's pockets. 'He used to be a polo pony so he got called Chukka,' Kirsty continued. 'Rather witty, don't you think?' she added sarcastically. She offered the horse a carrot and he took it immediately, swallowing silently without even a crunch. 'Here, give him one,' Kirsty urged, handing Lily another carrot.

The bone-crushing hooves took a step closer as the horse immediately moved in on Lily. She held her ground and timidly stuck out a hand, flat, as she had always been instructed, and before she knew it her fingers had been delicately avoided and the carrot was gone. The horse stood tall above her, crunching happily, a trail of saliva swinging out of its mouth. Laughing, Lily ducked out of range, but the horse suddenly sneezed and bits of carrot and froth sprayed straight into her face. 'Disgusting!' she spat, picking bits off her tongue.

'Riding him is like sitting in an armchair,' Kirsty went on. 'Wouldn't you like to try?' She looked at Lily persuasively. 'Go on! It'd be a laugh – we need to do something wild and crazy today . . . And, let's face it, there's not a lot of choice.'

'What do you mean?' Lily said, suspiciously, latching on to the *wild* and *crazy*.

'We need something to take your mind off Miss Home Alone.'

'I didn't know you liked horses.' Lily made it sound like she was accusing her.

'Like them, yes. Like *riding* them, not much. Unless it's a special occasion.'

'Why? Is there something wrong with them?'

Kirsty shook her head and smiled. 'Lily, don't fuss! It's just I hate breaking my nails and smelling of manure. Poor things,' she went on sadly, aware she'd lost ground, 'they're so sweet, and they spend their lives looking over the fence, just waiting for someone to take them out.'

'Oh,' Lily sympathized, heartstrings successfully pulled.

'And there really is no one else. They're both in their nineties – in horse years – and so they're a bit too slow for most people.'

Lily shrugged.

Taking her response as a definite yes, Kirsty had them tacked up almost before Lily realized what she was doing.

'Here, give me your foot,' Kirsty demanded, leading Chukka over. She stood beside the horse and linked her fingers to take Lily's weight and toss her up into the saddle.

Lily knew she had no choice.

'I thought polo ponies were meant to be small,' she said, as Kirsty gave her such a powerful leg up that she nearly flew straight over the horse's back.

The next thing Lily knew, she was charging backwards at high speed, the horse's hooves slipping dramatically on the cobbled stableyard. She glanced across to Kirsty in wide-eyed terror, and let out a little scream, but Kirsty took one look at Chukka and immediately started to run, heading for the large open gate that led out of the yard. Chukka meanwhile, still managing to canter backwards, took one stride too many and backed solidly into a wall, whereupon he leapt forward again as if someone had stuffed a firecracker up his backside.

Desperately hanging on, Lily watched the scene around her unfolding in slow motion. Ahead of her, Kirsty was still running, her head thrown back, arms and legs pumping, occasionally casting desperate glances over her shoulder, valiantly trying to get to the gate before Chukka. But beneath her Chukka rose to the challenge and determinedly extended his stride. As Kirsty reached the gate and sent it swinging shut, Chukka reached it too. As his escape route closed in front of him he seemed almost to hold in his breath, managing to squeeze himself and Lily through with barely six inches to spare.

Puddles of ice cracked and split under the pressure of

his galloping hooves, sending pistol cracks echoing out across the empty fields. With Lily still aboard, he left the track behind and moved on towards a large grass field, spread white with frost and boxed in by high black hedges.

This horse is having the time of his life, Lily thought furiously. And probably at the expense of mine. Her hat was tipped low over her eyes, her empty stirrups clanked against her ankles and she felt as if her teeth were being shaken out of her head.

'Slow down you bastard horse, slow down,' she yelled at Chukka, thinking how this was the stuff of too many bad films, wishing all the same that a rugged hero on a black stallion was waiting in the wings to materialize at a gallop beside her. Instead, all she could hear was Kirsty shouting her name over and over again.

Lily looked down at the ground, hard and stony and blurring with the gathering speed and took in the two stirrups, swinging beneath her. Without much hope she thought she might as well try to stuff her feet into them and, before she knew it, it had worked. Straight away the canter felt very different and she cautiously looked up again, realizing with surprise that she could now stay on quite easily. The relief flooded through her, filling her with euphoria, and instead of pulling on the reins she forgot herself and leaned forwards into Chukka's mane, pushing back her hat and encouraging him on. Giving herself up to the ice-cold air, the warm sun on her face and the wonderful, flying freedom of the gallop.

From the sound of drumming hooves behind her she

knew that Kirsty was now managing to give chase. She sat as still as she could in the saddle, not wanting to unwittingly send some signal that would cause the horse suddenly to change direction, or turn on a sixpence, like she'd heard polo ponies could.

'Stop!' Kirsty gasped desperately, the wind whipping away the sound of her words. 'He'll jump the hedge. Stop! Pull up. Pull on the reins!'

Lily felt herself wobble alarmingly. The horse, aware that Kirsty was creeping up alongside, put his ears back aggressively and then barged suddenly sideways, nearly losing Lily and forcing Kirsty to back off.

And ahead of her, on the brow of the hill, loomed the hedge, wide and huge and unyielding.

I can do this, Lily thought confidently, gathering herself up for the leap.

The horse barely checked his pace. He met it cleanly and Lily was shot high up into the air. For one exhilarating moment she knew what it felt like to fly.

By the time Kirsty's head popped up on the other side of the hedge Lily had managed to sit up. At the sight of her, still in one piece but covered in mud, with Chukka standing guiltily by her side, Kirsty's face broke into a huge smile of relief.

'Chukka, you fucker!' she admonished the horse.

Chukka hung his head, still blowing hard.

Before Lily could speak she had disappeared again, making her way down the other side of the hedge to reappear in an opening just a little further down. Lily hadn't known it was there. She heard Kirsty click her tongue at her tired horse, encouraging him to trot over to Lily. When he drew alongside, Kirsty leant over and took a strong hold of the nearest rein, but there was no likelihood Chukka was about to take off again. Both horses stood, still recovering, sending huge white plumes of breath into the frosty air.

'I didn't ask him to jump that fuck-normous hedge,' Lily said despondently, carefully standing up. 'I thought I would stay on.'

'You were brilliant.' Kirsty winced on her behalf. 'Totally brilliant. You stayed on for ages,' she paused for a second. 'Forgive me?' she asked pleadingly. 'I am so sorry he did that! It was as if he'd taken speed!'

Lily laughed.

'You know,' Kirsty went on and nodded earnestly at Lily as she spoke, 'I think it was at least as awful for me. At the beginning, it was quite funny, the sight of you bouncing out through the gateway. But suddenly, you were going so fast! And then, when I knew you were going to jump the hedge . . .' Kirsty shuddered. 'It was *horrible*!'

Kirsty leant across to Chukka and slapped his neck. The horse's ears flickered forwards. 'Useless animal. I thought I could trust you!'

'And we weren't meant to be going that way,' Kirsty told Lily as they eventually rode back into the stableyard. 'I suppose I'll understand if you say you've had enough . . . But we could carry on. There are no more fields, just lanes. And I *promise*, I promise that they're so knackered now they won't go faster than a walk.'

'Oh, I really believe you! About as much as I believe that this horse is ninety years old.'

They wandered slowly out of the yard again, down into the drive beside Little Venus Farm, Kirsty's home. Then they followed a long snaking lane that took them low across the hills.

Side by side the two horses ambled contentedly down the middle of the lane, their eyes half shut, their heads drooping, flicking back the occasional ear at the conversation that ebbed and flowed above them. It was hard to imagine Chukka had any other speed. Soothed by the gentle, swaying rhythm of the walk, it wasn't long before Lily and Kirsty were lulled into silence.

The pale winter sunlight splintered through the bare hedgerows, and the dark tarmac of the lanes, still dusted softly with early morning frost, caught the sun and sparkled. Behind them, dark imprints of the horses' hooves stood out sharply against the white of the road, marking their passing by. From her new-found height Lily could look out over the hedges and across the quiet fields. Kirsty was right, she thought. There probably was no better way to empty her mind.

As soon as she'd thought it, Grace was there, filling it again. But this time, perhaps for the first time ever, Lily felt no accompanying twist of pain. It was as if Grace's power, which had grown so strong as to overshadow Lily's entire life, had finally been stemmed. Her ivy-like ability to smother and reshape had been taken away. This time Lily could disregard Grace and not crucify herself in the process.

She had acknowledged more than once how strange it was that such an intense relationship had sprung up between them, aware that theirs was the kind of relationship one might have associated with couples rather than siblings. How it had become so all-consuming she didn't know, recognizing only that it was born out of tensions that had been there since the very beginning, that all Jeremy had done was expose vulnerabilities between them that had always been there.

Grace was seven years older and had bossed and mothered Lily from the moment she had been born, a relationship that could not survive comfortably into adulthood. As Lily had grown up, Grace had always fought off any threat to her dominant position, had seemed more and more insecure every time Lily showed signs of going her own way, especially when it seemed she was choosing a better route than Grace.

'Why don't you go back and get your things,' Kirsty chipped in, intuitively, 'and make sure she's all right.'

'You really think so?'

'No,' Kirsty laughed. 'But if you go back you'll put your mind at rest and find it easier to move on *for good*. And then, we're going to find a house together. It's high time I left home, and this is the ideal opportunity.'

'Yes, please!' Lily exclaimed, making Chukka suddenly start in fright.

'Then we'll do it. Let's start looking this afternoon.'

*

When they re-entered the stableyard, Kirsty's mother came walking out of her kitchen to catch them. She was tall and pretty, in Armani jeans and a heavy cream jersey, and she looked as though she meant business. She held up a bit of paper to Kirsty and raised her eyebrows.

'Simon Campion called,' she announced in a low, hopeful voice, allowing a suitably momentous silence to follow her words.

Kirsty lifted her feet from the stirrups and cast a quick look across to Lily.

Lily shrugged. 'Chukka here says Simon's a good bloke, and you should call him back.'

'Chukka's had his balls chopped off, so he doesn't know anything about it ... Oh God! This is not what I wanted to hear,' Kirsty moaned. She swung her leg over the front of the saddle and slid off her horse.

'Kirsty. You *are* going to call him back?' her mother said worriedly.

Kirsty ignored her and led the horse towards its stable.

What is the matter with you, Kirsty thought. You haven't even met him. You know nothing about him.

'He sounded *terribly* nice.'

'I'm sure the wolf sounded terribly nice when he knocked on the door of the three little pigs. He probably sounded just like Hugh Grant,' Kirsty said sharply, disappearing into the dark stable. 'What's wrong with you?' she shouted from inside. 'Why are you so desperate to get rid of me?'

Kirsty's mother looked at Lily helplessly.

Kirsty appeared again, a saddle over her arm. 'Well, don't be surprised if this little pig gets served up for dinner,' she said, stalking towards the house. 'Roasted by the great chef. With a little balsamic vinegar and a sweet apple sauce.'

8

The wind changed, blowing in from the east, and the wide blue sky was hidden once more by racing black clouds. With nothing better to do, Grace spent most of her days watching the rain slide down the windowpanes as the wind blew wildly down the chimneys. Her only diversion was to go out walking, which she did most afternoons. She wore black wellingtons and wrapped herself up in a huge orange rubber coat that she'd bought a long time ago, when she'd been keen on someone who'd wanted to take her sailing. The relationship had lasted only a few days but the coat had stubbornly stuck around for a good ten years and showed no signs of getting lost. Grace expected it to outlive her. She knew it only added to her already rather eccentric image but she didn't care.

Day by day, she began to map out the hills and valleys around her, putting together a dark web of steep lanes, overgrown footpaths and muddy bridleways, and slowly she began to feel better. Each day she ventured further, walking fast and silently up the dauntingly steep hills, sometimes plunging down again into low-lying cloud that prevented her from seeing more than a few feet ahead of her. She thought she should have a dog to keep an eye on her and give the walks a purpose.

Occasionally she would meet other walkers but she

never stopped to talk. It had been so long since she'd had a passing-the-time-of-day kind of conversation with anyone that, now she found she quite wanted to again, she couldn't think of what to say.

She knew she was being self-indulgent, acknowledged that without a little money of her own and the indefinite loan from her parents she could never have chosen to hole up for so long. And yet, without money, she'd have been forced back to people and the clutter and pressure of a job, and that might have made a difference. As it was, she reminded herself most days that she was wasting her life but still the admission was an idle one, not something she felt ready to do anything about.

Since the awful morning with the flowers, she had treated herself like an out-patient, battered and bruised, who needed pampering and fussing over. With no one to indulge her, she became her own nurse, filling a hot water bottle each night, putting fresh sheets on her bed every other day and keeping well stocked up with chocolate and magazines. And yet, even as she did this, she was aware that the days of playing the invalid were drawing to a close. She couldn't ignore the fact that since Lily had gone, she had finally felt stronger, and that a new restless energy was now trickling through her, sending her prowling around the house, making the long walks addictive. Miserable as she still was, the tight-lipped anger against the world had finally begun to lessen its hold. That morning had marked the moment when the torrent of panic and tension that had coursed through her for so long finally burst its banks and began to drain away.

In theory she wanted to see Lily before too many more weeks went by, but in practice she still felt a strong need to keep to herself. It was as if her recovery was still so new and fragile that it could break apart again if she got the slightest buffeting, even one harsh word, and so, apart from a brief call to her parents to check where Lily had gone and to make sure that she was all right, she continued to let the days pass by.

She could afford just a few more months before she would have to find a new job. Before the fiasco that was Jeremy, Grace had taught maths at a large school for girls in London and it was only because of him that she'd given it up. After their wedding, they had been going to live in Scotland and she had saved enough to give herself a few months to settle in before she found another school, somewhere in Edinburgh. Now she began to keep an eye out for jobs in the local papers and, at the same time, renewed her subscription to the *Times Educational Supplement*. She knew there was only a slim chance she'd actually follow up anything but at least she could feel she was starting out again.

She also pored over the small ads, fascinated by the things people wanted to sell, overcome by insane urges to buy a knitting-machine or a Belling cooker or even a catering pack of luxury disposable glasses in the unlikely event that she ever had a party.

Then, one Friday morning as she lay in bed drinking tea and reading the papers, an ad caught her eye that she couldn't resist. The address was a farmhouse about a mile and a half from Green Lane and there were five puppies for sale. I have to have one, she thought with instant conviction, absolutely certain that this was what she needed to turn her life around. Before she could doubt what she was doing, she made a quick telephone call to let the owner know she was on her way, hurriedly got dressed and within fifteen minutes had left the house.

As Grace neared the farmhouse, what she was planning finally caught up with her. She stopped the car in the middle of the lane and sat for a moment. She heard her mother's voice telling her it was ridiculous. That she had absolutely no idea what she was letting herself in for.

But, even as she forced herself to think sensibly, all she was aware of was that she wanted one now, that she couldn't wait. That it was *because* dogs were for life that she wanted one, that she'd noticed it was the boyfriends who were just for Christmas. Her life hadn't turned out quite as rosily as she'd imagined it would. She shouldn't be living in a dark wet lane in mid-Wales all on her own. She should be in bright, noisy Edinburgh, blissfully happy. She wanted a dog more than anything in the world. She would buy a dog that she would grow to love, and yet would never have met if everything had happened as it should. She started the car again, imagining him sitting beside her on the front seat.

The address led her to an old black and white farmhouse that looked as if it had sunk two feet into the mud spread all around it. She stopped the car and watched a few hens clucking and pecking in the verges of the lane beside the house, while others charged hopefully through the mud towards her. She pulled on the handbrake and got out. There was a thin line of smoke curling out of a wobbly chimney and she noticed that the roof was missing over half its ancient slate tiles.

She picked her way gingerly towards the house, avoiding rolls of uncoiled barbed wire, tractor tyres and sodden bales of rotting straw, and knocked gently on a front door that looked as if it would fall off its hinges if she pushed it. At her knock it opened immediately and a white-haired old woman poked her head around the door at Grace.

'I've come about the puppies. I called you about ten minutes ago.'

The woman stared at her for a few moments. 'I know who you are,' she said irritably. 'You'd better come in.' She put a hand to her head as if to wiggle it back into place and re-establish an unreliable current, then she turned and disappeared back inside.

Grace followed her uneasily, quickly sliding off her wellingtons, reminding herself as the front door slammed that no one knew where she was, suddenly picturing herself still there six months later, chained up and being fed Pedigree Chum.

They made their way along corridors tiled in cracked and curling linoleum, the walls getting narrower and narrower the further they went, the ceiling so low that spiders' webs hung down and brushed against Grace's forehead. Finally, they halted outside a heavy oak door.

Looking at her properly for the first time, Grace saw that the woman would once have been rather beautiful. She was tall and imperious with clear light blue eyes, a straight nose and a haughty aristocratic arch to her eyebrows. As she looked appraisingly back at Grace, she slowly wound a long loose strand of white hair back into a green jade hairclip.

'Emily Hodge,' she said, offering Grace a half-hearted smile. 'I can't stand letting them go. It's not you.'

'It must be hard,' Grace said smiling back at her.

'I've been breeding dogs on and off for fifty years,' she said with pride, 'and so I've done this many a time.' She spoke in clipped cut-glass tones. 'But it doesn't get any easier.' She stuffed her fists into her jacket pockets and thrust forward her hips. 'Know anything about looking after them?'

'No, not a lot,' Grace admitted.

'Then when you've chosen him, or her, you get straight down to Kirsty Williams's in Montgomery. Tell her I sent you. If you're quick you'll catch her before she goes for lunch. You know where I mean?'

Grace nodded briefly and looked away. The woman put her hand on the door's handle.

'She's a wonderful, wonderful girl. And she'll sell you everything you need to buy, and tell you everything you need to know.'

Oh, what a pleasure that would be. Grace smiled grimly and nodded. 'Thanks for the tip,' she said.

'Right then, let's go and have a look at them.' Emily Hodge threw her bony frame against the heavy door, which opened stiffly.

To Grace it was abundantly clear that she was living on the breadline. Her suit was worn and shiny with age, her skin had that thin translucence that spoke of lack of nourishment, her house was freezing cold and falling down all around her, her chickens were starving. One glance through the door told Grace where what little money she had was surely going. The room was warm and bright and newly painted, with a big wooden bed for the bitch. While Emily Hodge didn't look as if she'd had a proper meal for weeks, the puppies were fat and shiny with good health and bursting with energy.

Grace dropped to her knees and opened her arms to them. Within seconds they were climbing all over her, licking and jumping, worrying her trouser legs, chewing and nipping at her fingers with their piranha sharp teeth.

Grace knew very little about dogs. Some were black, some were chocolate and others were black and white and they were all tiny and incredibly sweet and that was about all she knew. After a few minutes playing with them, she picked one black and white one out and held him up in front of her, wondering how she was ever going to choose one. He responded with a tiny high-pitched bark at her, and a desperate wriggling in her hands as he struggled to get closer to her. She brought him in against her chest and he reached up to her face, managing to get in several quick licks to her nose and mouth before she held him away again.

'We're going to have to have some rules,' Grace told him. She smiled over at Emily Hodge. 'But I think it's got to be this one.'

With the puppy loose in her car, looking out of the window and whining continuously, and falling off the seat whenever she went around a corner, Grace left the farm-house with repeated reminders to visit Kirsty ringing in her ears.

She felt both elated and terribly nervous. It was so long since she'd had anything new to think about, to look *at*, let alone look *after*, that, once home again, as she watched the puppy scamper clumsily around the kitchen, then lie down to whine at the space under her kitchen door, she found herself suddenly wanting to rush away, finding his loneliness and misery at being taken away from his brothers and sisters too much to take.

And, overwhelmingly, Grace wanted to see Lily again. Lily was so capable. Lily would know how to look after the puppy, would love the puppy. And it would bring them together, happy again too.

She sat beside the puppy in her kitchen for what felt like hours, both of them pushed up against the Aga, drawing comfort from its warmth. She touched his long satiny ears and told him that it was going to be okay, living with her. That she was going to look after him, that he didn't really want to run away from her and go all the way back to Emily Hodge's because he was going to have a lovely life. As she rhythmically stroked his coat, and watched as he fell asleep, she thought he was the loveliest thing that had happened to her for ages, and that she'd even stomach a trip to Kirsty's warehouse if that was what he needed her to do.

She would go to Kirsty as Emily Hodge had suggested and see which way the wind blew. Perhaps she might even venture a question or two about Lily. For all their differences, Grace trusted that Kirsty was a good friend to Lily and wouldn't deliberately scupper a genuine attempt by Grace to make things up. If Lily would allow a thaw, Kirsty would have to let her know. But, for the first time, she knew that she couldn't count on Lily wanting peace between them, that their last argument had been so terrible that it could well take months to patch it up again.

Lily had made it clear that Grace had run out of chances, had used up her nine lives, and Grace had no way of knowing for sure unless she talked to Kirsty.

She stood up, careful not to wake the puppy, found him an old blanket and made him a temporary bed in her scullery. She shut him in there, took her car keys off the kitchen table and left the house.

*

She had to sit outside the Warehouse in her car, steeling her nerves. She unclipped her seat belt and studied the building ahead. She felt as nervous as if she were about to storm it. It was just one storey, she noticed, but big and impressive, built of old red brick and probably once part of the farm next door. It had high wide doors positioned at each end, tall enough to allow horses and carts, and later tractors and trailers, to drive straight in. She could see through the corner of one of the doors into the cavernous space within. It would make a stunning house, she thought.

At the far end a couple of men were unloading sacks of grain from the back of a lorry, a forklift truck moving neatly back and forth between them. Grace watched them for a moment, taking in their sweat-streaked faces and their dusty clothes, bemused that Kirsty would choose to work in such a place, but thinking, nastily, that everyone found their level sooner or later. Finally, she told herself to move. She switched off the radio and looked at herself in the mirror. In the glove compartment there was a stick of lipstick that had seen better days and she found it and put some on. Then she slammed shut the car door and strode confidently across the forecourt, presuming that the shop itself would be empty and that she'd have Kirsty all to herself.

She was wrong. Just inside the door, a man was half turned towards her, casually studying a row of bottles of Organic Tick Treatment for sheep. As she entered the shop he looked up at her and grinned. Completely unexpectedly, she felt herself flush with sudden warmth and a raw awareness that she had forgotten she could feel. Behind her the door shut with a clunk.

He was gorgeous. Gorgeous enough to make her want to throw herself at him and beg him to carry her away. Wow! she thought, in a moment of stunning clarity. You would make me so, so much better. Lift me up in those strong arms and never let me go.

Seconds passed and she found she couldn't take her eyes off his face, but, having smiled so irresistibly, he then dropped his gaze back to his bottle and didn't notice the effect he was having on her.

Kirsty had noticed. 'Can I help you?' she said, coming over from the other side of the shop. *Bitch*, she wanted to add, seeing the love-stricken look on Grace's face. 'What are you doing here?'

'Perhaps you can,' Grace replied, coming back to reality with a bump and trying hard to sound normal. But she couldn't bear the distraction of Kirsty straight away and so she left her and wandered off, looking half-heartedly around the shop. She touched things lightly with the tips of her fingers, trying to concentrate on what she was looking at but unable to stop herself staring back again at the man.

She loved the way his dark hair curled gently on to the back of his collar as he bent forward slightly to read the label, the brightness of his warm brown eyes and the shape of his long fingers as they held the bottle. But it wasn't as if there were just one or two things that stood out about him. It was an overall impression – a strong sense of promise. Promise that time spent with him would be full of fun and wonderful, and that if you were the one he fell in love with, you could never do better.

Grace sighed. 'I've just bought a puppy,' she announced eventually, turning back to Kirsty. 'Tell me what I need.'

'A muzzle,' Kirsty said.

Grace saw the man suppress a grin. She flushed with embarrassment and stared at Kirsty with complete, open dislike. How could she have thought she would ever, *ever* broach the subject of Lily with her? She'd rather drink the bottle of tick treatment. One day, she was going to make sure that Lily saw this girl for what she really was.

'A puppy!' Kirsty repeated more gently, a pasted-on smile on her face, trying not to be too harsh. 'So, how are the carpets?'

Grace glared back at her.

Don't do that to your face, Kirsty thought. It really does you no favours.

'What sort is he?' Kirsty went on, continuing the attempt at conversation, the smile staying in place. 'Or is he a she? Is it very sweet?'

If it hadn't been for the man, Grace would have already marched out of the shop. But because of him she wanted to stay, had to stay. And if that meant she had to talk to Kirsty she was prepared to endure it.

She gritted her teeth. 'It's a he. And yes, thank you, very sweet.'

Rather than continue the conversation, she stalked away again, over to a selection of dog beds and dragged a large wicker basket from out beneath a shelf. It was lined with a deep blue and white gingham quilt, soft and inviting.

With her arms folded, Kirsty watched Grace from across the room.

How come I'm so useless that I don't know what breed my dog is, Grace wondered? I never thought to ask and Emily Hodge must have thought I knew.

'What's your puppy's name?'

'Hodge.'

Kirsty's attention was caught. 'Is that who you got him from?' she asked, coming over immediately. 'Emily Hodge?'

'Yes. I was there this morning,' Grace told her, taken aback by her sudden interest.

'And Mrs Hodge sold him to you?' Kirsty persisted.

'Yes,' Grace told her impatiently. 'Why shouldn't she have done?' Despite everything between them, Grace wanted to know more. 'Why are you asking me that? Why shouldn't she sell me the puppy?'

'No reason,' Kirsty told her. 'Don't worry. It's good news.'

'But why?' Grace insisted.

'Because,' Kirsty said, 'the fact that she's started to sell her puppies again . . .' Grace saw with amazement that her eyes were full of tears. 'I didn't know. It's important. It means that she's carrying on.'

'Carrying on what?' Grace shook her head. 'I don't understand.'

'Her son died eighteen months ago,' Kirsty told her shortly.

'Oh God, that's terrible!' Grace thought back to the dignified, determined strength of frail Mrs Hodge. 'How did he die?'

'On the farm.'

Grace could tell that Kirsty did not want to say any more to her. She was looking at her in a way that made Grace cringe. As if she was thinking, what do you really care? What do you know about tragedy, sitting there in your lovely house, distraught because your boyfriend left you? Grace didn't like that look. She turned away, back to the dog beds, hurt and defensive and angry that Kirsty could make her feel that way.

'You don't want a wicker one,' Kirsty called after her dismissively, walking away from her. 'That's for older dogs. He'll chew it to bits.'

Grace looked glumly again at the dog bed and realized that Kirsty was right. She supposed she should get something plastic or wooden. She bent down and tried to put it back where she had found it, but got it solidly wedged between two shelves. Trying hard to drive it back in, she eventually got to the point where however she angled her tugs it wouldn't move at all. Let the witch sort it out, she told herself angrily, still unable to stop herself wrestling on.

'Don't expect her to help, she never does,' said a deep voice from high above her. 'I wonder if she could be sent somewhere to be genetically modified?'

Grace looked up. The man stood over Grace as he spoke but he was smiling and looking at Kirsty, not at her. She stood up and stepped out of his way, blowing her fringe off her hot flushed face. Then he crouched down at her feet and carefully studied the bed.

In a wild, fairytale moment Grace imagined him looking up at her, gently taking hold of her hands and pulling her down beside him, tumbling them both backwards into the gingham quilting. Instead, he quickly pulled the bed free and then slid it smoothly back into place.

'Thanks,' she said shyly, wishing she could think of something more interesting to say.

'Pleasure,' he replied, standing up again.

But the fact is, there wasn't a line that would have worked any better, she realized. The way that his eyes immediately slid away from hers told her plainly, painfully, that she was not holding his attention at all.

In the old days, I would have had a good shot at him,

Grace thought sadly, as he wandered back to Kirsty at the other end of the shop. But clearly not any more. Somewhere along the way she had lost whatever it was that made men like him sit up. So when he'd come over to help her there had been friendliness in his face and nothing more. It was a shock. All her adult life she had floated in the soft warm water of admiration, effortlessly attracting any man she liked. But this was like standing under a bitterly cold shower. She wondered where he lived and if she'd ever see him again. The thought that he could simply be driving through her life, on his way to somewhere else, dropping in for just a few minutes in the course of her eighty or so allotted years, was unbearable.

'For God's sake, can't you pick up some of this stuff? Does everything have to be on the floor?' Grace snapped at Kirsty, making her way back towards her. She pointed to some cases of Puppy Chum and a few bags of Winalot stacked up around the till. 'I want some of this. But do I dare pull a bag out? It looks as if the whole lot would come down!'

Kirsty bit back something far more insulting. She didn't want to descend into some sort of cat-fight, she just wanted Grace out of her shop as swiftly as possible. She glared back at her, grimly hoisted a bag of biscuits up into her arms, added a tray of puppy food and, balancing awkwardly, went to the till and started totting up. From behind her, Grace quickly picked out a collar and lead, a water bowl, a food bowl and a book on puppy care. When Grace had paid, Kirsty wasted no time in holding the door open for her.

Grace walked over to her car, followed at a distance by Kirsty carrying the dog bed. Neither of them offered to break the silence. Walking around to the boot Kirsty chucked the bed down on the ground beside her and turned away.

'I'm sorry about all that,' Grace blurted out, surprising herself as much as Kirsty. 'I really am.'

Kirsty turned back towards her. 'What did you say!' Kirsty was wide-eyed, staring at her, surprised. 'I don't think I heard right!' She grinned at Grace.

Grace tried but couldn't quite follow through. For all her good intentions, she couldn't say anything more. Didn't want to put away all the protective thorns and spikes that had marked out their boundaries for so long.

'I do care about Mrs Hodge. And her son,' she said instead. 'I thought she was wonderful.'

'Yes, she is,' Kirsty agreed. 'It wasn't an accident,' she added abruptly. 'He killed himself in the barn. He couldn't make the farm work any more.'

'Oh no!' She'd known it had got bad enough to make such awful things happen, but being confronted with the reality of it was completely, unbearably different. 'The farm where I was this morning?'

Kirsty nodded. 'He'd taken it over when his father died. He was their only child. After he died Mrs Hodge moved back in. She said it was a matter of honour.' Kirsty sighed. 'But of course she couldn't do anything with it. The farm's finished.'

Grace was terribly touched. Not just by what Kirsty was telling her, but by Kirsty herself, by all the intensity in her voice that she'd never had the chance to hear before.

'She likes you,' Grace told Kirsty hesitantly, not sure if she was going to get her head bitten off. 'I could tell straight away. Whatever you're doing for her,' she smiled, 'I think it must be helping her a little.'

Kirsty shrugged. 'Thanks. But in the end, she's lost her son. What can anyone do? Nothing that will bring him back to her. But if she's got the puppies, I think it's a good sign.'

Grace nodded.

'I'll see you around,' Kirsty told her and she turned and walked back to her shop.

When she had finished loading the car, Grace opened the driver's door and got in, then sat for a moment watching the key tremble in her hand, not yet able to drive away. She breathed deeply, forcing her nerves to steady, taken aback by the reaction that Kirsty had provoked in her, surprising herself by how much she cared about what Kirsty thought of her. She'd always known that Kirsty thought very little, and she'd always told herself that it didn't matter. But of course it hadn't been true and she'd resented Kirsty for taking Lily away from her, and resented Lily for appealing to Kirsty, for winning Kirsty's respect in a way that she knew she couldn't.

First poor Mrs Hodge, then Kirsty herself, two emotional encounters that made her desperate for the quiet safety of her house. She rubbed at her face. But she would go back soon and visit Mrs Hodge, she decided. Maybe take her a present and show her how well she was looking after her puppy. It couldn't hurt and she might just like the company.

She started the car. And then there'd been that man. Who could he be? Kirsty's little warehouse wasn't exactly a motorway service station. Not the kind of place one would pop into on the way to somewhere else. He had to live, or at least be staying, nearby.

She drove home, knowing she was going to get another chance with him. Perhaps not straight away but some time when she was more prepared, when she could focus on him properly. He might not have noticed her today but one day he would. And in the meantime she'd better shape up, buy some make-up and fake tan. Get a hair cut and some highlights and spend the last of her savings on some new clothes.

Because my heart is set on you, she sang out, suddenly inspired. She took a corner much too fast and a huge hedge loomed in her windscreen, forcing her to brake hard and concentrate on her driving. Stop fantasizing, she told herself sharply, concentrate on Hodge! And for a while after that she did. But long before she reached home her mind was elsewhere again. She had morphed back into the butterfly she'd always been before. Honed from long sessions at the gym, wearing new clothes, with her hair shining in the sunlight, she saw herself walking, bright and beautiful, towards him.

*

One down, one to go, Kirsty thought, turning back to Simon.

'I've been waiting,' he said, 'for rather a long time. The service here is terrible.'

Kirsty didn't smile, even though her heart had been hammering in her chest from the moment he'd first walked through the door. She busied herself with tidying up after Grace, wishing she didn't have to do this now.

'Did your mother say that I called? Again.' He paused, waiting for a response. 'God, I must be desperate.' There was amusement in his voice.

Still Kirsty did not reply.

'I've missed you.' He followed her about the shop, trying to get her to look at him.

'Lie down for a moment and I'm sure the feeling will pass,' Kirsty snapped. She turned around, wanting the whole thing over and done with as quickly as possible.

'Is that an offer?' Then his smile disappeared as he saw that she was serious. 'Looking at your face, I somehow don't think so.'

Kirsty pursed her lips. 'Just give up,' she said sadly.

Simon came closer. 'Why do you say that?' He frowned. 'I don't understand.' He lifted a curl of her hair and wound it gently around his finger, then tucked it slowly behind her ear.

Nor do I, she thought. Not really. Bracing herself, she stared back at him silently, her face impassive, hands by her sides.

'You and your friend managed to eat all my food and drink all my wine ... so it can't have been my cooking,' he mused.

'It isn't that,' she murmured, her ear burning at the

touch of his fingertip, momentarily torn between pushing him away and falling into his arms. Pushing him away won.

'No, it isn't,' Simon agreed, sounding sad. 'So it has to be me. Yes?'

It was as if, now that he had looked into her eyes, he had seen with shock that she was serious.

'I don't want to see you any more.'

He shook his head. Kirsty turned away because she couldn't bear the look on his face.

'Well,' he said, eventually. 'Rest assured. The message is received, loud and clear. That doesn't mean I understand a word of it. But if you want me to go, I'll go. I'm not the sort to hang around.'

He walked away, wishing she would respond, even to look at him, then stopped and looked back at her again. 'This is it, you know? No more chances. I won't be back for more.'

'I'm sorry, Simon,' Kirsty said miserably, keeping her eyes down. 'But I mean it. I can't. I don't want to get involved.'

Yet even as she was saying it, she was feeling none of the usual sense of relief. Instead she felt stupid and cowardly and couldn't bear what she was doing. But she didn't say anything, and then it was too late.

When, a moment later, she did look up, Kirsty saw that Simon was picking up his wallet and keys, which he'd left on a table by the till. And she saw straight away that everything had changed. He was a stranger again, not hostile, not aggressive, but suddenly unfamiliar and completely impenetrable. He looked at her and she saw with a nasty shock that there was now no reaction at all in his eyes. Either that or he's a bloody good actor, she thought. It was as if he had successfully withdrawn from her everything she had ever touched, taken back any part of him she had ever laid claim to. And she found she felt no relief at all, just sickness at what she'd done.

As he walked towards the door, she saw him afresh; the springing black hair no longer hers to slide her fingers through, the broad shoulders that were now turning away from her, no longer hers to wrap her arms around. His mouth that had once closed, smiling, over hers, now as unapproachable as a stranger's in the street.

She wanted to tell him that she was sorry, that she hadn't meant what she'd said, that she'd panicked because he was so serious about her so soon and that was all, but she couldn't do it. She watched through the window as he got into his car, thinking of all the things they would never do again and all the things they had never done. And with a sharp twist of pain she wondered how quickly he would fall into bed with someone else. She imagined his bed, rumpled white sheets half covering an unknown female form.

Out beside his car he looked at her once more through the window and raised a hand in goodbye, then drove away.

9

All Hal could remember was the name of the road. He had hoped that perhaps he could stand outside all the houses on Green Lane, one by one, and that her house would give off a different aura so that he could divine which one it was. But instead he'd walked up and down the little lane several times, sizing up too many possibilities, and had had no helpful jolt of recognition. And there was nobody about to ask. He'd expected it would be quiet, but not so deserted that in three-quarters of an hour of loitering he'd seen no one at all. Now there was nothing for it but to start knocking on all the doors. And if that didn't work he'd find his way to the Little Goose and see if anyone recognized her name.

He had tried a couple of houses without luck when he saw a car turn the corner into Green Lane and drive towards him. He stared at it gratefully, waiting as it swished through the puddles and came to a halt about fifty yards away. Then a fair-haired girl got quickly out and walked around to her boot. Hal watched as the girl stood with her hands on her hips, staring down into her car, then roughly began tugging at whatever it was she had inside. He watched her struggle for a few seconds, trying to decide what it could be, and then he strode towards her, wanting to help.

He'd known almost immediately that the girl wasn't Lily, but as he got closer he decided that she had to be Lily's sister. They were the same height and they shared the same colour hair and there was something about the way she swung her head at the sound of his footsteps. But whereas he guessed Lily would have then sauntered towards him with a grin, this girl looked quickly down again, as if she hoped he might change his mind and disappear before he reached her.

'Can I help?' he offered with a smile.

'Be my guest,' she replied from the depths of the boot, wondering what it was about herself and dog beds and tall, thirty-something men.

'I thought you were someone else. Actually someone I'm trying to find,' he said, stepping around her and tugging it out.

She shrugged and forced herself to look up at him. 'Tell me who and I might be able to help.'

'She's called Lily,' he paused. 'And she looks like you. Do you have a sister?'

'Yup,' the girl said, moving to the back seat and bringing out a tray of tins of Puppy Chum, answering as if she didn't really care either way. 'And she's called Lily. But you should have called first. She doesn't live here any more. You need to get back in your car, drive down the hill, through the town and out the other side. She's staying at Little Venus Farm. Ask someone when you get closer and they'll tell you which one it is.'

Relief shone for a moment in his face. But still he hesitated. He could do as she suggested, leave it at that, jump back into his car and have nothing more to do with her, but something held him back for a second longer. He wanted to know if this girl was always so awkward, why she spoke of Lily so sharply, why Lily no longer lived there?

Hal took the bed in one hand. 'Lead on,' he said. 'I'll help you get everything inside.'

Grace led the way to her front door. It had rained all night and she stretched over several large puddles on her way. Not wanting footprints on her pristine wooden floors, she hoped Hal would notice them and do the same. She turned the lock and pushed her way in and she could hear him following her down the hall.

What she wanted to do was go straight to Hodge, but she didn't want this man to see Hodge too. If she opened the scullery door, she'd be giving him an excuse to hang around and she absolutely didn't want him to. And yet, without opening the door, how was she to know if Hodge was all right? If he'd survived all that time away from her? She stopped in the doorway to the kitchen and listened but could hear nothing.

'So tell me who you are and where you come from,' she snapped at Hal, sounding like a bad-tempered Cilla Black. She added more softly, 'And why you're looking for Lily.'

Hal didn't answer and her words hung on in the air.

'Perhaps I should have asked you that before I told you where she was?' she encouraged.

'Yeah, you should have done,' Hal agreed. 'And probably before you let me in. But don't worry about it.'

He followed her into the kitchen and placed the dog bed gently on the floor. He didn't know how to answer her, how far to go. He thought about why he'd come, the hope he had that somehow, by bringing Lily back into his cocked-up life, she would make it all better. He looked around the room thinking how outrageous it would be if he started to cry.

'My name's Hal,' he started, 'and I need Lily's help.' He went over to a window. 'I'm calling on her, in an hour of need.'

Grace was shocked at the hopelessness in his voice. This was not what she'd expected, not at all what she wanted to hear. She'd been so certain he would be just another pushy guy who fancied his chances with Lily. Someone momentarily entertaining who could then be sent on his way. Instead, here he was, in her kitchen, a man she'd never met, needy and sad and obviously gearing up to bare his soul to her. She wished she hadn't let him in. She wanted to be with Hodge, not him, wanted to preserve what remained of her fragile good humour, which she could feel was already fast slipping away.

But Hal was oblivious.

'She's the only one who can make things better,' he said, still staring out of the window. 'Lily is the only one she might listen to. Because everyone else is tarred with the same brush.' He turned away from the window and looked at her. 'But you don't want to hear about all this, do you?' he realized, belatedly. 'Why should you?' He frowned and rubbed at his forehead. 'I'm sorry. It's driving me crazy. And so I find myself talking about it to complete strangers.'

He moved away from the window, making for the kitchen door.

'What brush is everyone tarred with then?' Grace asked, stepping around him and beginning to put away her shopping, thinking that as he'd got the message, she could afford to be rather more sympathetic. 'What did you do?'

'What I did, and what my fiancée, Amber, thinks I did are very different things.'

'Oh, I see. And Lily could put her straight,' Grace finished the sentence for him. 'Well, go on. You have to go and ask her. I'm sure she'll want to help.'

'You think she will?'

'Of course she will.' She waited for him to move on.

Hal nodded. 'Down the hill, through the town and out the other side,' he recited back to her. 'Thanks.'

She stood up to follow him out, relieved that it had been so easy.

'So what does Amber *think* you did?' she asked impulsively, thinking it was definitely safe because Hal was now moving purposefully through the door.

Hal looked back at her bitterly. 'Ruined our wedding day.'

'Oh!' Grace still had no sense of what was coming, thinking he was probably about to describe a lost ring, or a drunken brawl in the middle of a speech.

'How?' she asked.

Hal stopped in the doorway.

'Oh, you know how it goes,' he said dryly. 'We were going to meet at the end of the aisle . . .' He paused. 'But we didn't.'

Grace caught her breath.

Immersed in his words as he was, Hal was aware that she'd reacted rather strangely, as if she'd been hit in the stomach by a well-struck rugby ball. He went on, actually revelling in the power of his words, almost as if it had all happened to someone else.

'We didn't get married.'

'What went wrong?' Grace croaked out. 'Come back and tell me.'

'My best man went wrong.' Hal came back eagerly and sat down at the kitchen table opposite Grace. Weeks on, he still had the compulsion to talk about it at every opportunity. 'On the morning of our wedding,' he swallowed hard, still completely unable to accept what Josh had done, 'he – my best man – drove up to see Amber, my fiancée, in Oxford. And he told her that I wouldn't be showing up.'

Grace stared back at him, as still as a statue.

'And she believed him. Well, you would, wouldn't you? Would you suspect the best man of lying about that? Of course you wouldn't. So by the time I showed up it was too late. There was nothing I could do. My wedding had been cancelled, postponed to be precise, most of our guests sent home, and my bride had gone on our honeymoon without me.' Hal smiled grimly. 'Superb story, isn't it! Until it happens to you.'

He looked at her, waiting for her reaction, confident

that she would be suitably outraged and disbelieving, but Grace didn't speak. He leant forward, wondering if she was all right, and the silence went on. For a moment it seemed as if she was fighting back tears. He sat quietly, touched that he'd had such a powerful effect.

'I don't believe it!' Grace said eventually not looking at him. She took a deep breath and Hal heard a strange break in her voice. 'I just don't believe it.'

Hal nodded solemnly in agreement.

Grace lifted her head and stared at him solemnly, and then unexpectedly she started to laugh.

Hal looked at her in amazement.

'I'm sorry!' she cried, the look of surprise on his face just making it worse. She covered her mouth with her hand and bit hard on her lip. 'I can't help it!' She could feel the muscles gathering around her mouth, trembling with the awful effort of keeping straight. 'I'm really sorry,' she said, her voice breaking again. 'You must think I'm a terrible person to laugh at you.'

She took a couple of breaths, telling herself that she couldn't do this to him. But then she caught sight of his sweet baffled face and had to turn away.

Hal smiled awkwardly, thinking she was mad.

Grace shook her head and tried again. 'I know you must think I'm mad,' she finally managed to get out, in a normal voice. 'Really, I'm laughing at myself, not at you.' She closed her eyes for a second. 'It's the coincidence. You and me. You sitting here and telling me that.' She shook her head. 'It wasn't funny at all. It must have been so awful for you.' She went on, her voice steadier, managing to look at him properly with no further threat of laughter. 'This time, you picked the wrong person to tell.' She paused. 'Oh,' she said wiping her eyes. 'I'm crying now!'

'If you cry now, I will have to walk out of the door.'

Grace smiled. 'I got dumped at the altar too.'

Hal's eyes widened. 'No,' he replied firmly. '*I* did not get dumped at the altar. And neither did Amber.'

Grace considered him for a moment, weighing up his words and the force with which he'd said them. Then she got up, walked over to the sink and filled up the kettle. Yes, you were dumped in a way, she thought. Because if she'd really loved you, she would have waited for you. She wouldn't have let this happen.

Wanting to diffuse the tension, Grace decided it was now the right time to open the door to her scullery, thinking that Hodge would bound out and buy her a little time, but he was at the other end of the room, lying fast asleep against the radiator, his eyes tightly shut, spotted tummy turned up to the ceiling, one fat paw giving an occasional paddle at the air.

She shut the door on him again and turned back to Hal. How to explain what she meant? How to explain how she could have laughed at what he'd just told her? She had laughed with relief. It was as if this strange meeting had been orchestrated for her benefit, set up to give her the final go-ahead to pick up the pieces of her life. It was proof that she wasn't crazy to think about the man in the warehouse, that it was okay to stop worrying.

That if she once turned her back and dropped her guard, her past wouldn't immediately spring on to her back and drag her down again.

'I owe you a proper explanation,' she said.

*

They were still talking two hours later. Grace offered him lunch and when he agreed, looking at his watch and deciding that Lily could wait just a little while longer, she made them fat omelettes with a tomato salad and French bread, flipping the omelettes over immaculately so that the melted cheese oozed out from underneath them.

When she'd eaten every last tiny speck of omelette it was all Grace could do to stop herself picking up her plate and licking it clean. But she restrained herself and sat, mopping up the last of the tomato juice with her bread, and listening to Hal, unable to ignore – in the midst of all his misery – how light-hearted she felt.

She felt so charged up she found it hard to concentrate on what Hal was saying. All she wanted to do in those moments that required a reply was shout that he should give up on Amber and get on with his life, that he should start again, just as everyone had always said to her. But *she* had never listened and she knew he wasn't going to either. She of all people knew it was far too soon for him to hear the truth. So she forced herself to shut up and let him talk on.

'Lily is my best hope,' he told her again. 'Because she saw what happened. She did all she could to help work it out for me.'

'She would,' Grace agreed.

'Eventually, of course, I will persuade Amber to listen to me, and then I can explain and we can pick up the pieces and get on with our life together. I don't doubt that. But first of all she needs to hear it from someone else. And that someone else is Lily.'

'Wouldn't Amber even read a letter from you? Give you just one chance?' Grace asked. *If she wanted you back she would.* She knew that if Jeremy had tried to make contact with her she'd have given him every opportunity, any time. Even yesterday she'd probably still have listened.

'Think what she's been through,' Hal defended Amber. 'Think how that arsehole must have made her feel. I'm not a bit surprised she doesn't want to have anything to do with me. But with Lily talking to her . . .' Hal sighed. 'If Lily talked to her, told her what really happened . . .' He was looking somewhat unsure. 'I know I'm asking a lot. And Lily doesn't owe me a thing. God knows she did enough at the time, taking me all the way to Oxford, zipping down the motorway in that little car. Getting caught by the police . . .'

'Oh, she did, did she?'

'She was wonderful,' Hal repeated. 'She was so furious with Josh, my best man. It was like she was going to do anything to stop him. She was on a mission.' He looked at her quizzically. 'Perhaps now I can understand where all that came from.'

Grace shook her head. 'It wasn't because of me. Lily's always jumped straight in. If she cares about something she always wants to get involved.' She looked at him, seriously doubting how much even Lily could do to help him now.

Hal drained his cup of coffee and stood up. 'Well, I suppose I should get on with asking her.'

Grace stood up with him.

'It was good to meet you,' she said, walking with him towards the door. 'I know you still feel awful, but you've done a great job cheering me up!' They moved out of the kitchen. 'So. There's some comfort for you.' She smiled at him.

By the door he pulled her close to him and gave her a hug. 'I hope you don't mind me doing that,' he said.

Grace shook her head, taken aback by how lovely it felt.

'And you'll be fine, you know that, don't you?' he said. 'Better than fine. You're going to do brilliantly.' He paused, looking down at her. 'Seriously, I'm pleased that I made you laugh about him. Even if you did completely freak me out in the process.' He let her go. 'Mad woman,' he said. 'No wonder he ran a mile.'

'Watch it, you! You've only just met me. I don't think you know me well enough to say things like that.'

'I'm sorry!' Hal grimaced. 'You're quite right.'

'I hope it works out for you too, Hal,' Grace said seriously. 'And if it doesn't . . .'

'Don't say it,' Hal said firmly, cutting her off. 'I'm going. Off to find your sister.'

She waited while he put on his coat.

'That's nice,' she said, touching it, now wanting to prolong the conversation, not wanting him to go.

'Isn't it?' he agreed, doing up the buttons. 'Amber gave it to me last Christmas.' He looked at her. 'I could pass on a message to Lily? From you.'

Grace shook her head.

Hal let it rest. 'Then wish me luck!'

'Good luck,' she said.

It was raining now in light little bursts that barely broke through the sun, and the wind was gusting, blowing his tawny hair into damp little peaks. He'd got half-way to his car when he turned back to her suddenly.

'How about coming with me?' he called.

Grace's heart leaped. 'What?' she shouted back, hearing him perfectly well.

'Come with me. Now! Take the plunge. While I'm here to break up the fight.' He put out his hand encouragingly.

Grace hesitated. She looked at him, so big and reassuring, and thought how much easier it would all be with him standing there beside her. But still she hesitated.

'No,' she called. 'There's stuff I need to sort out. I'm not ready to see her yet.'

Hal shook his head. 'Not true.'

He waited in the rain, sure she would come.

She looked at him, agonized for a moment more, then ran out towards him, jumping over puddles as the door slammed shut behind her.

10

Hal stopped beside a navy blue TVR and opened the passenger door.

'So this is what she saw in you,' Grace joked as he guided her into the soft leather seat.

'Yes, if all my friends are to be believed.'

Hal got in and the engine started with a throaty growl.

'By the way,' he said, following signs for the town centre, 'put me straight. If you and Lily fell out about three weeks ago and she moved out, and you haven't spoken to her since . . . I presume it was you who enjoyed my hugely expensive bouquet of flowers?'

Grace looked across at Hal and shook her head. 'You don't want to know.'

They drove down the hill, through the town and out the other side. Concentrating on the narrow twisting roads, Hal could not take in much of the landscape around them, but as they began another steep climb he allowed himself an occasional glance between the hedges. When he'd mentioned to Lily that he wanted to come back here, he'd meant it, and it was because he'd got a few tantalizing glimpses of the places he was now being led through.

Just as they neared Little Venus Farm they had to pull over and stop for a passing tractor, and for a few seconds Hal could gaze around him. The southern counties were overrun with cars, carpeted with concrete, but here there was little sign that the landscape had changed in the last thousand years. Hal could see just one or two houses below him and, to the west, what looked like a small village, but overwhelmingly his impression was of the thick woods, deep valleys and rich green hills, stretching away further than he could see, rippling out across the horizon, powerful and reassuring. With bright sunlight beaming through the bruised black clouds, heightening the purple of the ploughed earth and the dazzling green of the rain-drenched grass, it was a magical sight.

'Sometimes I hate it,' Grace admitted.

'I can't believe it!'

'No, I do! You look at it and think it's all so idyllic, but you're going back to London tomorrow. You have no idea how peace and quiet can crack you up. How empty it makes you feel.'

Hal glanced across at her.

'Give me a great big traffic jam any day.'

'I didn't realize. I'm sorry.'

'Don't be. I can get away when I want to. I've got money and a car and a family to go to. But there are some people who don't ever get away.' She was thinking of Mrs Hodge. 'Peace and quiet's not what they need.'

'No. Of course it's not.'

She smiled at him, wanting to lighten the atmosphere.

'And it rains so much. That's why everything's green, even in August. It's our own form of water torture.'

They drove on, following the lane until they neared Little Venus Farm. 'What am I going to do if she's not there?' Hal asked as they pulled to a halt. 'Do you think she'll be there? What does she do with herself all day?'

And what am I going to do if she doesn't want to see me, Grace wondered.

'I don't know,' she shrugged. 'When she lived with me, she potted, or whatever she calls it. She was in her shed for most of the day. But here, I don't know.'

From a window, Lily watched them get out of the car. She saw Grace staring up at the house, looking nervous, biting her lip and Hal by her side in a chocolate sheepskin coat.

Lily didn't know what to do. Her brain whirred and clicked, putting together the information faster than she could consciously think it through. Hal on her doorstep. Hal and Grace side by side. How close? Look at the way she leans into him. How had it happened? How had it happened? At the awful thought that Grace was involved with Hal, Lily's heart plummeted. Stay away from her, she wanted to yell at him. You're a disaster zone. Don't do this to her! She can't take it! Grace, stay away from him!

She very nearly shouted it from the window. She saw Grace pause as they made their way to the front door and touch Hal's hand, and then she couldn't wait any longer and threw herself down the stairs just as the bell rang.

Having asked Grace to come with him, Hal knew that by doing so he'd almost certainly done away with any opportunity to talk to Lily immediately. Even before Lily opened the door, he had already decided that he would stay only to fix up a time to meet her later, knowing that she would not be able to concentrate on him with her estranged sister standing over his shoulder.

He knew he would find it desperately hard not to start talking to her straight away. For the four hours of the car journey from London he'd thought about nothing else – which nuggets of information he could give Lily to help her convince Amber of his love, the heartfelt words he would ask Lily to say on his behalf.

It had come to him suddenly that morning, as he had sat at his desk at work, that Lily was his best and perhaps his only chance. He had stared blankly at the meaningless words on his screen, and then suddenly there was Lily. Far removed from everything, untainted by all that had happened. As his idea had begun to form he had been filled with an exultation which immediately transformed itself into a blind panic that if he didn't get to her straight away, circumstances might change and she would somehow be prevented from helping him. He had paced his office for a few moments, letting his run of thoughts assemble themselves, and then he had left the office, stalking down the long corridors until he was outside and running the short distance to his car.

And now here he was outside her house, knocking on the door, anticipating the moment when it would finally open. And now it *was* opening and she was there, standing in front of him. Seeing her, so lovely and reassuring, it was all he could do not to push his way in front of Grace and grab hold of her, but he forced himself to hang back for just a few moments more.

Lily looked from him to Grace and back to him again.

'You!' She laughed in wonder, leaning into him for a kiss and taking hold of his arm, ignoring Grace for just a moment longer.

Hal grinned. 'Yes, me.'

'And you!' she said to Grace, forgiveness already twitching her cheeks into a smile. 'What are you doing here?'

She turned back to Hal again, asking the silent question.

'No,' he answered, shaking his head. 'I couldn't sort it out. I haven't managed to see her. Not yet.'

Lily's face crumpled in sympathy. 'Oh God, Hal. I so hoped it would be all right.'

She'd forgotten what he was like. How sincere and straightforward he was. Seeing him now, the notion that he might have got together with Grace was ridiculous.

'But you can't have come all the way from London just to tell me that it didn't work out?' Lily asked. 'Have you?'

'Don't make it so hard!' Grace butted in. 'He has come all the way from London to see you. He needs you—' she paused and said emphatically, 'you *have* to find a way to persuade Amber to give him another chance.'

Lily turned back to her, finding it hard to take in what she was hearing.

Grace stared back. 'I know. I know. You must think all this is really weird.'

But it wasn't what Grace was saying, it was who she'd become, that Lily could hardly believe. She could hear enthusiasm and confidence in Grace's voice, see a new sparkle in her eyes, and the fact that she showed any concern at all for someone else marked a radical improvement on past form.

'What is going on here?' she demanded indignantly. 'I turn my back for just a second, and the next thing I know, my agoraphobic sister is walking up the drive, practically hand in hand with someone I would say she should steer clear of at all costs.'

Grace laughed delightedly. 'I knew this would freak you out. It was why I couldn't resist coming too.' She turned to Hal. 'But Hal's lovely! Why do you say that about him?'

'Yes, bloody hell,' Hal agreed, 'what have I done?'

Lily said, 'No! I'm sorry. It's not what you've done, it's just . . . you're in the middle of a crisis, and I don't think Grace needs that right now!'

'Because I'm terribly ·delicate. Is that right, Lily? And being involved in a crisis might just send me jumping over the precipice?' Grace laughed but there was a defiant edge to her voice. 'Seriously, you don't need to worry. And I've only just met Hal. Literally, just today, because he turned up at home, looking for you. And he and I talked a bit.' Grace paused. 'Then we had some lunch and then the only thing left to do was to come and find you!'

'Fine. Absolutely fine,' said Lily, feeling rather ticked off, still catching up with the new Grace.

And the new Hal, too. Changed almost as dramatically, but in his case definitely for the worse. Trying to be bright and happy and falling in with the banter, he couldn't quite cover up his desperation. In the weeks since she'd seen him, it didn't look as if he'd thought to wash his hair, and his eyes were red and tired, his skin looked grey, and he looked very thin under his heavy sheepskin coat.

There was too much going on here, Lily thought looking from one to the other, not knowing who to start with. There was so much Lily and Hal needed to talk about and so much to say to Grace. But she and Grace could catch up any time. It had to be Hal she took care of first.

She started decisively. 'We can't talk here,' she told them both. 'Kirsty's parents are inside and Kirsty will soon be back.' She stopped and considered what to do. 'Hal, I'm on for it. I'm with you, whatever you want me to do. Of course I am. I'll do anything. And Kirsty too,' Lily went on. 'I'm sure she will help too, if you need her.'

'Maybe, although I have the feeling it's you Amber will listen to.'

Lily raised her eyebrows. 'Oh! I wondered what it was, exactly, that you were going to ask me to do.'

Hal nodded. 'Please,' he said, his voice full of intensity.

'Yes,' Lily said again, firmly. 'Of course I will. But we need to talk about it properly, discuss what I should say. How I get her to meet me. When and where.' She paused. 'How long are you here for?'

'I've got the day off tomorrow so I'm staying the night in the Little Goose. How about meeting me there? I'll buy you some supper. Bring Kirsty with you.'

'But not me,' said Grace. 'Definitely not me.'

'No,' said Lily, grinning at her, 'you are not invited.'

Lily turned back to Hal. 'There's one other thing,' she said, more seriously, 'something I just have to know.' She found herself holding her breath. 'The fact that you're here, the fact that there's hope for you and Amber. It must mean that Josh didn't go with Amber on her honeymoon?'

Ever since Amber's sister had told them that Josh had left with Amber, Lily had suspected that the true cause of the wedding-day fiasco was that Amber and Josh had never been able to give each other up. That it had been carefully set up by the two of them. A desperate last-minute plan to ditch Hal. By holding Hal in Wales, Josh had saved Amber from an excruciating confrontation on her wedding day. He had given her the chance to run away rather than face the music and admit to Hal and everybody else that she couldn't go through with her marriage. Whatever she and Josh would have to contend with when they finally did come home, it would, at least, be done in private.

But Hal was aghast at the question. 'What? Of course not!' he said, bristling and defensive. 'Why ask me that? He and Amber were finished ages ago. Of course he didn't go on the fucking honeymoon!'

'I'm sorry. It was just something Mel said at the reception.'

'You went to the reception? You met Mel? What else don't I know?'

Lily flinched. 'So what?' she said defensively. 'It's not that terrible! We only wanted to make sure you were okay.'

Hal winced at the look on her face. 'I'm sorry,' he said. 'I'm so wound up. And I was taken aback at the thought of you in there with all of them.' He grimaced. 'So, what did sweet little Mel say to you?'

'Nothing much.' Lily was panicking that she was about to put her foot in it again, that maybe Hal was the only one still in the dark about Josh and Amber. 'Just that she thought Josh might have . . . might have taken Amber to the airport.'

'Mel thought he took her to the airport!' Hal looked stunned. 'No,' he said emphatically. He shook his head. 'No. He wouldn't do that to me. And anyway, I'd have known about it. He might have taken her to the airport but he didn't jump on the plane.'

'Then they're definitely not—' Lily stopped. Hal hadn't ever thought that they were.

So Lily still didn't know if Josh had taken that final step on to the aeroplane that would have put him completely, permanently out of bounds. Hal seemed sure he hadn't, but Hal had been wrong about Josh before. And yet, she agonized, wouldn't Hal have heard about something as important as this? It wasn't the sort of thing that could have been kept away from him. It had to be true, she decided, trying not to grin into Hal's face. Then, as fast as she acknowledged the thought, she stamped it out. Josh didn't interest her. Even if he hadn't taken Hal's place on the honeymoon with Amber he was still a deceitful, double-dealing, untrustworthy scumbag. Not the sort of guy she would ever waste her valuable time thinking about. She had her standards, and whatever he looked like, however he had made her feel, she would stick to them. And in any case, she reminded herself sharply, there was absolutely no likelihood of ever seeing him again. He lived hundreds of miles away in London and the only person they had in common was never going to speak to him again. But you know where he works, a little voice reminded her, because he'd told her in the Little Goose. He worked in South Kensington, just off the Fulham Road, and one day, perhaps, she might find herself there and bump into him again.

'You can rest assured that Amber and Josh are not living together on an island paradise,' Hal told her. 'Actually he turned up at my flat a few days ago.'

Lily leaped upon the information. So he *had* spoken to Josh again.

'But I'm not telling you about it now.' Hal turned back to Grace. 'Because I am going to check in at the Little Goose and leave you two in peace.' Seeing Lily's face, he grinned at her. 'You're just dying to know, aren't you? But you'll have to wait.'

As he walked to his car he called back to her, 'I will tell you about it tonight. And don't savage each other. Be nice!'

He opened the door and then looked at Grace. 'And I'll come and say goodbye to you tomorrow, before I go.'

As Hal's car took the first bend, Grace let out a deep sigh. Lily looked across at her and guessed that with Hal no longer there she wasn't feeling so strong, daunted by the possibility that they might now have to confront the awfulness of the night Lily left.

'Isn't it cold?' Lily said to break the silence. She jumped up and down. 'We should get into the house. Come and have a cup of tea?'

'I came without my coat. I'm completely freezing,'

Grace agreed, still staring vacantly down the road. Then she turned to Lily. 'I don't want to go inside. Do you mind? I can't face making polite conversation with Kirsty's mother. Can you lend me a jumper or a coat? Then maybe we could go for a walk.' But before Lily could answer, a look of sudden panic crossed Grace's face. 'Oh, I have to go home.'

'Why?'

'Because,' Grace said, 'I've left someone at home waiting for me.'

Lily's eyes widened.

Grace smiled. 'I love him and he loves me. And if I don't get back soon he will probably be up the stairs and tearing down my bedroom door with his teeth in frustration.'

Lily laughed. 'You've gone and bought a dog!'

Grace looked crushed. 'How did you guess?'

'But Grace, you're completely mad!' Lily told her without thinking. 'You'll never look after him! It's ridiculous. You have no idea what you're letting yourself in for.'

'What!' Grace spluttered. 'Was that you or my mother speaking just then?'

'I didn't mean it,' Lily cried hastily. 'Honestly!' She didn't want to remind Grace that only a few weeks ago she'd barely been able to get herself dressed.

'You mustn't speak to me like that,' Grace insisted. 'Or you'll spoil everything. I'm fine now. I'm perfectly capable of looking after a puppy.'

*

The further they walked, the more Grace and Lily relaxed. At first the conversation between them came in fits and starts, but gradually Grace began to talk. As it had been so long since Lily had seen her like this, she shut up and let her keep going, limiting her responses to the occasional 'hmmm' or nod, all that was necessary to let Grace know that she was listening.

When they reached the bottom of the hill, Grace finally paused for a moment to catch her breath. The strong wind and the effort of talking and walking at the same time had brightened her eyes and pinked her cheeks and the rain had washed her face clean of make-up.

'Do I sound better?' Grace asked unexpectedly. She breathed deeply and swallowed. 'You must be able to tell. I feel so much better. Not just because of the puppy, but meeting Hal today. It was strange.' She paused, struggling to find the right words. 'Like I'd come full circle.'

'It's closure,' Lily told her.

'Oh,' Grace said doubtfully. She paused for a moment and started to smile. 'I'm sorry,' she bit her lip, 'for that evening. And for calling you Mother Superior. And for saying all those terrible things. I didn't mean any of them. You've been everything to me. You're my rock. But even so I had to push you away and stand up on my own.'

Lily looked back at her. 'I'm sorry too.'

'Do you know?' Grace said brightly, changing the subject. 'Today, I met . . .' She stopped again. It was on the tip of her tongue but she changed her mind at the last second, torn between wanting to talk about him, and superstitiously imagining that her chances would disappear if she spoke about it out loud. 'I suppose,' she said instead, 'that what I needed to realize was that everyone else wasn't leading such perfect lives either. I realized it, talking to Hal.'

Lily nodded. Looking at Grace, she felt old, with an overwhelming desire to protect her sister, to keep her safe and make sure that nothing could interfere or spoil it all.

'I want to say something,' Lily said quickly. 'We must hang on to how we are now. I don't think we should ever try to analyse why we fell out. I don't think we should talk about it at all. There's no need, is there? Neither of us really meant those things.'

Grace paused before replying. She saw the point and yet at the same time she hoped that one day they would be able to talk about the past again. Not just to go over why Lily left, and certainly not to dredge up old hurts, but because there were things she wanted to talk about. About her engagement. She had questions that still needed answers, impressions that maybe Lily hadn't always been honest about what had gone on, suspicions that important things had been swept under the carpet because, per- haps, it was felt that Grace couldn't deal with them. And the doubts and questions were still there between them, unresolved.

But it could wait. For the time being, she knew that Lily was right. That if they talked about it now this fragile *détente* would be shattered. They were not yet on firm enough ground to have a conversation rather than a row and she didn't want to lose Lily again so soon. So she shut up, and smiled back.

'I've missed you,' she admitted, turning towards Lily. 'I really have. And I don't want to talk about that night either. Apart from to say that I'm sorry. Again.' She screwed up her face. 'Tell me I wasn't as awful as I think I was.'

Lily opened her mouth to reassure her, but Grace went straight on. 'No. Don't! Please.' She winced. 'I was as awful as I think I was! Talk about something else. I want to hear about everything that's been going on while you've been away. Tell me how it's been, living with the lovely Kirsty.'

Lily laughed. She's amazing, she thought. Unbelievable. How can she be like this? And why, why if it's all so simple, couldn't she have been like this a few weeks ago, when I was still living with her? Those six months had been so grim that Lily, despite her best intentions, couldn't quite forget them. Not because she resented Grace any more, but because the psychological bruises Grace had given her had still not entirely faded. She had been left with a wariness that she couldn't drop to order, a new sense of self-preservation that told her not to let down her guard too soon, because, despite Grace's best intentions, it could all start up again. As it had done before.

I'm rushing everything, Lily decided. And it has to happen slowly. Let's see the puppy and make another date and leave it at that for now.

But running through Lily was a new awareness that it wouldn't be so easy to pick up where they had left off as and when they felt like it. That as much as she wanted to protect and nurture and preserve her sister's new state of happiness, a bombshell had arrived in the post that morning, forwarded on unwittingly by Grace. Something which meant it might no longer be possible to pop in and see Grace whenever she wanted.

Lily cursed the timing. The letter from the Registry was in response to an earlier one from her. Just after she had left Grace, Lily had enquired whether they were still interested in the possibility of her designing a range of kitchenware for them. They were. It seemed that by turning them down all those months ago, she had only fanned their interest. Now they were suggesting the possibility of a whole range of work that would keep her fully employed by them for at least the next three years. Crockery, tiles for the walls and for kitchen floors. It was an amazing opportunity, at once massively exciting and deeply terrifying. If she pulled it off it would bind her to them through what would probably be the most important stage of her career. She would emerge at the other end so well established and well connected that, she imagined, she could then turn in any direction she wanted and be sure of a certain level of success.

To design for the Registry would be a huge coup. Their products combined quality with cutting-edge designs that inspired worldwide devotion. Based on the Fulham Road, in an old art deco furniture warehouse, the Registry called itself a general store but it had a globetrotting faithful clientele that would think nothing of flying in for a Saturday afternoon browse around its five exquisite floors. It was the sort of place that Lily might have hoped to work in several years after having left college, at the peak of her career. That they had suggested she might go there straight away was the most flattering thing that had ever happened to her. The fact that she'd had to turn them down, the most galling. And yet some of her wasn't at all sure she wanted to rise to the challenge right now.

Having read their letter, she'd sat at the kitchen table, holding it in her suddenly sweaty hand, feeling like she was sitting not just at the other end of the country to them but on another planet. Much as she knew she should call them immediately and arrange a meeting, she couldn't bring herself to do it, panicking that she didn't want to give up the cosy undemanding world she had built for herself. She wondered whether her doubts were simply because she was extremely lazy and didn't like the idea of being tied down to work of any sort, or if she was right to doubt whether it was really for her. And there was Kirsty and the cottage they were just about to rent together. What would happen to it? Where she might work from hadn't been mentioned in the letter but, if they did give her the job, Lily wondered if they'd be content for her to live in Welshpool.

How badly did she want to stay? How much did she want to go? What if the two were mutually exclusive? She had been wondering and worrying throughout the day, and had got nowhere. Eventually she'd realized that without meeting them she simply couldn't know the answer to either question. So finally she had called them and had set up an interview, and then she'd sat at her window, drumming her fingers on the ledge, and had waited for Kirsty to come home. And then Hal and Grace had walked back into her life instead. At least now she'd be able to kill two birds with one stone, she comforted herself. Perhaps the Registry in the morning, Amber Aisling in the afternoon.

Walking with Grace, Lily decided not to tell her about the Registry. Whatever else came up between them, she knew this was one ingredient to leave out for now. And later, as she sat beside Grace and the puppy, she knew she'd definitely made the right decision. She didn't need to work out that she couldn't just slip her news casually into the middle of a conversation. It was going to change everything between them, all over again, and it could wait at least until she'd had the interview and found out if she'd really got the job.

*

When Kirsty arrived home she quietly shut the door of her car so as not to alert her mother that she was back and ran silently up the two steps to the front door. She trod lightly past the kitchen door, through the hall and up a flight of stairs to Lily's bedroom, and saw the closed door that told her that Lily wasn't in.

'Where are you, where are you? Where the fuck are you?' she hissed at the door before charging back down the stairs again and outside once more. This time she slammed the front door and then jumped back into her car, calling Lily's number with her mobile as she backed out of the drive. But Lily's phone was switched off and Kirsty didn't know where to find her.

She drove aimlessly along dark roads trying to decide

what to do, turning randomly left and right until she had no idea where she was. Finally, she turned into a little lane so narrow it was practically impassable. Brambles and nettles so tall and strong that they had grown out from each side to meet in the middle. They scratched and pulled at her car as she passed, slowly ripping a way between them. Her headlights picked out puddles so deep and huge she worried that the car wouldn't make it through them. When one threatened to block out her headlights she conceded defeat and pulled over into a boggy gateway. She turned off the engine, opened her window and lit a cigarette, inhaling deeply enough to make her lungs flinch in surprise at the sudden bombardment of smoke.

Thank God she'd got rid of him, she thought. She really couldn't bear clingy men. No more pressure, no more dopey, love-sick looks, no more horrible feelings of being trapped. She was free of him. He wouldn't call her mother ever again. And thank God the town would have to find some other source of excitement. Miserable sad people, eaten up with interest in her because there was nothing going on in their own boring lives. Urghh, she shuddered. That awful moment in the warehouse, when she'd felt as if she might die with the agony of watching him drive away, was only a reaction to the shock. She wasn't denying he was a nice guy, just not the one for her.

Where the fuck have you got to, Lily? she thought again, chain-smoking another cigarette. She urgently needed to tell Lily about what she'd done. As if by speaking about it out loud she could convince herself that she'd done the right thing. Having not wanted to talk to Lily about Simon at all in the past few weeks – because she'd known Lily would have encouraged her to hang on to him – she now felt safe telling her all that had happened. By chucking him, she'd earned the right to some emotional support. It had been a traumatic day, and Lily couldn't knock her when she was already down. If she could only find her.

She finished the cigarette and started the car again, turning around and driving back along the dark lane until, eventually, she recognized where she was and found her way home. It was only six thirty but as black as midnight.

This time she got out of the car and didn't hurry, walking to the front door and pausing on the way in to call hello to her parents.

'Lily's gone to her sister's,' her mother shouted from the kitchen. 'She told me to tell you she'd be back about six thirty.' There was a pause. 'So, about now.'

Kirsty raised her eyebrows at the news and stalked slowly on towards the stairs.

'And she also said to tell you that Hal has turned up. That he's taking you both out for supper to the Little Goose.'

Kirsty stopped on the first stair and bit hard into the soft skin of her thumb. No way, she panicked. There was no way she could face the Little Goose. She couldn't bear to see Simon again so soon.

She dragged herself up the stairs towards her bedroom, ignoring her mother's friendly call to join her in the kitchen. And then, as she opened her bedroom door, the second piece of news belatedly arrived at her brain and she found herself turning mechanically and making her way slowly back towards the kitchen and her mother. 'Did you say Hal?' she asked, standing in the doorway.

*

Ten minutes later, Lily poked her head around the door and waved hello.

'Lily,' Kirsty snapped, standing up immediately, 'I've been waiting so long. Where have you been?'

'To see a man about a dog. You know where I've been!' Lily smiled, not noticing Kirsty's pinched face. 'I asked your mum to tell you, so don't get stroppy and pretend you don't. And I guess you've also heard that Hal's here and that he wants to take us out tonight?'

'Yes. But I can't.' Kirsty ushered her out of the kitchen and into the hall. 'I can't go to the Little Goose tonight, not now.'

Lily looked at her and said nothing. Instead she led her upstairs and into her bedroom and sat her down on the bed.

'I just can't do it,' Kirsty said. 'It's too soon.' She closed her eyes and fell back on the pillows and groaned. 'Simon came around to the warehouse today. And I told him I didn't want to see him again.'

'So?' said Lily cautiously. 'You told him that ages ago. I didn't know you were still seeing him.'

'Well, I was.'

'You're so secretive! When? How many times? How many times since we had dinner at the Little Goose, the night we met Hal?' She looked at Kirsty, tilting her head sideways, her eyes questioning. 'And why didn't you tell me?'

Kirsty shrugged. 'He's turned up at work a few times. And we went out, maybe three or four more times. It was nothing serious. And I haven't seen him since you moved in here. Not until today.'

'Why didn't you tell me?' Lily asked again. Kirsty didn't answer. 'I know why,' Lily said. 'Because you didn't want me to interfere when you decided his time was up. That's right, isn't it? You knew we all liked him and you didn't want anyone to give you a hard time. And now, today, you've done the dirty deed and you want me to tell you what a brilliant thing it was to do. That it's all okay.' Kirsty, shocked, couldn't think of what to say. 'How do you feel about it?' Lily asked, an edge to her voice. 'Was it difficult? Easy? Was he upset?'

'I feel crap,' Kirsty burst out angrily, pushing herself up against the back of the bed. 'How do you think I feel!' She looked at Lily, still surprised that Lily was reacting like this. 'I didn't expect to but I do.' Then she heaved a sigh, hating her admission. 'No. That's not true. I'm okay. It was the only thing I could do and I'm glad it's all over. And Simon was fine about it too.'

Lily pulled a chair out from under a dressing-table and sat down. 'Had you slept with him?' she asked curiously.

Taken aback, Kirsty stood up abruptly and went to the other end of the room, over to a chair piled high with clean clothes. With her back to Lily she started matching socks and didn't answer for a few moments. 'It's got nothing to do with it,' she said eventually. 'And, anyway, none of your business.'

'Sorry.'

'But yes. Actually,' Kirsty said defiantly, now turning around, 'I did. Make something of it!'

'You're like one of those bugs, aren't you? A praying mantis. I think it's them that do that,' Lily said.

'God! Thanks a lot. What was that for? I haven't done anything wrong. I haven't hurt you! No, don't you smile at me like that now, you little cow!'

'I'm sorry,' Lily apologized. 'Okay, you don't actually kill the men off. But you know what I mean. Know that it's true. You should sort yourself out.'

'And what do you mean by that?' Kirsty replied, her voice trembling, not liking the patronizing tone. 'Lily, I've got a tidy knicker drawer but I haven't got a life. At least I do something. At least I'm alive!'

'Really,' Lily said, anger rising. 'Thanks so much. You should think why you need to attack anyone who makes you feel uncomfortable. Attack them, or in Simon's case, get rid of them.'

'Not true! I don't,' Kirsty exclaimed. She stopped pairing the socks and started putting them away in drawers, telling herself to calm down. She hadn't wanted to hurt Lily. It had burst out before she'd known what she was saying. She knew that much of what Lily was telling her was the truth.

'I do it,' Kirsty told Lily in a quiet voice, 'when they

make me feel claustrophobic and panicky and pressured into being someone I'm not. And Simon did all those things.'

'Oh, crap,' Lily scoffed. 'How can you say that? He adored you! And he was lovely to you.'

'I know he adored me,' Kirsty told her smartly. 'And that's what I didn't like. He didn't know me. He had me down for someone I wasn't, and it was impossible. And he was too old and serious and he'd read too many clever books and he had had too many high-powered girlfriends and I didn't like it.' Kirsty stopped at the disbelieving look on Lily's face. 'He's thirty-six, Lily. He's so much more grown-up than me. And we weren't suited in other ways too,' she said firmly. 'We didn't have similar interests. We weren't into the same things.'

'Like what?'

'Things like TV and shopping,' said Kirsty, now starting to smile too. 'Oh, stop looking at me like that! Stop doubting what I'm saying.' She threw a balled-up pair of socks at Lily's head. 'Listen to me and believe me,' she demanded. 'What I'm saying is that I'm much better off without him and you should trust me on that. Now stop asking me about him and tell me about Hal.'

'Thirty-six is so old, isn't it?' Lily said sarcastically. 'You're mad,' she told her, going over to the corner of the room to retrieve the socks and tossing them back to Kirsty. 'Mad to let him go. Why didn't you have some fun? Get to know him a bit better. You haven't given it a chance.'

'It's a shame he didn't meet you first. You'd have made a perfect couple.'

'Oh, Kirsty, shut up,' she said, coming to join her on the bed.

'Simon and I are over. And don't try to analyse me, Lily, because you're not very good at it.'

'I'm sure you're right,' Lily snapped back. 'But I can't say what you want me to say.' She sat back too quickly and banged her head against the wall. 'You don't really want it to end with him. You sounded convincing for a while but only because you're trying your best to convince yourself.' She paused and rubbed her head, and looked up at Kirsty. 'Ow!' Kirsty didn't respond. 'What is it with you? On the one hand, you're happy to pull men left, right and centre. And yet the minute someone like Simon comes on the scene you run a mile.'

'It's true.' Suddenly all the fight went out of Kirsty and she gave up. 'Actually, I feel totally shit about it. I don't know why, but I've never really cared about any boyfriend I've had. I used to look at my friends, desperately in love, and think, that looks nice. But always from a distance. I could never imagine feeling like that myself.'

'What are you afraid of?'

'I don't think it's that I'm afraid of anything. It's not as if I've had a traumatic experience or a bad childhood to blame it on. I just don't want it like everyone else does.'

'Well, looking at the arseholes I've seen you with, I don't blame you. But you have to admit Simon was different.'

Kirsty smiled sadly. 'I know. Why did I think I wanted *him* to go?'

'Poor Kirsty,' Lily said sympathetically.

'This morning, it was almost as if I was playing a game, trying out different phrases on him.' She shook her head. 'Why didn't I see how I'd feel now? I so want to tell him I didn't mean it. That I've come to my senses.'

'What shall we do with you?' Lily said smiling.

'Don't joke about it,' Kirsty said flatly. 'I miss him and I wish I hadn't done it.' She looked away and Lily saw a fat tear slide out from under her eyelashes. She had never seen Kirsty cry before. 'I didn't realize in time. But I knew it as soon as he drove away. And now he's gone.'

'Oh no,' Lily cried. 'Stop it! I can't bear it. It's not so bad. Don't be so sad! You have to get him back. That's what you've got to do. Tell him you've made a mistake.'

'It's not a question of telling him anything, doing anything differently. I think it's a question of how I get over him.' Another tear slid down Kirsty's face. 'Because he made it absolutely clear that I wasn't going to have another chance. Oh, what's the matter with me?' she demanded angrily, turning to Lily.

Lily sat in silence.

'The End,' Kirsty said abruptly, to finish the conversation. 'I don't want to talk about it any more. I definitely don't want to hear your plans for winning him back. And tonight,' she went on firmly, 'you are going to the Little Goose on your own. I'll wait up for you and you can come home and tell me everything that Hal said. I want to know everything that is going on.' She paused, wondering if Lily had forgiven her for the earlier outburst. 'Why exactly is he here?' she asked, curiously, turning the conversation away from Simon once and for all. 'I suppose she wouldn't have him back?'

Lily shook her head.

'How can I possibly not come and hear what he says? But I can't, I can't. Oh, God, the timing!'

'We could go somewhere else.'

'No, go there, without me. I wouldn't be good company tonight and, anyway, I think it's you Hal wants to talk to.'

'He'd like to see you. I know he would.'

Kirsty shook her head. 'No, not tonight.'

'If you're sure.' Lily got up. 'I'm sorry if I said all the wrong things just then. I think you should get him back. But I'm doing what you want. I'm not talking about it any more.'

Lily leaned down and touched Kirsty's shoulder. 'You'll be okay?'

Kirsty nodded and opened her bedroom door. 'For now. Have a good time. I'll see you in the morning.'

11

You can't help but see good-looking men on the Fulham Road. As Lily paused for a moment, tucking herself into a shop doorway, she saw another one striding towards her. He was in the middle of a conversation on his mobile and he was walking with his head bent, not looking where he was going. At his side a girl in a pink coat with long shiny brown hair and spindly legs encased in long shiny brown boots trotted to keep up with him. As the two of them swept past her, Lily's heart skipped a beat as she saw that the man was Josh.

Although she knew that she was near where he worked, and although a tiny bit of her had been longing to see him, when it really happened it was still such a surprise that she found herself holding her breath as he walked by. She watched the two of them stop just beyond her and saw him take his phone away from his ear and pull the girl to a halt. Smiling down at her, Josh planted a kiss upon the girl's upturned forehead and then another, more tenderly, on her cherry red lips. The girl leaned in to him, obviously hoping for more, but Josh laughed and put his hands on her shoulders, steering her slowly around until she was turned away from him, facing back the way they'd come. Then he gave her a gentle push and immediately went back to his mobile, walking away down one of the side streets without turning back. The girl stood as still as a statue for a few moments, watching him disappear, and then with a little secret smile of success she bounced into a jaunty walk, passing by Lily once more before making her way down Walton Street and out of sight.

Lily didn't expect the sight of Josh to have such an effect on her. Irrationally and overwhelmingly, she longed to be that girl.

She wandered down the road feeling let down and lonely. She was having an interview, the interview, with the Registry in less than half an hour. People would kill for such a chance. She slid the palms of her hands down her skirt. She couldn't let him spoil it, not Josh.

But he was so gorgeous. The memory of him didn't do him justice at all. Maybe it was the dark suit, cut so that it set off every beautiful line and angle of him. Or the tender, sexy smile that he'd given his knock-kneed girlfriend. And probably, she admitted, it was something to do with the fact that, this time, he had been completely oblivious to her.

She walked on, focusing on the dramatic art deco building that housed the Registry, just a few hundred yards away from her, forcing her mind to start to concentrate on what lay ahead. She would spend her last few minutes wandering through the store, slowly working her way up the floors towards her interview on the fifth, preparing herself by getting a sense of some of the things they had on sale.

She walked up a couple of shallow stone steps and in through two frosted-glass doors and found herself in a vast central atrium. She was in the heart of the store. She stood still for a moment, taking in the bustle and the buzz, the expectant purposeful looks on the faces of the shoppers as they made their way towards the escalators, or tap-tapped across the mosaic floor to the ground-floor departments. And dotted among them were others like her, standing still and allowing the atmosphere to wash over them.

Lily had been to the Registry before, many times, but this time she was seeing it with a different eye. As she stood in the middle of the atrium, she couldn't believe that she was here to become part of it, that her designs could possibly be good enough to be displayed in the huge lit-up alcoves she could see all around her. Josh faded from her mind as she began to concentrate on how to convince them that they were right to be after her.

She turned slowly, looking all around, and then tilted backwards to stare up at the pale blue and white stained-glass dome of a ceiling, glistening miles above her. She knew it was time to go. She took a slow trembling breath, told herself to be cool, that she could do it, and moved towards the escalators.

There were three of them to interview her. One man with hair dyed grey and long fingernails cracked a few terrible jokes at the beginning and then, when she didn't laugh, turned nasty, passing her pieces to identify from their stupendously expensive 'antique corridor' on the fourth floor. She thought about dropping one on his toe and asking, politely, what it had to do with her own work, but she wanted the job too much. His two colleagues were much nicer. She'd met them once before, when they'd come up to her stand at her end-of-year show and had embarrassed and flattered her with their noisy interest in her work. Today they gracefully sidelined their colleague, reiterating their own excitement ten times over, stressing how perfect Lily was for them, making it impossible for the other man to speak up and for her not to relax and blossom and tell them all about what she did and the sort of things she'd like to work on next.

Afterwards she stood outside, dazzled by the sunlight, feeling euphoric and released and slightly disorientated too. She looked down the street, suddenly feeling buffeted by all the sounds. She looked around, wanting to find somewhere quieter where she could think about it all. It had been so straightforward that already she was beginning to feel a little disconcerted, almost wishing that they'd given her a harder time, or held back a little on the enthusiasm so that she might have had more to work on. She heard a clock chime and realized that she had been inside with them for forty-five minutes. Long enough, then, for them to get a good sense of her, however relaxed it had been.

She started walking without thinking where she was going. She'd already killed an hour in the Fulham Road before the interview and there was nothing she hadn't seen before, but she set off again anyway. She was finding it hard to recall the details of the interview. She remembered that the nice two had explained that they would bring her up at their next directors' meeting and how the grey-haired man had illustrated the point by pretending to gag. She knew he'd caught her look of disdain and she wondered whether he'd try to sabotage her application. If he failed, and she did manage to get the job, any position made available to her would be for an initial six months. They'd explained that the successful applicant's brief would be to provide the Registry with several one-off pieces, whatever she liked, that they could display and sell on the fourth floor, and also to create a series of dummies, the idea being that these would, eventually, replace some of their current in-house designs. If okayed by the board, her dummies would then be sent on to one of the factories in Stoke-on-Trent to be mass-produced and sold under the Registry logo across the country. She would be providing the staple range for all their kitchenware. How amazing it would be, Lily thought with a surge of excitement. And it *could* be her. They had definitely liked her. All she had to hope for was that they didn't like everyone they saw as much.

Hal had promised her lunch that day but at the last minute he had had to stand her up, and now that she thought about it, she realized that the bubbling in her stomach wasn't only due to nerves. On the way to the tube she stopped at a deli and bought herself an enormous baguette. Then she turned up Pelham Street, keeping her eyes open for somewhere to stop, and eventually veering off course to sit down on a bench under a flowering cherry tree. The sun was warm on her face, and when she'd finished her baguette she sat on, happy to enjoy the sun, and put off the evil moment when she faced the sweat and stink of the underground. I love being back, she thought, closing her eyes and tipping back her head. And not just in safe, pretty Chelsea either, but in all of London. Not for the first time, she wondered if she should come back for good, give up Welshpool now that Grace didn't need her any more.

She got on the tube and as the train rattled towards Hammersmith some of her euphoria dissolved. By the time she got off again and headed towards the bridge she realized that she was tired. Not so much footloose as footsore. She walked over the bridge towards Barnes, and half-way across she stopped beside a green and gold-leaf lamp-post and leaned out over the river, looking down to the slick black water flowing fast beneath her. There was a group of seagulls just below her, bobbing amidst the driftwood and the plastic bottles, and further upstream a bony heron hunched down on a rock.

There'd been other questions she'd wanted to ask the Registry people, she remembered now. Did they care where she lived? How often would they want to see her? How much feedback would they give her? Would she be part of a team of designers or was she on her own? How quickly would they want her to start? Imagining actually starting work, she felt a great lurch of panic. She sniffed in the salty river smell and breathed out again, aware that she was on the cusp of a huge change, that everything she knew was turning around and reordering, settling down again in new formations. Looking out at the river, she felt as if she was leaning out on the edge of her life.

The water swirled hypnotically beneath her and the bridge shifted slightly under her feet. She jumped back in alarm, grabbing hold of the lamp-post, and the moment was broken. I don't want it, she suddenly panicked. This shouldn't be my first job. I haven't any experience. It's too much. I don't want this job.

She made herself let go of the lamp-post and looked around self-consciously, wondering if anyone had noticed her, or had worried that she'd been about to jump, but there was nobody else about.

She walked on, leaving the bridge behind, then turned right and set off up Lonsdale Road. She was borrowing the flat of an art-school friend who had left that morning for a long weekend with her boyfriend. It was on the ground floor of a big white stuccoed house, with high ceilings and lovely light rooms.

Josie, her friend, had crossed over with Lily for just one night, long enough to find her the spare key, to clear some hanging space in her wardrobe for the interview clothes, and to ensure that she got Lily wrecked the night before her interview. She could stay for as long as she wanted to, Josie had reassured her, it was all hers, apart from the slim chance of Beth, her little sister, turning up to sleep on the sofa on Friday night. But Beth had her own keys so Lily was not to worry about her.

It had been wonderful for Lily to see Josie again. Lily could tell her about the giant steps that Grace was finally taking, without needing to explain anything about the past. Josie had known Grace for years and had been one of the guests waiting with mounting dread for the denoue-ment in the church, as the rumours about Jeremy had escalated until they had zig-zagged and bounced around the pews like bolts of forked lightning.

And then, after a bit, the conversation had moved away from Grace and on to Lily, Josie demanding that Lily bring her up to date with her sex life. 'Non-existent, of course.' Josie refused to believe there was still no one that Lily fancied. To shut her up, Lily eventually told her about Josh, not that there was anything much to tell. She described the night when she had sat beside him in the Little Goose, and then having started to speak about him she, of course, had to explain why they'd met. And so she told Josie about the stag do, and how strange it was that she had become embroiled in another wedding-that-wasn't, albeit a different version.

Josh caught Josie's attention. Although she was, of course, interested in what he'd engineered for Hal, far more it was because he seemed to have got under Lily's skin. Josie had always found it disconcerting, the way Lily could slip along seemingly so unruffled, never falling in love, leaving each relationship completely unscathed, never knowing what it felt like to be hopelessly infatuated by someone. Hearing Lily unsuccessfully masking her interest in Josh, floundering around as everyone else did when she tried to sound nonchalant and unconcerned, even disapproving, Josie wanted to shout a great 'Yes!' in triumph.

'But you must see him again,' she insisted. 'You've got to find him while you're in London, hunt him down! I've never heard you talk like this about someone before.'

Lily looked at her incredulously and shook her head. 'Hunt down Josh! No way. That is *not* my style.'

'Oh, *Lily*!' Josie shouted, full of exasperation. 'You know, sometimes I could . . .'

'You could what?'

'I don't know,' Josie said, deflating again. 'Something bad.'

'Don't you do anything,' said Lily, taken aback. 'Don't you dare!'

'Don't worry. I won't. But don't you ever think you're missing out? You should live a little! Do the wrong thing for once.'

Lily laughed uncomfortably and brushed it away and started to tell her about other things.

While Lily talked, Josie had cooked her the one meal she knew how to do – grilled chicken and fried potatoes – and listened through the doorway. Afterwards she had lain on the sofa smoking, a glass of wine in one hand, letting Lily wash up.

She was impressed with Josh. Perhaps it was because Lily's description of him had unwittingly given him a heroic quality but, whatever the reason, she found herself intrigued by him. She liked him for doing something rather than just talking about what a disaster the girl was, for being prepared to take the flak. She'd never heard anything like it before. And she warned Lily against underestimating his resolve. What would he do if he knew Lily was about to play negotiator between Hal and Amber?

'He's gone this far already,' she said theatrically, think-

ing aloud and suddenly sitting bolt upright on the sofa.
'So how much further would he go a second time?' What
might he do when he realized that Lily was still determined to set Hal and Amber back on course? It might not
be a question of Lily hunting him down after all! Was Lily
safe?

She got off the sofa and appeared in the kitchen
doorway.

'Does anyone know where you're staying in London?
Is there a way he can find you if he wants to?'

Lily had whispered back that she was becoming para-
noid, and what had she had to smoke?

Josie had gone early the next morning and so Lily was
left to open the door later that same Thursday afternoon
to a blast of cold air and silence. It was like walking into a
completely different place. She unbuttoned her coat and
hung it at the bottom of the stairs, then walked through
into the sitting-room and over to a window that she'd left
a few inches open. Then she bounced down on the sofa.
As soon as she landed she was up again, moving over to
the wall to flick a switch on the central heating and then
into the kitchen to make a cup of tea.

She had one further ordeal to get through. In its way,
it was something she was as nervous about as her interview at the Registry – but she wasn't quite up to it yet.
She flicked on the television. *Pet Rescue* was about to
start. She would watch *Pet Rescue* and then she would do
it. Make the dreaded telephone call to Amber. Take the
plunge and see if there was any chance of persuading her
to meet up while Lily was in London. And once she'd

done that, she could start to think about other things, like the Registry and calling Kirsty and Grace, and seeing if there was any chance of an evening out with some friends.

She had Amber's number programmed into her mobile by Hal, ensuring that she couldn't lose it, and so, when the suitably sentimental theme tune started to play, she went through to Josie's kitchen and keyed it in, still with no idea of what she was going to say if it was picked up.

When somebody answered the phone she started in shock, but she managed to inquire, in her best caring, gentle tone, whether she could speak to Amber Aisling.

'Who is that?' a girl asked suspiciously.

'My name's Lily. But you . . . she,' Lily fumbled, 'you . . . she . . . you . . . won't know me.' Lily pulled herself together. 'I wanted to talk to her. Not for long. But I wanted to tell her something important.'

There was a long, suspicious pause. 'Okay, hang on and I'll see if she's free.'

Lily heard the receiver being put down and then a whisper, cut off by a hasty hand over the receiver.

Then the receiver was picked up again. 'This is Amber,' said the same voice. She now sounded clipped and rather confident. 'What did you want to tell me?'

Lily knew the next sentence was make or break but it had to be done.

'Well,' she said gently. 'Hal's asked me to get in touch.' She waited but the girl didn't respond. Lily went on. 'He asked me to call you because he knows you won't speak to him, and you don't trust any of his friends. And he can understand why. But I'm not a friend. I've only met him once before. So he thought you might listen to me.' She paused and swallowed, then proceeded again, still speaking as gently as she could, as if Amber's response was entirely dependent on how she said the words.

'I met him on the Friday night of his stag do. The night before what should have been his marriage to you.' She waited again, allowing Amber an opportunity to come back at her with something. To shout at her and tell her to get lost, perhaps, or even to break down and sob with relief that Hal had made contact. There was nothing.

'I'm calling because I think you should know the truth about what happened.' She hoped Amber was still there. 'And the truth is that Hal was terribly deceived by all his friends. So were you, I know,' she added hastily. 'And if only you hadn't left so fast,' Lily speeded up, thinking she'd said enough, 'none of this would have happened.' The last bit was hers but she thought it was worth pointing out. There was more long silence on the other end of the phone. 'He loves you, Amber. All this is crucifying him.'

At least she's let me say it, Lily thought, as she waited for a response. And now it can never be unsaid. Even if I get no further, I have passed on Hal's message.

'Lily,' the voice spoke very gravely. 'Thank you very much.'

Lily waited for more. 'Is that all?' she said, desperately not wanting her to hang up so soon.

There was another long pause and then the girl whispered, 'Don't let's make this worse.'

'But is there anything I can tell him?'

The voice spoke up again. 'I suppose you could tell

him that there's no point him doing this? That getting friends to make phone calls on his behalf is not going to help anything. That it's not, actually, going to make a blind bit of difference.'

'Don't you love him any more?' Lily asked sadly.

There was another long silence.

'Thanks so much for calling.' The girl now obviously felt it was time to go. 'I really don't want to talk about it.'

'Wait!' begged Lily.

'It's much better if we end this conversation now.'

'Why?'

'Because!'

'Tell me why, please.'

'Oh my God! Leave it alone!' She sighed in exasperation. 'What do you want me to say? That I've realized in the time we've been apart that he's not the one for me?'

Lily was taken aback at the way she trotted out the corny, awful phrase. 'Can't you do better than that?'

'Okay, how about I hope we can still be friends? What do you want me to say? You tell me!'

'I wouldn't know. I'm surprised you don't know. I'm surprised you don't know what to say to someone you were prepared to marry,' Lily said bitterly. 'Who you know still loves you and doesn't deserve to be treated like shit.'

There was silence on the other end of the telephone.

'What's wrong, Amber?' Lily asked.

'Oh, please!' The voice snapped back. 'Don't tell me you still think you're talking to Amber!'

Yes, Lily thought helplessly, I do. I did.

She could hear the girl breathing on the other end of the phone as she waited for Lily to respond but Lily couldn't think of anything to say. Then the voice spoke again, now mimicking Lily's words.

'*He loves you, Amber,*' she sighed theatrically. 'Oh, he's absolutely *crucified* without you.' She paused. 'Well, actually there *is* something you can tell Hal. From me. You can tell Hal that Amber was standing right beside me throughout this entire conversation. And that she suggests he gets on with his life now, and forgets about her. But you know what? She doesn't much care either way!'

'You shouldn't be enjoying this so much,' Lily told her bitterly. 'You're not in a soap opera.'

'Thanks for calling,' the girl said just before Lily hung up.

'Urgghhh!' Lily shouted in frustration. You bitch! If Amber was anything like her friend, thank God Josh got Hal out of the wedding. And fuck Hal for getting her involved like this. She hated them all. She lifted up her hands and saw that they were shaking with tension. Immediately she called Kirsty to let rip.

Kirsty, having initially thrown up her hands in horror as Lily recounted what had happened, was, in the end, philosophical. At least after a call like that they were left with no doubt that Hal was well rid of a monster. Even if it wasn't Amber herself on the phone, anyone with friends like that did not deserve Hal.

'This is good,' Kirsty told Lily confidently, 'because now you can come straight home.'

Kirsty didn't like Lily being in London. It made her

insecure. 'There's nothing else Hal can ask you to do and now you've done the interview you may as well come back. Oh my god! I can't believe I haven't asked you about it! How was it? Did they sign you up on the spot?'

Lily couldn't bring herself to contradict her or admit that being in London had been far better fun than she'd remembered and that the thought of coming back didn't fill her with quite as much glee as Kirsty would have hoped.

'So when *are* you coming back?' Kirsty demanded.

'Sunday. It's not long, Kirsty. And while I'm here I want to see a few friends. And Hal's taking me out for supper on Saturday night. He wanted me to have lunch with him today but he had to cancel me.'

'Which friends would those be then?' Kirsty asked.

Lily laughed. 'Oh, you don't know any of them,' she said, winding her up. 'But there's Linds and Charlie and Charlotte and Toe and Tracey and Martha and Hels. My proper friends. You know, the ones I wish lived in Welshpool.'

'Oh all *those* friends. I wouldn't bother calling them. They've been on the phone to me, actually, to say that they think you're really boring. Apparently you go on about Welshpool all the time and they're a bit sick of it.'

'Piss off!' Lily laughed.

'Lily,' Kirsty said, suddenly serious, 'remember the cottage we were going to get together? I've just seen the most perfect place. It's called Owl Cottage and it's in Montgomery, right in the town, and it's got a stream running through the bottom of the garden. And it's black and white and so pretty and about four hundred years old. It belonged to an artist. But he's just died, left his studio in the garden all ready for you. You will be coming back, won't you?'

How did she know there was any doubt? Lily wondered, touched that Kirsty was so in tune with her. The studio in the garden whetted her interest. And Montgomery was absolutely lovely. Why not at least have the summer there to decide where she was going to go next? She didn't want to be in London in the summer.

'We could have barbecues and parties in the garden.'

'With all our hundreds of friends,' said Lily drily.

Kirsty laughed. 'Well, invite some of yours down from London. Or we could always borrow Grace's!'

'What do you mean?'

'She's suddenly a different person. I see her everywhere I go.'

'I didn't realize there were so many places to go to. And how's Simon, by the way? Seen him anywhere?'

'Oh, no,' said Kirsty breezily. 'I'll tell you more when I see you. Talk about Grace, not me.'

'But has something else happened between you two? Have you sorted it out? Just tell me that?'

'Not with me, no. He's met someone else.'

'No!'

'Yes. Her car's parked in his drive.'

Simon couldn't have met someone else, Lily told herself, furious, not taken in by Kirsty's easy tone. Not so fast. He and Kirsty had barely been apart three weeks. What the fuck did he think he was doing? Kirsty and

Grace could do with poison tasters to check out their men, she thought, wondering how she might set up the service.

*

That night Lily had arranged to meet two of her former art college friends, Stella and Steph, who were living with a guy called Badger in a stark, trendy warehouse conversion in King's Cross. There'd been space for Lily too, and she'd still been considering whether to move in with them when she and Grace had had their fateful telephone conversation and she'd decided with some relief that she had to go to Welshpool instead.

What was it? she thought now, as Badger handed her a beer and showed her around. Had she changed so much since she'd last seen them, or had they? Or was it just that what little they'd had in common had been lost once the familiarity of day-to-day life in college was gone? Whatever it was, she felt now as if she hardly knew them.

'King's Cross,' Steph told her smugly, coming over to join her, 'has become the new Hoxton. Not,' she hastily reassured Lily, 'that Welshpool doesn't sound dead cool. Some of my best friends live in Wales.'

Lily thought Steph would find it much more dead than cool and thank God she was unlikely ever to make the two-hundred-mile journey to find out. But the warehouse was amazing and Lily had to admit it would have been fun to live there, if she could have got used to the complete lack of privacy. All the internal walls were suspended and had gaps of at least a foot at the top and bottom. Whatever happened in either the bathroom or the bedroom would be heard everywhere else.

A state-of-the-art internal lift took them up to the most spectacular roof terrace, and immediately she thought she could live with the floating walls if she could have this too. It was wonderful, and as she stood there sipping her beer and looking out across London she could understand why they felt they had arrived on the top of the world.

When Lily told them where she was being taken by Hal on Saturday night they laughed, taking it as an invitation to draw up a hit list of all the fabulously cool places that they frequented. Places like Aqua and Marley's and VoiceMail, they told her. Lily had nodded blankly. Then they would take her on to a couple of clubs.

They started off in the early evening in the West End, then moved deep into Soho, Steph, Stella and Badger moving her purposefully around the town as strategically as if she was the queen on a chessboard. By eleven, Lily was gliding down the streets in an intoxicated haze. She knew she'd never be able to remember where she'd been taken but, as she carefully selected another cocktail, a delicious pear daiquiri, in a slick bar somewhere in Wardour Street, she decided she didn't care. It simply felt wonderful to be out.

Later, she laid her hot cheek against the cool white-tiled walls of a loo somewhere deep in the bowels of Soho. They were brilliant people, she thought smiling. They were genuinely kind people who she could live with for ever. But she did miss Kirsty. It would have been fun to have had Kirsty with her now.

By half-past one they had moved across the Monopoly board of London, ending up in a club not far from where they had started out, full of dramatic deep shadows and candlelight, with vast high ceilings and glinting stone floors. As they queued to get in she could feel the beat of the music thumping through her, so loud her heart seemed to re-set to beat in time to the music.

For a while Lily danced and drank a little water, and then a huge wave of tiredness swept through her and she knew she had to go home. The others would stay until seven or eight and usually she'd have joined them, but all she wanted was her bed.

She motioned to her friends that she was going and they led her away from the dance floor, mouthing to her to keep in touch and smiling and kissing goodbye, then disappeared back into the heaving crowd. She left the club, grateful for the air and for the sight of a long line of taxis waiting to ferry her home.

She paid off the taxi driver and stumbled through the front door, the steady beat of music in her head already being drowned out by the insistent beat of a hangover, brewing before she'd even had the chance to sleep. Somehow she managed to pull off her tiny skirt and skimpy T-shirt, drop them on the floor, then drag on another T-shirt to sleep in and to make it to the bathroom. They'd drunk nothing like as much as her, she thought, looking at her haggard face, picturing them still dancing. She slung herself across Josie's bed, too out of it even to get under the duvet, and let the welcome clouds of sleep immediately gather her up and float her away.

A little later, she found she was still half awake. Through the daze she took in the fact that somewhere in the room a high, persistent peeping, like a half-hearted alarm clock, had stopped her from dropping off to sleep. She climbed out of bed and padded around the room in the shadowy grey light and traced the insistent peep to her mobile. She pulled it out of her bag and squinted at it suspiciously. What the hell? What did it want? She was sure she'd turned it off before she'd gone out. She looked more closely and saw that she was being warned that the batteries were low, and also that she had a text message.

If you are interested, she scrolled down, *in my side of the story*, she scrolled down again, *call me tomorrow*.

She pressed and pressed, not registering the message at all, and with relief she saw the lights go out. Then she threw the phone into her handbag, padded back to the bed and slid under the duvet, too sleepy to take the message in, or to think whom it might have been from.

12

Kirsty couldn't believe that Simon had met someone else so fast. The fact that it was someone with such a ridiculous name as Mimosa McAlpine would have made her laugh if she hadn't been so miserable, because he had so obviously fallen back into old habits. She would be a stunning size eight and as thick as a barn door. Obviously not someone who should get too fond of Pond House, but no doubt having some fun while she kept his interest.

Three weeks had gone by since she and Simon had split up. Whereas every break up in the old days had prompted a celebratory party with her friends, this time all she wanted to do was stay at home. Initially she tried to deny that it was Simon keeping her there and still made the odd effort to keep in touch with other friends, but without Lily around to distract her she quickly began to give in, finding herself thinking about Simon obsessively, all the time. Without Lily there to encourage her into action, there was no possibility at all of Kirsty making contact with him. She was too much of a coward to do it on her own. And now that Mimosa had arrived with the spring, it seemed to confirm that their relationship was truly over.

Her mother's constant refrain, *it's such a shame about Simon*, and the fact that it never occurred to her mother that this was any worse for Kirsty than it was for her, that she might be twisting the knife every time she mentioned his name, made it easier for Kirsty to decide once and for all that she was leaving home. She was too old to have to put up with it. When her mother proceeded to tell Kirsty all about Mimosa, Kirsty left the house and promptly joined the books of all the local estate agents, determined that if the Montgomery cottage fell through she would have alternatives already lined up.

Maybe I'm finally growing up, Kirsty thought miserably, when she realized she was recognizing most of the contestants on *University Challenge* as they returned to do battle in the later rounds. Maybe this despair was a necessary evil. Perhaps she had to go through all this heartache in order to ensure that she never lost another Simon, if she was lucky enough to meet someone half as good as him ever again.

Kirsty didn't want to come face to face with him but she was not averse to spying on him, particularly if there was a chance of a glimpse of Mimosa. She cruised several times past his house but never saw her. All she saw, every time, was her car. A scarlet, shiny, in-your-face Mercedes sports car, sitting there on the gravel, smug and proprietorial. Why didn't Mimosa ever drive her car, Kirsty wanted to know? Why didn't it ever, ever leave Simon's drive? Probably because Simon was keeping her housebound. Housebound and knickerless, she thought bitterly. She wanted to push the car out between the gates and down the hill that stretched away from Pond House, down to the conveniently placed Montgomery Canal lying at the bottom. Now she understood why the scorned lovers she read about in the *Daily Mail* so often focused on the cars, daubing them in pink paint, or better still, paint-stripper, or setting them on fire.

Having spoken to Lily in London, Kirsty found herself once again edging towards Pond House in her car. This time, for once, it was a valid journey. The conversation with Lily had finally stimulated some desire to see people, and she'd called up some friends and was on the way to meet them in a pub near Simon's village, for a drink.

It was seven thirty as she drove towards Simon's house, and very dark, much too dark to hope to see anything of interest, like Mimosa. But as she got close to the delicate wrought-iron gates, she saw that there were bright lights coming on in the drive and then the door of the house opened in front of her. This was it, she thought, this time she was going to see her.

Kirsty slowed and changed down into first gear. It was frustratingly hard to get a proper look, as there was a huge bank forcing a sharp right-angled turn just a few hundred yards ahead of her. At the most there was just four seconds' staring time.

The front door was open, spilling light out into the drive, and she watched fascinated, expecting some leggy, tarty human equivalent to the car to come stepping out into the darkness. But the girl who suddenly appeared was wearing jeans and wellingtons and a thick stripy jumper and, even over the noise of her engine, Kirsty could hear her laughing.

Kirsty just had time to take in a face shining in the lamplight and then the solid black bank came up hard and terrifyingly huge in her windscreen. She hit it at about ten miles an hour, with her mouth open in shock, and heard herself make a painful *oof* of protest as the steering-wheel shoved into her, knocking all the breath out of her chest, and then the engine died.

She slowly lifted her head. She could hear that she was groaning in desperate breaths as her shocked lungs struggled for air, and her ribs felt so painful that she wondered if one of them was broken. She sat for a moment, trying to stop herself making such an awful noise, willing herself to recover before Simon emerged to find out what had happened. But in the wing mirror she could see she was too late. Simon was already appearing through his gates, and then, when he saw her car, was breaking into a run. Lovely, lovely, darling Simon, Kirsty thought miserably, as he raced towards her, completely unattainable.

And behind him, more hesitantly, came the girl, chubby-faced and fluffy-haired, sweet-looking and appalled.

Oh please no, Kirsty thought despairingly, more affected by the sight of Mimosa than by the crash. It was worse, far worse than crashing the car, to realize that Mimosa was not the red-taloned, predatory bit of totty she'd conveniently presumed her to be.

Simon came around to her side of the door and opened it swiftly.

'What happened?' he asked, looking grey in the light of the car. 'Are you all right?'

'It's okay,' Kirsty groaned, feeling utterly humiliated. 'I'm fine.'

'You'll have to come inside.' He straightened up, glancing away from her back down the lane to where Mimosa was cautiously making her way towards them. He ran his hand through his black hair. Then he turned back to her. 'Looking at your car, we don't have much choice.'

'Surely I was going too slowly to do any damage?'

Kirsty stared up at him with miserable eyes. She bit her lip at his brusque words, feeling tears start to wet her cheeks. Yet even when he was being curt, Simon was still more capable and reassuring than anyone else she'd ever known. At that moment, in pain and shock, she would have died for the comfort of being wrapped up in his arms.

Mimosa arrived and leaned in over his shoulder.

'Don't cry,' she said, smiling. 'You'll be okay. Come in to the house and I'll give you a drink. I'm sure Simon can get the tractor to pull your car into our drive.'

Kirsty shook her head. 'I'll phone my dad. I've got my mobile.'

'That's ridiculous,' Simon snapped at her. 'You're outside my house.'

In the darkness Kirsty saw Mimosa shoot Simon a surprised, questioning look.

Any mental agility that Kirsty could usually rely on seemed to have departed her brain. She was sure there was a brilliant reason why she should wait, alone and vulnerable in the dark lane, for her dad to come and pick her up, but somehow nothing came to mind. Much as

Kirsty did not want to walk up 'our' drive into the Happy Families household that was now Pond House, she seemed to have no choice.

And it was much worse than she thought. Mimosa took her arm and helped her out of the car, leaving Simon to jog back to the house to find a rope and get the tractor. She led her through the front door, and there, just inside, in the flickering hall she knew so well, was an open bottle of champagne on the dark oak table and two glasses sitting on the flagstones beside the crackling fire.

No, no, this is what we *did. You can't be doing it too. Not like this.*

She looked around the hall, half expecting to see a pair of knickers dangling off the huge stone mantelpiece.

'I can't come in. I don't want to interrupt your evening,' she said woodenly.

'Oh, that doesn't matter.' Mimosa waved it away. 'We were staying in anyway. We were just going to fetch more logs when we heard you crashing your car.'

She took Kirsty over to the fire. 'Come on, warm yourself up,' she suggested. She drained one of the glasses of champagne, refilled it and handed it to Kirsty. 'Don't worry,' she smiled. 'I haven't got germs.'

Kirsty took it from her and gave her a sidelong glance. No, she thought. Mimosa wouldn't have germs. She was nothing like Kirsty had expected. Pretty but not knock-out, with heavily mascara'd eyelashes and determined blue eyes. She wasn't slim but she had athletic legs and big breasts. And if the firelight revealed the stripy jumper to be definitely more Laura Ashley than Kookai, that,

sadly, was no reason to dislike her. Under different circumstances they might even have become good friends.

Outside Kirsty could hear Simon opening heavy doors,
and then the tractor spluttered into life and chuff-chuffed
past the window, out through the front gates and on
towards her car.

'Come and sit down, you poor thing,' Mimosa told her
with a beaming smile.

Kirsty did as she was told, thinking how much Mimosa
seemed to be enjoying the situation. Not if you knew
about me and your boyfriend, she thought wearily.

She sank into a deep tartan armchair and leaned forwards to warm her hands on the fire.

'And you mustn't worry about Simon. Now he knows
you're all right, he'll be having fun. Doing the knight in
shining armour bit.'

Not for me he won't be.

There was a pause.

'Do you know, that was how Simon and I met?'
Mimosa told her enthusiastically. 'He was my knight in
shining armour too.'

No doubt she wanted to sound bright and conver-
sational but her words came out unnaturally loud, and
after she'd said them she swallowed hard. It left Kirsty in
no doubt that Mimosa did know about her and Simon.
Knew exactly the score between them. More than that, it
was as if she was telling Kirsty that she knew, wanting to
show that she wasn't about to be intimidated by her.

You've got it wrong, Kirsty thought, if you're thinking

like that. I'm not about to challenge you for him. You're nothing to me.

'I'd got a flat tyre in the Safeway car-park, and Simon offered to change it.'

'How romantic,' said Kirsty.

'Yes. It was actually!' Mimosa smiled determinedly at Kirsty. 'Come on, baby, change my tyre! He was perfect.'

As Mimosa talked, she started to relax, leaning back in her chair, and settling herself down to tell the story.

'It was dark and pissing down with rain, I'd found the jack and the spanners but I'd been working up the courage to get the wheel off for about half an hour! And then, suddenly, there he was! His car was parked right next to mine and he was on his way home. God, I was so grateful!' She heaved a happy sigh at the memory. 'And then the most amazing thing was, we went for a quick drink at the Little Goose and realized we knew each other already! We hadn't seen each other for years but we'd been at nearby schools and we'd been to all the same parties. I couldn't believe my luck! When I was fourteen I'd fancied the pants off him.' She drifted off, a fatuous smile now on her face. 'And then before I knew it, I was moving in here. Of course he tells everyone that it was only my car he was interested in!' She laughed.

'And was it?' Kirsty asked without thinking.

'No!' Mimosa looked surprised and then rather irritated. 'Of course not!'

She disappeared into the kitchen and then came back out again a few moments later with another glass of champagne and an enormous bowl of crisps. She sat down opposite Kirsty.

'That was very quick,' Kirsty ventured, 'you moving in.'

'I don't think so,' Mimosa told her swiftly. 'It felt right. And if I see something I want, I tend not to let it out of my sight.'

Ho hum, Kirsty thought. She supposed she should have thought the same.

She wondered what had led Mimosa to the Safeway car-park in Welshpool. Why had she come at all? Had she been passing through the town on her way to somewhere else, and had only decided to stay because of Simon, or was she always going to stay on? But she couldn't bring herself to encourage more conversation and find out.

'You were lucky,' Mimosa told her, an evil look in her eye. 'That could have been a very nasty bump.' She knocked back some more champagne and took a handful of crisps, then said deliberately, 'And you must have got to know the roads around here so well . . .'

Kirsty glanced at her, surprised that Mimosa would say something so barbed. But Mimosa immediately dropped to her knees to throw the last log on the fire. Still, a blotching red flush was spreading up from her neck.

Oh, so I do bother you, do I? Kirsty thought wearily, her head and back and ribs aching even more. I'm not surprised. It's horrible having me in your new house, is it? Well, actually, it's horrible being here too. And as soon as I can I'll be on my way.

'No,' Kirsty reassured her, 'not much time to get to know the roads. I was hardly ever here.'

It wasn't the truth. Kirsty had driven or been driven around there all her life, and in the brief time with Simon had had many opportunities to practise the turn into his drive. But while she decided that she didn't much like Mimosa, she didn't hate her for feeling competitive. If anything, Kirsty felt sorry for her. Kirsty was angry with herself for losing Simon and she wanted him back, but she wasn't going to get any relief from hurting Mimosa.

'I hope nobody drives into him,' Kirsty said, changing the subject. She rubbed her neck, wondering if she had whiplash.

'You don't need to worry about that!' Mimosa told her readily, now glad to move on to safer ground. 'And if anyone does, Simon will come off best. You may be surprised to know that tractors have excellent headlights.'

No, I won't be surprised, Kirsty thought irritably. I know that. I grew up on a farm.

'Although why they need them I can't imagine. Have you ever seen a farmer working at night?'

And don't say that either.

'Yes, of course,' Kirsty replied, 'all the time.'

'Pooh,' said Mimosa. 'They're too busy filling out their subsidy forms.'

What was that? Taken aback, Kirsty felt that at last things were looking up. Mimosa had definitely said 'pooh', and her last comment was rather unpleasant. Kirsty was relieved that there were now some good grounds for disliking her. She followed Mimosa into the kitchen, staring after her hopefully.

'I adore the countryside,' Mimosa told her melodramatically. 'And around here is as good as it gets. I could never live in a city again.'

Oh hurrah! Kirsty thought grimly.

'Which is lucky,' Mimosa went on, back to her old self, 'because Dad's offered to buy us some land. He's dying for me to put down some roots – literally! And we'll be able to show everyone how it should be done. I want to provide all the meat and veg for the Little Goose. Simon doesn't know about it yet, so don't say anything.'

Noticing the expression on Kirsty's face, Mimosa pulled a chair out from the kitchen table for her to sit down on. 'Look how pale you are! You need some Nurofen.' She now seemed genuinely concerned. 'I should have got them for you ages ago.'

Kirsty shook her head. 'Honestly, I don't have a headache, I'm fine.'

'I'm going to have a horse, too,' she told Kirsty, looking as if she was going to burst with enthusiasm for her wonderful new life.

It gets better and better, Kirsty thought. 'But do you know anything about horses?' she asked. 'Or farming?'

'Not much,' Mimosa admitted, opening a drawer. 'We'll be organic, of course. And I'm willing to learn. You're going to have to give me lots of tips.' She was sounding much brighter, as if she'd assessed Kirsty, and was pleased to find that she was no threat after all.

'I don't think so.'

'Oh yes, you must,' Mimosa insisted. She walked over and put a glass of water and two Nurofen into Kirsty's hand. 'Plough the fields and scatter. You're quite the local hero, aren't you,' she said, smiling down at her, an irresistible little dig that was out before she'd thought about it.

'What do you mean?'

At the tone of Kirsty's voice, Mimosa looked uneasy. 'I was talking about your job,' she insisted quickly. 'And about how much everyone seems to love you.'

Kirsty knew it wasn't true but she hadn't the energy to retaliate. She felt suddenly very vulnerable, bruised and bumped and unable to cope with the undercurrents and barbs being thrown at her. She longed to be away.

'Come into the Warehouse some time,' Kirsty suggested, 'not that I know the first thing about the important stuff. You'll have to get a farm manager to help you with that.'

Mimosa laughed in relief. 'God, yes! Of course I will. Don't think it'll be me wading through the cow shit or biting the balls off the young lambs.'

Just don't push your luck, Little Miss Chirpy, Kirsty thought. Or I might still find the energy to strangle you.

Mimosa glanced at her and didn't like what she saw. She moved to the other end of the kitchen. 'Feeling better now?'

'Much better, thank you,' Kirsty replied politely. 'I don't think I've done any permanent damage.' She rotated her head to the left and then the right, massaging her neck with one hand. 'I should call my friends and tell them where I am. Do you mind?' She dug into her bag and found her mobile.

'No, not at all. Give Simon a chance to bring back your car and I'm sure he'll drop you home.'

Kirsty called her friends and her parents, then sat back to wait for Simon. She even accepted Mimosa's offer of another glass of champagne.

Mimosa took her back through to the fire and they sat opposite each other in the throne-like armchairs and sipped champagne and stared into the flames.

'So, when do you think the farmers around here will wake up and smell the coffee?' Mimosa asked Kirsty, making a last attempt at conversation, still under the impression that this was a subject Kirsty would enjoy chewing over with her.

'What do you mean?'

'Realize that they have to stop waiting for someone else – us – to bail them out. Doesn't it annoy you?'

Kirsty didn't respond.

'Well, it annoys *me*! We've paid out a complete fortune for foot and mouth, and they're still exactly the same. Moaning, moaning, moaning. If BSE didn't ruin them, foot and mouth did, or the strong pound, or whatever else they can come up with to complain about. They forget that no one's making them do it!' Her eyes were wide and indignant-looking. 'They should find something more profitable if they can't afford to farm. Open a golf-course, or breed llamas or something. Don't you think?'

She was so far away from Kirsty then, that Kirsty knew

it was hardly worth arguing with her, and yet Mimosa was so appallingly ignorant and lacking in compassion that Kirsty found she couldn't keep quiet.

'If you let me take you to visit a few of the farms around here, you would never say something like that again. You have absolutely no idea what you're talking about.'

Mimosa was momentarily thrown, taken aback by the warning in Kirsty's voice, and the real emotion in her eyes. She looked back at her defiantly, but then turned and left the room.

Why did I bother, Kirsty asked herself. Why bother to explain to someone who didn't understand, and who wasn't interested anyway, that golf-courses depended on hundreds of people to come and play on them and that they cost hundreds of thousands of unattainable pounds to set up. That it wasn't llamas that could eat the short wiry grass but sheep. And that the farmers who'd battled through the soul destroying foot and mouth epidemic were fighting against the odds for their survival. That while everyone still wanted lamb and pork and beef on their tables, kept potatoes and carrots in their cupboards, needed sugar in their tea, and bread in the bread bins, there was now barely a role for farmers, as once there had been. How hard it was to understand that if they continued to care for their animals and cultivate the crops, it wouldn't be possible for them to be paid enough to survive on. Enough to have hope for the future and to stem the tide of suicides and bankruptcies and end the prospect of much of the countryside becoming a scrubby, deserted landscape, marked just occasionally by a groomed, green golf-course.

How had Simon managed to avoid hearing all this, Kirsty wondered? Or perhaps she'd got him wrong and he couldn't care less as long as he carried on getting hold of the produce he wanted for the Little Goose. Perhaps he would agree with Mimosa? Especially when he found out that Daddy was buying them land. Maybe it made Mimosa adorable? No. She couldn't pretend she didn't know Simon well enough to know he'd surely never think like that.

As if she had summoned him by thinking about him, Simon lifted the heavy iron latch and came in through the front door. The cold night air and the exertion had left him with a wild, windblown, Heathcliffian look. Simon must have known that she was waiting for him on the other side, and yet Kirsty caught a startled look that said he still hadn't prepared himself for seeing her there beside the fire. Kirsty smiled at him and he immediately disappeared into the kitchen.

'You okay, babes?' Mimosa called.

'Yes, of course.' Simon stood in the doorway with what Kirsty guessed was a Jack Daniels in his hand. He seemed to have got himself under better control now and even managed the briefest of smiles at them both.

He came and sat down on the rug at Mimosa's feet, leaned back against her legs and looked up at Kirsty. 'How are you doing?'

'She's fine,' said Mimosa.

'I think I'm fine.' Kirsty gazed at him. 'How's my car?'

'It'll cost more than it's worth to have the dents knocked out. At least fifty quid.' He smiled at her until she swallowed and looked away.

It was so hard, so bloody hard, to see him sitting there like that with Mimosa.

Behind him Mimosa started rubbing the back of his neck with her foot. He caught it in one hand, holding it still in its pale green angora sock while she wiggled her toes in delight.

Kirsty wondered how much Mimosa knew about her and Simon. She doubted that Mimosa would be sitting there quite so comfortably if she knew that Simon had once run naked out of the room where the three of them were sitting now, up to his bedroom to fetch the duvet and pillows off his bed, and had made him and Kirsty a nest in front of the fire, on the big square rug now acting as No Man's Land between her and Mimosa. He'd lifted Kirsty up in his arms, then dropped her gently into the goose-down before leaning over to kiss her in the fire-light's soft glow. And that it had been their first time together, and perfect enough for her to think that she would never let him go.

Looking at him, she was sure he was remembering too.

'You shouldn't drive something so flimsy,' Mimosa told Kirsty quietly, obviously emboldened by Simon's touch. 'You had absolutely no protection.'

Simon started to smile at the sight of Kirsty's angry face.

'Yes, I think Mimosa's right,' he told her seriously. 'Perhaps you should get a Land Rover? Something more robust.'

Kirsty glared at him.

'Or a tractor?' Mimosa giggled.

Kirsty had had enough. 'Will you take me home now, Simon?' She stood up abruptly. 'They'll be waiting for me. Thanks, Mimosa,' she added, 'it was good to meet you.'

Mimosa took hold of Kirsty's hand. 'All I can say is, thank God it happened outside our front door.' She shook her head. 'And thank God you're all right. I am so glad we were here to help and that I had the chance to meet you. And I hope you feel better in the morning.'

'I feel fine now,' Kirsty told her, removing her hand. 'Much better. But I want to go home.'

Kirsty slipped on her coat and walked slowly outside ahead of Simon, grateful for the dark. Simon followed her out and Mimosa waved him goodbye at the front door, then closed it, leaving them alone.

Simon's car was parked in an old stable building just a hundred feet or so from Pond House and they walked there slowly, side by side, their hands occasionally brushing together. There was an unbearable intimacy about him being so close. Heightened awareness meant she could feel the hairs on her arm nearest to his rising in excitement. Her heart thumped in pointless anticipation and she felt as if the dark night, the stars, the moon, were there only as a backdrop to her and Simon.

But all too soon they'd reached his car and nothing had

happened, nothing had been said, and there were only seconds left before the noisy engine and bright headlights broke the intensity of the moment.

She grabbed for his hand, surprising herself as much as him. It was a strong warm hand and at the touch a great flood of longing poured through her.

His hand stayed resolutely unresponsive in hers, but at least he didn't pull away and that gave her hope. Slowly she threaded each of her fingers through each of his and held on to him, and waited, and after what felt like forever, his hand sprang shut around hers. It was the most charged, erotic moment she had ever known.

In the darkness she moved to face him, saw him open his mouth to say something, his white teeth bright in the moonlight, the last glimpses of anger and vulnerability disappearing from his face, and desire growing in his eyes.

Before he could change his mind, she turned to him, pressing his hand between both of hers, but he pulled himself free and grabbed her roughly towards him, his hands touching her thick dark hair, kissing her so hard that their teeth clashed against each other.

She shoved her hips against him, feeling him hard against her, and his hands slipped down her back to cup her buttocks, holding her there. She wanted to sink to the ground with him there and then, to pull him down on top of her, guide his fingers through the zip on her jeans to pull aside her pants, to feel the ground cold against her back.

But almost before he'd started Simon stopped again.

Even though he still had his arms wrapped tightly around her, he lifted his head and rested his chin on the top of her head and she knew that she'd lost him.

'I'm sorry, darling Kirsty, but I can't do this again.'

He gently pushed her away from him, holding her at arm's length for a moment before letting her go. This was rejection. Kirsty had never been turned down at such a critical point before, never been turned down at all before.

'Why?' she almost cried.

'Because,' he said, 'you and I, for whatever reason, didn't work out. Whatever caused it to go wrong the first time hasn't gone away. It's probably not the coolest thing to say but I don't want to get hurt by you again.'

'Oh, Simon!' Kirsty said desperately, looking up at him. 'You can't say that! I don't know why I didn't come running after you but I know now it was the stupidest thing ever. Please!' she begged, 'can't you give me another chance?'

'No,' Simon shook his head. 'I'm not saying it because I want to play games. You know that's not my style. And I don't want to hurt you.' He looked down at her and smiled sadly. 'Even though you completely gutted me. But I don't believe it would work any better second time around than it did the first.'

'It would.'

'No, it wouldn't,' Simon said gently.

'It would.'

He didn't say anything.

'You're being so stubborn.' She looked pleadingly up at him. 'But I suppose there's Mimosa now. Of course,' she added bitterly when he didn't answer, 'let's not forget Mimosa.'

Simon nodded. 'Let's not forget Mimosa.'

She turned away from him then and opened the car door, so disappointed she couldn't speak. Once sitting beside her, Simon accelerated away so fast that gravel was flung wildly against the house.

'Slower, please,' she snapped. 'I've already had one accident tonight.'

He nodded and slowed down but there was still an urgency to the way he drove, an obvious eagerness to get her home.

I can't ever try again, Kirsty vowed, watching his profile as he concentrated on the road and wanting him more than ever. Or think about him any more. I will get over him and on with my life. And I'll meet someone else, and be just as happy.

'Has Mimosa moved in?' she asked despite herself, throwing Simon a quick sidelong glance.

'Yup.'

'That was quick.'

'Not especially.'

She tried to catch the expression on his face but he wasn't giving anything away.

'I didn't like her.'

'Well, how grown up of you.'

Kirsty smiled despite herself. 'Forget you and me. She's a Nazi bitch and I can't believe you've let her stay three days, let alone three weeks.'

Simon didn't answer.

'Okay, I'm sorry,' Kirsty said. 'You're right, I'm being childish.' She bit her lip. 'But I still don't like her. And tell me you two haven't slept beside the fire, like we did.'

'Not yet, but thanks for reminding me.' He turned to her. 'Don't play games, Kirsty,' he said sharply. 'You told me what you wanted and you got it. I've done only what you asked me to do. You can't get jealous when I meet someone else.'

'I know I can't but I have! And don't act like you don't understand what I'm talking about!' Kirsty told him angrily. 'You had your tongue down my throat less than ten minutes ago!'

'I know I did!' He looked at her and grinned. 'But I still don't want another relationship with you.'

'Okay,' Kirsty said with a sigh, 'just the sex, then.'

She made him laugh, restoring a little of her pride, but still she felt utterly miserable. Thank God they were nearly at Little Venus Farm and she could leap out of the car and get away from him.

He pulled up outside her parents' house and unclipped her seat belt.

'I didn't think you'd be like this.' He said it as a question, as if he was surprised that he could be hurting her. 'You seemed so sure.'

There was nothing else to do. Without replying, she opened her door and slipped out of the car, kept her head down and walked away.

You kissed me like you meant it, she thought stubbornly, booting open the front door. Now you're telling me you can walk away, but you're pretending that it meant nothing. Because, for a few moments there, I know I had you back. You can drive away from me but I don't believe you really want to go.

In answer, Simon's black Porsche swung past her in a fast circle and then left her alone.

13

Afterwards it seemed to Kirsty that she saw Mimosa all the time. Kirsty could never be sure if it was deliberate or not. Mimosa never showed any sign of noticing her, and yet she was always coming out of shops as Kirsty went in to them, or passing her on the street or in her car when Kirsty drove to work, and Kirsty couldn't quite believe that Mimosa didn't once register her presence. She wondered again what it was that had brought Mimosa to Welshpool in the first place. Asking around, she learned that Mimosa worked for an antique dealer somewhere in the south of England and that she was supposed to be recceing her way through Shropshire and mid-Wales, sniffing out bargains.

Whenever she was asked, Mimosa was always completely open about the fact that she wasn't very interested in antiques. She'd found herself falling into the job because she didn't know what else to do and because she fancied her boss – a friend of her father's – and because she liked the idea of telling people she was an antique dealer. Preoccupied with making money, and highly competitive, she was really motivated by the buzz of finding the bargains ahead of someone else, picking things up for a fraction of their value. And although bargains were no longer easily found, it was in the country houses, antique shops and auctions of Wales and the North of England where she found most of the little gems she could sell in the south for ten times more than she'd paid.

This time, she had been concentrating her efforts on Hope Castle, a tiny, perfect, russet-red castle dating back to the 1300s, built to withstand the murderous Welsh, and now to be converted into a luxury hotel. During the afternoon on the day she'd met Simon, and after painstaking spadework, she'd managed to wangle a private view with the frail Lord Hope, who, with no children to pass the castle on to, had sold his castle and was now disposing of its contents after living there for all his eighty-seven years. What had particularly caught the interest of Mimosa, and a good many other dealers too, was the fact that Hopes had lived at Hope Castle for four hundred years and had never before sold anything of value. Until the contents were listed and catalogued, nobody had any idea of what might be inside. Mimosa had won the chance of an invaluable private view – but then she'd met Simon and hadn't turned up.

Standing in the rain in the Safeway car-park, watching Simon working at her wheel with his coat off and his jersey pulled up to the elbows, her first thought had been, what a waste. What a waste that she'd found such a man here, because in her dismissive way that meant he was either an impoverished antiquarian bookseller or a struggling market gardener who had downsized because he hadn't been able to cope with real life. But then there had been that wonderful moment of surprise, as they had talked in the Little Goose and she had realized he wasn't the hopeless yokel she'd had him down for. She'd found herself thinking how attractive he was, and then he'd said something that made her realize that she knew him already, that he was the same impressively cool Simon Campion she'd known briefly at school. But the best moment had been when she'd peeped through the heavy velvet curtain that divided the restaurant from the pub, and watched Simon go over to talk to the manager on duty that night, and she had finally clicked that he was dynamic and stylish and booming with energy and that the dynamic and stylish Little Goose was all his.

She was thirty-four and tired of her single-girl's life-style in London. Tired of her little flat and of sleeping with her greying, fifty-five-year-old boss. The day after meeting Simon, she'd rung Lord Hope to be told that there was no possibility at all of rearranging her meeting. Where once she would have cried at the lost opportunity, now she didn't care at all. And a week after meeting Simon she'd rung her boss to tell him that she wasn't coming back.

One of the few things she worried about was Kirsty. Even before she had met her, she had realized from one or two idle lines of Simon's that she should classify Kirsty in the danger category, and the look on Simon's face when he'd realized whose car had hit the bank outside his house only confirmed what she'd already guessed. But, even worse, there was something powerfully alluring about Kirsty herself that nobody needed to tell her about. Something in the way she moved, something in the way she spoke, whatever it was, it had the power to make men buckle at the knees. What was strange for Mimosa was that more often than not she'd had that same effect on men and had never, until now, had to battle it out with someone like herself. Girls had often been far more beautiful than her but she'd always been the one to get the man she wanted. And although she must have come up against other Kirstys before, this was the first time that it had really mattered, that she'd been made to feel hopelessly vulnerable.

And so, just as Kirsty had stalked Pond House in the hope of catching sight of Mimosa, now Mimosa found herself watching out for Kirsty.

The morning after the accident, Mimosa came into the Warehouse, ostensibly to check that Kirsty was feeling better.

'Yes, thank you very much,' said Kirsty briskly, wanting the chat over and done with, aware of two other customers in the shop whose ears were already pricking up expectantly.

Mimosa didn't appear to notice. She played for time, looking behind Kirsty at the shelves of goods.

'I'm sorry,' Kirsty told her after one or two more inane attempts at conversation on Mimosa's part, 'I really have to get on here.'

'Oh well, maybe we can have a drink some time.'

Kirsty ignored the offer and Mimosa reluctantly left.

*

All the time, Kirsty missed Lily miserably. They'd spoken only once since she'd gone to London, following Lily's conversation with Amber, but after that there'd been the car accident and meeting Mimosa and the excruciating time with Simon, and Kirsty hadn't yet had a chance to tell Lily any of it.

In the days since Lily had gone, Kirsty had been to see Owl Cottage in Montgomery twice more, and had registered her serious, serious interest, feeling that if she put down roots for both of them she could ensure that Lily stayed. But even if Lily didn't stay, Kirsty knew that she herself was finally leaving home. On her salary she could just afford the rent on her own, and although there was another cheaper cottage that she was due to see that evening, she'd set her heart on moving to Owl Cottage.

Every third Saturday, Kirsty had to work at the Warehouse, and with Lily due back the next day, working this particular Saturday was a welcome distraction. That said, it was so quiet that by eleven nobody had been in to see her. Then, in the late morning, one of her farmers came in, Fred Gittins, an old man who'd decided after their first meeting that Kirsty was the most wonderful creature he'd ever laid eyes on and had made regular visits to the Warehouse every week since.

He came hesitantly through the door, glanced around the shop and rubbed his hands with satisfaction when he saw that she was alone.

'Hello, Fred,' Kirsty said, delighted to have some company, getting up to greet him and knowing from the look on his face that he had something to tell her.

Fred waved her to sit down again and then gave all his

attention to getting over to her desk, forcing his bandy, arthritic legs to move a great deal faster than they were used to. When he arrived, he put both hands on her desk in relief and leaned towards her.

'You've not been looking after yourself,' he told her gruffly, studying her face with watery blue eyes.

'No. You heard I bumped my car?'

'Arr,' he nodded, 'and hit your head.'

He took his time, looking over her face, and then when he was satisfied there was nothing seriously wrong, came and lowered himself slowly down in the chair beside her.

She waited, enjoying the fact that there weren't going to be any words of sympathy. Happy in the knowledge that he would do anything he could for her, at any time.

'You've come to tell me something, haven't you?'

'Arr,' Fred agreed, not giving any more away for the moment.

Kirsty waited. This was part of the Fred routine.

'You know that new filly over at Pond House?' he said eventually, looking down at his boots.

'Oh, he hasn't got her one already?' Kirsty burst out with disgust. 'Mimosa was telling me about it.'

When Mimosa had told Kirsty she was getting a horse, she must have had a horse in mind, Kirsty realized. She and Simon must have picked it up already.

'Bugger!' Kirsty told Fred. Simon must be keener than she'd realized. 'So where's Simon going to stable her?'

'In the house, I should hope!' Fred said, a delighted smile stretching across his face.

Kirsty looked at him blankly and then she laughed. 'So

you're talking about Mimosa, are you, Fred?' she checked. 'There isn't a new horse?'

'Mi-moh-sar,' Fred said slowly, repeating her name. 'Arr. That's her name. That's the one I'm talking about, Kirsty.' He fished a handkerchief out of his trouser pocket and coughed deeply. 'I'm not going to say that it should be you there.' He folded up his handkerchief and stuffed it back in his trousers, then leaned forward conspiratorially. 'But what I've got to tell you just might make you feel a little bit better about all that.' He nodded again, eyes watering, relishing what he was about to say.

'Mi-moh-sar,' he told her with glee, 'is being stabled in the spare bedroom.'

Kirsty sat back, wanting to pretend that this news didn't matter either way, but at the same time a warm trickle of hope began to flow through her veins.

'That's right,' Fred told her, puffed up with pleasure at her reaction, noticing everything. 'Simon agreed to put her up for a few nights around the time when she had that meeting arranged at Hope Castle. And he's never managed to get her out again.'

'But how do you know this?' Before she really believed it, Kirsty wanted to hear that the news was on good authority.

Fred thought about it. 'I wouldn't know how I know,' he told her slowly and earnestly, 'but I expect it was Beth Linden told Mary.'

Now Kirsty could see it might all be true. Mary was Fred's wife, and Mrs Linden cleaned Pond House for

Simon. It was Mrs Linden who'd first set the tongues wagging when she'd encountered Kirsty slinking down the stairs one morning, trying to avoid her, and her beady eyes would definitely take in evidence of Mimosa sleeping in the spare bed rather than Simon's.

'And so we were thinking, Mary and me, that you should let your Simon know that you're still soft on him. Otherwise you might find Mi-moh-sar never leaves. You can do that, now as you know you're not stepping on any toes.'

Not that that ever bothered me, Kirsty thought. But I don't mind you thinking it did.

Mimosa had been the evidence and proof that Simon had moved on and away from her. Now, if what Fred said was true, there was reason to hope again after all. But imagining baring her soul to him once more, putting herself again in the firing line, she thought that she couldn't bear to do it. That if anything ever did happen again, it would have to be because he made the running.

*

After Fred had left the shop she tried to settle down to clear some invoicing, but she couldn't concentrate and time and again she found herself at the window, imagining that if she waited long enough she would see Simon pulling up outside.

So Mimosa was a fraud, she thought with gleeful pleasure. She should have guessed. She remembered Simon catching Mimosa's foot as the three of them sat beside the fire and wondered if he'd done it deliberately to punish Kirsty? Or had it been a spontaneous gesture of affection, to someone who was perhaps a true old friend?

It was a pearl-grey day, the air hard and cold, and Kirsty had to search the sky to find the pale light of the sun. It was going to snow, she realized, looking up at the laden, low clouds. How lovely would that be? A childish rush of hope and excitement gripped her and she felt she had to get away from the Warehouse. She wanted to go for a walk, to climb high up to the ruins of Montgomery Castle and watch the snow arrive.

But she couldn't leave. Although customers were thin on the ground this morning, she couldn't close the shop until four. She continued to gaze out of the window, occasionally stretching her back and neck, trying to relieve the stiffness she'd felt since the accident and thinking obsessively about Simon. Thinking again and again about how he'd kissed her, convincing herself that she was going to get him back, particularly now that she knew he hadn't promptly fallen in love with somebody else. That even if he told himself he didn't want to get involved, he wouldn't be able to resist her, and that gradually she would wear him down, persuade him to trust her again. And Mimosa? Mimosa could now be cast aside. She didn't deserve him.

The stiffness in her back was bad and with her all the time, and with her legs straight she let her arms swing towards her toes, feeling the muscles in her back burning and then gradually starting to loosen up. Despite the aches and pains, she knew it had been only a relatively gentle bump, and apart from a round bruise on her forehead and a longer, deeper one just below her collarbone there was little to show for it. She swung her arms backwards and forwards a few times more, then stood up again and checked her watch, yawned and looked back out of the window. Then shut her mouth again in shock. Jogging towards her, in white lycra running shorts with a minidisk attached to her belt and a baseball cap on her head, was Mimosa.

Oh, not again, Kirsty thought, ducking away from the window. Who did she least want to see that day?

She raced to the door, flipped the Open sign to Closed, and swept the desk clear of her bits. Just off the main room of the Warehouse was a tiny annexe, more a cupboard than another room, housing three metal feedbins. She lifted the lid off the first and climbed clumsily inside, dropping the lid gently down over her head. Only a day ago it had been three-quarters full of Flash Nuts for Show Ponies and she thanked the competitive, Sloaney mother who had cleaned it out the evening before.

She heard footsteps outside the shop and pictured Mimosa coming panting up to the glass door, taking in the sign, peering in and seeing nobody there, turning and jogging away again. How long should I give her, Kirsty wondered? The last thing she wanted was to be caught climbing out of a feedbin. But then, just as she thought she might risk a quick look, she heard the shop door opening.

Didn't you read the sign? Kirsty thought, incensed. The sign that said, quite clearly, Closed. She heard the door quietly closing, then silence. Are you in here now? Kirsty wondered.

'Kirsty?' Mimosa called, answering her. 'Are you in the back?' And then, 'Are you there?' Footsteps passed the bin and made their way cautiously through the Warehouse. 'Kir-sty,' Mimosa called again.

Kirsty crouched, prepared to wait it out, trying to gauge how far Mimosa had got by the sound of her footsteps. Then, just as she could hear Mimosa approaching, there was the sound of a car coming slowly down the lane beside the Warehouse. It changed down a gear and turned in and she knew that she was about to have a second customer to contend with. She heard the engine die, then the sound of a slamming door and more footsteps. She prayed that whoever was arriving now would see the sign and not Mimosa, and leave. But it was not to be. She heard the door open again and she sank down in the bin with her hands covering her mouth, fighting back the urge to start giggling.

'Hi there,' she heard a woman's voice say, 'any sign of Kirsty?'

'No. Nowhere!' Mimosa replied. 'I'm a bit worried about her, actually. She hit the bank outside our house in her car a couple of days ago and I thought I'd see how she was doing. It's strange she's left the place unmanned!'

'I thought she left every place unmanned,' the other girl said dryly.

Oh, you bitch, Kirsty thought, in surprise. Whoever you are.

Mimosa laughed. 'You know her, do you?' Kirsty could hear the interest in her voice.

'Not really. She's a good friend of my sister's.' There was a pause. 'I'm Grace Somerville.'

Kirsty immediately recognized Grace's voice. Great! Now she had both her best friends – *not* – in her shop together, and she was stuck in a feedbin and couldn't welcome them in.

'Mimosa McAlpine.'

Kirsty couldn't resist taking a chance. She popped her head around the door and looked out. They were standing just around the corner from her, a few feet away, both with their backs to her, Grace with a small black and white puppy quivering at her feet. As she watched, it began to piddle on the concrete floor. That's okay, she told it. Do some more. It might mean she has to take you outside.

'I'd better watch what I say about her then,' Mimosa laughed.

'No, no, just say it quietly, she's probably in the store-room listening.'

'There's her scarf on the chair. She can't have gone for long.'

Kirsty crouched down again in her feedbin, holding the lid open just enough to squint through. She watched as Mimosa walked down to the other end of the shop, looking for her. Under the tight white shorts she was wearing only a G-string, and her surprisingly large bottom wriggled and jiggled with each thud of her feet. Not a pretty sight, Kirsty thought with satisfaction.

'*Kirsty*,' Mimosa boomed from the other end. She waited a few seconds. 'No, she's not there,' she said to Grace, striding back, hands on hips. 'She must have left the scarf behind when she went. We can say what we like.'

Why don't you, Kirsty thought, bracing herself.

'Actually, I quite like her,' Grace said to Kirsty's surprise. 'She makes me laugh.'

Kirsty couldn't quite imagine Grace laughing but still she was touched.

'Oh, me too,' Mimosa insisted, immediately. 'We've only met briefly but she seemed so nice.'

'I hope she's okay. I was bringing Hodge to meet her.' Grace bent down to pick up her dog and realized with horror that she was standing in a large pool of pee. 'Oh Lord. Look what he's done. I'd better clear it up.'

There was a pause as they both studied the floor then high-stepped away. Don't worry about it, Kirsty thought insistently. I'll do it. Go now, she willed them both. I'll mop it up.

Then Kirsty heard another car pulling into the yard outside. She couldn't believe it. She wondered whether to cut her losses and jump out of her hiding-place shouting, 'Here I am!' She pictured the wonderful look on their faces as she popped out of the feedbin like a jack-in-the-box.

'That'll be Simon,' Mimosa said. Kirsty sighed deeply and crouched lower into the bin.

'I got him to come and pick me up.' Mimosa moved to the window and waved. 'I always get knackered half-way around and this way it saves me one last bastard of a hill.'

But why meet here? Kirsty thought, despairingly. Of all places.

The door opened.

'Hullo babes,' Mimosa welcomed him in. 'Thirsty Kirsty's not here. Isn't it strange?'

'No,' Simon told her. 'Not if you see the big Closed sign on the door.'

'Oh! Is there?' Mimosa moved around the door to check. 'I wonder where she's gone? And why didn't she lock up?'

Why are you always so keen to see me? Kirsty wanted to ask her.

Mimosa shut the door again and draped herself around Simon's neck. 'Thanks for coming to get me.'

'Well, hello again,' Simon said to Grace, disentangling himself from Mimosa. He grinned. 'Do you come here often?'

Grace laughed nervously. 'No, actually! This is only my second time.'

'And both times I've been here too.'

Mimosa took Simon's arm proprietorially. 'Sorry to interrupt, babes, but as Kirsty's not here, it'd be great to get home. I'm dying for a shower.'

Kirsty watched Grace immediately back off. 'Of course,' she said, turning to Mimosa, 'don't let me hold you two up.'

Simon shrugged and went over to the door, opening it to let them both through. Mimosa and Grace stepped outside together.

'On second thoughts,' Simon said suddenly from the

doorway, 'you go home.' He threw Mimosa the car keys. 'I'm going to hang around a bit and see if she comes back. I don't like leaving the place unlocked.'

'But it's not your problem,' Mimosa snapped at him.

'I know,' he said calmly. 'And I won't stay longer than five minutes and then I'll walk home. You go on and have your shower. I'll see you soon.'

Mimosa nodded, obviously disappointed, and a little while later Kirsty heard first one and then another engine start, and then both cars pulled away.

Simon wandered over to the window and watched the cars go. Kirsty felt as if she shouldn't breathe in case he heard her. How long would she have to wait like this? Would it be hours more? She had to hope that five minutes was all he really did have in mind. She watched him leave the window and move over to her desk and chair and sit down, and she felt uncomfortable watching him, as if she was intruding. She hoped he wouldn't do anything that she'd rather not see, imagining how she'd feel if he farted or picked his nose while he waited. Instead he took her diary off the shelf beside the desk, placed it in front of him and flicked carefully through the pages. But that was okay, Kirsty thought – presumably he was checking if she had had anything planned that would have taken her away from the Warehouse.

When he had looked through several pages, he snapped it shut again and got up and slowly walked the length of the room, peering into corners, lifting lids, obviously looking for her, or for signs of her. He didn't seem unduly worried and yet she could tell he was puzzled by her absence and didn't want to let it go. She loved him for wondering, for showing concern for her.

When he came back again, he stood right in front of her bin. He looked at his watch and seemed to make up his mind to go, but then, just as he was moving towards the door, he turned and sat down heavily at her desk again. He felt behind him for her long red scarf, dragged it off the back of the chair and slowly wound it around his neck. Then he leaned back, looking more comfortable and comforted, and swivelled, lazily, around and around in her chair.

Watching him, Kirsty's heart squeezed with tenderness. More than anything, she wanted to climb out of the bin and into his arms, but she knew that it absolutely wasn't one of her options.

Eventually he'd had enough and came to a stop with his back to her. She watched him, fascinated, hardly daring even to blink in case she missed something. Then he turned towards her and dramatically pulled the scarf off his neck and buried his face in its folds.

'Drive me crazy,' she heard him say into the scarf.

'Hi!' she said loudly, unable to stop herself, rising out of the feedbin in front of him.

Simon jumped at least a foot. He looked at her, speechless for a few seconds. Then he banged his forehead down on the desk and covered his head with his arms.

She laughed at his reaction.

'*What-are-you-doing?*' he said, looking up at her again.

'Hiding from Mimosa!'

She looked at him sitting there, so shocked, and started

to laugh again, making him laugh too, until both of them were doubled up and Kirsty had to collapse back into her bin. When she could finally breathe again, she stood up and looked pleadingly across at him. 'Stop! Come and give me a hand getting out. Please.'

'How long were you planning to stay in there?' he asked, coming around from the desk. 'Do you have some food?'

'A few pony nuts. Enough to keep me going! But I don't think I can get out.'

'So you want me to lift you out, do you?' he asked, coming up to her and shaking his head. 'I don't think so.'

'Please,' she repeated. 'Come on. I've been in here too long already.'

'But I like you there. It makes me feel safe.'

As soon as he came into range, she clasped her arms around his neck.

'Pull me out, Mr Gorgeous,' she ordered, looking up at him through her eyelashes and thinking how perfect it would be if he kissed her now.

Simon put his hands around her waist and she leaned into him and climbed slowly out. Once free, she took her time regaining her balance, then reluctantly unhooked her arms.

'So what were you doing with my scarf?'

'Nothing,' he said, smiling, slowly letting her go.

'You were nuzzling it.'

'No, I was blowing my nose,' he said, still standing close to her. 'I've got this terrible cold.'

'Oh, right,' she said.

His face was very, very close to hers now. I think he wants me, she thought, feeling faint with longing and relief.

*

'Fancy a coffee?' Mimosa asked as she and Grace left the Warehouse.

'Sure!' Grace answered, wanting to talk to her some more, even if she could hardly bear the thought that this girl was not only going out with Simon but living with him too.

Mimosa was asking her at just the right time. In the past weeks it had struck Grace repeatedly that she had no friends, never had anyone to do anything with, and until she found a job she would love to have a girlfriend to share some of her time. Even in her moments of deepest despair, she had watched Lily and Kirsty together and had imagined how good it would be to have a Kirsty of her own. Now, feeling better, she felt pathetically grateful for Mimosa's offer of company, even if it did mean that she would have to bear the constant reminder of Simon.

'Come back to Pond House.'

Grace frowned. 'Sorry?'

'Oh.' Mimosa was surprised, used to everybody knowing the house. 'I'll lead, you follow.'

They left Welshpool and ten or so minutes later turned in through the gates and pulled up outside Pond House.

Looking at the house, Grace was caught by a surge of jealousy of Mimosa that almost prevented her from getting out of the car. Not because she particularly wanted Pond

House, but because it seemed that Mimosa had every aspect of her life perfectly in place. She could summon her beautiful man to meet her at the end of her no-doubt effortless run through the Montgomeryshire countryside, to pick her up and take her back to this beautiful, beautiful house.

She made herself get out, and walked around the car to let out Hodge.

'It's absolutely gorgeous,' she breathed to Mimosa, standing back to take it in properly. Hodge, nose to the ground, immediately zig-zagged away from her, running through a great arch cut out of a yew hedge and out of sight.

'He'll be okay. He can't go anywhere,' Mimosa told Grace. 'Come on, I'll show you around.'

Pond House was a small Elizabethan manor house, built of old red brick, warmed and weathered and faded over the years. Now at times it was more pale rose than red, and it sat secure and low against the ground. Today the uneven roof was white and glittering with frost and it hung protectively over the upper windows, almost like a thatch, or a low brimmed hat, seeming to push the house down even more securely into the ground.

'I didn't know it was here,' Grace said in wonder.

'Let me show you the garden.'

They followed Hodge through the archway, and there was the garden. It was on three levels, dropping down and down, each time linked by a gentle flight of stone steps. Today, set against the pale grey sky, with the grass frosted white and the heavy dark yew trees slipping in and out of the mist, it was magical, so still and white that Grace felt as if she'd stepped into a garden from Narnia. The yew hedge ran all the way down one side of the garden, once clipped into a dramatic row of globes and spires but now growing wild. In the centre of the first level there was a formal garden of box and thyme and lavender, planted out in formerly neat geometric patterns, but again the box had bushed out and the thyme and lavender had combined at some stage to overflow their beds and had never been cut back, and now their bare winter stalks trailed in all directions, spilling over on to the frost-patterned brick pathways that divided them.

'Garden,' Mimosa said after a moment, sweeping her arm to encompass it all. Then she turned back through the yew hedge and Grace followed her. She pointed at a range of buildings to the left of the house.

'Sheds, garages, log stores, kennels.'

Then she pointed to the right. 'Stables, more sheds and below that, orchard and a couple of paddocks.'

Grace smiled at her. 'Not much but it's home.'

'Anyway, come inside,' Mimosa told her briskly, leading the way in.

And inside was stunning too. Grace wondered whether it was Mimosa who had chosen the colour of the ochre walls, vivid against the ancient dark beams, and the thick mulberry curtains and wonderful rugs. She pictured Mimosa and Simon discovering Pond House together and slowly, lovingly, putting it back in order again.

'Have you lived here long?' Grace asked, in awe of it all.

'This is our first spring.'

'Gosh, so not long. To have made it so beautiful.'

Mimosa shrugged. 'Actually the place is falling down. The whole of the back wall is crumbling away. We're going to have to do some major rebuilding once the weather improves.'

She led the way into the kitchen and started to make coffee for them both. She always hated it when people went over the top about Pond House because she had had no part in making it as beautiful as it was. Mimosa liked to think of herself as someone with an excellent professional eye, and a good deal of creative flair, and it infuriated her that Pond House had already been done so well without her.

The fact that her father would definitely buy her some nearby land if she asked him to – and a house too if she wanted it – filled her with relief, because it would all come from her. She imagined the hills around Pond House filled with her sheep and horses, hers not Simon's, and she knew it would make her feel more secure. But she wouldn't be thinking like this if Simon would only give her a sign that he was falling in love with her.

Mimosa hadn't started out to mislead everybody about her relationship with Simon, but as most people thought she was his girlfriend anyway, and as she was so certain that he would, eventually be hers, she had started to gloss over the fact that it hadn't happened yet, at times even convincing herself. They got on so well together, were such a brilliant couple, he was always so affectionate and charming and thoughtful, that she told herself he was only being cautious and that it was just a matter of time. The odd comments he made about her needing to find a place of her own, she took with a pinch of salt. She was not about to move out. She needed to work on him and she needed to keep him in her line of vision, especially with Kirsty around.

*

Grace and Mimosa sat and chatted for half an hour about nothing in particular, neither of them wanting to lead the other towards dangerous ground by revealing anything very detailed about themselves. And then, just as Grace was thinking she should find Hodge and leave before she outstayed her welcome, Simon came bursting through the front door obviously in a wonderfully good mood.

'No sign of her, then?' Mimosa said.

'Actually, yes,' he grinned. 'She turned up just as I was leaving.'

'Where the hell had she been?'

'In a feedbin.'

'God, I don't know how she does that terrible job,' Mimosa told Grace. 'She must be permanently filthy.'

Simon caught Grace's eye and smothered a smile.

'I'm glad you found her,' she told him. 'I was wondering what had happened to her.'

Simon nodded, moving over to the coffee jug. 'I haven't even said hello to you properly,' he said turning back to her. 'I'm Simon Campion.' He held out a hand.

'Grace Somerville,' she said, taking it.

'And you live round here too, do you?'

There was a distracted look in his eyes, Grace thought. He was polite enough to seem interested in the answer and yet she could sense a suppressed energy in him that told her his mind was somewhere else.

'In Welshpool. On Green Lane.'

Simon nodded. 'Well, good to meet you!' He turned to Mimosa. 'I've got five minutes and then I'll have to go over to the Little Goose.' He drained his coffee mug. 'And by the way, I think you should call Nutt and Bower's again. There's a great little house in their window.'

'Oh, don't tell me you're leaving this beautiful place!' Grace cried.

Simon laughed. 'No, not me. But Mimosa is having the most terrible time finding somewhere to rent. You wouldn't think it would be so hard.'

Mimosa blinked in surprise. 'Oh goody, goody,' she said evenly, moving over to pick up his mug. She took it with her to the sink and bent her head low as she rinsed it out. 'Thanks. I'll ring them up and go and see it today.'

You poor thing, thought Grace, hearing the thickness of defeat in Mimosa's voice, at the same time riveted by what was going on. You didn't expect that to happen, did you?

Simon looked from Mimosa to Grace then back again. Then he went over to Mimosa and squeezed her shoulder. 'Got to go,' he told her ambiguously.

Mimosa continued rinsing out the mug. She would have to go, she realized. There was no point hoping for anything different.

Simon ran up the stairs and then they heard him striding across the room over their heads.

'He's going to the Little Goose,' Mimosa said awkwardly. 'Did you know it was his?' Grace looked blank. 'The one on Vincent Street,' she said shortly, avoiding Grace's eye.

Grace nodded. 'I've never been in.'

'And yes,' Mimosa added flatly. 'I'm finding a place to live.'

'Do you mind me asking? Are you two splitting up?'

'Good God! There was never any of that going on,' Mimosa laughed bitterly. 'We're just old friends. Simon offered to put me up for a bit. But obviously he's now got other plans.'

Is that so? Grace was unable to summon up real sympathy for Mimosa. If Simon wanted Mimosa out, who was Grace to argue? And then just as she was saying goodbye to Mimosa and slipping on her coat, she heard Simon thundering back down the stairs. He came into the kitchen and joined her at the back door, leaning past her to open it for the two of them.

They left the house together.

Thank God she'd started to make more effort to look good when she went out, she thought. She'd put on some mascara that morning and although she was only in old jeans and a black polo-neck jumper she knew she didn't look too bad. She gave Simon a quick sideways glance and tucked her hair behind her ears.

'I don't know you, do I?' he asked her, narrowing his eyes and considering her.

'No, you don't.'

'But I do remember that I met you that morning in Kirsty's shop. And you and Kirsty were definitely not getting on.'

Grace laughed awkwardly. 'You could say that. But I hope that's all over and done with now.' She wondered distractedly where Hodge had got to.

'Good,' he told her. Unexpectedly, his face broke into a wonderful, gleeful smile.

What did I say? thought Grace. Did I say something funny?

'And how's the dog bed? Or I should say, how's the dog?'

'What a memory!' Grace was pleased that he'd remembered. 'He's around here somewhere. God knows where. And he's lovely. Lots of work, like having a toddler apparently – although I wouldn't know about that – but worth every minute.'

She looked at him, not knowing what else to say, and at that moment Hodge reappeared, slinking up to join her, sliding around her legs guiltily, then, when he knew he'd been forgiven, bounding over to inspect Simon, licking his hands slavishly before tearing off around the yard at a hundred miles an hour.

Simon laughed as he watched him go. 'I do want a dog,' he said longingly.

Grace remembered a magazine article identifying the four most attractive types of men. They were supposed to be Scottish men, men with babies, men with fast cars and men with dogs. Simon liking *her* dog was good enough.

Getting into his fast car and driving away was not so good.

'So you run the Little Goose?' she said.

'Yes,' he smiled at her, humour twinkling in his eyes, as if she'd again said the funniest thing in the world, 'and I'm late so there will be nothing to give anyone to eat. I have to go.' He opened her car door for her.

Was there a note of regret in his voice? Grace couldn't tell. And, once he'd said goodbye, he'd almost run away from her to his car, revving up and shooting off at great speed, so she had to suppose he had other things on his mind than her. She opened the back of the car for Hodge and shut it again gently, surprised by how little the thought hurt. *Men – who needs them*, she thought, making a face at Hodge through the window.

14

If Lily could have planned the day, she would have woken at nine thirty, and would then have run herself a bath. She would have unhurriedly wiped all last night's make-up off her face and would have got into the bath with a piece of toast and a cup of coffee, where she would have soaked, letting the water slowly wash away last night's grime. Then she would have got dressed and would have opened the front door, not to a head-splitting dazzle but to a soft, misty morning. She would have strolled over the bridge and made her way to Starbucks in King Street where she would have slowly revived, drinking more coffee and reading the paper.

Instead, she was forced up through the layers of sleep into a pitch-dark and silent room. Deep in her warm pillows someone still smiled and beckoned her to him, but he was growing weaker by the second, the magic of her dream broken by her need to head for the bathroom. Lily took as short a time as possible but once back in bed her cold feet and beating heart put paid to any chance of slipping back to sleep and finding him again.

Eventually she gave up, sat up and looked with heavy-lidded eyes around the shadowy room. Her head wasn't quite as bad as it should have been, she thought, gingerly moving it from side to side. And she could still have the bath and the toast. She looked at her bedside clock. It was seven thirty. She shut her eyes again and dozed.

Later she went back to the bathroom and ran the hot tap, feeling the water pass between her fingers, nearly hot, slightly hot, warm, slightly warm, getting cooler, cooler, cold. So she would have to do without the bath. She washed sparingly, shoved deodorant under her arms and jumped straight into her clothes.

But, she thought, resolutely optimistic, Starbucks have surely not gone bust, and I didn't hear Hammersmith Bridge being bombed in the night. She could, at least, count on her coffee. That was the moment that she remembered her text message. What linked the two, she didn't know, but the coffee shop was momentarily put on hold.

Despite the condition she had been in when she read it, she could still remember each word. *If you are interested in my side of the story call me tomorrow.* Could it have been from Amber? Somehow Lily knew that it wasn't her. The conversation of the night before had had a definite ring of finality. She couldn't imagine Amber wanting to say anything more. Not Grace. Not Kirsty. Not likely to be one of her King's Cross friends. Who else? Who else with a story they might want to tell? Perhaps it was the awful man at her interview?

Or it was Josh. It made sense to think it could have been from him. He could have heard she was in London, and he had a story, one he had good reason to believe she might still be interested in hearing. And yet it somehow didn't fit with the Josh she thought she knew. From all she'd seen him do, he wouldn't care what people – what she – thought of him.

Perhaps that one brief kiss outside the Little Goose had seduced him, changed his life, got so under his skin he was going mad and needed an excuse, any excuse, to see her again? Unlikely as she knew it was, her stomach gave a great flip like a fish leaping out of water. It couldn't be Josh, she thought, because if Josh had been even the tiniest bit interested in her he'd have called her up before now. He wasn't the sort to need excuses, he would call a girl whenever it suited him. She was sure of it.

She got ready to leave the house. Somehow the horrible humiliating phone call with Amber's friend had changed everything. It had been the final straw, and all she wanted to do now was put them all behind her. She'd been embroiled in Hal's life for too long. She wanted to get on with her own. There was the date with Hal that she couldn't break and then she would have no need for anything more to do with any of them.

She knew that if Kirsty were here she would have told Lily she was being wet, would have grabbed the mobile off her and keyed 'reply'. She would have argued that the only reason Lily didn't want to call the number was because she was too scared it might be Josh at the other end. But Kirsty wasn't there and without her Lily could get away with it. And so, before she could change her mind, Lily deleted the message from her phone.

It was now nearly ten, with none of the glorious blue sky of the day before. She walked over the bridge heading towards Hammersmith and Starbucks feeling more and more hung over and listless, and realized halfway across that Starbucks too had lost its appeal. She didn't want to sit watching London through a window, it was too much of a waste when she was here so rarely, and yet she felt too fragile and too broke to do much else. Everyone she knew was working, so there was nobody to see. She didn't fancy window-shopping, and she certainly didn't feel up to stretching her legs and walking anywhere far. She wanted somewhere safe, yet distracting, somewhere to go that wasn't wasting her time, where she could kill a few hours.

She made her way towards the Victoria & Albert Museum. There was something wonderful if rather dusty and tame about it, perfect for the way she was feeling that morning. She was sure there were several collections there that it would be important for her to see, and she remembered Tippoo's Tiger, a mechanical man-eating tiger that had terrified her as a child, and wondered if it was still there. Once she had got off the tube and had made her way through the Exhibition Road entrance she began to feel uplifted at the thought of wandering among it all with the time to take as long as she wanted. This wasn't an over-indulgent hangover cure, she told herself. If she was going to work at the Registry this would surely be the first of many visits she'd make in order to undertake serious research.

There was so much that she'd forgotten about, or had never known was here – collections in the basements, dresses and seventeenth-century masks, modern British ceramics and china dolls – and looking confusedly at her map she didn't know where to start.

She chucked her map in a bin and strolled up two steps, deciding to wander, and there in front of her was the tiger, not quite as impressive as he'd been when she was a little girl but still gory enough. She remembered how she and Grace had stood where she was now, side by side, transfixed by his long fangs piercing the soldier's body. And then, in the hush, her mobile began to ring.

Around her people flinched and then stared at her accusingly. What a terrible *faux pas*, she thought, thinking how pompous they looked in their outrage. A mobile phone in the Victoria and Albert! So much worse than in the Tate Modern.

'Hi,' said a voice, and she stood still among them. She knew immediately who it was.

'Hello.'

'It's Josh here.' She could hear him smiling down the phone. 'Do you remember me?'

What a voice, she thought. I can't resist such a sexy voice.

One of the museum attendants was making his way towards her, a finger over his lips.

'Did you get my message? I sent you one last night.'

'How did you get my number?'

'I borrowed Hal's mobile . . .'

'And why are you calling me?' Lily asked, dropping her voice and turning her back on the attendant.

'Because I heard you were in London,' Josh whispered back, 'and I wanted to take you out while you're here. Put you straight about a few things.'

Lily walked away from the guide towards the café at the main entrance. 'Put me straight about what?' she asked. She stopped beside a small, exquisitely beautiful carving of the Madonna and child and absent-mindedly stroked her under the chin with one finger.

The museum attendant looked as if he was going to explode with outrage and Lily suddenly felt terribly embarrassed. How awful that she'd touched the Madonna like that. She was nearly a thousand years old.

She found a chair tucked behind a column and sat down.

'I've got to go. I can't talk to you now and anyway all that's over and done with.'

'Not quite all over, actually,' Josh told her, 'but that's not why I've called. You probably think it's ridiculous, but I care that you're walking around thinking I'm a son of Satan. I wanted to meet you while you were here, to talk about it.'

'Don't flatter yourself! I haven't thought about you for weeks.'

Josh laughed. 'You've seen a bit of Hal. I imagine my name might have come up once or twice. And I wanted to explain to you why I did what I did.'

'You don't need to explain to me,' she muttered, looking away as the attendant caught her eye again. 'You thought you were right. I thought you weren't. But I don't hold it against you. You don't need to explain. It's nothing to do with me any more. It's between you and Hal. And I can't talk now.'

'Yes you can. Please, Lily. Talk now,' he begged, laughing at her.

Get this man off the phone, Lily told herself, aware that she was now smiling inanely at the attendant, who had started walking, grim-faced, towards her. Get off the phone, and off the scene, for good. She knew the score, that he saw her as unfinished business. That if she said yes to a drink, the next thing she knew she'd be jumping into bed with him, and yet she couldn't bring herself to cut short the conversation in a way Josh would take seriously.

'Is there any point suggesting supper tonight?'

'No, there isn't.'

'Or lunch tomorrow?'

She took the phone away from her ear and looked beseechingly at the attendant.

'Two seconds,' he told her firmly, but disarmed a little by her smile. 'You know it's not allowed.'

The attendant turned his back on her and walked away.

'No,' she told Josh quickly, turning back to him, wishing she were a different sort of girl, someone who could cope with a guy like him, use him to have some fun and then forget all about him – because she didn't doubt that it would be fun.

'Lily, you don't have to sound so determined not to see me. It's not a problem. Get back to Welshpool. And forget about us all. It's probably for the best.'

There was a long pause.

'Thanks for calling, though.' Lily couldn't help herself.

'Where are you now?' Josh said.

'In the Victoria & Albert Museum.'

'Of course you are. Why haven't you got a job? How come you can wander around the V & A in the middle of a Friday morning?'

'What makes you think I'm wandering? I'm doing some research.'

'And I work just around the corner,' Josh said as if the two statements neatly coincided. 'So you can meet me for a cup of coffee. I'll come to the V & A so you don't need to waste any valuable research time.'

'Okay, I could manage that,' she said, relieved that she hadn't got rid of him after all. 'I'll wait for you in the café by the main entrance.'

She waited, burning her mouth on a coffee she bought to have something to do with her hands. She wouldn't be too frosty, she told herself, but at the first sign of any smouldering, at any whiff of a seduction routine, she'd get away from him. And she wasn't going to fancy him. She wouldn't give him the pleasure. It would do him good to see that not every woman tripped over herself in the rush to flirt with him.

But then, as she thought it all through, it was as if she could suddenly see herself, sitting there, one foot tucked tightly behind an aluminium table leg, her lips pursed, about to take a prim sip of coffee, thinking her tangle of suspicious thoughts about Josh and wondering how quickly she should get rid of him. And with awful self-recognition, she realized that she didn't like what she saw, and hadn't for a long while. She wondered what a stranger would make of her now, sitting there at the café table. Attractive, perhaps, but she didn't much care about that. She wanted warm and vibrant and interesting, she wanted to be someone who looked like they were good company, someone passionate, a lover of life. She wanted to be more of a Kirsty: exuberant and carefree. And she knew she didn't look like that at all.

She glanced self-consciously around the room but no one was watching her. In a few minutes Josh was coming and suddenly the thought of sitting next to him and behaving as she'd planned made her feel unutterably depressed.

Guys like Josh had always been out of bounds. The ones she had always warned herself off. She'd always played so safe, congratulated herself on being somebody who never got hurt, who always chose the decent, dependable Hals instead of the devil-may-care bastards like Josh. She had never had a fling, never allowed herself a relationship that was volatile or insecure – but, maybe, all the more exciting for being so. She'd never been hurt but she'd never been swept off her feet either. Both her long-term relationships had been with dull, boring guys and had been ended, of course, by her. She had been so careful not to hop into bed with somebody disreputable that she'd ended up hardly hopping in with anyone at all. Never with anyone who had the upper hand, and definitely never with anyone remotely as attractive as Josh. She'd looked at Grace, at the way she threw herself into every relationship she began, blind to everything, and had felt terribly superior. Perhaps it was that which Grace had hated so much.

And now, Lily wanted to be different. She wanted Josh. She wanted to throw caution to the wind and let herself go, just once, with Josh. Have some fun without worrying about the other girlfriends, or how little she could trust him. Take him on on his own terms, just to find out what it was like. If she didn't get involved, then she wouldn't get hurt.

A ripple of excitement rolled through her because there was nothing to stop her. And yet at the same time she was panic-stricken at the thought of changing the habits of a lifetime, especially where someone like Josh was concerned.

Why had it happened now? she wondered. Something to do with both Kirsty and Josie choosing almost the exact same moment to hint that she was missing out, that she was too strait-laced, even a bit of a killjoy. When they'd said it, she'd flinched but had then batted both of them away without a second thought. Now, with Josh's arrival imminent, it was as if she was hearing them again, and listening for the first time. She wished she could tell them what she was thinking now, and could have them to talk to, to tell her what she should do.

Josh arrived as he had said he would, just five minutes later. He strode around the corner of the coffee area without spotting her straight away, allowing her a few fist-clenching moments to watch him unaware. He was wearing a beautifully cut charcoal-grey suit with a pale pink shirt open at the throat, and he looked wonderful, a potent combination of rumpled sexiness and detached high-flying glamour.

When he finally caught her eye he raised a hand and smiled a loose, easy smile, and all the other women in the café swung round to look at Lily to see if she deserved him.

Oh Josh, Lily thought, breathing him in as she stood up and leaned slowly towards him, brushing her lips against his cheek. The problem with you is I know I couldn't walk away again.

He put a hand on her shoulder and kissed her cheek.

'I'll get us some coffee.'

In the queue she watched him make a quick quiet phone call and never once try to catch her eye.

Who are you ringing? she thought suspiciously, convinced it was a girl. Then she told herself sharply to stop it. She was not going to be that person.

He came and sat down opposite her and they started to talk. He made her laugh straight away, which she hadn't expected, and then listened more than he talked, which she hadn't expected either, so that gradually she found herself relaxing and almost forgetting the role she'd had him down to play. He was gentle in a way Lily had never imagined he would be and it took her aback, the flashes of sensitivity and compassion far more seductive than any chat-up line. They talked, inevitably, about Hal, and then she found herself telling him about Grace, about their childhood, and their parents, about her interview at the Registry and perhaps coming back to live in London.

Occasionally, she'd stop herself and think *I'm talking too much*. And yet, all the time, she knew that it was all right. That he wasn't sitting there thinking *how do I make this girl shut up*? But was enjoying being with her. And she was aware of every tiny part of him, of every movement that he made. Of the soft rise and fall of his pink shirt and how the muscles in his strong tanned throat contracted as he swallowed each sip of coffee.

She could remember every detail of the evening in the Little Goose, squashed up against him, thigh to thigh. The hand that was now lying so still on the table in front of her was the hand that had caressed her cheek, stroked her back. And the beautiful sensitive mouth now speaking about Hal was the one that had kissed her gently at the end of the evening with lust glittering in his eyes.

But Lily had to admit, as one coffee became two, that this time there was no sign that Josh had anything but the very best of intentions where she was concerned. Far from tumbling her into his bed, there was not a single attempt at a lingering look, not one flirtatious *double entendre* or anything else that she could have taken as a sign.

'Think about it,' he was saying.

She nodded. She was. She was imagining him standing up, crashing through the clutter of aluminium chairs to catch her in a Rodin-like kiss among the café tables.

'Hal is so innocent – you know that – he doesn't understand that women like Amber exist, let alone that they're going to make a beeline for him. And he does get these mad infatuations. He goes from nothing to passionately in love in a matter of days. He always has.

There've been so many others he might have married. But Amber was the clever one. And she grabbed him while she could.'

'What did you do to the others, then?' Lily asked suspiciously. 'Did they find themselves with faulty brakes on high mountainous roads? Or were they prodded with poison-tipped umbrellas as they walked down the Kings Road?'

'Nothing! I did nothing!' Josh insisted, laughing.

'Amber is very beautiful,' Lily said. 'Everyone says so. Hal must have thought he was in heaven. Especially after all those Sloaney-ponies he'd been out with before.'

Josh smiled and stretched both his arms up above his head, the smile turning into a long yawn. He rubbed his eyes and dislodged an eyelash which stuck out at a right-angle from all the others. She couldn't help herself leaning forwards to brush it gently away. At her touch Josh raised his eyebrows, but didn't say anything.

'Amber's very pretty,' he agreed. 'From a distance. Up close, there's definite wear and tear. You can't behave like her and not get a few cracks and chips along the way.'

'Those cracks and chips that miraculously don't show up on you anywhere.' She paused, considering him. 'If you're going to knock Amber, I think you should at least acknowledge that you're just the same as she is.'

Josh said quietly, 'You're right. But I wasn't quite as bloke-ish as you think I was. I didn't know the details of what was going on with Hal for a start, or I'd never have got involved.'

Lily was surprised by the sadness in his voice. She'd

not imagined he could sound so vulnerable. She looked back at him and he shrugged, then yawned again and stretched back in his chair.

'Sorry. I've had one too many late nights – at the office,' he added deliberately. 'I need a good night's sleep.'

Lily imagined waking up beside him.

'Seriously. What would you have done if one of those other girls had tried to lead him up the aisle?' she asked, clicking the bedroom door shut on the thought. 'You can't have imagined Hal would have been any happier with them? Would you have stepped in then too? Done the same to one of them?'

'No.'

'Why not? If you choose to judge Amber, why not judge all of them? Give them all scores between nought and ten. Amber scored a nought for being such a bitch. But would another have got a nought for looking like a dog? And another perhaps only a two because of her rugby player's thighs, or her obsession with dust? Or just, perhaps, because she was boring? And what was the pass rate?' Lily went on, warming to her point. 'What if someone scored a four? Would that be good enough to win the wedding day? Perhaps only a ten-out-of-ten girl was ever going to be good enough for you?'

'No! Of course not,' Josh protested. 'But I do think he'd have been happier with any one of those other girls. I don't hate Amber. She's quite endearing at times. But she would have made Hal miserable.'

'But that was for Hal to find out! And he may have done in years to come, but isn't that the risk anyone takes when they get married? He still thinks she's a ten-out-of-ten girl,' Lily said, 'he really does. Even now. And it isn't your scoring that matters, it's his.'

'Yes,' Josh looked steadily back at her, 'of course you're right. But if we're talking score cards, on hers Hal never scored higher than a two. We could all see it straight away. And Hal would have done so too if he'd only had a little time. But he wasn't going to get that time without us finding it for him. So we dashed in. Took him away. Got him out before it was too late.'

'You dashed in, did you?' said Lily. 'I knew it! You thought you were in the Rolf Harris song. You wanted to be like those two little boys!'

'Oh no, do you think so?' Josh said mortified, laughing.

'Yes,' Lily said smartly. 'But it wasn't ever going to work because Hal is still hell bent on running straight back into her arms.' She asked curiously, 'What are you going to do about that?'

'Do about it? Do you think I'd tell *you*? No, I don't need to do anything. This time around Amber's doing it all for me.'

'What do you mean? How do you know what she's up to?' Lily was intrigued.

Josh shrugged non-committally.

'Don't they both have a bit of a problem with you at the moment?'

'No, actually,' he said. 'Hal was pissed off with me, but even he is coming around now. And Amber . . .' Did she imagine it, or did Josh look rather uncomfortable? 'When I went to talk to Amber that morning she kissed me and smiled and said thank you very much and was off on that aeroplane before I'd finished the first sentence,' Josh told Lily.

Without you, please. Let it be that she went on her own.

'I was her new best friend,' Josh went on. 'Don't you see, Lily? It was exactly what she wanted to hear.'

'Why?'

'Because she'd got cold feet too. She didn't ever really want Hal. He was what she thought she should want. And I was gently letting her off the hook. If you'd met her, even once, you wouldn't be asking me this. Reliable is not one of Amber's middle names.'

From what she'd learned from the phone call with Amber's friend, Lily thought Screwed and Up probably were.

'You know,' he said, 'you're the first person who's ever challenged me about all this. Apart from Hal and Charlie, I haven't talked to anyone else about what we did.'

'So?'

'So, when you talk about it, of course it's impossible to justify. There's no getting away from it.'

'No,' Lily looked mortified. 'Don't say that. I'm just beginning to be convinced.' She laughed at herself. 'I don't believe I said that! 'Let's have more coffee?' She jumped up. 'It's my turn.' She wanted to ensure he wasn't about to say he had to go. She had little idea of the time, whether they were still talking in minutes since Josh had sat down opposite her, or if whole hours had gone by.

Later on she found herself telling him more about Grace, wanting him to know how she'd been through the same dilemma, how she still felt that she'd let Grace down. In the mood she was in now she wanted to tell him everything about everyone she'd ever known.

'You couldn't win that one,' he said, seeing how much it still bothered her. 'However you said it.'

'I barely said a thing,' Lily said defensively. 'Nothing like you!'

'Either you lie, tell them nothing at all apart from what a lovely couple they make, or stick your neck out and be damned.'

'Perhaps I should have done what you did.'

'I can't see you masterminding a successful kidnapping.'

'It's taken Grace two whole years to realize Jeremy's a bastard. I suppose I'd have had to hold on to her for a very long time. Someone might have come to rescue her.'

'Yes. People might have wondered where she'd gone. I can't see you doing anything like we did. You're too considered. Too measured.'

'Oh, please, don't you start. Not you too!' Lily groaned.

'Why do you say that?' Josh was amused. 'It's not a bad thing. I'm just saying you're not one to do something impulsive.'

As he said it he held her look, and the suggestion was suddenly there.

'It's not true,' Lily blurted out. 'I am.'

'That's very good news.' Josh smiled at her.

'I jumped out of a plane, once.'

'But I bet you had a parachute on.'

'Of course I bloody did!'

'Then I'm not sure that counts.'

'I don't care! I want nothing to do with your challenges. Not with your track record.'

Neither of them seemed able to look away. He caught hold of one of her hands.

'Please cancel it,' he said, suddenly very serious, 'whatever it is you're doing tonight,'

She looked in wonder at her hand in his, feeling it wouldn't now move if she wanted it to.

'I could take the rest of the day off. And spend it with you . . . it's Friday, I can do that . . .'

'Okay,' she agreed.

'Don't look like that,' he laughed. 'It'll be fun.'

15

As Josh and Lily moved to cross Exhibition Road he took her hand and kept it. They walked for about fifteen minutes, striding fast, hardly speaking, with little idea where they were heading for, and then, because it was lunchtime, and they were passing by, Josh stopped her outside an Italian restaurant just off the King's Road.

They ordered *pappardelle al cinghiale* and a bottle of wine, but when the food arrived Lily found she couldn't bring herself to swallow a single mouthful. She looked across at Josh and saw that he wasn't touching the food either.

'Have a cigarette if you want one,' she suggested. 'Don't mind me.'

'Don't tempt me. I gave up a few weeks ago.' Then he said, 'Let's go. Do you mind? It's ridiculous being here if we can't eat anything.'

She nodded and he jumped up immediately and pulled her to her feet, called over the bill and hurried Lily outside. As she came out of the restaurant after him, she tripped down the little step out on to the street and Josh reached out and just managed to catch her. Once she was in his arms he didn't let her go.

'Got you,' he said, his mouth instantly against hers.

He kissed her lightly and gently and yet immediately

a tidal wave of lust and excitement rose inside her, the warmth spreading through her, up through the soles of her feet, taking her over completely. She'd always been self-conscious about kissing in public, but standing on the pavement in Langton Street with Josh, Lily could have been standing there stark naked and she wouldn't have cared as long as he didn't stop.

She slipped her hands through his thick hair, stroking the nape of his neck where his hair was soft and clipped close like bristling velvet, touching the expensive wool of his suit and his well-muscled back beneath the thin material, then down again to touch his bottom, making him grab her harder and let out an involuntary groan in her ear, feeling his narrow hips and long lean thighs beneath her hands.

'What did you say?'

'That you were driving me mad.' Josh stopped and wrapped his arms around her, his cheek against her hair. 'And I want to kiss you again and again and again. You know, I've been going mad for quite a long time now. You have no idea.'

She felt her heart do a great trampolining somersault of delight.

'Since when?'

'Since I saw you in the Little Goose. How could you kiss me like that and then leave me to stew for four weeks?'

'You should have got in touch sooner.'

Even in the light-hearted laughter of the moment she wished she hadn't said that. Because it sounded as if she'd been waiting for his call when she hadn't. And if she knew one thing, it was that Josh would be bored by girls waiting for his call.

But Josh brushed it aside, slipping his arm around her shoulders and they walked down the street, back on to the King's Road.

'So what shall we do now?' he asked her, pulling her close against him. 'We can't eat. And I doubt that you'll come to bed with me. What have you never done before? Have you been on the Millennium Wheel?'

'I don't think I'd get to see much of London, would I?'

He kissed her cheek. 'It might qualify us for the mile-high club.'

'I meant because of the weather.'

Josh looked doubtfully at the sky. 'Then would you like to come back to my flat?'

They walked some more and she didn't answer and then he paused and looked at his watch and then across at her.

'If you're not coming back with me, Lily, I might as well head back to the office, if you don't mind. You know where you are, don't you?'

Lily stared at him gobsmacked. She couldn't believe it.

'Lily!' Josh laughed at her. 'Who do you think I am? I'm joking. Really, I'm joking! I want to spend the day with you, outside. And with as many other people as possible.'

'Bastard,' she laughed.

'Millennium Wheel,' Josh said. 'Tate Modern. Or the Wetland Centre?'

'You must be joking.'

'I'm serious. It's a great place.'

'Don't we need swimming costumes?'

'No, Lily,' Josh told her patiently, 'it's not a waterslide park, it's a nature reserve. It's in Barnes. Where you're staying.'

'Oh,' Lily said cautiously. 'I don't know.'

'I thought you'd appreciate it, coming from all that rain. I'm trying to think of somewhere you'd feel at home.'

Lily shook her head. 'I've just got away from it,' she said. 'Definitely the Millennium Wheel.'

*

The mist hadn't lifted properly and only a few people were queuing to get on the Wheel. They picked up their tickets straight away, bore the obligatory photograph and were joined by less than six others in a pod. They stood close together, looking out at the wonderful stretching view, but aware of nothing much but each other, lacing their fingers but otherwise not touching. 'I'll come back one day with my grandfather,' Josh told her. 'I can't take it in properly with you beside me.'

Then he leaned in close to her. 'So where next?' he said. 'I suppose you want the Tate Modern?'

'No,' said Lily, thinking of his flat. 'Nowhere else.'

Afterwards they walked slowly to the river and stood looking out at the Thames, Josh standing behind her with his arms around her, a light drizzle wetting her face, barely anybody else in sight, and Lily thought how it had to be the most romantic day of her life.

'Who'd have thought it?' she said to him, leaning back against him. 'That I'd be here today, doing this with you.'

Josh didn't answer but tightened his arms around her.

'Shall we come back again tomorrow?'

'No,' he said, 'we don't get another day like today.'

Lily turned in his arms. 'Don't say that!'

'I didn't mean it like that,' he said, kissing her gently on each fine blonde eyebrow, thinking how lovely she looked with her huge eyes and her pink cold cheeks. 'We'll have other days together, and they'll be even better.'

They got a taxi back to Josie's flat.

Once inside, Lily left him for a moment in the sitting-room and went through to the kitchen. Toast, she thought. I'll make some toast and tea. She cut a couple of slices of bread, wanting something to do to dilute some of the potency between them, and give herself a chance to think straight. How had it got like this? This wasn't how it was meant to be. Josh was so different that she couldn't think straight. Couldn't remember how she was supposed to be behaving. And yet she couldn't bear to be away from him, she thought, spreading the butter as quickly as she could. What was it that she hadn't anticipated, that was sending her spiralling away from how she'd planned to be? She felt in love. Already. Just like that.

She took the tea and toast through to the sitting-room and found him stretched out on the sofa, waiting for her. She put the plate down on the table and realized that she still couldn't imagine eating anything herself. Instead, she took a piece to Josh and leaned over him, holding it to his mouth. With three bites it had gone and he held her hand and licked the butter off her fingers.

'Come here,' he told her, putting down his tea and holding out his arms.

She climbed on top of him, sitting with her knees on either side of his body, and felt as if she was diving down into his sea-green eyes. He lifted a hand and carefully stroked back her hair and she collapsed on to his chest. They lay close together, two blond heads, his arms wrapped around her and her face buried in his neck.

Oh, Josh, she wanted to sigh. I wasn't meant to feel like this. I meant to have some fun, take advantage of you and then forget all about you, but I know now that I want to stay. That I like being here too much. She pushed herself up on her elbows and looked down into his face, running her fingers across his cheekbones and down across his lips. Stay with me, please. I don't want this to be just a fling.

He reached up for her and kissed her again. Everything was changing now, all the emotion and desire building up fast in both of them, as this time they both knew that they were going to see it through. She kissed him passionately back, hungrily, desperately, leaving cautious Lily far behind, clutching quick, urgent instructions that whatever happened next, she must never ever forget how wonderful, magical, utterly right this moment felt.

And then came the sound of a key turning in the front door lock of Josie's flat and a girl's voice calling out *hello*.

Lily saw her own disbelief mirrored on Josh's face,

remembering at the same time Josie's warning her that her little sister might be using the flat.

'So this happens in real life, too,' Josh said flatly.

'Is that you, Beth?' Lily called, still lying spread out on Josh but managing to sound quite normal.

'I'll get rid of her,' she whispered to him.

'Oh, Lily, great! I wasn't sure if you'd be in,' came the cheerful voice back again, followed by a heavy thud. 'Hang on a minute and I'll come and join you. It's a bit mad out here.'

'Yes, come and join us, why not?' Josh called and Lily covered his mouth with her hand.

'Who is she?' Josh whispered.

'She's a pain,' Lily hissed back. 'I can't believe this has happened.'

The door banged shut again.

'She's obviously your guardian angel.'

Lily glowered. 'A guardian angel wouldn't do this to me.'

She stood up and Josh got off the sofa and stood up behind her. When there was no further sound, she turned back to him but then they heard the front door slam again.

Lily immediately slipped out of the sitting-room and closed the door between Beth and Josh. She couldn't face the polite introductions straight away.

'Hi,' Lily breathed, covering the door. Beth was Josie's younger sister, just eighteen and someone she'd known since she was a child. She was standing in the hall in a sarong, a T-shirt and a pair of pink flip-flops.

'Hi you too!' Beth grinned back, then took in the

dishevelled hair, the bright eyes and stubble-burned chin. 'Oh no,' she said in horror, 'I'm interrupting, aren't I? I *thought* I heard a man's voice!'

'No, it's fine! Josie mentioned that you might be coming.'

Beth's face had flushed a bright crimson. 'I'm so sorry!' She sounded completely mortified.

'Beth,' Lily insisted, laughing despite herself, 'stop it!'

Beth made a face at the sitting-room door. 'I'll go out again. I'm going. Right this second.'

'It doesn't matter,' Lily lied, wanting to make it easy for her. 'We weren't doing anything.'

Beth was having none of it. 'My friends are having a drink on the other side of the bridge,' she gabbled, almost tripping over her sarong in her haste to get back out of the door. 'They're in one of the pubs on the river. And they're dying for me to join them. After tonight I'm not going to see them for ages,' she said, only adding the slightest of embellishments to what was, essentially, completely true. She rubbed her jangling bangled arms in agitation, and grabbed at a moth-eaten canvas bag, glancing again at the closed sitting-room door. 'I'll come back later?' She raised her eyebrows meaningfully. 'In about an hour? Is that long enough?'

'I'm in tonight,' Lily told her laughing. 'Are you? Can we catch up then?'

'Yes,' Beth said, desperate to be off as soon as she could. 'I'll show you my photos from India!'

'Can't wait.'

Before she could say another word, Beth was gone.

Lily opened the door, ran into the room and launched herself into Josh's arms.

'You can't get rid of me so easily,' she told him.

'Thank you, Beth, for your hour, whoever you are!' He pushed the door shut with his foot.

'She's sweet. And she was so embarrassed. And she was wearing a T-shirt and flip-flops. It's going to snow!'

'Don't talk about her any more.'

With Lily still in his arms he led her over to the sofa and dropped her gently down. She caught him by the lapels of his suit and pulled him on top of her.

'How long were you gone for, do you think?' he asked her, kissing her collarbone.

'About a minute? Definitely less than two.'

'That's the foreplay done then, don't you think?'

She laughed. 'Not on your life.'

*

Afterwards he propped himself up on an elbow and looked down at her.

'Lovely Lily. I can never let you go.'

They were lying on the floor, half covered with a cotton throw that usually lay along the back of Josie's sofa, which had at some point been dragged with them to the floor. Josh ran a finger gently down her cheekbone. 'I always want to be with you.'

Lily nodded, thinking am I mad to believe you're serious?

He kissed her again and she breathed in his warmth and sighed lazily and closed her eyes.

'But Lily,' he said and this time his tone of voice told her he was about to say something she wouldn't like. 'I'm going to have to go.'

'Why? Where?'

He winced. 'Can you believe I'm meant to be going to another stag night tonight?'

Lily sat up and looked at him disbelievingly.

'I know. Do you think I want to go? Do you think I want to leave you now?'

She reached for her jumper. *Maybe*, she thought.

'It's all right. You can't help it,' she said, feeling in a strange way unsurprised.

He leaned over to her, but he was already starting to get up. 'I'm so sorry. But it's something I can't miss.'

She nodded.

'I didn't know this was going to happen to us,' he said, stepping into his boxer shorts. 'I'd have got out of it.'

'Cancelled the stag night,' she managed to smile. 'Presuming you're the best man.'

'No, no one's ever going to want me for that job again.'

She got up and came close to him, surprising herself by how calm she was, how she almost didn't mind him going because she wanted some time to think about him.

'Shall we do something tomorrow? I'm leaving for home on Sunday.'

Josh didn't react.

'No. You have plans for tomorrow,' Lily answered the question herself, feeling sadness slip over her as doubt crept into her mind.

'Tomorrow and Sunday. Can you believe I'm escorting

a client on to the set of a film? I have to be in Brighton for the whole of tomorrow, home for the evening, and then back to Brighton for the whole of Sunday too.'

'A client?'

'A neurotic screenwriter who can't be let out on his own. Even at the weekend. But I could see you tomorrow night.'

'You know I'm seeing Hal. I told you.' She looked away, wondering if it would be so bad to cancel Hal for Josh. 'And I can't cancel him,' she said. Josh nodded. 'We've had this set up for ages. I feel I must see him. And I wouldn't have been able to see you on Sunday anyway because I'm leaving. I'm getting the train back in the morning.'

'Oh, Lily!'

'Shall we get together again in about six months?' She tried to sound light-hearted.

Josh shook his head. 'You won't get rid of me that easily. Hal's asked me to come back to the Little Goose for Easter.'

'What? Why?'

'He says it's important to him.' Josh shrugged. 'I was going to try to get out of it.'

Oh, Lily thought. Were you just?

'I didn't see the point.' At her face he stopped. 'Of course I wanted to see you again, but I didn't think you'd want to see me. I imagined going there with Hal – lots of long walks in the fresh air and endless conversation about Amber – and I have to say I can think of better ways to spend my time. But now, of course I want to come. That is, if you're still going to be there?'

Lily nodded.

'Then it's the only place I want to be.'

'Why do you think Hal wants you to go back?' she asked.

'He cares a lot that we patch things up. And I think he has a twisted sense of humour.'

'He's very forgiving.'

'Isn't he? He wants to stay in the Little Goose and try to see you two again.'

'You'll have to tell him about me. Otherwise we'll never get any time away from him.'

'I will, but I have to be careful!'

'Because he'll be worried for me?'

'No. Because he fancies you himself.'

Lily laughed. 'Hal! I don't think he's up to fancying anybody but Amber. Not yet.'

It was nearly an hour since Beth had gone and Lily guessed she'd soon be back. And knowing that Josh had to go, Lily realized that she wanted him out of the house quickly, needing a little time alone before Beth returned.

'I'll call you.' He hugged her hard but she could feel he was thinking about his stag night, ready to go.

She turned away from him and dressed quickly, but even as she was going through the sitting-room door, Lily heard the slap of Beth's flip-flops as she approached the front door again. Damn, she thought, as the key moved in the lock.

'I'll leave you both to it. Be friendly,' Josh instructed her. He gave her a last swift kiss goodbye.

Lily opened the front door for her.

When Beth saw Lily she jumped nervously.

'Has he gone now?' she asked, making it sound as if Josh was a dangerous animal, and then jumped again in alarm as Josh appeared behind Lily.

'Hi,' she mumbled, looking away, her face colouring again.

'This is Josh,' Lily told her, grinning at her reaction, 'and Josh's just leaving.'

*

'Isn't he lovely,' Beth said passionately, her pink and white complexion still more pink than white at the thought of him.

Lily turned back to her and smiled and the warmth inside spilled out through her face and Beth immediately caught her arm.

'You are a lucky cow,' she hissed, leading her back up the hall. 'Has Josie met him yet?'

'She knows about him but she hasn't met him. *I* hardly know him.'

She walked back into the sitting-room and Beth stood in the doorway and looked after her thoughtfully, taking in the throw still lying on the floor.

'But better than you did before I left, perhaps!'

Beth's confidence was obviously growing now that the reality of Josh had gone through the front door.

'Respect, please! You're far too young to talk to me like that.'

'If I wasn't so sad and single myself, I'd be very pleased for you.'

Beth went back out into the hall and dragged in a bright blue nylon rucksack, then opened a zip and pulled out a long string of dirty T-shirts and paisley cotton pyjama bottoms.

'Beth!' Lily exclaimed. 'You're not eligible for sad and single when you're only eighteen. It's the privilege of the twenties and thirties.'

Beth laughed, scrabbling deeper into her bag. 'I'm looking for something,' she explained. 'Josie said I can leave my stuff here. I'm going to Peru for six months on Monday.'

Lily looked at the mountain of moccasins and flip-flops and tie-dyed sarongs, at the cameras and jumpers and toe-rings and beaded photo frames that now engulfed Josie's tidy hall and spilled into the sitting-room, and wondered just how much of Beth Josie was expecting.

From deep in one of the bags, Beth unearthed a leather beaded necklace and matching bracelet and handed them both to Lily with a smile. 'Here,' she said. 'They're skitti beads – trust and love. Have them.'

'Thanks,' said Lily.

*

Josh didn't call Lily the next day. She told herself not to mind but still she did. Would it have been so impossible to call her from his mobile? She didn't think so, and a tiny bit of her took stock of the fact that he hadn't, and worried at it.

And then evening came and it was time to get ready to go out with Hal. As she put on her make-up she chatted to Beth, enjoying the distraction after a day spent trying not to think about Josh. And yet, as she chose what to wear, he was still with her. She wished that it was Josh she was dressing to meet, wished that she'd been able to see him again after their one wonderful day together, to reassure her that he had cared, that she wasn't mad to think the day had meant something to him too. A day without him, and with no word from him, had released the demons in her head and they were already whispering to her that she was being taken in, like so many others had been taken in before her. Telling her that he'd only got in touch because he'd already agreed to go to Welshpool with Hal and wanted to set himself up with a little distraction for while he was there.

But still she couldn't imagine changing anything. Already she was dying to see him again, willing away the days between now and Easter, and she didn't doubt that he wanted to see her again too, that at that moment she was as interesting to him as he was to her. But what she had to remember was not to hope it would last.

She was not going to let on to Hal what had happened between her and Josh, she decided, sitting on her bed in a pale pink satin camisole and painting pearly pink varnish on her fingernails. She waved dry her hands and considered them. If she told Hal, she thought, shaking the bottle again before adding a second coat, he'd be bound to be annoyed with her. He'd feel betrayed and upset, and would warn her away from him. And she didn't want to hear it.

To go with the camisole she had a beautiful vintage

fifties lace skirt that she'd found the year before in the Portobello Road, and she stood up and lifted it carefully out of Josie's cupboard and put it on. She added boots and a diamanté bracelet and was ready. She collected up her keys, shouted goodbye to Beth and left the house.

Across the room of the restaurant she saw him watching her and she caught his eye and waved, surprised by how good it was to see him waiting for her there. She handed away her coat and walked quickly over to him, and he stood up and put his arm around her shoulders and gave her a great warm smacker of a kiss.

'You're in a good mood,' she laughed.

'Who wouldn't be if they were waiting for you?'

'You smoothie!'

She sat down and he ordered them both a glass of champagne.

'Okay, let's get it out of the way,' he said determinedly, the moment the waiter had left their table, 'and then we can talk about something else.'

'What do you mean?' she said, looking down at her napkin, visions of her and Josh tumbling naked off the sofa filling her mind.

'Amber?' Hal helped her. 'Remember her? You were going to make a call for me.' He sighed, 'Oh, Lily, do I take it you still haven't managed to sort out my life?'

She looked up at him, hoping that she had heard a trace of humour in his voice.

'Hal, I'm sorry. I did call but it didn't go well.'

He tipped back his chair, considering her.

'I'm not surprised.'

'You're not?'

'No,' he said bringing his chair straight again. 'And don't worry. I think I'll survive.'

'It's been a long time now, Hal. Can you start to forget her?'

'I know I should,' he shrugged, 'and pretty soon I will, I'm sure I will. I'm still hurt but I'm used to that and I'm certainly not devastated any more.' He took a heavy breath. 'I can almost call her a silly bitch but not quite,' he sighed. 'But I still want to know what she said.' He said the last bit firmly, but there was a distinctly brave look in his eye.

'No you don't. She didn't say anything that would make you feel better. In fact, *she* didn't say anything at all. I spoke to a friend.'

'Barbie,' Hal nodded knowingly. 'Poor you.'

'What?' said Lily, surprised. 'How did you know?'

'They're always doing that, pretending to be each other. They've lived together for ages and they've got it down to a fine art. In fact, that's one good thing to come out of all this! I will never have Barbie's face peering around the bathroom door at me ever again!'

Lily laughed. 'Barbie as in the doll?'

'They could be sisters! And if it was her you spoke to, I'm not interested in hearing what she said.'

Lily nodded. 'Only her.'

'I knew nothing good was going to come out of it, but I was hoping that you'd somehow persuade Amber to get in touch with me.' He sighed heavily again. 'I know, I know, that's not going to happen now. But all I wanted was to apologize to her,' he said.

Lily raised her eyebrows. It was on the tip of her tongue to tell Hal what Josh had said about Amber practically dancing on the ceiling with relief at the news that her wedding was off.

'But that's it,' he said with finality. 'No more talking about Amber. I am going to get on with my life!'

'Good! Drink to that!' She clunked her glass with his.

'It's not as if we were together for years. Three, four months ago, I didn't even know her.'

'No more talk about Amber,' Lily echoed him.

He smiled and finished his champagne in two long swallows.

'I'm even starting to think . . .' he paused, 'that I was a bit of an arse to get so involved in the first place.'

Lily laughed.

'See. I'm not doing such a bad job of being normal, am I?' he demanded. 'I'm making you laugh, I'm taking you out, holding down my job – for a little while longer. *And* I'm bringing Josh with me to stay at the Little Goose over Easter. To patch things up with him.'

Lily felt herself reddening. 'Hey! You *are* forgiving!'

'Well, if I'm going to move on, I have to be. He's a good friend. And he was right, Amber didn't love me. I'd have been miserable.'

Lily shook her head. 'You're willing to forget what Josh did to you?'

'Probably. One day. Aren't I a pushover?'

A waiter appeared at their table, Hal ordered more champagne and the waiter passed her a menu.

'What about those other guys? Charlie and Richard and Alex?' she asked. 'Are you forgiving them too?'

Hal shrugged. 'Richard and Alex haven't been in touch since that weekend. Can you believe it! I've known them since we were seven . . .'

'I'm sorry,' Lily said.

'But Charlie and I will get together some day. It's just taking longer than it is with Josh. He's more ashamed about it all.'

'I understand.'

She picked up her menu.

'Lily, I wouldn't be in such good shape now, if it wasn't for you.'

She glanced up. Hal was looking at her earnestly and Lily thought what a fool Amber had been. Not to see what she'd got, and to hold on to him and to look after him properly.

'It wasn't me,' she told him.

'Yes it was. I was talking to you – and your sister – when I couldn't talk to anyone else.'

'But it didn't get you anywhere.'

'How do you know?'

'I don't believe you, but thank you for saying so.'

If Hal had been about to say more, he changed his mind.

'After Easter, I'm going away,' he told her. 'I've handed in my notice and I'm going travelling.'

'How fantastic. Where?'

'West Indies? Galapagos Islands? Wherever takes my fancy. I'll go for about six months.'

'That's brilliant. You are so lucky that you can do that. It sounds amazing,' said Lily wistfully. 'My plans are Welshpool, bit of London, Welshpool, bit of London, Welshpool.'

Hal laughed. 'Come with me, then?'

Lily raised her eyebrows at him. 'Seriously?'

He nodded.

'No, of course I can't,' she said.

There was something in his expression that meant she had to look away.

'Have you ever been away? I mean far away?' he asked her then.

'Portugal and Spain and France, but never outside Europe. Never to a sugar white beach with palm trees and turquoise water.'

'Then come with me!' Hal insisted.

'Okay, tell me when and I'll be there,' she joked, then looked at him again and wished she hadn't. Back off! She wanted to tell him, wrong-footed by the new look in his eyes, and by a sudden awareness of Hal as someone more than just the jilted bridegroom. You're messed up and vulnerable, she wanted to say. Don't even think of turning your attentions on me.

'When are you going away?'

'After Easter. And you will be in Welshpool over Easter, won't you? If Josh and I come down? You and Kirsty, and Grace too. Can we all have supper, in the Little

Goose over the weekend?' Hal said it eagerly. 'Would Friday night be okay? Good Friday?'

'We might be in our new cottage by then, Kirsty and I. But of course we'll come!'

At least if Josh and Hal were friends again, she thought, it wouldn't be so awkward when Hal realized what was going on between Josh and her.

'And we'll drink a toast to Amber for getting us all together. You never met her, did you?'

'I met her sister, but never her.'

'If you had, I think you'd have understood why I was so deranged,' he laughed bitterly.

'I understand now.' Lily reached out and touched his sleeve. 'Don't blame yourself for falling for her.'

It was still early when they left. Hal found her a taxi and helped her inside, then insisted on covering the cab fare home.

'I'll see you soon,' he said, leaning in through the open window and reaching for her hand.

'Thanks for tonight. It was lovely.'

He looked at her wistfully and then kissed her hand. 'Get home,' he said and turned away.

16

She was out of the door by eight the next morning. As she closed it quietly so as not to wake Beth her mobile rang, piercing in the silence of the sleeping street. She looked at the number and saw that it was Josh.

'Hello,' she said cautiously. Longing for him enveloped her. 'How was the film set?'

'Bloody awful.'

'And the client?'

'Spent the whole day in tears.'

'Oh no,' Lily laughed. 'Why?'

'Because they're messing with his script. What are you doing now, right now? Where are you?'

'Leaving the house, shutting the front door.' Lily did as she said and set off down the street. 'Walking down Lonsdale Road.'

'I thought you would be. Why don't you stay another day and wait for me. I could see you tonight.'

'I have to go back. I want to. I've things I have to decide . . .'

'Like what?'

'Like what I'm going to do. Where I'm going to live. Little things like that.'

'Where else would you live?'

'London, I suppose,' she said cautiously. 'If I get the

job at the Registry it would make sense if I moved nearer to it.' She couldn't say that what had happened between them made it hard not to think of moving to London just to be nearer to him.

As she talked, she turned left out of Lonsdale Road, heading towards the bridge.

'What are you doing now?' she asked Josh.

'Talking to you. Getting ready to pick up the dreadful Mr Barnsley for a second day of mental torture.'

'Why do you have to do it all over again?'

'Because he wants me to. And he's an important client.'

'Oh, I see,' she teased. 'So it's all about money.'

'Absolutely.'

She'd reached the bridge now. Sunday morning and it was empty. She liked it like that. She could see people jogging along the towpath below her and just one other person crossing the bridge from the other side.

'So have you missed me at all?' she asked, suddenly brave, not wanting the entire conversation to be one that he could have been having with his sister.

He was silent for a moment, thinking about it. 'Yes,' he said quietly.

'How much would that be?'

'Truly, madly, deeply. Masses and masses,' he laughed. 'More than I miss cigarettes.'

She laughed. 'Oh, thank you!'

'And I'd do anything, *anything*, to see you now.'

'Oh, right.' That's why you've cancelled your client, Lily thought.

'But you're going home and I'm going to Brighton. Will Kirsty be there to meet you at the station?'

The person walking towards her was very close now, she thought. If he didn't lift his head up and look where he was going he was going to walk straight into her.

'Why are you smiling?' Lily demanded.

'I'm not!'

'Yes, you are, I can hear it in your voice . . .' Josh didn't reply, but she was sure she'd been right. 'Josh,' she said again, 'are you there?'

'Where?' Josh said, standing there in front of her on the bridge and grinning at her. She felt her stomach do a great leap of shock and outrage as she struggled to take it in.

'I took a chance that you'd walk rather than get a cab,' he said, reaching for her, laughing delightedly because he'd managed to make it all the way up to her without her realizing it was him.

She was so surprised that she felt completely disorientated, dumbstruck. It was Josh, there, right in front of her. She stood back from him for a moment, then started to laugh with him, because now that she could see him all her old fears and insecurities vanished. The Josh she didn't trust, the cold-hearted seducer, was banished by the reality of the Josh who was obviously so pleased to see her now. In the quiet early morning, freshly shaved but with his hair still showing signs of having been slept on, he looked more endearing, more gorgeous than ever. Lost for words, she threw her arms around his neck and kissed him.

'You taste of peppermint,' she told him.

'Lily, I couldn't stay away. Mr Barnsley will have to wait.'

'You're crazy,' she laughed.

'No I'm not.' He shook his head. 'When are you going to take us seriously?'

She didn't reply but pulled him close to her and kissed him again.

'Oh baby,' he groaned, running his hands up her back. 'Can't we go back to your flat?'

'One-track mind,' She said, deep in his arms, thinking how nice that would be.

'Is that a yes?'

'What about Mr Barnsley? Won't he get tired of waiting?'

'I don't care.'

She looked up at him. 'I don't care about my train either.'

He took her hand and they ran back over the bridge together, back to Josie's flat. Distracted by Josh's phone call, Lily had forgotten to post her key back through the letter-box so she was able to let them both in. With Lily's bag still in his hand, Josh started to kiss her the moment the front door was open, turning her so that they stepped slowly backwards together to close it again. With their combined weight the door moved much too fast and then shut with such a loud clunk that it echoed through the flat, and for a second they stopped, certain that Beth was going to appear at the sitting-room door and spoil every-thing for the second time. But there was no sound. Josh dropped her bag to the floor.

'Where's the bedroom?'

'Behind me.'

He pushed her in and kicked the door shut. 'She can't disturb us now.'

'At this rate, I might still make the train,' Lily laughed as she fell backwards on to the bed.

*

Her train arrived at teatime and Kirsty was there at the station to meet her.

'I couldn't wait to see you,' she told Lily elatedly, taking her bag, beaming at Lily, at the station supervisor and at almost every other passenger that happened to be in range. 'So much has happened since you left!'

'Too right,' Lily nodded, but Kirsty didn't hear her. She took Lily's arm and steered her away from the platform and down the station steps to the car-park.

She unlocked the car and opened the door for Lily, slinging her bags into the boot. Then she drove them both quickly away, squeezing through a set of red traffic lights in her impatience to leave the station and reach a bit of clear road so that she could concentrate on Lily rather than the driving.

Before Kirsty could start, Lily turned to her. 'Actually, I've got a few things to tell you too.'

Kirsty raised her eyebrows.

'But I'm not going to tell you yet, because first *you're* going to tell *me* what's happened with Simon.'

'Oh, Lily!' Kirsty said in frustration.

'I know, I shouldn't have said anything. But you have to tell me first. You've got together again, haven't you?'

'But I want to know what's happened to *you*.'

Kirsty looked at her mutinously but she knew she wasn't going to win. And so she began to tell Lily what had happened, starting with the visit from Fred, and then Mimosa and Grace, and then, finally Simon.

'Poor Simon,' Lily said, 'you must be driving him insane. No wonder he's determined to stay away from you! Tell me what happened afterwards? After they'd all gone. After he'd helped you out of the feedbin. Tell me!'

Kirsty had been determined to make Simon kiss her. Every ounce of experience, all her powers of seduction, had gone into those few seconds where she had him again in her grasp. But he had known what to expect and he had broken free, laughing. She'd joined him at the window and they'd looked out together at the leaves spiralling around the yard in the wind.

'It's going to snow,' Kirsty said.

'Do you think so? Isn't it nearly summer?'

'No! And we don't often get summer up here, not in these parts.' She smiled up at him. 'It'll snow tonight, I'm sure.'

'Are *you* sure, country girl, or is Michael Fish sure?'

Kirsty turned to him. 'Look at the cattle,' she ordered, pointing across to a nearby field. 'When one puts its tail in the air like that, it always means snow.'

'Yeah, right!'

Kirsty nodded.

'Really?' He said, believing her. 'How funny!'

She looked up at the ceiling, trying to keep a straight face.

'I am such a mug.'

'Come for a walk with me tomorrow afternoon, after you leave the Little Goose,' she said impulsively. 'If it snows it will be wonderful. We could go up the Long Mountain. I bet you haven't ever seen it in the snow.'

'Why?' he asked her softly, but there was a soft, smitten look in his eyes that told her she was right to hope, that she was still on his mind.

Kirsty shrugged.

'I'll come and pick you up,' he'd said, 'and you can show me the way.'

'And so,' Kirsty said now, glancing gleefully over to Lily, 'we're going up there this afternoon.'

Lily looked out of the window. 'There's still time for it to snow.'

*

On the way home Kirsty made a detour via Montgomery.

Of all the places that Lily had grown to know so well, Montgomery was her favourite. And of all the places that could most tempt her to stay on there, it was Montgomery, with its pretty Georgian square, pink and olive and pastel blue houses and lovely gallery and shops. Kirsty had taken Lily there soon after she had arrived, knowing that she would fall for the little town and the old ruined castle sitting high above it. Lily had looked up at it from the square, listening as Kirsty had told her how it had been built in the early twelve hundreds and had been fought over for the next four hundred years until it had been won from the royalists in the Civil War and orders had been put through for its demolition in 1649. Lily had looked up at it, seeing it not as a ruin but as imperious and secure again, with horses and soldiers galloping under its arches, flags held high, ready to defend the town below.

Kirsty took Lily straight through the square and down a little lane that Lily had never noticed before, and stopped and pointed out Owl Cottage backed up against the craggy rock of the steep hillside at the end of a little path.

'What do you think?'

Lily looked at the cottage. It was hidden behind wildly overgrown creepers and ivy and a tangle of a garden, but was still incredibly pretty. Chocolate-box pretty if it were ever done up too neatly, with the old roof reaching half-way down the house and the stream running through the bottom of the garden. The wide borders were already full of promise, daffodils and tulips just starting to bud in readiness for the spring. For the size of the cottage, there was lots of garden, some of it hidden behind old apple trees and a yew hedge, and more spreading out in front of the cottage, divided in half by a pretty herringbone brick path that led away from the porched front door. In any other mood, at any other time, Lily would have fallen for it straight away, but now Josh had messed up everything. She didn't want to be anywhere he wasn't. And he was in London.

'Isn't it sweet!' she said, unable to feel anything at all. 'But I don't know what I'm going to be doing this summer . . .' She tailed off, knowing how awful it would be sounding to Kirsty.

'I do understand, you know,' Kirsty interrupted. 'I knew the minute you went that you'd come back feeling differently. When or if you decide it's time to move away from here, I'll still rent it – on my own. And you'll still be allowed to come and stay,' she went on. 'For a small fee. And if you've already decided and you need to tell me you're moving away, you mustn't feel guilty,' Kirsty told her, avoiding her eye. 'But you should let me know.'

Lily turned away. 'I'm sorry, I'm sorry. And I haven't decided anything. I think it would be lovely to live here with you. Forgive me? Please. When I tell you what happened in London you'll understand. But at the moment I promise you I have no plans to leave.' She shrugged. 'I have no plans.'

'There's only four weeks' notice in the contract so it's not as if I'm making a lifelong commitment. And if you can come too, then come. But if you don't it doesn't matter because I think it's perfect for me and I'm moving in. If you're thinking about your job and you need to wait and see what they say, do that. They may not want you. And if they do, then perhaps it *would* be better for you to move nearer to London. What did we agree?' Kirsty reminded her. 'That we'd take it for the summer and then we'd think again. Either way, I am doing that. What ever happens with me and Simon. With you or without you. I have to leave home. Big deal!' she laughed. 'Five whole miles away from my parents.'

'It's great that you get on with them so well,' Lily said, taken aback by how easy Kirsty was making it all. 'Look at Grace and me. As far away from ours as possible.'

They got out of the car and leaned side by side over the little wooden gate at the bottom of the path that led up to the cottage.

'Come on,' Kirsty said. 'Nobody lives there now. Let me at least show you around.'

Lily, panicking that some hidden owner might leap out and shout at them, ran lightly up the path after Kirsty.

She peered in through the kitchen window at the low-beamed ceilings and made out an old-fashioned Rayburn and a terracotta-tiled floor. And, despite what she thought she'd feel, something turned over inside her and shook itself out, a determination not to put her life on hold just for Josh, whom she hardly knew. She'd been happier here than she'd been anywhere else. And Kirsty and she had planned to move in together. Whatever she felt for Josh, she'd known him for just a few days. There was no hurry. She would move in as planned.

She would give herself the summer here, she thought, looking away from the cottage and down to the studio at the bottom of the garden. Where else was she going to go? And she'd still have Kirsty for some of the time, even if she was about to get it together with Simon.

She visualized herself and Kirsty out in the garden in bikinis, sunbathing and having barbecues, splashing in the stream when it was hot enough. Saw herself coming out of the studio, her hands caked in clay, having produced her first pieces for the Registry.

'I do want to live here,' she said to Kirsty as they opened the gate again and left the cottage. 'I definitely do. When do you want to move in?'

'Pheww!' Kirsty grinned in relief. 'We'll have a laugh, Lily, I promise you.' She paused and fixed Lily with a determined eye. 'And now you are going to tell me what's been going on.'

How should I put it, Lily thought? 'When I said I didn't know where I wanted to be, I wasn't only thinking about my job,' she started tentatively.

Kirsty listened, transfixed.

'I saw Josh again.'

'How did you manage that?'

As they drove away from the cottage and Montgomery, Lily told her about the wonderful, perfect day with Josh. How quickly and intensely she had felt for him. And then how he'd met her on the bridge, how it was the most romantic thing that had ever happened to her. And how now that she was home again, back in Welshpool, she felt as if she'd fallen in love and she had to keep reminding herself that she couldn't have done, mustn't have done, not with Josh.

'If I wish I was in London again, it's only because of him. Because I want to see some more of him, find out if he is as I think he is. You don't mind me saying that?'

'I don't. I understand what you're saying,' Kirsty insisted immediately. 'But Lily . . .'

She looks frightened for me, Lily thought in surprise, and disappointment rose up inside her, making her bite her lip and turn away.

'Don't hate me,' Kirsty begged, leaning around her to look at her face. 'I know it's not what you want me to say. But I have to say it!'

Lily nodded, not trusting herself to speak.

'Don't take him too seriously, Lily, that's all. Please,' Kirsty continued, 'have some fun with him but don't let him get to you. He could hurt you so badly.'

Lily gave a curt little nod.

'Don't get me wrong. I'm excited for you,' Kirsty said, desperate to make amends. 'I think it's fantastic that you've met someone.'

'But you don't trust Josh.' Lily nodded slowly. 'I don't think you'd say that if you'd seen him with me. I know how he seemed when we saw him here but he wasn't like that at all in London.'

'That's great.' Kirsty shrugged, thinking *never again* will I put myself in this position. Next time I will be dishonest. I will not risk my friendship. I will not alienate myself from her. Better that I'm there at her side when he dumps her than not at her side at all.

'I wanted you to tell me it was all going to be okay.'

'It probably is,' Kirsty said. 'All I'm saying is I think you're right to be wary. That he's used to having lots of fun, with lots of girls. Maybe you're the one to change that,' she shrugged. 'Why not? But I don't think you can know that yet.'

'He's coming down for Easter with Hal,' Lily said, feeling better. 'They want us to have supper with them! They want to stay at the Little Goose.'

'Oh, do they now!' Kirsty laughed.

'Who are you, getting all proprietorial already? Business is business. Simon will be pleased.'

'And then you will know,' Kirsty said simply. 'You'll have proper time together. And how fantastic if Hal is coming back again too,' Kirsty smiled. 'It makes it even better.'

*

Ten minutes before Simon was due at Little Venus Farm Kirsty set out to meet him, walking rather than driving because the snow had finally arrived, coming down slowly, in fat, fluffy flakes. Wearing jeans and a jumper, wellingtons and a brown oilskin with a hood, she set off along the long, twisting lane that led away from Little Venus Farm. The snow was already creaking under her boots, high in the hills she knew it would be deep. She wondered whether Mimosa had realized who Simon was going walking with, wondered how desperate she was under the steam-rolling exterior and whether she might try to stop him.

With the snow's arrival, the wind had stopped, but still the air was icy cold and Kirsty shivered inside her coat, wishing that she'd brought some gloves and a scarf. She wondered how far she would have to walk before she met Simon's car, hoping it wouldn't be all the way to Pond House. She'd set off impulsively, almost to ensure that he had to come out to meet her, to avoid the possibility of him phoning her to say, for whatever reason, that he wasn't able to come.

As she walked she listened for the sound of his car, following the lane as it twisted sharply left and right, and after what felt like ages she saw him slowly making his way towards her, struggling on the slippery narrow road, his lights on and the windscreen wipers on full too. She walked faster to meet him, sliding rather than walking, until she was level with the car. He stopped and opened his door.

'Want a lift?' he called.

She nodded and came around to the passenger side and got in beside him.

'This car hates the snow,' he told her, turning up the heater. 'It's already tried to take me over one precipice on the way here.' He gingerly let off the handbrake and the car started to slide forwards. 'Are you cold? How long have you been walking for?'

'Not long,' she said, on edge now that she was with him again.

He drove on for a moment longer and then suddenly said, 'So where are we going, Kirsty, you and me?'

'What?' she exclaimed, not expecting him to get so heavy so soon.

'There's no way we'll make it up on to the Long Mountain. Watch.' He touched the foot brake and the car didn't react at all, gliding slowly on down the road in a perfect straight line.

Kirsty's eyes widened. 'Are you serious? Can you really not stop?'

'No. But it's okay, isn't it?' He carefully took her hand

and looked at her and laughed. 'Because we're together again.'

'Don't do that! Keep them on the steering-wheel,' she said, thinking, damn him for joking about it.

'Don't worry,' he said reassuringly. 'The hedges will stop us falling over the edge. That's what they're there for.'

'Does your steering-wheel work? Can you turn the wheel?'

'A little.'

'I can't be in another accident. I've only just got over the last one! Turn into the hedge before we go any faster.'

'No way!' Simon protested. 'It'll scratch the car. It was your idea to come out.'

'I hadn't realized how bad it was.'

'We'll be fine. Watch me.'

He lifted his hands off the steering-wheel again and the car responded by slowly turning off the road and into a gateway. It bumped carefully over the raised verge and came to a gentle halt.

'It's always better if you let them find their own way.' Simon turned off the engine.

'Good car. Thank you, car,' Kirsty said shakily, patting the dashboard.

'I'm sorry if you were scared,' he said after a moment's silence. 'Are you okay?'

Kirsty nodded, not looking at him.

The falling snow had moved up a gear now, coming down in a swirling mass, and for a while they both looked out at it. Then Simon turned to Kirsty questioningly, and she looked back at him, waiting for him to speak, but he didn't say anything and so they sat silently together, cocooned in the car, still not talking.

Why didn't he talk? Or at least make some effort with her? Why had he come? Perhaps he didn't realize what she wanted. Perhaps he didn't want anything to happen between them? Now it was awkward and awful and she wished she hadn't assumed it was all going to be wonderful, because the disappointment was gut-wrenchingly horrible. She wondered if he was laughing at her for bringing him out like this.

She glanced sideways at him, willing him to make a move, but he continued to stare impassively through the windscreen.

'I'm off then,' she said irritably.

She opened her door and stepped outside and snowflakes immediately bombarded her, settling in her eyelashes and on her cheeks and hair.

She shut the door hard behind her and wiped the snow away and then, when there was no sign that Simon was following her, she strode away down the lane, turning a corner and quickly disappearing from his sight.

She heard a click and a slam in the distance but she didn't turn around, and then at last he came up alongside her and slid his arm around her shoulders.

'What's the matter with you?' he said.

Kirsty turned on him. 'I didn't want it to be like this!' she retorted, making Simon jump back with alarm. 'I don't want to have to feel that it's all up to me. For fuck's sake.

What did I do? Nothing so terrible.' She started walking faster. 'And I've said sorry, and tried to explain, not that there's a lot of explaining to do. And I've told you how I feel – which is horrible, by the way.' She turned to him, furiously. 'And yet you're still punishing me. You kiss me and then you tell me, actually no. You wait in the Warehouse for me and then walk away the minute you find me. Do you want to be with me or not? Because if you do, I think it's *your* turn to show *me* now. Horrible man,' she added.

'Why do I always forget what a bolshie pain in the arse you are?' Kirsty looked away to hide her grin. 'It's always the same. You go away, and all I can think about is my adorable, scrumptious Kirsty, with her little turned-up nose,' he paused, 'and her lovely blue eyes, and her beautiful, sweet lips. And then I see you, and you swear and shout and stomp around me, and I think: remember this next time, stupid man! Remember what she's really like. Stay away from her!'

'And then?' Kirsty said, slowing down.

'And then,' he said, putting out his arms to stop her, 'I can't do it. I never could.'

Kirsty felt relief wash through her.

'And if it's okay, I'm not even going to try any more. Because I'm not very happy if I'm not with you.' He put his arms over her shoulders and looked down at her. 'And I'm very happy if I am.' He paused. 'You know why I had to try to be without you for a while? For my pride, and for you to have a chance to sort yourself out, and to realize what you were missing out on.'

She moved closer to him and slid her arms around his waist. 'Don't tell me you deliberately got hold of Mimosa to make me jealous?'

'What?' he sounded amazed. 'But of course!'

Kirsty laughed and shoved him backwards. 'Poor Mimosa.'

'I know. But I think she's got the message now. Even if she hasn't, she's not my problem and I don't want to think about her. I want to think about you. And me.' He held her still.

They stood there in the middle of the lane, oblivious to everything else but each other. She lifted her face to his and he kissed her with all the hungry passion that Kirsty could ever have hoped for, with the snow falling fast and silently on their heads, on Simon's shoulders and Kirsty's black wellington boots, and piling up around them.

For a long time neither of them moved, until finally Kirsty looked down at her feet, and laughed to see how much snow had fallen around them. She turned in Simon's arms, sliding one of hers around his waist.

'Look at us,' she said softly. 'Another ten minutes and we'd have been buried alive.' She kicked the snow off her boots.

'I can think of worse things.'

Slowly they walked over to a gap in the hedge and stood together, Simon pulling her close, and they looked out at the snow, spreading soft and silently across the hills. After a while, Kirsty turned to watch him instead. He was standing so close and yet she could see that he was far away from her. She watched him as he looked

out across the rolling, snow-covered hills and was transfixed. It had been like that all along, she thought, he had
always been like that. But here, in the silence and the
peace of the moment, it was intensified. There was a
stillness, a wonderful calmness, about him that she loved.
That didn't make him detached or solitary, but was a
sign of his strength. However much he needed her and
wanted her, she thought, he would always have that
about him. He was always going to be independent of
her too.

From the start he'd had the strength of character not to
need to play games with her but to tell her straight away
that he'd fallen for her. What she'd mistaken for over-
dependence was actually his confidence, a willingness to
be open about what he felt for her. But before she'd
realized how good that was, she'd run away.

She'd always seemed to attract needy men, those who
would latch on to her and who made her feel as if they
were dragging her down, holding her back. And at first
she'd thought Simon was like that too. But she'd been
wrong. She stretched up and kissed him gently on his
cheek and then again on the corner of his mouth, making
his lips twitch into a smile.

'Back to the car now?' he said, turning to her. 'Shall we
go home?'

She nodded and started to walk away from him,
moving ahead and out of sight as she turned the corner
and he followed her slowly, wondering why she hadn't
waited for him. When a snowball hit him on his shoulder
he shouted in surprise.

'It's romantic,' she laughed. 'It's what people like us are meant to do.'

'And this, are we meant to do this too?' He took a handful of snow and bit into it, then ran after Kirsty down the lane towards the car, and grabbed her and kissed her again, bending her backwards over the bonnet, making her gasp with shock, but his mouth was already over hers and no sound came out. The cold snow and his hot tongue sent waves of desire throbbing through her as the snow melted, turning their lips slippery and wet, and Kirsty felt as if she was going to collapse with longing for him.

'I love you,' he told her, still leaning over her.

Her eyes widened. 'Surely not.'

'And I've loved you for as long as I've known you.'

She bit her lip, feeling her eyes burn with tears at the look in his eyes. 'I love you too.'

She couldn't believe it was happening, this miraculous, perfect moment she'd never dared to hope would happen to her.

'And I'm taking you home.'

'What about Mimosa?'

They got into the car and slid their way carefully back to Pond House.

'Don't worry about Mimosa,' Simon told her as they pulled to a halt. 'I'm sure she said she was going out.'

The front door was locked. Simon found the key and opened it for them and together they walked into the kitchen. There on the table was a note for Simon.

'What did I say? It's from Mimosa,' he told her. 'I knew something was up.' He read it out loud.

Simon, I'll admit I didn't want to go! He looked up at Kirsty and grinned at that. *But I know now that I've definitely outstayed my welcome.*

'Oh, you haven't!' said Kirsty.

Don't worry, Kirsty, I won't be moving in on your doorstep! And Simon, thanks a million for putting up with me for as long as you did. I'll keep in touch, love, Mimosa.

'Why's she talking to me?'

'Because she's a thoughtful considerate person. I suppose she guessed you might be coming back with me after our walk.'

She kissed him gently. 'So you told her who you were meeting, did you?'

'Yes, I did. I don't think she was surprised. Once she'd realized it was never going to happen between me and her, she didn't want to hang around to watch.'

Kirsty stood in front of Simon. 'Nothing ever happened between the two of you?'

'No, of course it didn't.'

'She never said, "Take me to bed or lose me for ever"?'

'No, she didn't,' he said seriously, coming towards her. 'Who did?'

'Kelly McGillis in *Top Gun*!'

He smiled. 'Say it again?'

17

The snow didn't settle, and almost as soon as it disappeared it felt like spring. In the week before Easter, the air turned softer and primroses and violets started to appear through the grass in the verges. There were pussy-willow and hawthorn in the hedges, and lambs in the fields. On good days, when the sun was out, Lily walked around feeling as if she was in a production of *The Darling Buds of May*, but with no part for herself. The longer she went without seeing Josh, the more she worried that there was no future for them. If she mentioned how she felt to Kirsty, hoping for some reassurance, Kirsty only nodded gravely, making Lily feel even more convinced that all her fears were well founded and that she should write off any hope of a future with Josh. And then, after he'd called her on the telephone, she told herself that she was being hysterical and ridiculous, that there was nothing wrong that seeing him again wouldn't cure. Around her everyone and everything seemed suddenly full of the joys of spring, and everyone and everything was joyfully pairing off, from Kirsty and Simon to the wood pigeons canoodling in the trees. Even the blackbirds who lived in the ceanothus bush next to her studio were passing her window at half height, their beaks stuffed with grasses and bits of twig.

Only a few days after Lily returned from London, she

and Kirsty moved in to Owl Cottage. For Kirsty it was a huge step, both practically and emotionally, and necessitated borrowing a van from a neighbour to transport all her things. For Lily it felt very casual and involved only the packing of a couple of bags and fetching her pots and portable kiln from Grace's. And somehow, even as they moved in together, both of them were acknowledging that their time together might be short-lived, that, however much they denied it, everything was changing for both of them. Much as Kirsty loved Lily and being with Lily, she was now happiest when she was with Simon.

For the first time since she'd arrived in Welshpool, there was no pressure on Lily to stay there. She and Kirsty had committed themselves to spending the summer together, which she was happy to honour, but the summer was only three more months and from the day she moved in the restlessness started to build inside her again. In this part of Wales, she'd found people and a place she would always know and love, but not somewhere she could live in permanently like Grace and Kirsty could.

Alone for so much of the day, Lily found herself working far harder than she'd ever done before. Using her pottery to divert her attention from herself and Josh and their future, she produced better work than ever.

Then, almost as a reward for her good behaviour, the Registry finally got in touch and offered her the job. Now there was a real reason to feel that her time here was ending. She felt that she was only marking time in Montgomery, that she had no roots anywhere any more, nothing to help her to stay.

As the days passed and Good Friday drew closer, she found she was spending up to twelve hours at a time in the studio. At the thought of seeing Josh again, she was tied into knots of anticipation and excitement and panic. She veered between thinking that she hardly knew him and that she couldn't expect anything from him at all, to feeling that something wonderful and special had happened between the two of them and that as soon as she saw him again everything was going to be all right.

He had called her every day since she'd left London, oblivious to all the heart-searching going on, and she had to admit that on the telephone he had said all the right things, that he missed her desperately and that he couldn't work or eat or sleep until he saw her again. And for a little while after the phone calls, she'd feel that it was all going to be fine, that Josh hadn't simply been making the words up.

Hal called her too, sounding bright and happy again. Thank God he's not with Amber, she found herself thinking every time she put the phone down. He's so much too nice for Amber. She wanted to see him again, and she recognized, before she dashed the thought away, that if Josh hadn't taken away her ability to fancy anybody else, perhaps something might have started to kindle between the two of them. As far as she knew, Josh had still not told Hal about her, and she wished that he would because she felt that she owed it to Hal not to mislead him. Hal's openness with her was not being reciprocated and she hated lying to him about anything, however much he'd understand. She imagined the moment when he found out, when he realized, yet again, that his best friend had not been straight with him, and she knew, even if he understood, that he would be hurt.

The night before Josh and Hal were due to arrive, Kirsty told Lily that Simon wanted to cook for them all at Pond House rather than at the Little Goose.

'If Simon thinks it's a good idea,' Lily agreed cautiously, thinking that actually she preferred the idea of the anonymity and noise of the Little Goose.

'Because, of course, then it *is* a good idea, isn't it?' Kirsty joked. 'He is, after all, always right in your book, isn't he? Simon says this is how to do it, Simon says that's a good idea. You're as bad as my mother.'

Lily laughed. 'It's true!'

She called Hal and told him about Simon's offer and gave him directions to Pond House.

'How's Josh?' she asked then, in a moment of weakness, before Hal put down the phone. 'Have you spoken to him recently?'

'He's great. Charlie thinks he's met someone.'

'Really!'

'I'll believe it when I see it.'

'You haven't met her then?'

'No,' Hal said. 'Charlie says she lives in New York. He's been over there a lot recently. And if she was a London girl I think we'd have met her.'

'Maybe she lives outside London?' Lily dared, sick at heart.

'Perhaps,' Hal laughed. 'I don't think she exists at all. Josh doesn't believe in keeping still where his women are concerned.'

'Doesn't he?'

'No, Lily,' Hal said rather sharply, 'he doesn't. We're not talking about girls like you. We're talking about the kind of girls Josh goes after. Anyway,' he changed the subject firmly. 'We're driving up together tomorrow. Josh wanted to leave early in the morning but I have to do some work. So we'll come straight to Pond House if that's okay with you?'

*

Next morning her first thought was *He's coming tonight*. She lay in bed, wondering if he was awake, imagining him and Hal packing the car, filling up with petrol and leaving London.

As the hours moved by, and she walked across the garden to her studio, she imagined their journey up the motorways. She saw them on the M25, travelled with them the hour on the M40, then the M54 and through Shrewsbury. She imagined them getting nearer and nearer, until she felt she couldn't bear to wait any longer to see him again.

After lunch Kirsty rang her from Pond House, guessing how she was and insisting that she went around to keep her company while Simon prepared the supper.

'But I don't want to. Josh might come around here to see me first.'

'Then don't be there.'

'I thought you said not to play games.'

'If you don't come, I'll send Chukka around to fetch you. You shouldn't sit around waiting for him. Do what you'd normally do. And Josh isn't the sort of guy that would expect you to hang around. He won't appreciate it.'

'I'll go out with Grace. I feel like a walk.' She felt she needed someone more soothing than Kirsty promised to be at that moment, and she owed it to Grace to tell her what was going on before she met Josh that evening.

'What's Simon cooking for us?' she asked. 'Is he preparing a feast?'

'I suggested he did something from Jamie Oliver.' Lily laughed.

'You didn't.'

'I didn't think he'd be so touchy.'

She walked through the wet grass to the studio, snapping off some branches of cherry blossom to stick in a vase. She let herself in, filled a vase with water for the blossom and then went over to the cup she'd been working on the day before. It was a loving cup, something she'd always meant to make but had never found the right reason to start before. She'd finished building it the day before and now she unwrapped it carefully from the polythene that she'd put on to prevent it from drying out. It was going to be beautiful. The traditional double handles were already in place and she held it up, looking at it critically, turning it around to check it from every angle, seeing if there was anything wrong with it that she hadn't noticed the day before. Then she sprayed it with a mist of water to soften the clay. Today she was going to paint it, first with a white slip and then, when that was dry, starting work on the spring flowers that she wanted to decorate it with. Some in relief and some two dimensional. She was going to wind them into the handles, cowslips and daisies and violets, and carry one or two of them and their stems down into the inside of the cup. When she'd finished inscribing it, decorating and painting it, she would biscuit fire it, then dip it into the glaze and leave it to dry again, rubbing it down to get rid of any tiny little blemishes in the glaze. Finally, it would be ready to glaze fire. And then she could give it to Kirsty.

Loving cups could be big business, she realized as she began work on it again. The Registry would definitely fall for them. They didn't take too long to make and she could picture them, filling up an alcove on the ground floor for Valentine's Day, each one unique. Then her mind grew full of Josh again and she saw him dumping his bag on the bed in the Little Goose, utterly carefree, leaning out of the window to stare down into the street, hurrying Hal up so that they could get down to the bar for a beer.

Would he call her straight away? Would it feel strange for him to be back here again? Wasn't it strange that he'd ever come? That he'd chosen this little place to spirit Hal away to? And strange that she'd ever come too. If she hadn't followed Grace here. If Grace hadn't got ditched, hadn't found her way to Welshpool in the first place . . .

Grace, she thought in agitation, her mind leaping on again. She really did want to go and see Grace. She wanted to be with her and to tell her all about Josh. In the old days Grace would have been the first person Lily would have turned to. Why hadn't she now? Since she'd come back from London, Lily had hardly seen her and had spoken to her only once on the phone. She felt horribly guilty and hoped that Grace hadn't been too hurt by the silence. Lily ran back to the house and rang her number, and Grace picked up the phone.

'Can we take Hodge out? Can I come with you for a walk?'

Grace agreed immediately, delighted at the need for her that she could hear in Lily's voice. She was back in the driving seat, literally, as she jumped into her car, turned it around in Green Lane and headed towards Montgomery.

Outside Lily's cottage she hooted and then waited, watching Lily come out through the front door, lock it and run down the path. Lily didn't ask where Grace was taking her, and Grace, apart from saying she knew a good place to walk, didn't elaborate. After ten or so minutes of driving extremely fast up tiny lanes that Lily had never noticed before, she parked the car in an unused gateway and turned off the engine.

They had stopped in the entrance to an old forestry track that wound, wide and inviting, into the hills, long since spread over with pine-needles and springing soft grass.

'Let's walk from here.' She turned to Lily and smiled. 'You haven't been here before, have you?' Lily shook her head, picturing the scene. Grace setting off alone up the track in her orange coat.

They got out of the car and climbed, one after the other,

over the old gate. Hodge was immediately off, jumping into an overgrown ditch, his tail waving ecstatically, and then he streaked away through the trees.

For about ten minutes Lily and Grace walked in silence, up the track that led them slowly higher and higher, winding them around the side of the hill. All that could be heard were the softly snapping twigs beneath their feet and then gradually, as Lily relaxed and concentrated on walking, her breath began to come hard as she and Grace started to fight it out between the two of them to be the fastest. Eventually Lily started to laugh, at the same time conceding defeat.

'Stop! Okay. You're much, much fitter than me!' she gasped, doubled over to get back her breath. 'I've got to have a rest.' She collapsed on to the grass at the side of the track, then pulled off her sweatshirt and pushed it underneath her.

'It's Hodge,' Grace said. 'If I didn't have to walk him I wouldn't be so fit.'

As soon as she'd caught her breath, Lily stood up again and looked around her. On her right the woods spread on above her, tall and dense and dark. But to her left, there was a gap in the trees. She walked slowly towards it, and looked, and there suddenly were the sky and the sun, and Housman's blue remembered hills.

'It's absolutely beautiful,' she called back to Grace. 'I'm so glad you've brought me here.'

'Wait until you see it from the top,' Grace said, taking off her coat and coming to stand and look at Lily's side. 'But let's have a breather here first.'

She went back to her coat and scrambled in her deep pockets.

'We have two classy plastic cups,' she said then, making Lily turn in surprise. She passed them both over to her.

'Two slices of lemon,' she pulled out a little sandwich bag with two pieces of lemon and dropped one in each of the cups, and Lily started to smile.

'And two cans of Vodka and Tonic, ready mixed.' She brought them out from the other pocket and twisted back the ring pulls, as calmly as if she carried such things around with her every day. 'Cold,' she said, holding the can against her red hot cheek. 'But sadly, no ice.'

She poured and both of the cups fizzed up and immediately overflowed. 'I got the impression you needed one.'

'You're wonderful,' Lily smiled.

'It's medicinal,' said Grace, taking a glass from Lily and catching the spill on her tongue, quickly drinking it down to a level that would stay in the cup. 'Drink it.'

'Thanks!' Lily said.

She drank far too quickly because she was so thirsty, and when she had finished she lay down, putting the cup on the grass beside her, and turned over on to her back.

'Now I'm pissed, Grace,' she said indignantly, staring up at the sky. 'It must be the altitude.'

'Or that you haven't eaten anything for God knows how long,' Grace said, looking at Lily's concave stomach and jutting hipbones exposed to the cold air.

They lay there silently for a moment longer.

'Give us a cigarette then,' Lily said.

Grace moved back to her coat pockets. She brought out a packet and lit and handed one to Lily and then sat back against a tree, watching the smoke curl from Lily's lips and drift upwards into the sky.

Slowly Lily started to tell her about Josh.

'I keep thinking how lucky I am to have found someone. Finally feel all those things I'm meant to feel,' Lily said, speaking so quietly that Grace could hardly hear her. 'You said things about me once. And you were right.' She looked over to Grace. 'Those things about me not feeling anything. You were right. I never had.'

'I shouldn't have said that.'

'No, you were right,' Lily insisted. 'And that was why it was fantastic to meet Josh, and finally feel it. I've felt what it's like now.' She stopped again.

'And?' Grace said, aware of a tightening in her chest, because Lily was finally talking to her like she'd always wanted her too, giving ground, conceding weaknesses and admitting a vulnerable side, giving Grace the opportunity to help her.

'Now I can't believe I'll be able to keep him.'

'I think that's part of the deal. Until you know him better. If you care about someone, a part of you is always going to imagine how much it would hurt to lose them. I think everybody does that.'

Neither of them spoke for a while and Lily eventually stubbed out her cigarette and dropped the butt in her empty can and stood up again.

Calling on Lily

'Why do you think you're going to lose him?' Grace asked looking up at her.

Lily didn't answer at first. 'Because he's a massive flirt,' she said, walking away a little. 'And I've seen it first hand. He did it to me when he was here. I was fun, a distraction. I know I didn't mean anything to him.'

'And then I saw him with another girl, just a few weeks ago. And she looked just like I think I would look – gazing up at him like she couldn't believe her luck. And I can't help wondering what happened to her, and whether I'm destined to be that girl too. I'm scared that there must have been at least another hundred and fifty girls like her. And another hundred and fifty to come.'

'But you didn't think that when you were with him?'

'No,' Lily agreed with a sigh. 'When I was with him, I couldn't think of anything apart from how wonderful he was. And I think he guessed how I'd doubt him now. He even warned me about it. Told me not to doubt him. Not to do exactly what I'm doing now. But I can't help it. I still think he's a serial seducer.'

'Oh, don't, Lily,' Grace told her emphatically. 'You'll do your head in. Don't think. Don't worry. You're seeing him again today, just get on with it!'

'But it's not that simple! I can't just say, yes Grace, you are absolutely right! I'm sure you are. But it doesn't work like that.'

'I know. But what's your choice?'

Lily bit her lip and shrugged. 'I have no choice. Even if I knew, absolutely *knew* that he was bad news, there's no way I'd get out first.'

'Lily!' Grace said impatiently. 'Stop it! I can't believe you're talking about getting out. Nothing has gone wrong!'

'I know,' Lily winced. 'Don't shout. I thought you of all people would think I should get away, but you're right. I'm being pathetic. Once I see him again it'll all be fine.' She fell silent again and then sat back against a rock and closed her eyes.

For all her common-sense talk, Grace's first thought had been that Lily should get away. That nothing and no one was worth the risk of being hurt like she had been. But before she'd said anything out loud she had managed to clamp down on herself, because she knew that Lily had no alternative but to see it through just like she had. The thought of Lily with someone who might mess with her just a tiny bit turned Grace's stomach. In the bad times, she'd even wished it upon Lily, thought that if Lily could only experience one tiny bit of what she was going through herself, she would be a better, more compassionate person because of it. Lily had seemed so strong, so insulated from pain that she'd wanted to puncture her. But now she felt ashamed that she could have imagined such a thing, wanting to protect her and yet knowing that only Lily could take the decision to get out, and that the likelihood of her doing so was zero. Because who in Lily's position had ever chosen to do that?

'I know it's nothing like what you went through with Jeremy,' Lily ventured, her eyes still closed. The words hung in the air. She hadn't raised the subject of Jeremy for a long while.

'Of course it's not. I never once doubted Jeremy. I wish I had,' Grace said. Lily smiled up at her. 'Well, if I did doubt him I pushed the doubt away again, because I thought married to Jeremy and miserable was better than not married to Jeremy and miserable.' Grace stopped for a moment. 'It was different. People were telling me to keep away from him. Nobody's saying that to you.' She looked down at her again. 'And now that you've mentioned Jeremy, I'm going to ask you something, Lily,' she said, coming to sit down beside her. 'And you've got to tell me the truth.' She took her time. 'Did something once happen between you two, something that you haven't told me about?'

Colour immediately flooded Lily's cheeks and she couldn't help herself looking away.

Oh my God! Grace thought in horror. I didn't mean an affair. In all this time I never thought *that*.

'Yes, in a way,' Lily said heavily. Then she saw the look on Grace's face. 'Not that! Not an affair!' Lily said, outraged, seeing the question on Grace's face. 'For God's sake, Grace! I'm your sister!' She moved away from Grace and rolled over on to her stomach.

'What then?' Grace asked, calming down.

'I told him what I'd said to you,' Lily said hesitantly. 'That I didn't think he loved you enough.'

'And?'

'And I told him I thought he should leave you alone . . .'

Grace's eyes widened. 'Did you? And what did he say?'

'That he wanted the pleasure of marrying you first.'

Grace sharply drew in her breath. Then she said in a quiet, sad voice, 'And then what did he say?'

'I'm so sorry, Grace.' Lily came and sat next to her and put her arm around her, seeing that she was starting to cry. 'I said that he couldn't do that to you. You know, I remember thinking at the time that he didn't mean it. That he said it because he knew I didn't like him, and it made him really hate me, and he wanted to hurt me. It wasn't anything to do with what he felt for you.' She touched Grace's arm, trying to reassure her. 'But then, he didn't show up, so God, I've always felt that perhaps he did it because of what I said.'

'That's what I've always felt too. I blamed you for frightening him off somehow. The fact that he was so spineless, so despicable that he could be frightened off, didn't matter. I'd rather he'd stayed. I really loved him . . .' Tears filled Lily's eyes too. 'What did I do to deserve him?' Grace smiled. 'I'm fine. Honestly. I'm not crying because I'm sad about him. Not any more. I'm crying because it took me so long to get over him, and I hate myself for it.' She sniffed. 'He means nothing to me now. I promise you. I can't even remember what it was like to be in bed with him.' She laughed, and wiped her nose and eyes with her sleeve.

'The vodka doesn't help!'

Grace nodded. 'Now I want to be strong. I don't want this hanging over me any more. I mean it, Lily. I was over him long before I was over what happened to me. It was the humiliation and the rejection and envying everyone else who seemed to be leading normal lives. But I needed to know. I needed to ask you.'

Lily nodded.

'It couldn't happen to me again because I'm so much stronger now. I don't need a man to make me happy. And you've got to be the same. Strong and confident. Go there for dinner thinking he's mad about you because he will be. Make him need you more than you need him.'

18

Lily had half hoped, half expected Josh to come and find her at Owl Cottage before dinner, but then at about six he rang from the car to say that the traffic was awful and that he and Hal would meet them at Pond House.

The previous afternoon, in her favourite shop in Welshpool, she'd found a 1940s lace and velvet top, fitted and very sexy, with a low scooped neck and tiny jet buttons at the cuffs. Not wanting to dress it up too much, she was going to wear it with her jeans.

Kirsty came into her bedroom while Lily was getting ready, and watched as she put some sparkle stick on her eyelids. She smiled at Lily's reflection, thinking how wonderful Lily always looked, with her own personal mix of modern and old, as always wearing her clothes with the cool they required.

'Josh won't know what's hit him! You look amazing.'

'Do you think?' Lily grinned happily back at her, moving on to the mascara.

'How's Grace going to cope tonight?' Kirsty asked, trying on the sparkle stick in the mirror over Lily's shoulder.

'I think she'll enjoy herself. As long as you don't give her a hard time.'

'Have I ever!'

Lily laughed uncomfortably.

'No, of course I won't. Grace and I understand each other now.' Kirsty smiled at Lily. 'And I was never horrible to her face, just behind her back. She never knew.'

'She's a different person now. And she needs you to be *very* nice.'

'I know. And I'm pleased she's coming. But when I said how was she going to cope,' Kirsty said, 'I was thinking of you and Josh. It won't be easy for her, seeing you with him. Won't it remind her of everything and make her worry about you?'

'We talked about it this afternoon. I think she'll be okay.'

Kirsty caught Lily's eye in the mirror and held it. 'She's got a lot to thank you for. Don't let her get in the way of you and Josh.'

'She wasn't ever going to! She's happy for me.'

Kirsty added some of Lily's lipstick, then turned to her for approval.

Lily nodded. 'Why is it, whenever I think about him I feel sick?' She fell back on the bed.

'You know you were so much more fun before you met him.'

Lily laughed. 'Really?'

'Really.'

'Come on. We'll be late.' Lily sat up again on the bed.

'No, Lily! It's half past six! But we can go now if you want to. Simon will be pleased to see us early.'

'To see you.'

'And you.'

'And we could give him a hand, couldn't we? Peel some vegetables or something.'

'Have you ever tried? He goes crazy if anyone gives him a hand. Carving knife crazy.'

'Well, let's go and sit with him in the kitchen and have a drink until they arrive. Grace will be there soon. She's early for everything.'

'We could have a little sherry together.'

'Stop teasing me.'

Kirsty was driving and was going to stay the night with Simon afterwards, and Lily was either going back to the Little Goose with Josh or would stay at Pond House with Kirsty and Simon if the disaster that she insisted she could now feel in her bones materialized. She felt that if she planned to stay with Josh she was tempting fate, but if she at least pretended that she was going to stay at Pond House, then it would turn out all right.

Simon had some lethal raspberry cocktails ready for them when they arrived, and as soon as she saw him and them, Lily felt better. She and Kirsty took up positions at the other end of the kitchen away from Simon, and watched him preparing supper.

'Don't you think it's odd,' Kirsty asked Lily in a low voice when Simon took a sip of something off a wooden spoon, 'how cooking is so sexy?'

'How can I answer that?' Lily demanded. 'You'll wonder about me if I say yes, and kill me if I say no.'

Kirsty drummed her fingers on the kitchen table and looked at Lily. 'They'll be here soon.'

'Really?' Lily said sarcastically.

'Stop winding her up, Kirsty,' Simon said, walking back to the other end of the room where two fat plucked ducks were sitting in a pan. He brought a bowl out of the fridge.

'What is that?' Lily asked, interested.

'Butter, zest of an orange, a little honey, some pancetta.' He began sliding the mixture expertly under the ducks' skin with his fingers.

Kirsty grimaced and looked away. 'Tell Lily what we're having,' she told him.

'I'm not hurt by that look, Kirsty,' Simon replied. He turned to Lily. 'Remember, when it comes to food, she knows nothing.'

'We're having roast duck,' Kirsty said bitterly. 'Two roast ducks, and I knew them both well. And it's not funny,' she snapped at Simon, noticing him catch Lily's eye. She turned back to Lily and said plaintively. 'I knew them when they quacked.'

Lily nodded, looking solemn. 'And now they've croaked.'

Grace arrived. She was led through into the kitchen by Kirsty and she looked thin and pretty in a little black top and dark red stretchy skirt.

'What happened to Mimosa?' she whispered later to Lily when Kirsty was out of earshot.

'She's gone,' Lily told her. 'Gone for good.'

Lily led Grace through into the hall and they sat down together in front of the fire and Lily told her what had happened – about Kirsty and Simon's walk, and how Mimosa had packed and left before their return – and there was nothing in Grace's face that gave her away. Nothing that could have given Lily any idea of the lovely lighting up inside when she heard that Mimosa had gone, and then, just seconds later, the horrible realization that Simon was now with Kirsty.

'There was something sad about Mimosa,' Grace said instead. 'I'm sorry for her, but Simon is better off with Kirsty.'

She wasn't going to let on to Lily what it took to say that. How when she'd first told Lily that she didn't need a man, secretly she'd still thought she might have Simon, because the more Lily talked about Kirsty and Simon, there was less and less for Grace to say. Hearing it all, she saw that, of course, Simon had been Kirsty's all along. Grace remembered the first time she'd seen him, there in Kirsty's Warehouse, and when she thought about it, how obvious it had been, even then, that Kirsty was the only girl he could see, the only one he was aware of. And somehow, realizing that she'd never had a chance made it easier to deal with now. She looked across at Kirsty, who was standing just through the doorway in the kitchen talking to him, and thought how again Kirsty was closest to the one person Grace wanted for herself. First Lily, now Simon. But she could give in this time. Could even look over at Kirsty and think how she was going to use this evening to get to know her, to get on with her, and do away with all the tension that had so dominated every moment each had spent in the other's company.

Once, soon after Lily had moved in with Grace, Lily had invited Kirsty around for supper, no doubt hoping it would jolly Grace up a little. Grace had refused supper and had instead left the table and stretched out on the sofa where she'd stayed, glaring at the television and feeling humiliated, while Kirsty and Lily had sat across the room, laughing and eating and ignoring her. But even then she'd wished that Kirsty was someone she could get to know. Known that if only Grace could have grabbed hold of her, Kirsty would have been good for her. That evening Grace had finally left the room and crept defeated up the stairs to her bedroom, with each step feeling as if she was sinking. Going down, slowly and invisibly.

But this evening, as she walked into Pond House, she knew straight away that Kirsty had been watching for her. When she'd knocked on the door, it had been Kirsty who had let her in, who had kissed her and squeezed her shoulder, told her how great it was to see her, put a drink into her hand and led her through to find Simon and Lily.

When there was a second loud knocking at the door, Lily's heart immediately started to do the same. She came out into the hall, wanting to hide behind Kirsty.

Simon opened the front door to Josh and Hal, and Grace immediately joined Lily and stood protectively at her side, narrowing her eyes suspiciously as she waited for first sight of Josh.

Vaguely Lily was aware that Hal was there in the house, and talking excitedly in her right ear, but she wasn't taking him in and she felt him move away, to envelop Grace in a great hug and then turn to Kirsty. She could hear him telling her how much he'd been looking forward to seeing her again. But all the time, she was standing still and looking for Josh, and he was there, looking back at her. He came over to her slowly, savouring the moment, staring at her with such unashamed delight that she collapsed inside, wondering why she had ever felt she needed to doubt him.

'Hello, my darling,' he said, pulling her against him, and kissed her long enough for nobody to misunderstand the situation.

'I've missed you so much,' she said, looking up at him.

He hugged her tighter. 'Tell me just one tenth as much as I've missed you.'

'I can't believe you're here.'

'We nearly weren't. I am never letting Hal drive me around these lanes again. And tell me we don't have to sit through a dinner party. Not now. Not when I haven't seen you for so long.'

Lily smiled at him. 'It's only Hal who'd call it that. It's just supper. I thought it would be good fun. And with Hal here and everything . . .'

'I don't mind! I'm still with you, aren't I? I'll just have to look forward to being on my own with you afterwards. In a big bed in the Little Goose.'

Lily looked around to see they had been left alone. She wondered what Hal had made of seeing them together, but when they walked back into the kitchen there was no sign of him. Before the evening was up, she decided, Josh or she was going to have to talk to him.

Supper seemed to cook itself while Simon sat, relaxing on the arm of Kirsty's armchair, chatting and laughing with Grace and Hal, only getting up once to make another jug of cocktail. And then, just as everybody was becoming aware of how hungry they were, he told them it was time to eat.

Lily got up with the others and noticed how Hal immediately came over to take Josh's arm and lead him purposefully out of the room. He *had* seen Josh kiss her, Lily guessed. She let them go ahead, wanting to give Josh the chance to talk to Hal. At the same time, she could hear Simon calling her to come through and she knew she couldn't leave it too long. She walked quietly out into the hall and caught them standing in the shadows. Hal didn't see her go by and as she passed he raised his glass to Josh.

'You're pinching someone from me yet again, Josh,' she heard Hal whisper. 'Congratulatons!'

What? Lily thought, as Josh glanced worriedly in her direction. She kept on walking. She was unable to tell from his voice whether or not he was joking. Could it be true? Could Hal really be thinking of her like that?

She found herself in the kitchen, where Grace was sitting alone at a round table waiting for the others, and she pulled out a chair and sat down opposite her. Very quickly Hal and Josh joined her. Josh immediately caught her eye and nodded his head gently, directing his look across to Hal. Then he gave her a tiny smile as if to say that all was well. Hal must have been joking, Lily decided. He couldn't have been thinking of her like that.

Looking across to Hal, Lily could see no sign at all that he was upset with Josh. And if Josh was happy that surely must mean that Hal was pleased for them. He wouldn't have started to think of her like that, she told herself again. Not so soon after Amber.

Josh came to sit next to her on her left-hand side. To her right there was an empty place waiting for Simon. Seconds later he appeared, carrying two succulent, crispy, perfectly roasted ducks, Kirsty behind him with bowls of vegetables and bubbling dauphinoise potatoes.

All through supper, as they picked over the last pieces of duck, licking their fingers and talking and laughing, Lily watched Hal carefully, and knew by the end there was nothing on his mind, nothing for her to worry about. Then, later on, Josh caught her eye and whispered quickly, *I've told him*, and she grinned back, relieved that it had all been so straightforward.

Sitting next to Josh and looking across the table to Grace, watching her as she started to giggle at something Hal was whispering to her, Lily felt suddenly aware that this was one of those precious moments, one that she would remember, like a photograph, for the rest of her life. That whatever was to happen later, in days, months, years to come, at that moment everything was perfect, a fleeting flash of true happiness. Josh must have seen something in her face because she felt his hand reach for hers, and she thought how different it was to be sitting next to him this time, how lovely it was to allow her fingers to entwine with his in a secret delight at what they had together.

A crème brûlée and a gooseberry tart later, Hal decided it was time to stand up and propose a toast.

Sweet, Lily thought, catching Kirsty's eye. I wonder what he's going to say.

'Simon,' Hal began, raising his glass, 'I should start with you, because that was the most delicious supper. You deserve a star, a Michelin Star.' He paused. 'Then Lily, for being so utterly sweet, but I've told you that already so I'm not going to say it again.' He moved on. 'Kirsty and Grace,' he said, 'thank you both for all your efforts to sort me out.' Then he turned to Josh and slowly raised his glass. 'Without whom I wouldn't be here today,' he said staring at him. 'And I'm glad I am. Very, very glad.' He relaxed and smiled. 'You might be dangerously self-opinionated, extraordinarily arrogant, and sickeningly attractive to women, but thank you. I mean it, I'm truly grateful. Finally,' Hal said, 'I think we should toast Amber. The girl who got us all together. But who isn't here tonight.'

He put down his wine and pulled his jacket off the back of his chair, fumbling slowly in its pockets. Then he brought out his wallet, opened it, and prised out a photograph.

'I haven't shown you this before, have I?' he asked Lily, who was sitting opposite him.

Lily shook her head.

Hal held the little photograph in one hand and then picked up a fork with the other. Everybody watched silently as he slid the photograph carefully in between its prongs so that the photo was held in place.

'I need a prop,' he said and looked around for what he wanted. On a side table was a bowl of fruit and Hal went over to it, picked it up and carried it carefully back to the middle of the table. He chose an orange from the bowl, cut a neat hole in it with his knife and pushed the handle of the fork straight into it so that the fork stood up out of the orange like a sword in a stone. Then he replaced the orange in the bowl and placed the bowl in the centre of the table.

'Hello, everybody,' Hal said, moving the bowl from side to side and making them all smile. 'I'm Amber, your new table decoration. Everyone raise your glass to me.'

Lily waited until the photograph was there in front of her and then she looked curiously at it. The girl was smiling straight at the camera, undeniably beautiful, with long smooth dark brown hair and full cherry red lips. But she was also, undeniably, the girl who'd been with Josh that day on the Fulham Road. The girl he had walked with, arm in arm, straight past her. The girl Josh had put his arms around and kissed just ten feet away from her. It was Amber, Amber, Amber, all along.

She controlled herself beautifully. 'Oh, she is gorgeous, Hal!' Lily said, disentangling her hand from Josh's grasp under the table.

On no account was she going to let Hal notice anything was wrong. She was not going to add to the pain that his bastard of a friend had put him through already and was no doubt going to put him through again.

She turned the fruit bowl away again. 'You don't need to see her in the flesh to tell that.'

Josh and Amber would have been carrying on together ever since the aborted wedding day, she thought dully.

He must have flown off with her on honeymoon, just as Amber's sister had suspected. And he must still be seeing her, stringing Lily along at the same time. Why, *why* bother with me too? she thought miserably. Unless it was simply because he could. Because she, Lily, had made it so easy for him to do just that. After the day they'd spent together, he'd probably gone straight from Lily to Amber. And she couldn't believe that she could be so stupid as to let this happen.

Hal looked at the photograph and talked as if she was the only person in the room.

'I'm not carrying your photo around because I think I can make things better. Not any more,' he said quietly. 'But it feels a bit like taking off a wedding ring, throwing you away. Even though I know it's over, it's a big step.'

'I would,' Lily told him, bitterly, breaking the silence. 'I'd throw it away. Tear it into little pieces and get on with your life.'

She picked up her glass of wine, drained it, then reached across the table for Hal's cigarettes and lit one.

You bastard, she thought, still looking anywhere but Josh.

Hal was staring at her, eyebrows raised.

'Just every now and again,' she told him. 'When I get desperate. I'll smoke it by the fire.' She stood up and quickly left the room, aware of the immediate resumption of laughter and conversation that told her the rest of them had noticed nothing wrong.

So, she thought bitterly, staring into the flames. The cracks and chips have shown up on Josh after all. How desperate he must be to do that to Hal! But perhaps he and Amber were so in love they couldn't do anything else. The thought that Hal had forgiven Josh and was now starting to put everything to do with Amber behind him, and was about to get hurt all over again made her angrier for Hal than for herself. She wanted Hal to know what a devious, gutless man he had for a friend. And yet she knew she couldn't do it to him.

She imagined them all sitting around the table unaware of what was going on inside her, and she wanted to go home. And never see Josh again. But she sat instead close to the fire, not feeling strong enough to stand up and leave, and pretty soon Josh came through the door and over to her chair, taking in the look on her face, concern growing in his eyes.

He crouched down in front of her. 'Are you okay?'

'Fuck off,' she hissed.

For a moment he looked as if she had knocked all the breath out of him. He dropped her hand but seemed not to know what else to do and continued to crouch there at her feet, speechless.

'I mean right now.'

His face went hard and he got up and turned away and left her.

Then the others realized that something was up and came through to join her. Only Hal seemed oblivious. He came and sat down in the armchair opposite Lily, with Amber's orange in his hand, and started to peel it, then offered it around. When nobody took him up on the offer he started to eat it messily, the juice trickling down his chin and on to his trousers.

Then Josh reappeared again in the doorway. Without looking at Lily, he announced to the room that he was going back to the Little Goose.

'But what about me?' Hal called. 'I don't want to go yet!' He looked at his watch. 'Come off it, Josh!'

To shut Hal up Grace offered to drop him off on her way home. Then she left her chair and came over to Lily, full of worry.

'Come outside. Please tell me what's wrong,' she begged her.

But Josh, his face angry and hurt, had turned his back on all of them and was starting to make his way out to the front door. That it was the end between them, Lily knew with terrible certainty. But still the thought of him leaving, and her never speaking to him again, was too awful to imagine. She couldn't let him go, and she got up and ran out of the room after him.

'Is there more?' Josh asked as she met him on the other side of the front door.

She stared back at him, still feeling as if she might burst with fury at him for being so stupid.

'Explain to me, please, why you said that,' he said quietly. 'I should know what's going on.'

'You and Amber are going on.' She watched him flinch and knew that, of course, she'd been right, and any last vestige of hope had to go. 'And I've only just realized.' Josh looked at her sharply. 'You must have thought I would never find out,' she went on. 'Or perhaps you wouldn't have cared if I had? And I suppose Hal doesn't know either. Even if you could do it to me, how could you do that to Hal? Your friend. How dare you do it to either of us?'

He walked away from her and looked up at the stars.

'I thought you knew. Something you said made me think you already knew . . . It never occurred to me that it was such a big deal. I wouldn't have kept it back from you either. It had nothing to do with you and me.'

'You thought I wouldn't mind! That it didn't matter? Of course it did.'

'Lily,' he looked back at her. 'It didn't.'

'But how can you say that? How can you not see that I'm not like all your other girls!' she cried. 'And I always knew what you were like! I was so stupid to get involved with you.'

'Really? You were so stupid why? What am I like?'

'Faithless, unfaithful . . .' Lily ventured.

'Anything else?'

'Shallow, unreliable.'

'No wonder you want to get away. But all I've wanted to do,' he said, 'from the moment I first saw you, is be loyal to you, faithful to you, to love you, to look after you. Only you!' He laughed bitterly. 'Do I deserve this? Is that why this is happening now? A punishment for never having felt anything like this before? I finally get to see what it's all about and then, instantly, it's taken away from me again?'

'How can you ask me that?' she spat out.

He waited for a moment, as if he still couldn't quite believe it. That if he waited long enough, she was going to apologize, or tell him that it was all one hugely unfunny joke at his expense. But she didn't, and eventually he turned his back on her and walked towards his car.

'No, don't go!' she called then. 'I deserve more than that.'

He turned back again.

'*You* deserve more than that? *I* deserve more than that! Amber has absolutely nothing to do with you and me and if you weren't programmed to be *quite* so suspicious of me, *quite* so sure that I'm so *faithless*, and *unfaithful*, we wouldn't even be having this conversation.'

'Oh really,' Lily said sarcastically. 'What would Hal say?'

'Hal knows. Amber told him months ago.'

'Told him what? That you took his place on the honeymoon?'

'I did not do that!' Josh said enunciating each word extremely clearly. 'That is ridiculous.'

'Josh!' Lily said, heart beating faster. 'I know that you're still having an affair with her.' She felt a grim thrill at the words because, horrible as it was, she knew she'd got him.

'No, Lily. I am not. Nothing has happened between Amber and me for months.'

'But I saw you kissing her on the street,' Lily blurted out. 'Just last week. I saw you both on the Fulham Road.'

'Oh, you did? What do you think you saw?' he said contemptuously. 'The most you saw was someone happy again. She's been let off the hook! She's enjoying herself! So she wants to kiss me! Big deal! What's wrong with that? You should be having this conversation with Amber, Lily. Not with me.'

'You were kissing her, too,' Lily insisted, wanting to hang on to the certainty, unable to face the awfulness of everything that she'd said to him if it wasn't true. 'It was obvious that you were more than just friends.'

'Oh, for Christ's sake Lily! Listen to yourself.'

All at once it was the last thing she wanted to do.

'You don't understand.'

She wanted to say that she'd seen Amber looking at Josh with love practically pouring out of her ears, that anyone would have thought like she had done. But she'd presumed everything from it, and already said so much that she couldn't bring herself to say anything else. She knew that she'd ruined all the chances for her and Josh. That the one day, that beautiful golden day, was all that they'd have. He was still angry with her. She could see it in the turn of his shoulders against her as he moved towards his car.

'You should have trusted me,' he said, opening the door.

'I know I should.'

She walked over to him and stood close by him and for a while neither of them spoke.

'If I said please forgive me. That I'll go crazy if I lose you. That I'm sorry. Would it make a difference?'

'*If* you said that? Or you *are* saying that?'

'I *am* saying that.'

He got into his car and looked at her through the open window. 'Then forgiveness could be in order.'

'When? Now? Tomorrow? Next month?' She couldn't believe that he was still prepared to drive away from her. 'Don't go yet.'

'I've things to do. It's late.'

'Josh! Wait!' she said aghast. She bent down and looked in through the window. 'When am I forgiven?'

'Lily,' he told her wearily. 'I forgive you now. How could I not? I completely adore you.'

'You haven't told me that before.'

'Well, I'm telling you now.'

'Then get out of the car,' she insisted. 'Let me tell you how much I adore you too. You've got to.'

'No. I haven't got to. This time you've got to trust me. Start practising!' He kissed her quickly on the cheek. 'I've got to go.'

Without saying anything more, or even looking at her again, he started the engine.

'But aren't you even going to say goodbye?' she called after him as the car shot forwards out of the drive.

When Lily walked back into the house, Kirsty and Grace looked at her anxiously but it was obvious that whatever had happened outside the house was an improvement on whatever had happened inside and that Lily was feeling better.

'I'll tell you later,' Lily mouthed to them both, nodding slightly at Hal, who was still sitting in front of the fire, eyes half closed.

Later, as she and Grace cleared up together, she caught

sight of Kirsty and Simon in the kitchen, kissing under a tea towel, and she turned away, busying herself with finding all the dirty glasses left in the hall. Josh and I could be like that, she thought. Why had he gone? How could he have said that to her and then disappeared? But she knew why. That after such a conversation, leaving her was the best thing to do. She'd have done the same.

Hal had obviously decided the best thing to do was to avoid the subject of her and Josh completely. Instead he talked to her about his holiday, which was scheduled to start almost as soon as he returned to London from Welshpool. Lily listened to his itinerary half-heartedly, her mind on Josh.

'I can't believe you've never travelled outside Europe,' Hal said.

'I don't think it's a problem,' she told him tiredly.

'But it is,' Hal insisted, 'it's a terrible gap in your education.'

She smiled. 'If you say so.'

'And I feel it is my duty to fill such a gap.'

'Really, Hal,' she laughed.

'Would you let me?'

Anything I say to you now, you'll forget in the morning, she thought, looking at his sweet face and his slightly bleary eyes. And anything you say to me you'll have forgotten too. 'Sort it out then,' she said in a moment of irresponsibility.

Hal smiled and nodded with satisfaction and leaned back for his jacket, now draped across his armchair. Again he reached for the inner pocket.

No more horrors, please, Lily thought as he pulled out

an organizer. He keyed something in that she couldn't read and then looked back at her with satisfaction.

'Done. Now I won't forget you in the morning,' he told her.

Suddenly, she couldn't bear it any longer. She wanted to bury her head in a cushion and sleep.

'Do you want me to take you home?' asked Grace, immediately standing up and coming over from the other side of the room.

'No, I think I'll stay the night here.'

Lily turned back to Hal. 'I have to go to bed. Do you mind?' She called through the door to Kirsty and Simon. 'If that's okay with you. Do you mind if I stay here?'

'Of course not,' Simon said.

'I'll dump Hal at the Little Goose,' Grace said.

'Dumping me at the Little Goose would be most kind,' Hal told her from his chair.

Lily leaned over to him and kissed him goodbye. He cupped her face in his large hands and looked carefully into her face. 'Don't worry,' he said. 'It's going to be okay.'

After Grace and Hal had left, Simon insisted that Kirsty take Lily up to bed and leave him to clear up the last things.

'It was absolutely awful,' Lily told Kirsty later in the bedroom. 'It was terrible. I was so horrible to Josh.'

'It wasn't your fault if you got the wrong end of the stick.'

'It was! I should have trusted him.'

'I didn't. I understand exactly why you said what you said.'

'But I'm supposed to know him better than you do!'

'I saw him in the Little Goose! You weren't so wrong.'

Lily sat down on the bed. 'What I'm saying, seriously, is that he was never like that. Not really. Not once I got to know him, and he got to know me. But I couldn't trust it. I was so scared I was going to be taken in.'

'But I don't think you've blown it. I think you've got another chance.'

'I think so too.' Lily smiled up at Kirsty.

'Give him tonight to get over it, then see him tomorrow.' Lily nodded.

Kirsty smothered a long yawn. 'Sorry!'

'Go to sleep. I'm sorry. I'll shut up.'

'It's okay. We can talk all night if it helps. But I don't think there's anything we can say. You'll see him tomorrow and talk it all though and everything will be fine. I don't think there's any doubt.'

'Thanks. Go to bed.'

'I'll drive you home as soon as you wake up. And then you can go and see Josh.'

*

Lily woke up the next morning to Kirsty shouting up to her from the bottom of the stairs.

'No thanks,' she called back, even though she couldn't hear a word, deciding this was the best way to shut her up.

It seemed to work. Peace returned to her bedroom. Lily waited for a few seconds then pushed her head deep into

the soft white pillow and closed her eyes again, wondering
if it had really worked, and how long she would be left
alone, and then what it was that she'd turned down.
She drifted, half awake, half asleep, aware of the breeze
tickling the edges of her bedroom curtain, and listening
to the gentle, musical woodwind of the doves cooing in
the trees outside her window, and thought what a lovely
house it was to wake up in, even if Kirsty did always
have to do it so raucously.

Then came the sound of Kirsty's feet, heavy and purposeful on the wooden stairs, and Lily braced herself. As
Kirsty came in she pushed herself upright in the bed.

'What do you mean *no thanks*?' Kirsty asked, indignantly, breathing hard, and she tossed a thick white
envelope on to Lily's lap.

Lily picked it up in surprise, and turned it over in her
hand.

'It's addressed to you, but why has it been sent *here*?'

Kirsty came and sat down on the bed beside Lily.
'What might it be?'

Lily looked down at her name neatly typed on the
front and shrugged and suddenly was completely awake.
She opened the envelope and pulled out a folded piece of
paper and glanced quickly up at Kirsty before opening it.
Inside, there was a sheet of Little Goose writing paper
with a short scrawled message.

Go home and get packing.
We're going on holiday.

347

'I don't believe it,' Lily cried in astonishment.

Kirsty took it from her and read it and looked over to her silently for a few seconds. 'Best get off home!' she said then. 'Get packing!'

'Don't go all flippant on me. What's going on?' Lily pleaded. 'When? What holiday?' She swung the duvet off her legs. 'Where on holiday?' But she was starting to smile as she said it, because the thought of a holiday with Josh was fantastic, wonderful. She leaped out of bed. 'I can't believe it. Isn't this what you dream about?' She looked at Kirsty then turned around in the room. 'I need to find my jeans!' she panicked. 'I've got to get home.'

It's as if her speed setting's been turned up, Kirsty thought, sitting on the bed and watching Lily run around the room gathering up her things and stuffing them into her bag, then seconds later pulling everything out again as she searched for deodorant and a clean jumper.

'What if it's from Hal?' Kirsty said casually from the bed. 'He was definitely very keen on you last night.'

'What?' Lily said. She stopped what she was doing and looked up, a pair of knickers dangling from one finger.

'How do you know it's definitely from Josh?' Kirsty asked. 'It might be from Hal.'

Lily's face sagged. 'It can't be from Hal!'

Kirsty looked back at her. 'Why? And would it be so bad? Hal's a really nice guy. A really nice, rich guy. You'd have a great time.'

'Kirsty! What are you saying! I don't want to go on holiday with Hal! I'm not going on holiday with Hal,' she insisted. 'It was Josh who sent this letter to me.'

'Okay. Forget I said it. 'It's Josh. Definitely Josh.'

Lily stared back at her. 'But you're right. Hal did keep asking me to go away with him. And he put me in his bloody organizer.'

Kirsty got off the bed. 'I'm sorry I said anything. Give me five minutes and I'll drive you home.'

Lily went on downstairs and sat in the kitchen waiting for Kirsty. She wondered whether she was right to think that Kirsty still didn't like Josh. She unzipped her bag and found her mobile and called Grace, needing somebody else to tell about the note, someone more on Josh's side. The phone rang for a long time.

'Hmm?' Grace said eventually, not sounding like Grace at all. Grace usually answered as if she just might be being judged on her phone-answering skills.

'Have you got your mouth full?'

'Hello Lily.'

'I'm sorry. Have I woken you up?'

'No.'

'I wanted to talk to you.'

'Okay,' Grace said sounding cagey. 'About what?'

'I've had this weird note,' Lily started, already wishing she hadn't. There were things in Grace's voice telling her that Grace was not on for a chat. 'I think it must be from Josh. He says that he wants to take me away on holiday. I wondered what you thought . . .' Lily tailed off.

'That's great. Go for it.'

'Is that all?'

'What else?'

'Kirsty thought it might have been from Hal.'

'Oh no,' Grace said immediately. 'I doubt it would have been Hal.' And as she spoke the words, there was a cough. A distinctly male cough in the background.

'Grace!' Lily cried. 'You were meant to take him back to the Little Goose! Not take him home and shag him!'

'Lily,' Grace exploded back. 'I did not do that!'

Lily started to laugh. 'Yes you did.'

'He's here. Okay. But he's just arrived. Do you want to ask him yourself?'

'No!' She wanted to get off the phone and leave them to it. 'If Hal's with you, it's answered my question.'

She was thrilled for both of them. Completely delighted that Hal was with Grace. She hoped he had stayed the night. That he would stay the next night too, and the one after.

'I'll call you soon.'

'Lily, Hal arrived ten minutes ago. He really did.'

'Of course he did. Have fun!' Lily put down the phone, just as Kirsty walked in through the door.

'Guess what,' Lily said.

*

'But maybe he had just arrived for coffee,' Kirsty said when they were in the car driving back towards Owl Cottage. 'It doesn't mean he didn't send you the note.'

'Why do you keep doing this to me? Of course he didn't. Why can't you just accept that Josh wants to take me on holiday. You've got Simon. Why can't I have Josh?'

'I want you to have Josh,' Kirsty said, looking at her.

'Don't think I don't. Of course I do. But I can't help saying these things. They're on my mind.'

'Well, they're not on mine. Not until you put them there anyway . . .'

'Honestly, Lily. It's nothing to do with what I think about Josh. I like him. I really, really like him and I can't think of anyone better for you. But I'm worried that he didn't send you that note. Why don't you call him now and ask him?'

'But then I'd spoil it. Wouldn't I? He's wanting me to trust him. That's the whole point. He won't want me to check it all out with him first.'

They'd arrived back at the cottage.

'Are you coming in?'

'What do you think? That I'd leave you on your own?'

They unlocked the door and walked tentatively into the cottage together, almost as if they were expecting Josh to jump out at them, or at the very least to find another white envelope lying on the mat. There was nothing there.

'Don't stay,' Lily told her then. 'You don't have to, and I know you promised Simon you'd be around this morning.'

Kirsty was obviously torn.

'Honestly. I promise I'm fine,' Lily insisted. 'What do I need you here for anyway? If anything happens you'll be the first to know. But I'm not going to start packing. Not without an idea of whether this is some joke.'

Kirsty took her arm, seeing in her face that Lily was losing her earlier certainty. 'Don't worry. It's not some joke.'

As she said that the letter-box rattled behind them and they both jumped around. In a flash Kirsty raced to the window.

'It's okay. It's just the postman,' she said turning back. But Lily was already standing in front of her, another envelope in her hand.

'He's a bit too clever by half,' Lily said, trying to sound unfazed. 'There's no postmark on this. One more of these and he'll start to give me the creeps.' She pulled open the envelope.

'He must have got the postman to drop it off. Why couldn't he just give it to you himself?' Kirsty asked her impatiently. 'No, I know,' she said immediately. 'It's kind of more fun this way.'

Lily hadn't replied. Seeing the dazed look on her face, Kirsty took the letter out of her hands and read it.

'Have you seen *when* you're going?' Kirsty asked at last.

Lily took it back again. 'What's today, Saturday? Oh, not today! He's mad. What if I couldn't? And how did he manage to sort it all out so fast?'

'It's possible. If you find the right sort of travel agent.'

'But I have to get ready. Packed. I have to find my passport!' Lily looked frantically around the room. 'And I have to get to the airport. Where am I meant to be flying from?'

'Birmingham International. I'd say we should leave in the next couple of hours. You should call Grace and say goodbye.'

'Oh Kirsty!' Lily shook her head. 'I had no idea. I thought he was talking about Devon, or the Lake District.'

'Shame! If only you'd known you could have got your legs waxed.'

'St Lucia,' Lily said, starting to laugh too. 'I don't *know* anyone who's been there. Will you really take me to the airport?'

Kirsty left her in Owl Cottage getting ready, promising to come and pick her up again within the hour. And once she'd gone Lily started circling the cottage, throwing together her things. She had no bikini, no sun tan lotion. Just a few grubby T-shirts and an old sarong. But she didn't care. Alone in the house, running around, up and down the stairs in her bare feet, she felt as if she could fly, full of anticipation and happiness and wild excitement.

She was ready for Kirsty when she returned to pick her up and then, almost before she'd settled down to the journey, they had arrived at the airport, pushing their way in together and making their way over to International Departures.

There was no sign of Josh. Twenty minutes later and there was nothing left to do but for Lily to leave Kirsty on the other side of passport control and make her way towards the plane.

'I just can't bear it!' Kirsty cried. 'I want to know so badly.'

'You do know. We both know it's him.'

Lily hugged her tightly and whispered goodbye. She left Kirsty then, not wanting to look back at her, and disappeared into passport control, and Kirsty waited another moment more and then turned back, out through the doors, willing Lily to remember to find a moment to call her and to tell her that it really had been Josh waiting for her on the other side, and that the whole thing hadn't been some terrible joke.

Lily moved hesitantly on towards the X-ray machines, thinking all the time that she could see him. But there was still nobody there that she recognized. She slid her handbag on to the checks, and then picked it up again the other side, still looking around her, nervously, still not finding him.

And then she did see something. Someone. A golden head, a foot taller than nearly everybody else, turning instinctively towards her. And it was Josh. When she caught his eye she started to laugh because he looked so delighted, and so relieved that she was there, and then she ran towards him.

'What are you doing here?' she said into his neck. 'I'm waiting for Hal.'

'Give up, Lily.' He bent to kiss her lips. 'You've been waiting for me.'

She looked up at him. 'Yes,' she said. 'It's true.'

Arms around each other, they started to walk away from passport control and on into the departure lounge. It was still half an hour before their flight was to be called, and Lily could see a tiny boutique out of the corner of her eye. She could see that they had sunglasses for sale, and some perfect Burberry bikinis.

Epilogue

They walked along a gently twisting path towards the hotel's reception, past tiny waterfalls and fantastic flowers and under great canopies of scented blossom. As they drew near a waiter came out to join them, with a silver tray and two long glasses of fruit punch.

'Welcome to La Mouskia – Mr Fairfax and Miss Somerville – we hope you will have a wonderful stay.'

At the hotel's reception their arrival caused a sudden burst of activity. What's the problem, Lily wondered, waiting patiently next to Josh. Eventually the hurried conversation stopped and the manager looked up, beamed at them both and came over.

'We would like to move you to another room,' he explained.

'Oh!' said Lily. 'Why?'

The manager paused, for a brief moment torn between professional discretion and an acute desire to spill the beans. 'Our honeymoon suite has unexpectedly become available.'

He looked at them both and sadly shook his head. 'It appears that the bride has decided not to marry her groom after all.'

Lily thought it was better if she didn't catch Josh's eye.

'We would be delighted if you would take the suite instead.'

Josh took a firm grasp of Lily's hand.

'That would be perfect,' he said.

Acknowledgements

Of course Kirsty is wrong and there are lots of good-looking men in Welshpool and I hope she hasn't offended male residents of Welshpool or anyone else. I owe my thanks to many of them for helping me with the book, especially Liz Wait, Sharon Sheppard and Heather Pugh. Thanks too to my family, particularly to Josie for swapping tea for vodka, to Hez for the details about Montgomery and to Charlotte Bevan who was such a brilliant sounding board, and also to friends who helped in so many ways, especially Edla Griffiths, Antonia Brooks and Louise Voss. Thank you to Clifford Evans of the Shropshire Rural Stress Support Network who provides an invaluable service and whose advice I greatly value. Thanks to everyone at Pan for their great ideas and hard work, especially my wonderfully supportive editor, Imogen Taylor. And to Jo Frank, a better agent and friend would be hard to find. And, most of all, thanks to dearest Ant. As he says himself, greater love hath no man than he who lives with a writer.